NUMBER 3
FALL 2018

BLACK Infinit

BODY SNATCHERS!

Lights out!

the extension is endless, the sensation of depth is overwhelming. And the darkness is immortal."
—Carl Sagan

COVER: CENTRAL IMAGE BY MAURICE WHITMAN
INTERIOR ILLUSTRATIONS: ALLEN KOSZOWSKI, VIRGIL FINLAY, KURT RÖSCHL, H. W. WESSO, DICK FRANCIS, ED EMSHWILLER, AND OTHERS

EDITOR AND PUBLISHER: TOM ENGLISH
COLUMNISTS: MATT COWAN; TODD TREICHEL

www.DeadLetterPress.com   ISBN-13: 978-1732434417

PLEASE STAND BY

elements in science fiction. After all, any race of beings intelligent enough to solve the problems of interstellar space travel are not going to be happy just fitting in with the locals. No, these strange visitors from other worlds are going to want to run the show, and may wish to seize power without raising a ruckus. If they can accomplish this through a little bit of mind control, or by inhabiting a few highly-placed officials, or—even better—by trading places with your annoying next-door neighbor, then so be it. Aliens are sneaky that way.

Televised science fiction during the sixties (and beyond) is filled with numerous, memorable examples of alien body-snatching. In fact, the creators and producers of just about every sci-fi series of the day relied heavily on this fantastic form of identity theft to propel their weekly adventures into the weird. Writer Rod Serling gave us one the first instances, in the 1961 episode of *The Twilight Zone*, "Will

A FULL-SCALE ALIEN INVASION IS ALWAYS A RATHER INCONVENIENT AND AGGRAVATING AFFAIR. UNINVITED VISITORS FROM OUTER SPACE DROP IN UNANNOUNCED WITH THEIR HIGH-TECH WAR MACHINES AND WORN-OUT EXCUSES FOR PLANETARY CONQUEST, AND TURN OUR CITIES INTO RUBBLE AND OUR NEIGHBORS INTO ASH. IT'S ENOUGH TO MAKE THE LOCALS RUN FOR COVER AND CALL OUT THE NATIONAL GUARD.

On second thought, large-scale destruction followed by widespread panic in the streets is actually a good thing, especially when one considers the unpleasant alternative: an alien attack can be far more subtle, an invasion so quietly covert that no one suspects a thing ... until it's too late.

In this issue of *Black Infinity,* we examine the devious methods extraterrestrials often employ to take over the earth neatly and discreetly—one unsuspecting victim at a time. Yes, dear reader, we explore the tactics of the Body Snatchers: alien *control*, alien *possession*, alien *replacement*.

These tactics have long been standard plot

the Real Martian Please Stand Up?"

Serling's story plays out in the close confines of an all-night diner, where a busload of strangers gather after their travel plans are interrupted by a winter storm. In walk two state troopers searching for the extraterrestrial survivor of a crashed UFO. The policemen *know* the intruder is hiding among the humans inside—they tracked the alien's footprints in the snow, leading from the flying saucer to the diner—but, according to the opening remarks of writer/narrator Serling, finding a Martian blending in with a roomful of characters will be even harder than finding "a needle in a haystack."

For this story and its opening narration, Serling may have drawn inspiration from Hal Clement's 1950 novel *Needle,* about an alien detective who resembles a four-pound green

jellyfish and is able to live symbiotically inside the host body of another life-form. This creature is in hot pursuit of another of his kind when both aliens crash-land their spaceships on earth. The Hunter, as he's called, soon inhabits the body of a fifteen-year-old boy (who is initially unaware of the Hunter's presence) and attempts to continue tracking his quarry.

The search is anything but easy, though: "...The criminal is a needle in a haystack of people," states a tagline in the May 1949 issue of *Astounding Stories* (in which the novel

debuted in serial form). "But this detective of an alien world had a terrible task indeed; his needle could become a wisp of hay in a haystack." Alas, as in Serling's "Will the Real Martian Please Stand Up?"—this is but one of the many perils encountered when dealing with body snatchers!

In 1963, *The Outer Limits* introduced American audiences to several others. In "Corpus Earthling," parasitic creatures that look like harmless specimens of rock—but are actually the vanguard of an alien invasion—creeped out an entire generation of viewers, when one of these wriggling crystalline life-forms crawled across the face of a struggling female lab technician, possessing her mind and disfiguring her in the process. The episode is based on a 1960 novel by Louis Charbonneau.

In the noir-ish and equally scary *OL* episode "The Invisibles," crablike monstrosities take control of their human hosts by clambering onto the backs of several willing (but nonetheless fearful) inductees to a secret alien cult. This memorable childhood nightmare

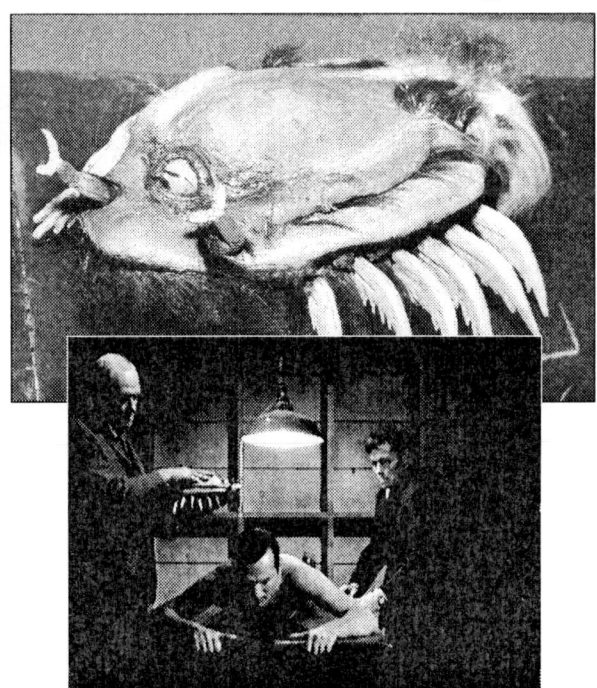

came courtesy of writer/producer Joseph Stefano, who penned many of the darkest segments of the first season. The creature (and its method of attachment) is similar to that of the 1994 movie *The Puppet Masters,* featured in this issues' edition of Matt Cowan's Threat Watch.

And in "The Special One," an alien disguised as a human arrives at the home of a gifted child, explaining to the parents that he's an educator sent by the government to help cultivate the boy's scientific genius. In reality, the nefarious Mr. Zeno has plans to equip his young student with unearthly knowledge, while slowly indoctrinating the boy to aid him in a plot to take over the world.

Also from the first season of *The Outer Limits* is "The Duplicate Man," which deals (in part) with the hunt for a deadly alien being called a *megasoid.* This episode doesn't exactly fit our theme of body snatchers, but it's based on an intriguing story by Clifford D. Simak which *does* fit; for the cunning megasoid is adept at mind control. We reprint the tale in this issue, and remind readers that it's the second "Outer Limits story" to appear in *Black Infinity.* (Jerry Sohl's "The Invisible Enemy" appeared in our first issue.)

Another iconic science fiction television series made its broadcast debut in 1966 with a frightening episode about alien control *and* replacement. In the *Star Trek* (TOS) episode "The Man Trap" a vampiric creature assumes the identity of one of Captain Kirk's crewmen and is beamed aboard the starship *Enterprise.* The creature, Kirk soon learns, has a

natural ability to control how people perceive it, and thereby can appear as anyone it chooses, including the ship's chief medical officer, Dr. McCoy. And all this simply so it can procure its next meal— by sucking the salt from the bodies of its mind-controlled victims. (With its effective "bear" and creepy atmosphere, this episode of *Star Trek* could just as easily have been an installment of *The Outer Limits.* And that, dear reader, is praise indeed.)

The *Star Trek* pilot "The Cage" (later edited into the two-part episode "The Menagerie") also features alien mind-control. Series creator Gene Roddenberry's Hugo Award-winning script recaptures the sense of wonder of the SF pulps of the forties and fifties, while introducing viewers to the gallant spacefaring men and women of earth's far-flung future—who are ill-equipped and unprepared to deal with a dying race of beings so mentally advanced that not only have they attained the power of telepathy but also the ability to conjure up an endless stream of convincing illusions.

Other 1960s shows featured episodes revolving around alien body-snatching, including the Irwin Allen series *Lost in Space;* but covert invasion through alien replacement is the entire premise of *The Invaders.* In the 1967 pilot, architect David Vincent witnesses the landing of a flying saucer, and then spends two full seasons trying to convince the world that it's in the midst of an alien invasion. People are skeptical, of course, because for the most part, Vincent has little or no proof. As

the show's opening narration intones, these tricky aliens have "taken human form."

With Vincent often unable to distinguish human from non-human, friend from foe, and usually unable to trust anyone, *The Invaders* managed to generate the same sense of dread and paranoia as the 1956 B-movie *The Invasion of the Body Snatchers, which was released at the height of the Red Scare.* Not surprisingly, Larry Cohen, *The Invaders* creator,

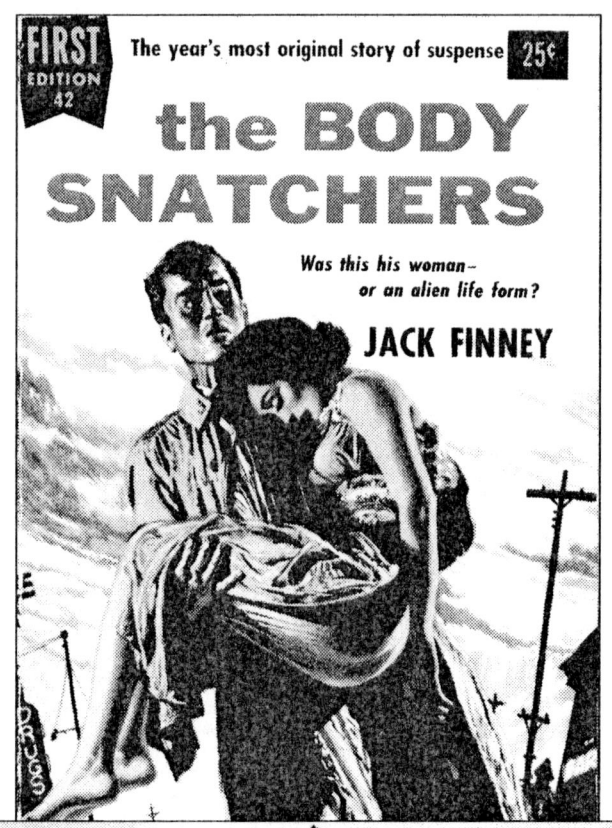

points to this cold-war classic, along with *Invaders from Mars* (1953), as two of his childhood favorites. (Matt Cowan discusses both films in this issue's installment of Threat Watch.)

The Invasion of the Body Snatchers is based on a 1954 novel by Jack Finney, which might be considered the quintessential example of alien replacement; except that the literary roots of the idea go back farther, to the year when pioneering editor John W. Campbell, Jr. published his novella "Who Goes There?" in the August 1938 issue of *Astounding Science Fiction*. The story is frequently anthologized and was faithfully adapted in 1982 by John Carpenter as *The Thing*. (We've reprinted Campbell's groundbreaking tale, along with Matt's take on *The Thing*, in this issue.)

Carpenter took his title from producer Howard Hawks, who helmed the less-than-faithful but nonetheless classic 1951 version, *The Thing from Another World*. There's no body-snatching in the Hawks' version, but the movie certainly captures the claustrophobic closeness of the snow and ice-bound research station. (By the way, the 1951 version helped inspire such films as *IT! The Terror from Beyond Space* (1958) and *Alien* (1979)— and other movies featuring a "deadly, monstrous menace in a confined space"—a good topic for a future issue of *Black Infinity*.)

In addition to Campbell's classic, this issue we present several vintage

tales of alien body-snatching in literature, including stories by Philip K. Dick, Jack Williamson, Lester del Rey, and others. Contemporary writers Douglas Smith, Kurt Newton, Gregory L. Smith, Marc Vun Kannon, and Rebekah Memel help round things out with their own unique takes on alien control, possession, and replacement.

In our comics section, we present a classic tale of the Space Rangers from issue 71 of *Planet Comics*.

The tale introduces the character of Borla, a Martian with uncanny mental powers.

Borla's appearance and Martian heritage remind us of another benevolent refugee from the Red Planet, one with shapeshifting abilities: J'onn J'onzz. Created by writer Joseph Samachson and artist Joe Certa, and introduced in *Detective Comics* #225 (Nov. 1955), J'onzz, the Manhunter from Mars, took on the human form of Police Detective John Jones.

Comics have been fertile ground for culti-

vating the seeds of alien mind-control and replacement. Perhaps the quintessential example is Marvel's *Secret Invasion,* which sported the tagline "Who do you trust?"

In Secret Invasion, a crossover story event running through most of Marvel's titles during 2008, readers learned that many of their favorite characters had long been replaced by the Skrull, a highly-advanced race of alien shapeshifters. (Not sure, but I seriously doubt the Skrull tried to replace Rocket Raccoon.)

Also in this stuffed issue, Todd Treichel feeds our fears by surveying the unsettling science behind mind control, in *How Weird Is That?* And, were this not enough, we also have ... uh, speaking of enough.... *Enough!*

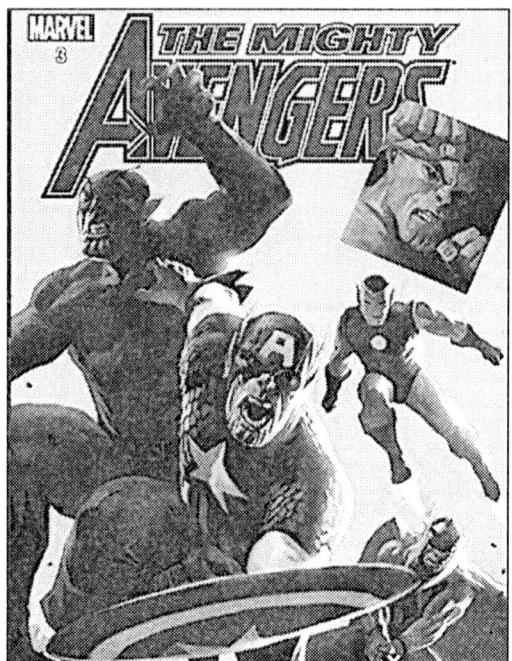

I always ask readers of these *usually* brief introductions to *please stand by* for the weird fact and fiction that follows, but this is absolutely insane. I've been running on like there's no tomorrow. Truth is, I don't know *what's* got into me lately.

I was fine—no, *really,* I was—until a few days ago when, late one evening, I saw those strange lights descending from the autumn sky. I can't explain it, but since then I just haven't been myself.

Tom English
New Kent, VA

Credits: page 2: Rod Serling helped legitimize TV fantasy with *The Twilight Zone*; p. 3 (clockwise): John Hoyt in "Will the Real Martian Please Stand Up?" (CBS, 1961); a mind-controlling, crab-like creature, from *The Outer Limits* episode "The Invisibles"; Submitting to alien control is hard work, but undercover agent Spain (Don Gordon) puts his back into it (MGM, 1964); p. 4: William Shatner as Kirk, paralyzed by the salt vampire, which assumed the identity of Nancy Crater (Jeanne Bal) in *Star Trek* series premiere, "The Man Trap" (Paramount, 1966); p. 6: Roy Thinnes as David Vincent; and the transformation process, from *The Invaders* (Paramount, 1967); p. 7: 1955 Dell "paperback original" of Finney's novel—from *Colliers Magazine,* 1954; ice-bound saucer, in *The Thing from Another World* (RKO, 1951); p. 8: awaiting their alien guest, in *TTFAW* (RKO, 1951); p. 9: (left) shapeshifter hero, the Martian Manhunter (DC Comics); homage to a classic *Avengers* cover, depicting Skrull replacements (Marvel Comics).

Is that really your closest friend—or a monstrous imitation, the spawn of a deadly alien world?

WHO GOES THERE?

by JOHN W. CAMPBELL, Jr.

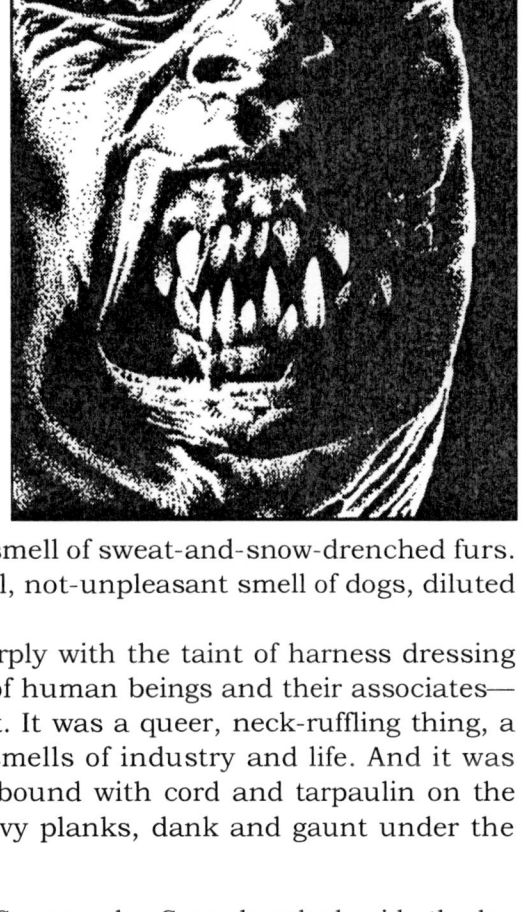

The place stank. A queer, mingled stench that only the ice-buried cabins of an Antarctic camp know, compounded of reeking human sweat, and the heavy, fish-oil stench of melted seal blubber. An overtone of liniment combatted the musty smell of sweat-and-snow-drenched furs. The acrid odor of burnt cooking fat, and the animal, not-unpleasant smell of dogs, diluted by time, hung in the air.

Lingering odors of machine oil contrasted sharply with the taint of harness dressing and leather. Yet, somehow, through all that reek of human beings and their associates—dogs, machines, and cooking—came another taint. It was a queer, neck-ruffling thing, a faintest suggestion of an odor alien among the smells of industry and life. And it was a life-smell. But it came from the thing that lay bound with cord and tarpaulin on the table, dripping slowly, methodically onto the heavy planks, dank and gaunt under the unshielded glare of the electric light.

Blair, the little bald-pated biologist of the expedition, twitched nervously at the wrappings, exposing clear, dark ice beneath and then pulling the tarpaulin back into place restlessly. His little birdlike motions of suppressed eagerness danced his shadow across the fringe of dingy gray underwear hanging from the low ceiling, the equatorial fringe of stiff, graying hair around his naked skull a comical halo about the shadow's head.

Commander Garry brushed aside the lax legs of a suit of underwear, and stepped toward the table. Slowly his eyes traced around the rings of men sardined into the Administration Building. His tall, stiff body straightened finally, and he nodded. "Thirty-seven. All here." His voice was low yet carried the clear authority of the commander by nature, as well as by title.

"You know the outline of the story back of

that find of the Secondary Pole Expedition. I have been conferring with Second-in-Command McReady, and Norris, as well as Blair and Dr. Copper. There is a difference of opinion, and because it involves the entire group, it is only just that the entire Expedition personnel act on it.

"I am going to ask McReady to give you the details of the story, because each of you has been too busy with his own work to follow closely the endeavors of the others. McReady?"

Moving from the smoke-blued background, McReady was a figure from some forgotten myth, a looming, bronze statue that held life, and walked. Six-feet-four-inches he stood as he halted beside the table, and with a characteristic glance upward to assure himself of room under the low ceiling beams, straightened. His rough, clashingly orange windproof jacket he still had on, yet on his huge frame it did not seem misplaced. Even here, four feet beneath the drift-wind that droned across the Antarctic waste above the ceiling, the cold of the frozen continent leaked in, and gave meaning to the harshness of the man. And he was bronze—his great red-bronze beard, the heavy hair that matched it. The gnarled, corded hands gripping, relaxing, gripping and relaxing on the table planks were bronze. Even the deep-sunken eyes beneath heavy brows were bronzed.

Age-resisting endurance of the metal spoke in the cragged heavy outlines of his face, and the mellow tones of the heavy voice. "Norris and Blair agree on one thing; that animal we found was not—terrestrial in origin. Norris fears there may be danger in that; Blair says there is none.

"But I'll go back to how, and why, we found it. To all that was known before we came here, it appeared that this point was exactly over the South Magnetic Pole of Earth. The compass does point straight down here, as you all know. The more delicate instruments of the physicists, instruments especially designed for this expedition and its study of the magnetic pole, detected a secondary effect, a secondary, less powerful magnetic influence about eighty miles southwest of here.

"The Secondary Magnetic Expedition went out to investigate it. There is no need for details. We found it, but it was not the huge meteorite or magnetic mountain Norris had expected to find. Iron ore is magnetic, of course; iron more so—and certain special steels even more magnetic. From the surface indications, the secondary pole we found was small, so small that the magnetic effect it had was preposterous. No magnetic material conceivable could have that effect. Soundings through the ice indicated it was within one hundred feet of the glacier surface.

"I think you should know the structure of the place. There is a broad plateau, a level sweep that runs more than 150 miles due south from the Secondary Station, Van Wall says. He didn't have time or fuel to fly farther, but it was running smoothly due south then. Right there, where that buried thing was, there is an ice-drowned mountain ridge, a granite wall of unshakable strength that has dammed back the ice creeping from the south.

"And four hundred miles due south is the South Polar Plateau. You have asked me at various times why it gets warmer here when the wind rises, and most of you know. As a meteorologist I'd have staked my word that no wind could blow at -70 degrees; that no more than a five-mile wind could blow at -50; without causing warming due to friction with ground, snow and ice, and the air itself.

"We camped there on the lip of that ice-drowned mountain range for twelve days. We dug our camp into the blue ice that formed the surface, and escaped most of it. But for twelve consecutive days the wind blew at forty-five miles an hour. It went as high as forty-eight, and fell to forty-one at times. The temperature was -63 degrees. It rose to -60 and fell to -68. It was meteorologically impossible, and it went on uninterruptedly for twelve days and twelve nights.

"Somewhere to the south, the frozen air of the South Polar Plateau slides down from that 18,000-foot bowl, down a mountain pass, over a glacier, and starts north. There must be a funneling mountain chain that directs it, and sweeps it away for four hundred miles to hit that bald plateau where we found the secondary pole, and 350 miles farther north reaches the Antarctic Ocean.

"It's been frozen there since Antarctica froze twenty million years ago. There never has been a thaw there.

"Twenty million years ago Antarctica was beginning to freeze. We've investigated, though, and built speculations. What we believe happened was about like this.

"Something came down out of space, a ship. We saw it there in the blue ice, a thing like a submarine without a conning tower or directive vanes, 280 feet long and 45 feet in diameter at its thickest.

"Eh, Van Wall? Space? Yes, but I'll explain that better later." McReady's steady voice went on.

"It came down from space, driven and lifted by forces men haven't discovered yet, and somehow—perhaps something went wrong then—it tangled with Earth's magnetic field. It came south here, out of control probably, circling the magnetic pole. That's a savage country there; but when Antarctica was still freezing, it must have been a thousand times more savage. There must have been blizzard snow, as well as drift, new snow falling as the continent glaciated. The swirl there must have been particularly bad, the wind hurling a solid blanket of white over the lip of that now-buried mountain.

"The ship struck solid granite head-on, and cracked up. Not every one of the passengers in it was killed, but the ship must have been ruined, her driving mechanism locked. It tangled with Earth's field, Norris believes. No thing made by intelligent beings can tangle with the dead immensity of a planet's natural forces and survive.

"One of its passengers stepped out. The wind we saw there never fell below forty-one, and the temperature never rose above -60. Then—the wind must have been stronger. And there was drift falling in a solid sheet. The *thing* was lost completely in ten paces." He paused for a moment, the deep, steady voice giving way to the drone of wind overhead and the uneasy, malicious gurgling in the pipe of the galley stove.

Drift—a drift-wind was sweeping by overhead. Right now the snow picked up by the mumbling wind fled in level, blinding lines across the face of the buried camp. If a man stepped out of the tunnels that connected each of the camp buildings beneath the surface, he'd be lost in ten paces. Out there, the slim, black finger of the radio mast lifted three hundred feet into the air, and at its peak was the clear night sky. A sky of thin, whining wind rushing steadily from beyond to another beyond under the licking, curling mantle of the aurora. And off north, the horizon flamed with queer, angry colors of the midnight twilight. That was Spring three hundred feet above Antarctica.

At the surface—it was white death. Death of a needle-fingered cold driven before the wind, sucking heat from any warm thing. Cold—and white mist of endless, everlasting drift, the fine, fine particles of licking snow that obscured all things.

Kinner, the little, scar-faced cook, winced. Five days ago he had stepped out to the surface to reach a cache of frozen beef. He had reached it, started back—and the drift-wind leapt out of the south. Cold, white death that streamed across the ground blinded him in twenty seconds. He stumbled on wildly in

circles. It was half an hour before rope-guided men from below found him in the impenetrable murk.

It was easy for man—or *thing*—to get lost in ten paces.

"And the drift-wind then was probably more impenetrable than we know." McReady's voice snapped Kinner's mind back. Back to the welcome, dank warmth of the Ad Building. "The passenger of the ship wasn't prepared either, it appears. It froze within ten feet of the ship.

"We dug down to find the ship, and our tunnel happened to find the frozen—animal. Barclay's ice-ax struck its skull.

"When we saw what it was, Barclay went back to the tractor, started the fire up and, when the steam pressure built, sent a call for Blair and Dr. Copper. Barclay himself was sick then. Stayed sick for three days, as a matter of fact.

"When Blair and Copper came, we cut out the animal in a block of ice, as you see, wrapped it and loaded it on the tractor for return here. We wanted to get into that ship.

"We reached the side and found the metal was something we didn't know. Our beryllium-bronze, non-magnetic tools wouldn't touch it. Barclay had some tool-steel on the tractor, and that wouldn't scratch it either. We made reasonable tests—even tried some acid from the batteries with no results.

"They must have had a passivating process to make magnesium metal resist acid that way, and the alloy must have been at least ninety-five percent magnesium. But we had no way of guessing that, so when we spotted the barely opened lock door, we cut around it. There was clear, hard ice inside the lock, where we couldn't reach it. Through the little crack we could look in and see that only metal and tools were in there, so we decided to loosen the ice with a bomb.

"We had decanite bombs and thermite. Thermite is the ice-softener; decanite might have shattered valuable things, where the thermite's heat would just loosen the ice. Dr. Copper, Norris and I placed a twenty-five-pound thermite bomb, wired it, and took the connector up the tunnel to the surface, where Blair had the steam tractor waiting. A hundred yards the other side of that granite wall we set off the thermite bomb.

"The magnesium metal of the ship caught, of course. The glow of the bomb flared and died, then it began to flare again. We ran back to the tractor, and gradually the glare built up. From where we were we could see the whole ice-field illuminated from beneath with an unbearable light; the ship's shadow was a great, dark cone reaching off toward the north, where the twilight was just about gone. For a moment it lasted, and we counted three other shadow-things that might have been other—passengers—frozen there. Then the ice was crashing down and against the ship.

"That's why I told you about that place. The wind sweeping down from the Pole was at our backs. Steam and hydrogen flame were torn away in white ice-fog; the flaming heat under the ice there was yanked away toward the Antarctic Ocean before it touched us. Otherwise we wouldn't have come back, even with the shelter of that granite ridge that stopped the light.

"Somehow in the blinding inferno we could see great hunched things—black bulks. They shed even the furious incandescence of the magnesium for a time. Those must have been the engines, we knew. Secrets going in blazing glory—secrets that might have given Man the planets. Mysterious things that could lift and hurl that ship—and had soaked in the force of the Earth's magnetic field. I saw Norris' mouth move, and ducked. I couldn't hear him.

"Insulation—something—gave way. All Earth's field they'd soaked up twenty million years before broke loose. The aurora in the sky above licked down, and the whole plateau there was bathed in cold fire that blanketed vision. The ice-ax in my hand got red hot, and hissed on the ice. Metal buttons on my clothes burned into me. And a flash of electric blue seared upward from beyond the granite wall.

"Then the walls of ice crashed down on it. For an instant it squealed the way dry ice does when it's pressed between metal.

"We were blind and groping in the dark for hours while our eyes recovered. We found every coil within a mile was fused rubbish, the dynamo and every radio set, the earphones and speakers. If we hadn't had the steam tractor, we wouldn't have gotten over to the Secondary Camp.

"Van Wall flew in from Big Magnet at sun-up, as you know. We came home as soon as possible. That is the history of—*that*." McReady's great bronze beard gestured toward the thing on the table.

II

BLAIR STIRRED UNEASILY, his little, bony fingers wriggling under the harsh light. Little brown freckles on his knuckles slid back and forth as the tendons under the skin twitched. He pulled aside a bit of the tarpaulin and looked impatiently at the dark ice-bound thing inside.

McReady's big body straightened somewhat. He'd ridden the rocking, jarring steam tractor forty miles that day, pushing on to Big Magnet here. Even his calm will had been pressed by the anxiety to mix again with humans. It was lone and quiet out there in Secondary Camp, where a wolf-wind howled down from the Pole. Wolf-wind howling in his sleep—winds droning and the evil, unspeakable face of that monster leering up as he'd first seen it through clear, blue ice, with a bronze ice-ax buried in its skull.

The giant meteorologist spoke again. "The problem is this. Blair wants to examine the thing. Thaw it out and make micro slides of its tissues and so forth. Norris doesn't believe that is safe, and Blair does. Dr. Copper agrees pretty much with Blair. Norris is a physicist, of course, not a biologist. But he makes a point I think we should all hear. Blair has described the microscopic life-forms biologists find living, even in this cold and inhospitable place. They freeze every winter, and thaw every summer—for three months—and live.

"The point Norris makes is—they thaw and live again. There must have been microscopic life associated with this creature. There is with every living thing we know. And Norris is afraid that we may release a plague—some germ disease unknown to Earth—if we thaw those microscopic things that have been frozen there for twenty million years.

"Blair admits that such micro-life might retain the power of living. Such unorganized things as individual cells can retain life for unknown periods, when solidly frozen. The beast itself is as dead as those frozen mammoths they find in Siberia. Organized, highly developed life-forms can't stand that treatment.

"But micro-life could. Norris suggests that we may release some disease-form that man, never having met it before, will be utterly defenseless against.

"Blair's answer is that there may be such still-living germs, but that Norris has the case reversed. They are utterly non-immune to man. Our life-chemistry probably—"

"Probably!" The little biologist's head lifted in a quick, birdlike motion. The halo of gray hair about his bald head ruffled as though angry. "Heh. One look—"

"I know," McReady acknowledged. "The thing is not Earthly. It does not seem likely that it can have a life-chemistry sufficiently like ours to make cross-infection remotely possible. I would say that there is no danger."

McReady looked toward Dr. Copper. The physician shook his head slowly. "None whatever," he asserted confidently. "Man cannot infect or be infected by germs that live in such comparatively close relatives as the snakes. And they are, I assure you," his clean-shaven face grimaced uneasily, "*much* nearer to us that—*that*."

Vance Norris moved angrily. He was comparatively short in this gathering of big men, some five feet eight, and his stocky, powerful build tended to make him seem shorter. His black hair was crisp and hard, like short steel wires, and his eyes were the gray of fractured steel. If McReady was a man of bronze, Norris was all steel. His movements, his thoughts, his whole bearing had the quick, hard impulse of a steel spring. His nerves were steel—hard, quick acting—swift corroding.

He was decided on his point now, and he lashed out in its defense with a characteristic quick, clipped flow of words. "Different chemistry be damned. That thing may be dead—or, by God, it may not—but I don't like it. Damn it, Blair, let them see the monstrosity you are petting over there. Let them see the foul thing and decide for themselves whether they want that thing thawed out in this camp.

"Thawed out, by the way. That's got to be thawed out in one of the shacks tonight, if it *is* thawed out. Somebody—who's watchman tonight? Magnetic—oh, Connant. Cosmic rays tonight. Well, you get to sit up with that twenty-million-year-old mummy of his. Unwrap it, Blair. How the hell can they tell what they are buying, if they can't see it? It may have a different chemistry. I don't care what else it has, but I know it has something I don't want. If you can judge by the look on its face—it isn't human so maybe you can't—it was annoyed when it froze. Annoyed, in fact, is just about as close an approximation of the way it felt, as crazy, mad, insane hatred. Neither one touches the subject.

"How the hell can these birds tell what they are voting on? They haven't seen those three red eyes and that blue hair like crawling worms. Crawling—damn, it's crawling there in the ice right now!

"Nothing Earth ever spawned had the unutterable sublimation of devastating wrath that thing let loose in its face when it looked around its frozen desolation twenty million years ago. Mad? It was mad clear through—searing, blistering mad!

"Hell, I've had bad dreams ever since I looked at those three red eyes. Nightmares. Dreaming the thing thawed out and came to life—that it wasn't dead, or even wholly unconscious all those twenty million years, but just slowed, waiting—waiting. You'll dream, too, while that damned thing that Earth wouldn't own is dripping, dripping in the Cosmos House tonight.

"And, Connant," Norris whipped toward the cosmic ray specialist, "won't you have fun sitting up all night in the quiet. Wind whining above—and that thing dripping—" he stopped for a moment and looked around.

"I know. That's not science. But this is, it's psychology. You'll have nightmares for a year to come. Every night since I looked at that thing I've had 'em. That's why I hate it—sure I do—and don't want it around. Put it back where it came from and let it freeze for another twenty million years. I had some swell nightmares—that it wasn't made like we are—which is obvious—but of a different kind of flesh that it can really control. That it can

change its shape, and look like a man—and wait to kill and eat—

"That's not a logical argument. I know it isn't. The thing isn't Earth-logic anyway.

"Maybe it has an alien body-chemistry, and maybe its bugs do have a different body-chemistry. A germ might not stand that, but, Blair and Copper, how about a virus? That's just an enzyme molecule, you've said. That wouldn't need anything but a protein molecule of any body to work on.

"And how are you so sure that, of the million varieties of microscopic life it may have, *none* of them are dangerous. How about diseases like hydrophobia—rabies—that attack any warm-blooded creature, whatever its body-chemistry may be? And parrot fever? Have you a body like a parrot, Blair? And plain rot—gangrene—necrosis if you want? *That* isn't choosy about body chemistry!"

Blair looked up from his puttering long enough to meet Norris' angry, gray eyes for an instant. "So far the only thing you have said this thing gave off that was catching was dreams. I'll go so far as to admit that." An impish, slightly malignant grin crossed the little man's seamed face. "I had some, too. So. It's dream-infectious. No doubt an exceedingly dangerous malady.

"So far as your other things go, you have a badly mistaken idea about viruses. In the first place, nobody has shown that the enzyme-molecule theory, and that alone, explains them. And in the second place, when you catch tobacco mosaic or wheat rust, let me know. A wheat plant is a lot nearer your body-chemistry than this other-world creature is.

"And your rabies is limited, strictly limited. You can't get it from, nor give it to, a wheat plant or a fish—which is a collateral descendant of a common ancestor of yours. Which *this*, Norris, is not." Blair nodded pleasantly toward the tarpaulined bulk on the table.

"Well, thaw the damned thing in a tub of formalin if you must. I've suggested that—"

"And I've said there would be no sense in it. You can't compromise. Why did you and Commander Garry come down here to study magnetism? Why weren't you content to stay at home? There's magnetic force enough in New York. I could no more study the life this thing once had from a formalin-pickled sample than you could get the information you wanted back in New York. And—if this one is so treated, *never in all time to come can there be a duplicate!* The race it came from must have passed away in the twenty million years it lay frozen, so that even if it came from Mars then, we'd never find its like. And—the ship is gone.

"There's only one way to do this—and that is the best possible way. It must be thawed slowly, carefully, and not in formalin."

Commander Garry stood forward again, and Norris stepped back muttering angrily. "I think Blair is right, gentlemen. What do you say?"

Connant grunted. "It sounds right to us, I think—only perhaps he ought to stand watch over it while it's thawing." He grinned ruefully, brushing a stray lock of ripe-cherry hair back from his forehead. "Swell idea, in fact—if he sits up with his jolly little corpse."

Garry smiled slightly. A general chuckle of agreement rippled over the group. "I should think any ghost it may have had would have starved to death if it hung around here that long, Connant," Garry suggested. "And you look capable of taking care of it. 'Ironman' Connant ought to be able to take out any opposing players, still."

Connant shook himself uneasily. "I'm not worrying about ghosts. Let's see that thing. I—"

Eagerly Blair was stripping back the ropes. A single throw of the tarpaulin revealed the thing. The ice had melted somewhat in the heat of the room, and it was clear and blue as thick, good glass. It shone wet and sleek under the harsh light of the unshielded globe above.

The room stiffened abruptly. It was face up there on the plain, greasy planks of the table. The broken haft of the bronze ice-ax was still buried in the queer skull. Three mad, hate-filled eyes blazed up with a living fire, bright as fresh-spilled blood, from a face ringed with a writhing, loathsome nest of worms, blue, mobile worms that crawled where hair should grow—

Van Wall, six feet and two hundred pounds of ice-nerved pilot, gave a queer, strangled gasp, and butted, stumbled his way out to the corridor. Half the company broke for the doors. The others stumbled away from the table.

McReady stood at one end of the table watching them, his great body planted solid on his powerful legs. Norris from the opposite end glowered at the thing with smouldering hate. Outside the door, Garry was talking with half a dozen of the men at once.

Blair had a tack hammer. The ice that cased the thing *schluffed* crisply under its steel claw as it peeled from the thing it had cased for twenty thousand thousand years—

III

"I KNOW YOU DON'T LIKE THE THING, CONNANT, but it just has to be thawed out right. You say leave it as it is till we get back to civilization. All right, I'll admit your argument that we could do a better and more complete job there is sound. But—how are we going to get this across the Line? We have to take this through one temperate zone, the equatorial zone, and halfway through the other temperate zone before we get it to New York. You don't want to sit with it *one* night, but you suggest, then, that I hang its corpse in the freezer with the beef?" Blair looked up from his cautious chipping, his bald freckled skull nodding triumphantly.

Kinner, the stocky, scar-faced cook, saved Connant the trouble of answering. "Hey, you listen, mister. You put that thing in the box with the meat, and by all the gods there ever were, I'll put you in to keep it company. You birds have brought everything movable in this camp in onto my mess tables here already, and I had to stand for that. But you go putting things like that in my meat box, or even my meat cache here, and you cook your own damn grub."

"But, Kinner, this is the only table in Big Magnet that's big enough to work on," Blair objected. "Everybody's explained that."

"Yeah, and everybody's brought everything in here. Clark brings his dogs every time there's a fight and sews them up on that table. Ralsen brings in his sledges. Hell, the only thing you haven't had on that table is the Boeing. And you'd 'a' had that in if you coulda figured a way to get it through the tunnels."

Commander Garry chuckled and grinned at Van Wall, the huge Chief Pilot. Van Wall's great blond beard twitched suspiciously as he nodded gravely to Kinner. "You're right,

Kinner. The aviation department is the only one that treats you right."

"It does get crowded, Kinner," Garry acknowledged. "But I'm afraid we all find it that way at times. Not much privacy in an Antarctic camp."

"Privacy? What the hell's that? You know, the thing that really made me weep, was when I saw Barclay marchin' through here chantin' 'The last lumber in the camp! The last lumber in the camp!' and carryin' it out to build that house on his tractor. Damn it, I missed that moon cut in the door he carried out more'n I missed the sun when it set. That wasn't just the last lumber Barclay was walkin' off with. He was carryin' off the last bit of privacy in this blasted place."

A grin rode even Connant's heavy face as Kinner's perennial, good-natured grouch came up again. But it died away quickly as his dark, deep-set eyes turned again to the red-eyed thing Blair was chipping from its cocoon of ice. A big hand ruffed his shoulder-length hair and tugged at a twisted lock that fell behind his ear in a familiar gesture. "I know that cosmic ray shack's going to be too crowded if I have to sit up with that thing," he growled. "Why can't you go on chipping the ice away from around it—you can do that without anybody butting in, I assure you—and then hang the thing up over the power-plant boiler? That's warm enough. It'll thaw out a chicken, even a whole side of beef, in a few hours."

"I know," Blair protested, dropping the tack hammer to gesture more effectively with his bony, freckled fingers, his small body tense with eagerness, "but this is too important to take any chances. There never was a find like this; there never can be again. It's the only chance men will ever have, and it has to be done exactly right.

"Look, you know how the fish we caught down near the Ross Sea would freeze almost as soon as we got them on deck, and come to life again if we thawed them gently? Low forms of life aren't killed by quick freezing and slow thawing. We have—"

"Hey, for the love of Heaven—you mean that damned thing will come to life!" Connant yelled. "You get the damned thing— Let me at it! That's going to be in so many pieces—"

"No! No, you fool—" Blair jumped in front of Connant to protect his precious find. "No. Just low forms of life. For Pete's sake let me finish. You can't thaw higher forms of life and have them come to. Wait a moment now—hold it! A fish can come to after freezing because it's so low a form of life that the individual cells of its body can revive, and that alone is enough to reestablish life. Any higher forms thawed out that way are dead. Though the individual cells revive, they die because there must be organization and cooperative effort to live. That cooperation cannot be reestablished. There is a sort of potential life in any uninjured, quick-frozen animal. But it can't—can't under any circumstances—become active life in higher animals. The higher animals are too complex, too delicate. This is an intelligent creature as high in its evolution as we are in ours. Perhaps higher. It is as dead as a frozen man would be."

"How do you know?" demanded Connant, hefting the ice-ax he had seized a moment before.

Commander Garry laid a restraining hand on his heavy shoulder. "Wait a minute, Connant. I want to get this straight. I agree that there is going to be no thawing of this thing if there is the remotest chance of its revival. I quite agree it is much too unpleasant to have alive, but I had no idea there was the remotest possibility."

Dr. Copper pulled his pipe from between his teeth and heaved his stocky, dark body from the bunk he had been sitting in. "Blair's being technical. That's dead. As dead as the mammoths they find frozen in Siberia. We have all sorts of proof that things don't live after being frozen—not even fish, generally speaking—and no proof that higher animal life can under any circumstances. What's the point, Blair?"

The little biologist shook himself. The little ruff of hair standing out around his bald pate waved in righteous anger. "The point is," he said in an injured tone, "that the individual cells might show the characteristics they had in life if it is properly thawed. A man's muscle cells live many hours after he has died. Just because they live, and a few things like hair and fingernail cells still live, you wouldn't accuse a corpse of being a zombie, or something.

"Now if I thaw this right, I may have a chance to determine what sort of world it's native to. We don't, and can't know by any other means, whether it came from Earth or Mars or Venus or from beyond the stars.

"And just because it looks unlike men, you don't have to accuse it of being evil, or vicious or something. Maybe that expression on its face is its equivalent to a resignation to fate. White is the color of mourning to the Chinese. If men can have different customs, why can't a so-different race have different understandings of facial expressions?"

Connant laughed softly, mirthlessly. "Peaceful resignation! If that is the best it could do in the way of resignation, I should exceedingly dislike seeing it when it was looking mad. That face was never designed to express peace. It just didn't have any philosophical thoughts like peace in its make-up.

"I know it's your pet—but be sane about it. That thing grew up on evil, adolesced slowly roasting alive the local equivalent of kittens, and amused itself through maturity on new and ingenious torture."

"You haven't the slightest right to say that," snapped Blair. "How do you know the first thing about the meaning of a facial expression inherently inhuman? It may well have no human equivalent whatever. That is just a different development of Nature, another example of Nature's wonderful adaptability. Growing on another, perhaps harsher world, it has different form and features. But it is just as much a legitimate child of Nature as you are. You are displaying that childish human weakness of hating the different. On its own world it would probably class you as a fish-belly, white monstrosity with an insufficient number of eyes and a fungoid body pale and bloated with gas.

"Just because its nature is different, you haven't any right to say it's necessarily evil."

Norris burst out a single, explosive, "Haw!" He looked down at the thing. "Maybe that things from other worlds don't *have* to be evil just because they're different. But that thing *was!* Child of Nature, eh? Well, it was a hell of an evil Nature."

"Aw, will you mugs cut crabbing at each other and get the damned thing off my table?" Kinner growled. "And put a canvas over it. It looks indecent."

"Kinner's gone modest," jeered Connant.

Kinner slanted his eyes up to the big physicist. The scarred cheek twisted to join the line of his tight lips in a twisted grin. "All right, big boy, and what were you grousing about a minute ago? We can set the thing in a chair next to you tonight, if you want."

"I'm not afraid of its face," Connant snapped. "I don't like keeping a wake over its corpse particularly, but I'm going to do it."

Kinner's grin spread. "Uh-huh." He went off to the galley stove and shook down ashes vigorously, drowning the brittle chipping of the ice as Blair fell to work again.

IV

"CLUCK," REPORTED THE COSMIC-RAY COUNTER, "cluck-burrrp-cluck."

Connant started and dropped his pencil.

"Damnation." The physicist looked toward the far corner, back at the Geiger counter on the table near that corner. And crawled under the desk at which he had been working to retrieve the pencil. He sat down at his work again, trying to make his writing more even.

It tended to have jerks and quavers in it, in time with the abrupt proud-hen noises of the Geiger counter. The muted whoosh of the pressure lamp he was using for illumination, the mingled gargles and bugle calls of a dozen men sleeping down the corridor in Paradise House formed the background sounds for the irregular, clucking noises of the counter, the occasional rustle of falling coal in the copper-bellied stove. And a soft, steady *drip-drip-drip* from the thing in the corner.

Connant jerked a pack of cigarettes from his pocket, snapped it so that a cigarette protruded, and jabbed the cylinder into his mouth. The lighter failed to function, and he pawed angrily through the pile of papers in search of a match. He scratched the wheel of the lighter several times, dropped it with a curse and got up to pluck a hot coat from the stove with the coal tongs.

The lighter functioned instantly when he tried it on returning to the desk. The counter ripped out a series of chuckling guffaws as a burst of cosmic rays struck through to it. Connant turned to glower at it, and tried to concentrate on the interpretation of data collected during the past week. The weekly summary—

He gave up and yielded to curiosity, or nervousness. He lifted the pressure lamp from the desk and carried it over to the table in the corner. Then he returned to the stove and picked up the coal tongs. The beast had been thawing for nearly eighteen hours now. He poked at it with an unconscious caution; the flesh was no longer hard as armor plate, but had assumed a rubbery texture. It looked like wet, blue rubber glistening under droplets of water like little round jewels in the glare of the gasoline pressure lantern. Connant felt an unreasoning desire to pour the contents of the lamp's reservoir over the thing in its box and drop the cigarette into it. The three red eyes glared up at him sightlessly, the ruby eyeballs reflecting murky, smoky rays of light.

He realized vaguely that he had been looking at them for a very long time, even vaguely understood that they were no longer sightless. But it did not seem of importance, of no more importance than the labored, slow motion of the tentacular things that sprouted from the base of the scrawny, slowly pulsing neck.

Connant picked up the pressure lamp and returned to his chair. He sat down, staring at the pages of mathematics before him. The clucking of the counter was strangely less disturbing, the rustle of the coals in the stove no longer distracting.

The creak of the floorboards behind him didn't interrupt his thoughts as he went about his weekly report in an automatic manner, filling in columns of data and making brief, summarizing notes.

The creak of the floorboards sounded nearer.

V

BLAIR CAME UP FROM the nightmare-haunted depths of sleep abruptly. Connant's face floated vaguely above him; for a moment it seemed a continuance of the wild horror of the dream. But Connant's face was angry, and a little frightened. "Blair—Blair you damned log, wake up."

"Uh-eh?" the little biologist rubbed his eyes, his bony, freckled finger crooked to a mutilated child-fist. From surrounding bunks other faces lifted to stare down at them.

Connant straightened up. "Get up—and get a lift on. Your damned animal's escaped."

"Escaped—what!" Chief Pilot Van Wall's bull voice roared out with a volume that shook the walls. Down the communication tunnels other voices yelled suddenly. The dozen inhabitants of Paradise House tumbled in abruptly, Barclay, stocky and bulbous in long woolen underwear, carrying a fire extinguisher.

"What the hell's the matter?" Barclay demanded.

"Your damned beast got loose. I fell asleep about twenty minutes ago, and when I woke up, the thing was gone. Hey, Doc, the hell you say those things can't come to life. Blair's blasted potential life developed a hell of a lot of potential and walked out on us."

Copper stared blankly. "It wasn't—Earthly," he sighed suddenly. "I—I guess Earthly laws don't apply."

"Well, it applied for leave of absence and took it. We've got to find it and capture it somehow." Connant swore bitterly, his deep-set black eyes sullen and angry. "It's a wonder the hellish creature didn't eat me in my sleep."

Blair started back, his pale eyes suddenly fear-struck. "Maybe it di—er—uh—we'll have to find it."

"You find it. It's your pet. I've had all I want to do with it, sitting there for seven hours with the counter clucking every few seconds, and you birds in here singing night-music. It's a wonder I got to sleep. I'm going through to the Ad Building."

Commander Garry ducked through the doorway, pulling his belt tight. "You won't have to. Van's roar sounded like the Boeing taking off downwind. So it wasn't dead?"

"I didn't carry it off in my arms, I assure you," Connant snapped. "The last I saw, the split skull was oozing green goo, like a squashed caterpillar. Doc just said our laws don't work—it's unearthly. Well, it's an unearthly monster, with an unearthly disposition, judging by the face, wandering around with a split skull and brains oozing out." Norris and McReady appeared in the doorway, a doorway filling with other shivering men. "Has anybody seen it coming over here?" Norris asked innocently. "About four feet tall—three red eyes—brains oozing out— Hey, has anybody checked to make sure this isn't a cracked idea of humor? If it is, I think we'll unite in tying Blair's pet around Connant's neck like the Ancient Mariner's albatross."

"It's no humor," Connant shivered. "Lord, I wish it were. I'd rather wear—" He stopped. A wild, weird howl shrieked through the corridors. The men stiffened abruptly, and half turned.

"I think it's been located," Connant finished. His dark eyes shifted with a queer unease. He darted back to his bunk in Paradise House, to return almost immediately with a heavy .45 revolver and an ice-ax. He hefted both gently as he started for the corridor toward Dogtown.

"It blundered down the wrong corridor—and landed among the huskies. Listen—the dogs have broken their chains—"

The half-terrorized howl of the dog pack had changed to a wild hunting melee. The voices of the dogs thundered in the narrow corridors, and through them came a low rippling snarl of distilled hate. A shrill of pain, a dozen snarling yelps.

Connant broke for the door. Close behind him, McReady, then Barclay and Commander Garry came. Other men broke for the Ad Building, and weapons—the sledge house. Pomroy, in charge of Big Magnet's five cows, started down the corridor in the opposite direction—he had a six-foot-handled, long-tined pitchfork in mind.

Barclay slid to a halt, as McReady's giant bulk turned abruptly away from the tunnel leading to Dogtown, and vanished off at an angle. Uncertainly, the mechanician wavered a moment, the fire extinguisher in his hands, hesitating from one side to the other. Then he was racing after Connant's broad back. Whatever McReady had in mind, he could be trusted to make it work.

Connant stopped at the bend in the corridor. His breath hissed suddenly through his throat. "Great God—" The revolver exploded thunderously; three numbing, palpable waves of sound crashed through the confined corridors. Two more. The revolver dropped to the hard-packed snow of the trail, and Barclay saw the ice-ax shift into defensive position. Connant's powerful body blocked his vision, but beyond he heard something mewing, and, insanely, chuckling. The dogs were quieter; there was a deadly seriousness in their low snarls. Taloned feet scratched at hard-packed snow, broken chains were clinking and tangling.

Connant shifted abruptly, and Barclay could see what lay beyond. For a second he stood frozen, then his breath went out in a gusty curse. The Thing launched itself at Connant, the powerful arms of the man swung the ice-ax flat-side first at what might have been a head. It scrunched horribly, and the tattered flesh, ripped by a half-dozen savage huskies, leapt to its feet again. The red eyes blazed with an unearthly hatred, an unearthly, unkillable vitality.

Barclay turned the fire extinguisher on it; the blinding, blistering stream of chemical spray confused it, baffled it, together with the savage attacks of the huskies, not for long afraid of anything that did, or could live, and held it at bay.

McReady wedged men out of his way and drove down the narrow corridor packed with

men unable to reach the scene. There was a sure foreplanned drive to McReady's attack. One of the giant blowtorches used in warming the plane's engines was in his bronzed hands. It roared gustily as he turned the corner and opened the valve. The mad mewing hissed louder. The dogs scrambled back from the three-foot lance of blue-hot flame.

"Bar, get a power cable, run it in somehow. And a handle. We can electrocute this—monster, if I don't incinerate it." McReady spoke with an authority of planned action. Barclay turned down the long corridor to the power plant, but already before him Norris and Van Wall were racing down.

BARCLAY FOUND THE CABLE in the electrical cache in the tunnel wall. In a half minute he was hacking at it, walking back. Van Wall's

voice rang out in a warning shout of "Power!" as the emergency gasoline-powered dynamo thudded into action. Half a dozen other men were down there now; the coal kindling were going into the firebox of the steam power plant. Norris, cursing in a low, deadly monotone, was working with quick, sure fingers on the other end of Barclay's cable, splicing a contractor into one of the power leads.

The dogs had fallen back when Barclay reached the corridor bend, fallen back before a furious monstrosity that glared from baleful red eyes, mewing in trapped hatred. The dogs were a semicircle of red-dipped muzzles with a fringe of glistening white teeth, whining with a vicious eagerness that near matched the fury of the red eyes. McReady stood confidently alert at the corridor bend, the gustily muttering torch held loose and ready for action in his hands. He stepped aside without moving his eyes from the beast as Barclay came up. There was a slight, tight smile on his lean, bronzed face.

Norris' voice called down the corridor, and Barclay stepped forward. The cable was taped to the long handle of a snow shovel, the two conductors split and held eighteen inches apart by a scrap of lumber lashed at right angles across the far end of the handle. Bare copper conductors, charged with 220 volts, glinted in the light of pressure lamps. The Thing mewed and hated and dodged. McReady advanced to Barclay's side. The dogs beyond sensed the plan with the almost telepathic intelligence of trained huskies. Their whining grew shriller, softer, their mincing steps carried them nearer. Abruptly a huge night-black Alaskan leapt onto the trapped thing. It turned squalling, saber-clawed feet slashing.

Barclay leapt forward and jabbed. A weird, shrill scream rose and choked out. The smell of burnt flesh in the corridor intensified; greasy smoke curled up. The echoing pound of the gas-electric dynamo down the corridor became a slogging thud.

The red eyes clouded over in a stiffening, jerking travesty of a face. Armlike, leglike members quivered and jerked. The dogs leapt forward, and Barclay yanked back his shovel-handled weapon. The thing on the snow did not move as gleaming teeth ripped it open.

VI

GARRY LOOKED ABOUT THE CROWDED ROOM. Thirty-two men, some tensed nervously standing against the wall, some uneasily relaxed, some sitting, most perforce standing as intimate as sardines. Thirty-two, plus the five engaged in sewing up wounded dogs, made thirty-seven, the total personnel.

Garry started speaking. "All right, I guess we're here. Some of you—three or four at most—saw what happened. All of you have seen that thing on the table, and can get a general idea. Anyone hasn't, I'll lift—" His hand strayed to the tarpaulin bulking over the thing on the table. There was an acrid odor of singed flesh seeping out of it. The men stirred restlessly, hasty denials.

"It looks rather as though Charnauk isn't going to lead any more teams," Garry went on. "Blair wants to get at this thing and make some more detailed examination. We want to know what happened, and make sure right now that this is permanently, totally dead. Right?"

Connant grinned. "Anybody that doesn't can sit up with it tonight."

"All right then, Blair, what can you say about it? What was it?" Garry turned to the little biologist.

"I wonder if we ever saw its natural form," Blair looked at the covered mass. "It may have been imitating the beings that built that ship—but I don't think it was. I think that was its true form. Those of us who were up near the bend saw the thing in action; the thing on the table is the result. When it got loose, apparently, it started looking around. Antarctica still frozen as it was ages ago when the creature first saw it—and froze. From my observations while it was thawing out, and the bits of tissue I cut and hardened then, I think it was native to a hotter planet than Earth. It couldn't, in its natural form, stand the temperature. There is no life-form on Earth that can live in Antarctica during the winter, but the best compromise is the dog. It found the dogs, and somehow got near enough to Charnauk to get him. The others smelled it—heard it—I don't know—anyway they went wild, and broke chains, and attacked it before it was finished. The thing we found was part Charnauk, queerly only half-dead, part Charnauk half-digested by the jellylike protoplasm of that creature, and part the remains of the thing we originally found, sort of melted down to the basic protoplasm.

"When the dogs attacked it, it turned into the best fighting thing it could think of. Some other-world beast apparently."

"Turned," snapped Garry. "How?"

"Every living thing is made up of jelly—protoplasm and minute, submicroscopic things called nuclei, which control the bulk, the protoplasm. This thing was just a modification of that same world-wide plan of Nature; cells made up of protoplasm, controlled by infinitely tinier nuclei. You physicists might compare it—an individual cell of any living thing—with an atom; the bulk of the atom, the space-filling part, is made up of the electron orbits, but the character of the thing is determined by the atomic nucleus.

"This isn't wildly beyond what we already know. It's just a modification we haven't seen before. It's as natural, as logical, as any other manifestation of life. It obeys exactly the same laws. The cells are made of protoplasm, their character determined by the nucleus.

"Only, in this creature, the cell nuclei can control those cells *at will*. It digested Charnauk, and as it digested, studied every cell of his tissue, and shaped its own cells to imitate them exactly. Parts of it—parts that had time to finish changing—are dog-cells. But they don't have dog-cell nuclei." Blair lifted a fraction of the tarpaulin. A torn dog's leg, with stiff gray fur protruded. "That, for instance, isn't dog at all; it's imitation. Some parts I'm uncertain about; the nucleus was hiding itself, covering up with dog-cell imitation nucleus. In time, not even a microscope would have shown the difference."

"Suppose," asked Norris bitterly, "it had had lots of time?"

"Then it would have been a dog. The other dogs would have accepted it. We would have accepted it. I don't think anything would have distinguished it, not microscope, nor X-ray, nor any other means. This is a member of a supremely intelligent race, a race that has learned the deepest secrets of biology, and turned them to its use."

"What was it planning to do?" Barclay looked at the humped tarpaulin.

Blair grinned unpleasantly. The halo of thin hair round his bald pate wavered in a stir of air. "Take over the world, I imagine."

"Take over the world! Just it, all by itself?" Connant gasped. "Set itself up as a lone dictator?"

"No," Blair shook his head. The scalpel he had been fumbling in his bony fingers dropped; he bent to pick it up, so that his face was hidden as he spoke. "It would become the population of the world."

"Become—populate the world? Does it reproduce asexually?"

Blair shook his head and gulped. "It's—it doesn't have to. It weighed 85 pounds. Charnauk weighed about 90. It would have become Charnauk, and had 85 pounds left, to become—oh, Jack, for instance, or Chinook. It can imitate anything—that is, become anything. If it had reached the Antarctic Sea, it would have become a seal, maybe two seals. They might have attacked a killer whale, and become either killers, or a herd of seals. Or maybe it would have caught an albatross, or a skua gull, and flown to South America."

Norris cursed softly. "And every time it digested something, and imitated it—"

"It would have had its original bulk left, to start again," Blair finished. "Nothing would kill it. It has no natural enemies, because it becomes whatever it wants to. If a killer whale attacked it, it would become a killer whale. If it was an albatross, and an eagle attacked it, it would become an eagle. Lord, it might become a female eagle. Go back—build a nest and lay eggs!"

"Are you sure that thing from hell is dead?" Dr. Copper asked softly.

"Yes, thank Heaven," the little biologist gasped. "After they drove the dogs off, I stood there poking Bar's electrocution thing into it for five minutes. It's dead and—cooked."

"Then we can only give thanks that this is Antarctica, where there is not one, single, solitary, living thing for it to imitate, except these animals in camp."

"Us," Blair giggled. "It can imitate us. Dogs can't make four hundred miles to the sea; there's no food. There aren't any skua gulls to imitate at this season. There aren't any penguins this far inland. There's nothing that can reach the sea from this point—except us. We've got brains. We can do it. Don't you see—*it's got to imitate us—it's got to be one of us—that's the only way it can fly an airplane—fly a plane for two hours, and rule—be—all Earth's inhabitants. A world for the taking—if it imitates us!*

"It didn't know yet. It hadn't had a chance to learn. It was rushed—hurried—took the thing nearest its own size. Look—I'm Pandora! I opened the box! And the only hope that can come out is—that nothing can come out. You didn't see me. I did it. I fixed it. I smashed every magneto. Not a plane can fly. Nothing can fly." Blair giggled and lay down on the floor crying.

Chief Pilot Van Wall made for the door. His feet were fading echoes in the corridors as Dr. Copper bent unhurriedly over the little man on the floor. From his office at the end of the room he brought something and injected a solution into Blair's arm. "He might come out of it when he wakes up," he sighed, rising. McReady helped him lift the biologist onto a nearby bunk. "It all depends on whether we can convince him that thing is dead."

Van Wall ducked into the shack, brushing his heavy blond beard absently. "I didn't think a biologist would do a thing like that up thoroughly. He missed the spares in the second cache. It's all right. I smashed them."

Commander Garry nodded. "I was wondering about the radio."

Dr. Copper snorted. "You don't think it can leak out on a radio wave, do you? You'd have five rescue attempts in the next three months if you stop the broadcasts. The thing to do is talk loud and not make a sound. Now I wonder—"

McReady looked speculatively at the doctor. "It might be like an infectious disease. Everything that drank any of its blood—"

Copper shook his head. "Blair missed something. Imitate it may, but it has, to a certain extent, its own body chemistry, its own metabolism. If it didn't, it would become a dog—and be a dog and nothing more. It has to be an imitation dog. Therefore you can detect it by serum tests. And its chemistry, since it comes from another world, must be so wholly, radically different that a few cells, such as gained by drops of blood, would be treated as disease germs by the dog, or human body."

"Blood—would one of those imitations bleed?" Norris demanded.

"Surely. Nothing mystic about blood. Muscle is about 90% water; blood differs only in having a couple percent more water, and less connective tissue. They'd bleed all right," Copper assured him.

Blair sat up in his bunk suddenly. "Connant—where's Connant?"

The physicist moved over toward the little biologist. "Here I am. What do you want?"

"Are you?" giggled Blair. He lapsed back into the bunk contorted with silent laughter.

Connant looked at him blankly. "Huh? Am I what?"

"*Are* you there?" Blair burst into gales of

laughter. "*Are* you Connant? The beast wanted to be a *man*—not a dog—"

VII

DR. COPPER ROSE WEARILY from the bunk, and washed the hypodermic carefully. The little tinkles it made seemed loud in the packed room, now that Blair's gurgling laughter had finally quieted. Copper looked toward Garry and shook his head slowly. "Hopeless, I'm afraid. I don't think we can ever convince him the thing is dead now."

Norris laughed uncertainly. "I'm not sure you can convince me. Oh, damn you, McReady."

"McReady?" Commander Garry turned to look from Norris to McReady curiously.

"The nightmares," Norris explained. "He had a theory about the nightmares we had at the Secondary Station after finding that thing."

"And that was?" Garry looked at McReady levelly.

Norris answered for him, jerkily, uneasily. "That the creature wasn't dead, had a sort of enormously slowed existence, an existence that permitted it, nonetheless, to be vaguely aware of the passing of time, of our coming, after endless years. I had a dream it could imitate things."

"Well," Copper grunted, "it can."

"Don't be an ass," Norris snapped. "That's not what's bothering me. In the dream it could read minds, read thoughts and ideas and mannerisms."

"What's so bad about that? It seems to be worrying you more than the thought of the joy we're going to have with a madman in an Antarctic camp." Copper nodded toward Blair's sleeping form.

McReady shook his great head slowly. "You know that Connant is Connant, because he not merely looks like Connant—which we're beginning to believe that beast might be able to do—but he thinks like Connant,

moves himself around as Connant does. That takes more than merely a body that looks like him; that takes Connant's own mind, and thoughts and mannerisms. Therefore, though you know that the thing might make itself *look* like Connant, you aren't much bothered, because you know it has a mind from another world, a totally unhuman mind, that couldn't possibly react and think and talk like a man we know, and do it so well as to fool us for a moment. The idea of the creature imitating one of us is fascinating, but unreal, because it is too completely unhuman to deceive us. It doesn't have a human mind."

"As I said before," Norris repeated, looking steadily at McReady, "you can say the damnedest things at the damnedest times. Will you be so good as to finish that thought—one way or the other?"

Kinner, the scar-faced expedition cook, had been standing near Connant. Suddenly he moved down the length of the crowded room toward his familiar galley. He shook the ashes from the galley stove noisily.

"It would do it no good," said Dr. Copper, softly as though thinking out loud, "to merely look like something it was trying to imitate; it would have to understand its feelings, its reactions. It is unhuman; it has powers of imitation beyond any conception of man. A good actor, by training himself, can imitate another man, another man's mannerisms, well enough to fool most people. Of course, no actor could imitate so perfectly as to deceive men who had been living with the imitated one in the complete lack of privacy of an Antarctic camp. That would take a superhuman skill."

"Oh, you've got the bug, too?" Norris cursed softly.

Connant, standing alone at one end of the room, looked about him wildly, his face white. A gentle eddying of the men had crowded them slowly down toward the other end of the room, so that he stood quite alone. "My God, will you two Jeremiahs shut up?" Connant's voice shook. "What am I? Some kind of microscopic specimen you're dissecting? Some unpleasant worm you're discussing in the third person?"

McReady looked up at him; his slowly twisting hands stopped for a moment. "Having a lovely time. Wish you were here. Signed: Everybody."

"Connant, if you think you're having a hell of a time, just move over on the other end for a while. You've got one thing we haven't; you know what the answer is. I'll tell you this, right now you're the most feared and respected man in Big Magnet."

"Lord, I wish you could see your eyes," Connant gasped. "Stop staring, will you! What the hell are you going to do?"

"Have you any suggestions, Dr. Copper?" Commander Garry asked steadily. "The present situation is impossible."

"Oh, is it?" Connant snapped. "Come over here and look at that crowd. By Heaven, they look exactly like that gang of huskies around the corridor bend. Benning, will you stop hefting that damned ice-ax?"

The coppery blade rang on the floor as the aviation mechanic nervously dropped it. He bent over and picked it up instantly, hefting it slowly, turning it in his hands, his brown eyes moving jerkily about the room.

Copper sat down on the bunk beside Blair. The wood creaked noisily in the room. Far down a corridor, a dog yelped in pain, and the dog drivers' tense voices floated softly back. "Microscopic examination," said the doctor thoughtfully, "would be useless, as Blair pointed out. Considerable time has passed. However, serum tests would be definitive."

"Serum tests? What do you mean exactly?" Commander Garry asked.

"If I had a rabbit that had been injected with human blood—a poison to rabbits, of course, as is the blood of any animal save that of another rabbit—and the injections continued in increasing doses for some time, the rabbit would be human-immune. If a small quantity of its blood were drawn off, allowed to separate in a test tube, and to the clear serum, a bit of human blood were added, there would be a visible reaction, proving the blood was human. If cow, or dog blood were added—or any protein material other than that one thing—human blood—no reaction would take place. That would prove definitely."

"Can you suggest where I might catch a rabbit for you, Doc?" Norris asked. "That is, nearer than Australia; we don't want to waste time going that far."

"I know there aren't any rabbits in Antarctica," Copper nodded, "but that is simply the usual animal. Any animal except man will do. A dog for instance. But it will take several days, and due to the greater size of the animal, considerable blood. Two of us will have to contribute."

"Would I do?" Garry asked.

"That will make two," Copper nodded. "I'll get to work on it right away."

"What about Connant in the meantime," Kinner demanded. "I'm going out that door and head off for the Ross Sea before I cook for him."

"He may be human—" Copper started.

Connant burst out in a flood of curses. "Human! *May* be human, you damned sawbones! What in hell do you think I am?"

"A monster," Copper snapped sharply. "Now shut up and listen." Connant's face drained of color and he sat down heavily as the indictment was put in words. "Until we know—you know as well as we do that we have reason to question the fact, and only you know how that question is to be answered—we may reasonably be expected to lock you up. If you are—unhuman—you're a lot more dangerous than poor Blair there, and I'm going to see that he's locked up thoroughly. I expect that his next stage will be a violent desire to kill you, all the dogs, and probably all of us. When he wakes, he will be convinced we're all unhuman, and nothing on the planet will ever change his conviction. It would be kinder to let him die, but we can't do that, of course. He's going in one shack, and you can stay in Cosmos House with your cosmic ray apparatus. Which is about what you'd do anyway. I've got to fix up a couple of dogs."

Connant nodded bitterly. "I'm human. Hurry that test. Your eyes—Lord, I wish you could see your eyes staring—"

COMMANDER GARRY WATCHED ANXIOUSLY as Clark, the dog-handler, held the big brown Alaskan husky, while Copper began the injection treatment. The dog was not anxious to cooperate; the needle was painful, and already he'd experienced considerable needle work that morning. Five stitches held closed a slash that ran from his shoulder, across the ribs, halfway down his body. One long fang was broken off short; the missing part was to be found half buried in the shoulder bone of the monstrous thing on the table in the Ad Building.

"How long will that take?" Garry asked, pressing his arm gently. It was sore from the prick of the needle Dr. Copper had used to withdraw blood.

Copper shrugged. "I don't know, to be frank. I know the general method. I've used it on rabbits. But I haven't experimented with dogs. They're big, clumsy animals to work with; naturally rabbits are preferable, and serve ordinarily. In civilized places you can buy a stock of human-immune rabbits from suppliers, and not many investigators take the trouble to prepare their own."

"What do they want with them back there?" Clark asked.

"Criminology is one large field. A says he didn't murder B, but that the blood on his shirt came from killing a chicken. The State makes a test, then it's up to A to explain how it is the blood reacts on human-immune rabbits, but not on chicken-immunes."

"What are we going to do with Blair in the meantime?" Garry asked wearily. "It's all right to let him sleep where he is for a while, but when he wakes up—"

"Barclay and Benning are fitting some bolts on the door of Cosmos House," Copper replied grimly. "Connant's acting like a gentleman. I think perhaps the way the other men look at him makes him rather want privacy. Lord knows, heretofore we've all of us individually prayed for a little privacy."

Clark laughed brittlely. "Not any more, thank you. The more the merrier."

"Blair," Copper went on, "will also have to have privacy—and locks. He's going to have a pretty definite plan in mind when he wakes up. Ever hear the old story of how to stop hoof-and-mouth disease in cattle?"

Clark and Garry shook their heads silently.

"If there isn't any hoof-and-mouth disease, there won't be any hoof-and-mouth disease," Copper explained. "You get rid of it by killing every animal that exhibits it, and every animal that's been near the diseased animal. Blair's a biologist, and knows that story. He's afraid of this thing we loosed. The answer is probably pretty clear in his mind now. Kill everybody and everything in this camp before a skua gull or a wandering albatross coming in with the spring chances out this way and—catches the disease."

Clark's lips curled in a twisted grin. "Sounds logical to me. If things get too bad—maybe we'd better let Blair get loose. It would save us committing suicide. We might also make something of a vow that if things get bad, we see that that does happen."

Copper laughed softly. "The last man alive in Big Magnet—wouldn't be a man," he pointed out. "Somebody's got to kill those—creatures that don't desire to kill themselves, you know. We don't have enough thermite to do it all at once, and the decanite explosive wouldn't help much. I have an idea that even small pieces of one of those beings would be self-sufficient."

"If," said Garry thoughtfully, "they can

modify their protoplasm at will, won't they simply modify themselves to birds and fly away? They can read all about birds, and imitate their structure without even meeting them. Or imitate, perhaps, birds of their home planet."

Copper shook his head, and helped Clark to free the dog. "Man studied birds for centuries, trying to learn how to make a machine to fly like them. He never did do the trick; his final success came when he broke away entirely and tried new methods. Knowing the general idea, and knowing the detailed structure of wing and bone and nerve-tissue is something far, far different. And as for other-world birds, perhaps, in fact very probably, the atmospheric conditions here are so vastly different that their birds couldn't fly. Perhaps, even, the being came from a planet like Mars with such a thin atmosphere that there were no birds."

Barclay came into the building, trailing a length of airplane control cable. "It's finished, Doc. Cosmos House can't be opened from the inside. Now where do we put Blair?"

Copper looked toward Garry. "There wasn't any biology building. I don't know where we can isolate him."

"How about East Cache?" Garry said after a moment's thought. "Will Blair be able to look after himself—or need attention?"

"He'll be capable enough. We'll be the ones to watch out," Copper assured him grimly. "Take a stove, a couple of bags of coal, necessary supplies and a few tools to fix it up. Nobody's been out there since last fall, have they?"

Garry shook his head. "If he gets noisy—I thought that might be a good idea."

Barclay hefted the tools he was carrying and looked up at Garry. "If the muttering he's doing now is any sign, he's going to sing away the night hours. And we won't like his song."

"What's he saying?" Copper asked.

Barclay shook his head. "I didn't care to listen much. You can if you want to. But I gathered that the blasted idiot had all the dreams McReady had, and a few more. He slept beside the thing when we stopped on the trail coming in from Secondary Magnetic, remember. He dreamt the thing was alive, and dreamt more details. And—damn his soul—knew it wasn't all dream, or had reason to. He knew it had telepathic powers that were stirring vaguely, and that it could not only read minds, but project thoughts. They weren't dreams, you see. They were stray thoughts that thing was broadcasting, the way Blair's broadcasting his thoughts now—a sort of telepathic muttering in its sleep. That's why he knew so much about its powers. I guess you and I, Doc, weren't so sensitive—if you want to believe in telepathy."

"I have to," Copper sighed. "Dr. Rhine of Duke University has shown that it exists, shown that some are much more sensitive than others."

"Well, if you want to learn a lot of details, go listen in on Blair's broadcast. He's driven most of the boys out of the Ad Building; Kinner's rattling pans like coal going down a chute. When he can't rattle a pan, he shakes ashes.

"By the way, Commander, what are we going to do this spring, now the planes are out of it?"

Garry sighed. "I'm afraid our expedition is going to be a loss. We cannot divide our strength now."

"It won't be a loss—if we continue to live, and come out of this," Copper promised him. "The find we've made, if we can get it under control, is important enough. The cosmic ray data, magnetic work, and atmospheric work won't be greatly hindered."

Garry laughed mirthlessly. "I was just thinking of the radio broadcasts. Telling half the world about the wonderful results of our exploration flights, trying to fool men like Byrd and Ellsworth back home there that we're doing something."

Copper nodded gravely. "They'll know

something's wrong. But men like that have judgment enough to know we wouldn't do tricks without some sort of reason, and will wait for our return to judge us. I think it comes to this: men who know enough to recognize our deception will wait for our return. Men who haven't discretion and faith enough to wait will not have the experience to detect any fraud. We know enough of the conditions here to put through a good bluff."

"Just so they don't send 'rescue' expeditions," Garry prayed. "When—if—we're ever ready to come out, we'll have to send word to Captain Forsythe to bring a stock of magnetos with him when he comes down. But—never mind that."

"You mean if we don't come out?" asked Barclay. "I was wondering if a nice running account of an eruption or an earthquake via radio—with a swell windup by using a stick of decanite under the microphone—would help. Nothing, of course, will entirely keep people out. One of those swell, melodramatic 'last-man-alive-scenes' might make 'em go easy though."

Garry smiled with genuine humor. "Is everybody in camp trying to figure that out, too?"

Copper laughed. "What do you think, Garry? We're confident we can win out. But not too easy about it, I guess."

Clark grinned up from the dog he was petting into calmness. "Confident, did you say, Doc?"

VIII

BLAIR MOVED RESTLESSLY around the small shack. His eyes jerked and quivered in vague, fleeting glances at the four men with him; Barclay, six feet tall and weighing over 190 pounds; McReady, a bronze giant of a man; Dr. Copper, short, squatly powerful; and Benning, five-feet-ten of wiry strength.

Blair was huddled up against the far wall of the East Cache cabin, his gear piled in the middle of the floor beside the heating stove, forming an island between him and the four men. His bony hands clenched and fluttered, terrified. His pale eyes wavered uneasily as his bald, freckled head darted about in bird-like motion.

"I don't want anybody coming here. I'll cook my own food," he snapped nervously. "Kinner may be human now, but I don't believe it. I'm going to get out of here, but I'm not going to eat any food you send me. I want cans. Sealed cans."

"OK, Blair, we'll bring 'em tonight," Barclay promised. "You've got coal, and the fire's started. I'll make a last—" Barclay started forward.

Blair instantly scurried to the farthest corner. "Get out! Keep away from me, you monster!" the little biologist shrieked, and tried to claw his way through the wall of the shack. "Keep away from me—keep away—I won't be absorbed—I won't be—"

Barclay relaxed and moved back. Dr. Copper shook his head. "Leave him alone, Bar. It's easier for him to fix the thing himself. We'll have to fix the door, I think—"

The four men let themselves out. Efficiently, Benning and Barclay fell to work. There were no locks in Antarctica; there wasn't enough privacy to make them needed. But powerful screws had been driven in each side of the door frame, and the spare aviation control cable, immensely strong, woven steel wire, was rapidly caught between them and drawn taut. Barclay went to work with a drill and a key-hole saw. Presently he had a trap cut in the door through which goods could be passed without unlashing the entrance. Three powerful hinges made from a stock crate, two hasps and a pair of three-inch cotter pins made it proof against opening from the other side.

Blair moved about restlessly inside. He was dragging something over to the door with panting gasps, and muttering frantic curses. Barclay opened the hatch and glanced in, Dr.

Copper peering over his shoulder. Blair had moved the heavy bunk against the door. It could not be opened without his cooperation now.

"Don't know but what the poor man's right at that," McReady sighed. "If he gets loose, it is his avowed intention to kill each and all of us as quickly as possible, which is something we don't agree with. But we've something on our side of that door that is worse than a homicidal maniac. If one or the other has to get loose, I think I'll come up and undo these lashings here."

Barclay grinned. "You let me know, and I'll show you how to get these off fast. Let's go back."

THE SUN WAS PAINTING the northern horizon in multicolored rainbows still, though it was two hours below the horizon. The field of drift swept off to the north, sparkling under its flaming colors in a million reflected glories. Low mounds of rounded white on the northern horizon showed the Magnet Range was barely awash above the sweeping drift. Little eddies of wind-lifted snow swirled away from their skis as they set out toward the main encampment two miles away. The spidery finger of the broadcast radiator lifted a gaunt black needle against the white of the Antarctic continent. The snow under their skis was like fine sand, hard and gritty.

"Spring," said Benning bitterly, "is come. Ain't we got fun! And I've been looking forward to getting away from this blasted hole in the ice."

"I wouldn't try it now, if I were you." Barclay grunted. "Guys that set out from here in the next few days are going to be marvelously unpopular."

"How is your dog getting along, Dr. Copper?" McReady asked. "Any results yet?"

"In thirty hours? I wish there were. I gave him an injection of my blood today. But I imagine another five days will be needed. I don't know certainly enough to stop sooner."

"I've been wondering—if Connant were—changed, would he have warned us so soon after the animal escaped? Wouldn't he have waited long enough for it to have a real chance to fix itself? Until we woke up naturally?" McReady asked slowly.

"The thing is selfish. You didn't think it looked as though it were possessed of a store of the higher justices, did you?" Dr. Copper pointed out. "Every part of it is all of it, every part of it is all for itself, I imagine. If Connant were changed, to save his skin, he'd have to—but Connant's feelings aren't changed; they're imitated perfectly, or they're his own. Naturally, the imitation, imitating perfectly Connant's feelings, would do exactly what Connant would do."

"Say, couldn't Norris or Vane give Connant some kind of a test? If the thing is brighter than men, it might know more physics than Connant should, and they'd catch it out," Barclay suggested.

Copper shook his head wearily. "Not if it reads minds. You can't plan a trap for it. Vane suggested that last night. He hoped it would answer some of the questions of physics he'd like to know answers to."

"This expedition-of-four idea is going to make life happy." Benning looked at his companions. "Each of us with an eye on the other to make sure he doesn't do something—peculiar. Man—aren't we going to be a trusting bunch! Each man eyeing his neighbors with the grandest exhibition of faith and truth—I'm beginning to know what Connant meant by 'I wish you could see your eyes.' Every now and then we all have it, I guess. One of you looks around with a sort of 'I-wonder-if-the-other-three-are-look.' Incidentally, I'm not excepting myself."

"So far as we know, the animal is dead, with a slight question as to Connant. No other is suspected," McReady stated slowly. "The 'always-four' order is merely a precautionary measure."

"I'm waiting for Garry to make it four-in-a-bunk," Barclay sighed. "I thought I didn't have any privacy before, but since that order—"

NONE WATCHED MORE TENSELY than Connant. A little sterile glass test tube, half filled with straw-colored fluid. One—two—three—four—five drops of the clear solution Dr. Copper had prepared from the drops of blood from Connant's arm. The tube was shaken carefully, then set in a beaker of clear, warm water. The thermometer read blood heat, a little thermostat clicked noisily, and the electric hotplate began to glow as the lights flickered slightly. Then—little white flecks of precipitation were forming, snowing down in the clear straw-colored fluid. "Lord," said Connant. He dropped heavily into a bunk, crying like a baby. "Six days—" Connant sobbed, "six days in there—wondering if that damned test would lie—"

Garry moved over silently, and slipped his arm across the physicist's back.

"It couldn't lie," Dr. Copper said. "The dog was human-immune—and the serum reacted."

"He's—all right?" Norris gasped. "Then—the animal is dead—dead forever?"

"He is human," Copper spoke definitely, "and the animal is dead."

Kinner burst out laughing, laughing hysterically. McReady turned toward him and slapped his face with a methodical one-two, one-two action. The cook laughed, gulped, cried a moment, and sat up rubbing his cheeks, mumbling his thanks vaguely. "I was scared. Lord, I was scared—"

Norris laughed brittlely. "You think we weren't, you ape? You think maybe Connant wasn't?"

The Ad Building stirred with a sudden rejuvenation. Voices laughed, the men clustering around Connant spoke with unnecessarily loud voices, jittery, nervous voices relievedly friendly again. Somebody called out a suggestion, and a dozen started for their skis. Blair. Blair might recover— Dr. Copper fussed with his test tubes in nervous relief, trying solutions. The party of relief for Blair's shack

started out the door, skis clapping noisily. Down the corridor, the dogs set up a quick yelping howl as the air of excited relief reached them.

Dr. Copper fussed with his tubes.

McReady noticed him first, sitting on the edge of the bunk, with two precipitin-whitened test tubes of straw-colored fluid, his face whiter than the stuff in the tubes, silent tears slipping down from horror-widened eyes.

McReady felt a cold knife of fear pierce through his heart and freeze in his breast. Dr. Copper looked up. "Garry," he called hoarsely. "Garry, for God's sake, come here."

Commander Garry walked toward him sharply. Silence clapped down on the Ad Building. Connant looked up, rose stiffly from his seat.

"Garry—tissue from the monster—precipitates, too. It proves nothing. Nothing—but the dog was monster-immune too. That one of the two contributing blood—one of us two, you and I, Garry—one of us is a monster."

IX

"BAR, CALL BACK THOSE MEN before they tell Blair," McReady said quietly. Barclay went to the door; faintly his shouts came back to the tensely silent men in the room. Then he was back.

"They're coming," he said. "I didn't tell them why. Just that Dr. Copper said not to go."

"McReady," Garry sighed, "you're in command now. May God help you. I cannot."

The bronzed giant nodded slowly, his deep eyes on Commander Garry.

"I may be the one," Garry added. "I know I'm not, but I cannot prove it to you in any way. Dr. Copper's test has broken down. The fact that he showed it was useless, when it was to the advantage of the monster to have that uselessness not known, would seem to prove he was human."

Copper rocked back and forth slowly on the bunk. "I know I'm human. I can't prove it either. One of us two is a liar, for that test cannot lie, and it says one of us is. I gave proof that the test was wrong, which seems to prove I'm human, and now Garry has given that argument which proves me human—which he, as the monster, should not do. Round and round and round and round and—"

Dr. Copper's head, then his neck and shoulders began circling slowly in time to the words. Suddenly he was lying back on the bunk, roaring with laughter. "It doesn't have to prove one of us is a monster! It doesn't have to prove that at all! Ho-ho. If we're all monsters it works the same—we're all monsters—all of us—Connant and Garry and I—and all of you."

"McReady," Van Wall, the blond-bearded Chief Pilot, called softly, "you were on the way to an M.D. when you took up meteorology, weren't you? Can you make some kind of test?"

McReady went over to Copper slowly, took the hypodermic from his hand, and washed it carefully in ninety-five percent alcohol. Garry sat on the bunk edge with wooden face, watching Copper and McReady expressionlessly. "What Copper said is possible," McReady sighed. "Van, will you help me here? Thanks." The filled needle jabbed into Copper's thigh. The man's laughter did not stop, but slowly faded into sobs, then sound sleep as the morphia took hold.

McReady turned again. The men who had started for Blair stood at the far end of the room, skis dripping snow, their faces as white as their skis. Connant had a lighted cigarette in each hand; one he was puffing absently, and staring at the floor. The heat of the one in his left hand attracted him and he stared at it and the one in the other hand stupidly for a moment. He dropped one and crushed it under his heel slowly.

"Dr. Copper," McReady repeated, "could be right. I know I'm human—but of course can't prove it. I'll repeat the test for my own information. Any of you others who wish may do the same."

Two minutes later, McReady held a test tube with white precipitin settling slowly from straw-colored serum. "It reacts to human blood too, so they aren't both monsters."

"I didn't think they were," Van Wall sighed. "That wouldn't suit the monster either; we could have destroyed them if we knew. Why hasn't the monster destroyed us, do you suppose? It seems to be loose."

McReady snorted. Then laughed softly. "Elementary, my dear Watson. The monster wants to have life-forms available. It cannot animate a dead body, apparently. It is just waiting—waiting until the best opportunities come. We who remain human, it is holding in reserve."

Kinner shuddered violently. "Hey. Hey, Mac. Mac, would I know if I was a monster?

Would I know if the monster had already got me? Oh Lord, I may be a monster already."

"You'd know," McReady answered.

"But we wouldn't," Norris laughed shortly, half hysterically.

McReady looked at the vial of serum remaining. "There's one thing this damned stuff is good for, at that," he said thoughtfully. "Clark, will you and Van help me? The rest of the gang better stick together here. Keep an eye on each other," he said bitterly. "See that you don't get into mischief, shall we say?"

McReady started down the tunnel toward Dogtown, with Clark and Van Wall behind him. "You need more serum?" Clark asked.

McReady shook his head. "Tests. There's four cows and a bull, and nearly seventy dogs down there. This stuff reacts only to human blood and—monsters."

MCREADY CAME BACK to the Ad Building and went silently to the wash stand. Clark and Van Wall joined him a moment later. Clark's lips had developed a tic, jerking into sudden, unexpected sneers.

"What did you do?" Connant exploded suddenly. "More immunizing?"

Clark snickered, and stopped with a hiccough. "Immunizing. Haw! Immune all right."

"That monster," said Van Wall steadily, "is quite logical. Our immune dog was quite all right, and we drew a little more serum for the tests. But we won't make any more."

"Can't—can't you use one man's blood on another dog—" Norris began.

"There aren't," said McReady softly, "any more dogs. Nor cattle, I might add."

"No more dogs?" Benning sat down slowly.

"They're very nasty when they start changing," Van Wall said precisely. "But slow. That electrocution iron you made up, Barclay, is very fast. There is only one dog left—our immune. The monster left that for us, so we could play with our little test. The rest—" He shrugged and dried his hands.

"The cattle—" gulped Kinner.

"Also. Reacted very nicely. They look funny as hell when they start melting. The beast hasn't any quick escape, when it's tied in dog chains, or halters, and it had to be to imitate."

Kinner stood up slowly. His eyes darted around the room, and came to rest horribly quivering on a tin bucket in the galley. Slowly, step by step, he retreated toward the door, his mouth opening and closing silently, like a fish out of water.

"The milk—" he gasped. "I milked 'em an hour ago—" His voice broke into a scream as he dived through the door. He was out on the ice cap without windproof or heavy clothing.

Van Wall looked after him for a moment thoughtfully. "He's probably hopelessly mad," he said at length, "but he might be a monster escaping. He hasn't skis. Take a blow torch—in case."

The physical motion of the chase helped them; something that needed doing. Three of the men were quietly being sick. Norris was lying flat on his back, his face greenish, looking steadily at the bottom of the bunk above him.

"Mac, how long have the—cows been not-cows—"

McReady shrugged his shoulders hopelessly. He went over to the milk bucket, and with his little tube of serum set to work on it. The milk clouded it, making certainty difficult. Finally he dropped the test tube in the stand, and shook his head. "It tests negatively. Which means either they were cows then, or that, being perfect imitations, they gave perfectly good milk."

Copper stirred restlessly in his sleep and gave a gurgling cross between a snore and a laugh. Silent eyes fastened on him. "Would morphia—a monster—" somebody started to ask.

"Lord knows," McReady shrugged. "It affects every Earthly animal I know of."

Connant suddenly raised his head. "Mac! The dogs must have swallowed pieces of the monster, and the pieces destroyed them! The dogs were where the monster resided. I was locked up. Doesn't that prove—"

Van Wall shook his head. "Sorry. Proves nothing about what you are, only proves what you didn't do."

"It doesn't do that," McReady sighed. "We are helpless because we don't know enough, and so jittery we don't think straight. Locked up! Ever watch a white corpuscle of the blood go through the wall of a blood vessel? No? It sticks out a pseudopod. And there it is—on the far side of the wall."

"Oh," said Van Wall unhappily. "The cattle tried to melt down, didn't they? They could have melted down—become just a thread of stuff and leaked under a door to re-collect on the other side. Ropes—no—no, that wouldn't do it. They couldn't live in a sealed tank or—"

"If," said McReady, "you shoot it through the heart, and it doesn't die, it's a monster. That's the best test I can think of, offhand."

"No dogs," said Garry quietly, "and no cattle. It has to imitate men now. And locking up doesn't do any good. Your test might work, Mac, but I'm afraid it would be hard on the men."

X

CLARK LOOKED UP from the galley stove as Van Wall, Barclay, McReady, and Benning came in, brushing the drift from their clothes. The other men jammed into the Ad Building continued studiously to do as they were doing, playing chess, poker, reading. Ralsen was fixing a sledge on the table; Vane and Norris had their heads together over magnetic data, while Harvey read tables in a low voice.

Dr. Copper snored softly on the bunk. Garry was working with Dutton over a sheaf of radio messages on the corner of Dutton's bunk and a small fraction of the radio table. Connant was using most of the table for cosmic ray sheets.

Quite plainly through the corridor, despite two closed doors, they could hear Kinner's voice. Clark banged a kettle onto the galley stove and beckoned McReady silently. The meteorologist went over to him.

"I don't mind the cooking so damn much," Clark said nervously, "but isn't there some way to stop that bird? We all agreed that it would be safe to move him into Cosmos House."

"Kinner?" McReady nodded toward the door. "I'm afraid not. I can dope him, I suppose, but we don't have an unlimited supply of morphia, and he's not in danger of losing his mind. Just hysterical."

"Well, we're in danger of losing ours. You've been out for an hour and a half. That's been going on steadily ever since, and it was going for two hours before. There's a limit, you know."

Garry wandered over slowly, apologetically. For an instant, McReady caught the feral spark of fear—horror—in Clark's eyes, and knew at the same instant it was in his own. Garry—Garry or Copper—was certainly a monster.

"If you could stop that, I think it would be a sound policy, Mac," Garry spoke quietly. "There are—tensions enough in this room. We agreed that it would be safe for Kinner in there, because everyone else in camp is under constant eyeing." Garry shivered slightly. "And try, try in God's name, to find some test that will work."

McReady sighed. "Watched or unwatched, everyone's tense. Blair's jammed the trap so it won't open now. Says he's got food enough, and keeps screaming 'Go away, go away—you're monsters. I won't be absorbed. I won't. I'll tell men when they come. Go away.' So—we went away."

"There's no other test?" Garry pleaded.

McReady shrugged his shoulders. "Copper was perfectly right. The serum test could be absolutely definitive if it hadn't been—contaminated. But that's the only dog left, and he's fixed now."

"Chemicals? Chemical tests?"

McReady shook his head. "Our chemistry isn't that good. I tried the microscope you know."

Garry nodded. "Monster-dog and real dog were identical. But—you've got to go on. What are you going to do after dinner?"

Van Wall had joined them quietly. "Rotation sleeping. Half the crowd sleep; half stay awake. I wonder how many of us are monsters? All the dogs were. We thought we were safe, but somehow it got Copper—or you." Van Wall's eyes flashed uneasily. "It may have gotten every one of you—all of you but myself may be wondering, looking. No, that's not possible. You'd just spring then, I'd be helpless. We humans must somehow have the greater numbers now. But—" he stopped.

McReady laughed shortly. "You're doing what Norris complained of in me. Leaving it hanging. 'But if one more is changed—that may shift the balance of power.' It doesn't fight. I don't think it ever fights. It must be a peaceable thing, in its own—inimitable—way. It never had to, because it always gained its end otherwise."

Van Wall's mouth twisted in a sickly grin. "You're suggesting then, that perhaps it already *has* the greater numbers, but is just waiting—waiting, all of them—all of you, for all I know—waiting till I, the last human, drop my wariness in sleep. Mac, did you notice their eyes, all looking at us."

Garry sighed. "You haven't been sitting here for four straight hours, while all their eyes silently weighed the information that one of us two, Copper or I, is a monster certainly—perhaps both of us."

Clark repeated his request. "Will you stop that bird's noise? He's driving me nuts. Make him tone down, anyway."

"Still praying?" McReady asked.

"Still praying," Clark groaned. "He hasn't stopped for a second. I don't mind his praying if it relieves him, but he yells, he sings psalms and hymns and shouts prayers. He thinks God can't hear well way down here."

"Maybe he can't," Barclay grunted. "Or he'd have done something about this thing loosed from hell."

"Somebody's going to try that test you mentioned, if you don't stop him," Clark stated grimly. "I think a cleaver in the head would be as positive a test as a bullet in the heart."

"Go ahead with the food. I'll see what I can do. There may be something in the cabinets." McReady moved wearily toward the corner Copper had used as his dispensary. Three tall cabinets of rough boards, two locked, were the repositories of the camp's medical supplies. Twelve years ago, McReady had graduated, had started for an internship, and been diverted to meteorology. Copper was a picked man, a man who knew his profession thoroughly and modernly. More than half the drugs available were totally unfamiliar to McReady; many of the others he had forgotten. There was no huge medical library here, no series of journals available to learn the things he had forgotten, the elementary, simple things to Copper, things that did not merit inclusion in the small library he had been forced to content himself with. Books are heavy, and every ounce of supplies had been freighted in by air.

McReady picked a barbiturate hopefully. Barclay and Van Wall went with him. One man never went anywhere alone in Big Magnet.

Ralsen had his sledge put away, and the physicists had moved off the table, the poker game broken up when they got back. Clark was putting out the food. The clicks of spoons and the muffled sounds of eating were the only sign of life in the room. There were no words spoken as the three returned; simply all eyes focused on them questioningly while the jaws moved methodically.

McReady stiffened suddenly. Kinner was screeching out a hymn in a hoarse, cracked voice. He looked wearily at Van Wall with a twisted grin and shook his head. "Uh-uh."

Van Wall cursed bitterly, and sat down at

the table. "We'll just plumb have to take that till his voice wears out. He can't yell like that forever."

"He's got a brass throat and a cast-iron larynx," Norris declared savagely. "Then we could be hopeful, and suggest he's one of our friends. In that case he could go on renewing his throat till doomsday."

Silence clamped down. For twenty minutes they ate without a word. Then Connant jumped up with an angry violence. "You sit as still as a bunch of graven images. You don't say a word, but oh, Lord, what expressive eyes you've got. They roll around like a bunch of glass marbles spilling down a table. They wink and blink and stare—and whisper things. Can you guys look somewhere else for a change, please?

"Listen, Mac, you're in charge here. Let's run movies for the rest of the night. We've been saving those reels to make 'em last. Last for what? Who is it's going to see those last reels, eh? Let's see 'em while we can, and look at something other than each other."

"Sound idea, Connant. I, for one, am quite willing to change this in any way I can."

"Turn the sound up loud, Dutton. Maybe you can drown out the hymns," Clark suggested.

"But don't," Norris said softly, "turn off the lights altogether."

"The lights will be out." McReady shook his head. "We'll show all the cartoon movies we have. You won't mind seeing the old cartoons will you?"

"Goody, goody—a moom-pitcher show. I'm just in the mood." McReady turned to look at the speaker, a lean, lanky New Englander, by the name of Caldwell. Caldwell was stuffing his pipe slowly, a sour eye cocked up to McReady.

The bronze giant was forced to laugh. "OK, Bart, you win. Maybe we aren't quite in the mood for Popeye and trick ducks, but it's something."

"Let's play Classifications," Caldwell suggested slowly. "Or maybe you call it Guggenheim. You draw lines on a piece of paper, and put down classes of things—like animals, you know. One for 'H' and one for 'U' and so on. Like 'Human' and 'Unknown' for instance. I think that would be a hell of a lot better game. Classification, I sort of figure, is what we need right now a lot more than movies. Maybe somebody's got a pencil that he can draw lines with, draw lines between the 'U' animals and the 'H' animals for instance."

"McReady's trying to find that kind of a pencil," Van Wall answered quietly, "but, we've got three kinds of animals here, you know. One that begins with 'M.' We don't want any more."

"Mad ones, you mean. Uh-huh. Clark, I'll help you with those pots so we can get our little peep show going." Caldwell got up slowly.

Dutton and Barclay and Benning, in charge of the projector and sound mechanism arrangements, went about their job silently, while the Ad Building was cleared and the dishes and pans disposed of. McReady drifted over toward Van Wall slowly, and leaned back in the bunk beside him. "I've been wondering, Van," he said with a wry grin, "whether or not to report my ideas in advance. I forgot the 'U animal' as Caldwell named it, could read minds. I've a vague idea of something that might work. It's too vague to bother with, though. Go ahead with your show, while I try to figure out the logic of the thing. I'll take this bunk."

Van Wall glanced up, and nodded. The movie screen would be practically on a line with this bunk, hence making the pictures least distracting here, because least intelligible. "Perhaps you should tell us what you have in mind. As it is, only the unknowns know what you plan. You might be—unknown before you got it into operation."

"Won't take long, if I get it figured out right. But I don't want any more all-but-the-test-dog-monsters things. We better move Copper into this bunk directly above me. He won't be watching the screen either." McReady nodded toward Copper's gently snoring bulk. Garry helped them lift and move the doctor.

McReady leaned back against the bunk, and sank into a trance, almost, of concentration, trying to calculate chances, operations, methods. He was scarcely aware as the others distributed themselves silently, and the screen lit up. Vaguely Kinner's hectic, shouted prayers and his rasping hymn-singing annoyed him till the sound accompaniment started. The lights were turned out, but the large, light-colored areas of the screen reflected enough light for ready visibility. Kinner was still praying, shouting, his voice a raucous accompaniment to the mechanical sound. Dutton stepped up the amplification.

So long had the voice been going on, that only vaguely at first was McReady aware that something seemed missing. Lying as he was, just across the narrow room from the corridor leading to Cosmos House, Kinner's voice had reached him fairly clearly, despite the sound accompaniment of the pictures. It struck him abruptly that it had stopped.

"Dutton, cut that sound," McReady called as he sat up abruptly. The pictures flickered a moment, soundless and strangely futile in the sudden, deep silence. The rising wind on the surface above bubbled melancholy tears of sound down the stove pipes. "Kinner's stopped," McReady said softly.

"For God's sake start that sound then; he may have stopped to listen," Norris snapped.

McReady rose and went down the corridor. Barclay and Van Wall left their places at the far end of the room to follow him. The flickers bulged and twisted on the back of Barclay's gray underwear as he crossed the still-functioning beam of the projector. Dutton snapped on the lights, and the pictures vanished.

Norris stood at the door as McReady had asked. Garry sat down quietly in the bunk nearest the door, forcing Clark to make room for him. Most of the others had stayed exactly where they were. Only Connant walked slowly up and down the room, in steady, unvarying rhythm.

"If you're going to do that, Connant," Clark spat, "we can get along without you altogether, whether you're human or not. Will you stop that damned rhythm?"

"Sorry." The physicist sat down in a bunk, and watched his toes thoughtfully. It was almost five minutes, five ages, while the wind made the only sound, before McReady appeared at the door.

"Well," he announced, "haven't got enough grief here already. Somebody's tried to help us out. Kinner has a knife in his throat, which was why he stopped singing, probably. We've got monsters, madmen and murderers. Any more 'M's' you can think of, Caldwell? If there are, we'll probably have 'em before long."

XI

"IS BLAIR LOOSE?" someone asked.

"Blair is not loose. Or he flew in. If there's any doubt about where our gentle helper came from—this may clear it up." Van Wall held a foot-long, thin-bladed knife in a cloth. The wooden handle was half burnt, charred with the peculiar pattern of the top of the galley stove.

Clark stared at it. "I did that this afternoon. I forgot the damn thing and left it on the stove."

Van Wall nodded. "I smelled it, if you remember. I knew the knife came from the galley."

"I wonder," said Benning, looking around at the party warily, "how many more monsters have we? If somebody could slip out of his place, go back of the screen to the galley and then down to the Cosmos House and back—he did come back, didn't he? Yes—everybody's here. Well, if one of the gang could do all that—"

"Maybe a monster did it," Garry suggested quietly.

"There's that possibility."

"The monster, as you pointed out today, has only men left to imitate. Would he decrease his—supply, shall we say?" Van Wall pointed out. "No, we just have a plain, ordinary louse, a murderer to deal with. Ordinarily we'd call him an 'inhuman murderer' I suppose, but we have to distinguish now. We have inhuman murderers, and now we have human murderers. Or one at least."

"There's one less human," Norris said softly. "Maybe the monsters have the balance of power now."

"Never mind that," McReady sighed and turned to Barclay. "Bar, will you get your electric gadget? I'm going to make certain—"

Barclay turned down the corridor to get the pronged electrocuter, while McReady and Van Wall went back toward Cosmos House. Barclay followed them in some thirty seconds.

The corridor to Cosmos House twisted, as did nearly all corridors in Big Magnet, and Norris stood at the entrance again. But they heard, rather muffled, McReady's sudden shout. There was a savage flurry of blows, dull *ch-thunk, shluff* sounds. "Bar—Bar—" And a curious, savage mewing scream, silenced before even quick-moving Norris had reached the bend.

Kinner—or what had been Kinner—lay on the floor, cut half in two by the great knife McReady had had. The meteorologist stood against the wall, the knife dripping red in his hand. Van Wall was stirring vaguely on the floor, moaning, his hand half-consciously rubbing at his jaw. Barclay, an unutterably savage gleam in his eyes, was methodically leaning on the pronged weapon in his hand, jabbing—jabbing, jabbing.

Kinner's arms had developed a queer, scaly fur, and the flesh had twisted. The fingers had shortened, the hand rounded, the fingernails become three-inch long things of dull red horn, keened to steel-hard, razor-sharp talons.

McReady raised his head, looked at the knife in his hand and dropped it. "Well, whoever did it can speak up now. He was an inhuman murderer at that—in that he murdered an inhuman. I swear by all that's holy, Kinner was a lifeless corpse on the floor here when we arrived. But when It found we were going to jab It with the power—It changed."

Norris stared unsteadily. "Oh, Lord, those things can act. Ye gods—sitting in here for hours, mouthing prayers to a God it hated! Shouting hymns in a cracked voice—hymns about a Church it never knew. Driving us mad with its ceaseless howling—

"Well. Speak up, whoever did it. You didn't know it, but you did the camp a favor. And I want to know how in blazes you got out of the room without anyone seeing you. It might help in guarding ourselves."

"His screaming—his singing. Even the sound projector couldn't drown it." Clark shivered. "It was a monster."

"Oh," said Van Wall in sudden comprehension. "You *were* sitting right next to the door, weren't you? And almost behind the projection screen already."

Clark nodded dumbly. "He—it's quiet now. It's a dead—Mac, your test's no damn good. It was dead anyway, monster or man, it was dead."

McReady chuckled softly. "Boys, meet Clark, the only one we know is human! Meet Clark, the one who proves he's human by trying to commit murder—and failing. Will the rest of you please refrain from trying to prove you're human for a while? I think we may have another test."

"A test!" Connant snapped joyfully, then his face sagged in disappointment. "I suppose it's another either-way-you-want-it."

"No," said McReady steadily. "Look sharp and be careful. Come into the Ad Building. Barclay, bring your electrocuter. And somebody—Dutton—stand with Barclay to make sure he does it. Watch every neighbor, for by the Hell these monsters came from, I've got something, and they know it. They're going to get dangerous!"

The group tensed abruptly. An air of crushing menace entered into every man's body, sharply they looked at each other. More keenly than ever before—*is that man next to me an inhuman monster?*

"What is it?" Garry asked, as they stood again in the main room. "How long will it take?"

"I don't know, exactly," said McReady, his voice brittle with angry determination. "But I *know* it will work, and no two ways about it. It depends on a basic quality of the *monsters*, not on us. 'Kinner' just convinced me." He stood heavy and solid in bronzed immobility, completely sure of himself again at last.

"This," said Barclay, hefting the wooden-handled weapon tipped with its two sharp-pointed, charged conductors, "is going to be rather necessary, I take it. Is the power plant assured?"

Dutton nodded sharply. "The automatic stoker bin is full. The gas power plant is on standby. Van Wall and I set it for the movie operation—and we've checked it over rather carefully several times, you know. Anything those wires touch, dies," he assured them grimly. "*I* know that."

Dr. Copper stirred vaguely in his bunk, rubbed his eyes with fumbling hand. He sat up slowly, blinked his eyes blurred with sleep and drugs, widened with an unutterable horror of drug-ridden nightmares. "Garry," he mumbled, "Garry—listen. Selfish—from hell they came, and hellish shellfish—I mean self— Do I? What do I mean?" He sank back in his bunk, and snored softly.

McReady looked at him thoughtfully. "We'll know presently," he nodded slowly. "But selfish is what you mean, all right. You may have thought of that, half sleeping, dreaming there. I didn't stop to think what dreams you might be having. But that's all right. Selfish is the word. They must be, you see." He turned to the men in the cabin, tense, silent men staring with wolfish eyes each at his neighbor. "Selfish, and as Dr. Copper said—*every part is a whole.* Every piece is self-sufficient, an animal in itself.

"That, and one other thing, tell the story. There's nothing mysterious about blood; it's just as normal a body tissue as a piece of muscle, or a piece of liver. But it hasn't so much connective tissue, though it has millions, billions of life-cells."

McReady's great bronze beard ruffled in a grim smile. "This is satisfying, in a way. I'm pretty sure we humans still outnumber you—others. Others standing here. And we have what you, your other-world race, evidently doesn't. Not an imitated, but a bred-in-the-bone instinct, a driving, unquenchable fire that's genuine. We'll fight, fight with a ferocity you may attempt to imitate, but you'll never equal! We're human. We're real. You're imitations, false to the core of your every cell."

"All right. It's a showdown now. *You* know. You, with your mind reading. You've lifted the idea from my brain. You can't do a thing about it.

"Standing here—

"Let it pass. Blood is tissue. They have to bleed; if they don't bleed when cut, then by Heaven, they're phoney from hell! If they bleed—then that blood, separated from them, is an individual—*a newly formed individual in its own right, just as they—split, all of them, from one original—are individuals!*

"Get it, Van? See the answer, Bar?"

Van Wall laughed very softly. "The blood—the blood will not obey. It's a new individual, with all the desire to protect its own life that the original—the main mass from which it was split—has. The *blood* will live—and try to crawl away from a hot needle, say!"

McReady picked up the scalpel from the table. From the cabinet, he took a rack of test tubes, a tiny alcohol lamp, and a length of platinum wire set in a little glass rod. A smile of grim satisfaction rode his lips. For a moment he glanced up at those around him.

Barclay and Dutton moved toward him slowly, the wooden-handled electric instrument alert.

"Dutton," said McReady, "suppose you stand over by the splice there where you've connected that in. Just make sure no—thing pulls it loose."

Dutton moved away. "Now, Van, suppose you be first on this."

White-faced, Van Wall stepped forward. With a delicate precision, McReady cut a vein in the base of his thumb. Van Wall winced slightly, then held steady as a half inch of bright blood collected in the tube. McReady put the tube in the rack, gave Van Wall a bit of alum, and indicated the iodine bottle.

Van Wall stood motionlessly watching. McReady heated the platinum wire in the alcohol lamp flame, then dipped it into the tube. It hissed softly. Five times he repeated the test. "Human, I'd say," McReady sighed, and straightened. "As yet, my theory hasn't been actually proven—but I have hopes. I have hopes.

"Don't, by the way, get too interested in this. We have with us some unwelcome ones, no doubt. Van, will you relieve Barclay at the switch? Thanks. OK, Barclay, and may I say I hope you stay with us? You're a damned good guy."

Barclay grinned uncertainly; winced under the keen edge of the scalpel. Presently, smiling widely, he retrieved his long-handled weapon.

"Mr. Samuel Dutt— *Bar!*"

The tensity was released in that second. Whatever of hell the monsters may have had within them, the men in that instant matched it. Barclay had no chance to move his weapon, as a score of men poured down on the thing that had seemed Dutton. It mewed, and spat, and tried to grow fangs—and was a hundred broken, torn pieces. Without knives, or any weapon save the brute-given strength of a staff of picked men, the thing was crushed, rent.

Slowly they picked themselves up, their eyes smouldering, very quiet in their motions. A curious wrinkling of their lips betrayed a species of nervousness.

Barclay went over with the electric weapon. Things smouldered and stank. The caustic acid Van Wall dropped on each spilled drop of blood gave off tickling, cough-provoking fumes.

McReady grinned, his deep-set eyes alight and dancing. "Maybe," he said softly, "I underrated man's abilities when I said nothing human could have the ferocity in the eyes of that thing we found. I wish we could have the opportunity to treat in a more befitting manner these things. Something with boiling oil, or melted lead in it, or maybe slow roasting in the power boiler. When I think what a man Dutton was—

"Never mind. My theory is confirmed by—by one who knew? Well, Van Wall and Barclay are proven. I think, then, that I'll try to show you what I already know. That I, too, am human." McReady swished the scalpel in absolute alcohol, burned it off the metal blade, and cut the base of his thumb expertly.

Twenty seconds later he looked up from the desk at the waiting men. There were more grins out there now, friendly grins, yet withal, something else in the eyes.

"Connant," McReady laughed softly, "was right. The huskies watching that thing in the corridor bend had nothing on you. Wonder why we think only the wolf blood has the right to ferocity? Maybe on spontaneous viciousness a wolf takes tops, but after these seven days—abandon all hope, ye wolves who enter here!

"Maybe we can save time. Connant, would you step for—"

Again, Barclay was too slow. There were more grins, less tensity still, when Barclay and Van Wall finished their work.

Garry spoke in a low, bitter voice. "Connant was one of the finest men we had here—and five minutes ago I'd have sworn he was a man. Those damnable things are more than imitation." Garry shuddered and sat back in his bunk.

And thirty seconds later, Garry's blood shrank from the hot platinum wire, and struggled to escape the tube, struggled as frantically as a suddenly feral, red-eyed, dissolving imitation of Garry struggled to dodge the snake-tongue weapon Barclay advanced at him, white-faced and sweating. The Thing in the test tube screamed with a tiny, tinny voice as McReady dropped it into the glowing coal of the galley stove.

XII

"THE LAST OF IT?" Dr. Copper looked down from his bunk with bloodshot, saddened eyes. "Fourteen of them—"

McReady nodded shortly. "In some ways— if only we could have permanently prevented their spreading—I'd like to have even the imitations back. Commander Garry—Connant— Dutton—Clark—"

"Where are they taking those things?" Copper nodded to the stretcher Barclay and Norris were carrying out.

"Outside. Outside on the ice, where they've got fifteen smashed crates, half a ton of coal, and presently will add ten gallons of kerosene. We've dumped acid on every spilled drop, every torn fragment. We're going to incinerate those."

"Sounds like a good plan." Copper nodded wearily. "I wonder, you haven't said whether Blair—"

McReady started. "We forgot him! We had so much else! I wonder—do you suppose we can cure him now?"

"If—" began Dr. Copper, and stopped meaningly.

McReady started a second time. "Even a madman. It imitated Kinner and his praying hysteria—" McReady turned toward Van Wall at the long table. "Van, we've got to make an expedition to Blair's shack."

Van looked up sharply, the frown of worry faded for an instant in surprised remembrance. Then he rose, nodded. "Barclay better go along. He applied the lashings, and may figure how to get in without frightening Blair too much."

Three quarters of an hour, through -37° cold, while the aurora curtain bellied overhead. The twilight was nearly twelve hours long, flaming in the north on snow like white, crystalline sand under their skis. A five-mile wind piled it in drift-lines pointing off to the northwest. Three quarters of an hour to reach the snow-buried shack. No smoke came from the little shack, and the men hastened.

"Blair!" Barclay roared into the wind and when he was still a hundred yards away. "Blair!"

"Shut up," said McReady softly. "And hurry. He may be trying a lone hike. If we have to go after him—no planes, the tractors disabled—"

"Would a monster have the stamina a man has?"

"A broken leg wouldn't stop it for more than a minute," McReady pointed out.

Barclay gasped suddenly and pointed aloft. Dim in the twilit sky, a winged thing circled in curves of indescribable grace and ease. Great white wings tipped gently, and the bird swept over them in silent curiosity. "Albatross—" Barclay said softly. "First of the season, and wandering way inland for some reason. If a monster's loose—"

Norris bent down on the ice, and tore hurriedly at his heavy, windproof clothing. He straightened, his coat flapping open, a grim blue-metaled weapon in his hand. It roared a challenge to the white silence of Antarctica.

The thing in the air screamed hoarsely. Its great wings worked frantically as a dozen feathers floated down from its tail. Norris fired again. The bird was moving swiftly now, but in an almost straight line of retreat. It screamed again, more feathers dropped, and with beating wings it soared behind a ridge of pressure ice, to vanish.

Norris hurried after the others. "It won't come back," he panted.

Barclay cautioned him to silence, pointing. A curiously, fiercely blue light beat out from the cracks of the shack's door. A very low, soft humming sounded inside, a low, soft humming and a clink and clink of tools, the very sounds somehow bearing a message of frantic haste.

McReady's face paled. "Lord help us if that thing has—" He grabbed Barclay's shoulder, and made snipping motions with his fingers, pointing toward the lacing of control cables that held the door.

Barclay drew the wire cutters from his pocket, and kneeled soundlessly at the door. The snap and twang of cut wires made an unbearable racket in the utter quiet of the Antarctic hush. There was only that strange, sweetly soft hum from within the shack, and the queerly, hectically clipped clicking and rattling of tools to drown their noises.

McReady peered through a crack in the door. His breath sucked in huskily and his great fingers clamped cruelly on Barclay's shoulder. The meteorologist backed down. "It isn't," he explained very softly, "Blair. It's kneeling on something on the bunk—something that keeps lifting. Whatever it's working on is a thing like a knapsack—and it lifts."

"All at once," Barclay said grimly. "No. Norris, hang back, and get that iron of yours out. It may have—weapons."

Together, Barclay's powerful body and McReady's giant strength struck the door. Inside, the bunk jammed against the door screeched madly and crackled into kindling. The door flung down from broken hinges, the patched lumber of the doorpost dropping inward.

Like a blue rubber ball, a Thing bounced up. One of its four tentacle-like arms looped out like a striking snake. In a seven-tentacled hand a six-inch pencil of winking, shining metal glinted and swung upward to face them. Its line-thin lips twitched back from snake-fangs in a grin of hate, red eyes blazing.

Norris' revolver thundered in the confined space. The hate-washed face twitched in agony, the looping tentacle snatched back. The silvery thing in its hand a smashed ruin of metal, the seven-tentacled hand became a mass of mangled flesh oozing greenish-yellow ichor. The revolver thundered three times more. Dark holes drilled each of the three eyes before Norris hurled the empty weapon against its face.

The Thing screamed in feral hate, a lashing tentacle wiping at blinded eyes. For a moment it crawled on the floor, savage tentacles lashing out, the body twitching. Then it struggled up again, blinded eyes working, boiling hideously, the crushed flesh sloughing away in sodden gobbets.

Barclay lurched to his feet and dove forward with an ice-ax. The flat of the weighty thing crushed against the side of the head. Again the unkillable monster went down. The tentacles lashed out, and suddenly Barclay fell to his feet in the grip of a living, livid rope. The thing dissolved as he held it, a white-hot band that ate into the flesh of his hands like living fire. Frantically he tore the stuff from him, held his hands where they could not be reached. The blind Thing felt and ripped at the tough, heavy, windproof cloth, seeking flesh—flesh it could convert—

The huge blowtorch McReady had brought coughed solemnly. Abruptly it rumbled disapproval throatily. Then it laughed gurglingly, and thrust out a blue-white, three-foot tongue. The Thing on the floor shrieked, flailed out blindly with tentacles that writhed and withered in the bubbling wrath of the blowtorch. It crawled and turned on the floor, it shrieked and hobbled madly, but always McReady held the blowtorch on the face, the dead eyes burning and bubbling uselessly. Frantically the Thing crawled and howled.

A tentacle sprouted a savage talon—and crisped in the flame. Steadily McReady moved with a planned, grim campaign. Helpless, maddened, the Thing retreated from the grunting torch, the caressing, licking tongue. For a moment it rebelled, squalling in inhuman hatred at the touch of the icy snow. Then it fell back before the charring breath of the torch, the stench of its flesh bathing it. Hopelessly it retreated—on and on across the Antarctic snow. The bitter wind swept over it, twisting the torch-tongue; vainly it flopped, a trail of oily, stinking smoke bubbling away from it—

McReady walked back toward the shack silently. Barclay met him at the door. "No more?" the giant meteorologist asked grimly.

Barclay shook his head. "No more. It didn't split?"

"It had other things to think about," McReady assured him. "When I left it, it was a glowing coal. What was it doing?"

Norris laughed shortly. "Wise boys, we are. Smash magnetos, so planes won't work. Rip the boiler tubing out of the tractors. And leave that Thing alone for a week in this shack. Alone and undisturbed."

McReady looked in at the shack more carefully. The air, despite the ripped door, was hot and humid. On a table at the far end of the room rested a thing of coiled wires and small magnets, glass tubing and radio tubes. At the center a block of rough stone rested. From the center of the block came the light that flooded the place, the fiercely blue light bluer than the glare of an electric arc, and from it came the sweetly soft hum. Off to one side was another mechanism of crystal glass, blown with an incredible

neatness and delicacy, metal plates and a queer, shimmery sphere of insubstantiality.

"What is that?" McReady moved nearer.

Norris grunted. "Leave it for investigation. But I can guess pretty well. That's atomic power. That stuff to the left—that's a neat little thing for doing what men have been trying to do with hundred-ton cyclotrons and so forth.

It separates neutrons from heavy water, which he was getting from the surrounding ice.

"Where did he get all—oh. Of course. A monster couldn't be locked in—or out. He's been through the apparatus caches." McReady stared at the apparatus. "Lord, what minds that race must have—"

"The shimmery sphere—I think it's a sphere of pure force. Neutrons can pass through any matter, and he wanted a supply reservoir of neutrons. Just project neutrons against silica—calcium—beryllium—almost anything, and the atomic energy is released. That thing is the atomic generator."

McReady plucked a thermometer from his coat. "It's 120° in here, despite the open door. Our clothes have kept the heat out to an extent, but I'm sweating now."

Norris nodded. "The light's cold. I found that. But it gives off heat to warm the place through that coil. He had all the power in the world. He could keep it warm and pleasant, as his race thought of warmth and pleasantness. Did you notice the light, the color of it?"

McReady nodded. "Beyond the stars is the answer. From beyond the stars. From a hotter planet that circled a brighter, bluer sun they came."

McReady glanced out the door toward the blasted, smoke-stained trail that flopped and wandered blindly off across the drift. "There won't be any more coming. I guess. Sheer accident it landed here, and that was twenty million years ago. What did it do all that for?" He nodded toward the apparatus.

Barclay laughed softly. "Did you notice what it was working on when we came? Look."

He pointed toward the ceiling of the shack.

Like a knapsack made of flattened coffee tins, with dangling cloth straps and leather belts, the mechanism clung to the ceiling. A tiny, glaring heart of supernal flame burned in it, yet burned through the ceiling's wood without scorching it. Barclay walked over to it, grasped two of the dangling straps in his hands, and pulled it down with an effort. He strapped it about his body. A slight jump carried him in a weirdly slow arc across the room.

"Antigravity," said McReady softly.

"Antigravity," Norris nodded. "Yes, we had 'em stopped, with no planes, and no birds. The birds hadn't come—but it had coffee tins and radio parts, and glass and the machine shop at night. And a week—a whole week—all to itself. America in a single jump—with antigravity powered by the atomic energy of matter.

"We had 'em stopped. Another half hour—it was just tightening these straps on the device so it could wear it—and we'd have stayed in Antarctica, and shot down any moving thing that came from the rest of the world."

"The albatross—" McReady said softly. "Do you suppose—"

"With this thing almost finished? With that death weapon it held in its hand?

"No, by the grace of God, who evidently does hear very well, even down here, and the margin of half an hour, we keep our world, and the planets of the system, too. Antigravity, you know, and atomic power. Because *They* came from another sun, a star beyond the stars. *They* came from a world with a bluer sun."

"Who Goes There?" first appeared in the August 1938 issue of Astounding Stories *(with illustrations by H. W. Wesso). John W. Campbell published his novelette under the pseudonym of Don A. Stuart, perhaps because he was also the editor of* Astounding. *(Frequently reprinted and thrice adapted for film, "Who Goes There?" is one of the most successful pieces of self-published fiction ever.) Campbell edited* Astounding *(later renamed* Analog*) from 1937 until his death in 1976, and discovered such greats as Asimov and Heinlein. According to* The Encyclopedia of Science Fiction, *"More than any other individual, he helped to shape modern SF." (photo:* The Thing from Another World*, RKO Pictures, 1951; new illustrations by Allen Koszowski)*

BY HER HAND, SHE DRAWS YOU DOWN

by Douglas Smith

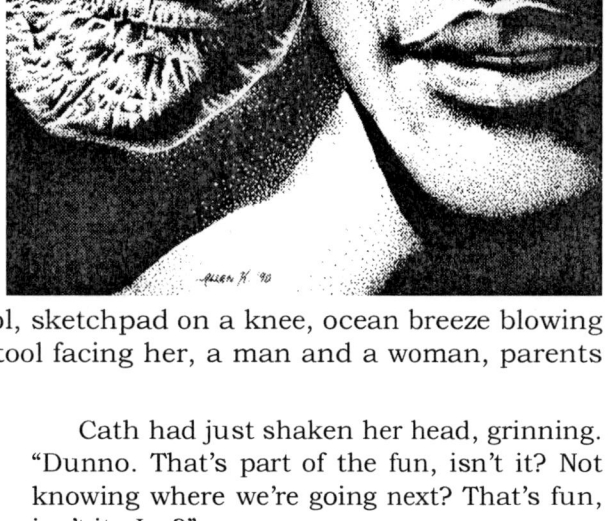

By her hand, she draws you down.
With her mouth, she breathes you in.
Hope and dreams and soul devoured.
Lost to you, what might have been.

By her hand, she draws you down...

JOE SWORE WHEN HE SAW CATH DO-
ING A KID. He had left her for just a
minute, to get a beer from the booth on
the pier before it closed for the night. Walk-
ing back now, he could see Cath on her stool, sketchpad on a knee, ocean breeze blowing
her pale hair. A small girl sat on another stool facing her, a man and a woman, parents
he guessed, beside the child.

Kid's not more than seven, he thought.
Cath promised me no kids. She promised.

The sun was long set, and the air had
turned cool, but people still filled the boardwalk. Joe wove through the crowd as fast as
he could without attracting attention. Cath
had set up farther from the beach tonight, at
the bottom of a grassy slope that ran up to
the highway where their old grey Ford waited.

"Last night tonight," Cath had said when
they had parked the car earlier. "*It* wants to
move on. I can feel the change."

Joe had swallowed and turned off the ignition. He was never comfortable talking about
it. "Where's it headed?"

Cath had just shaken her head, grinning.
"Dunno. That's part of the fun, isn't it? Not
knowing where we're going next? That's fun,
isn't it, Joe?"

Yeah, loads of fun, he thought now as he
approached Cath and her customers. It *had*
been fun once, when they'd met, before he
learned what Cath did, what she had to do.
When his love for her wasn't all mixed up with
fear of what she would do to someone.

Or to him.

The child's parents looked up as Joe came
to stand beside Cath. The father frowned. Joe
smiled, trying to hide the dread digging like
cold fingers into his gut. Turning his back to

them, he bent to whisper in Cath's ear. That flowery scent she had switched to recently rose warm and sweet in his face. *Funeral parlors,* he thought. *She smells like a goddam funeral parlor.*

"Cath, she's just a kid," he rasped in her ear.

Cath shook her head. Her eyes flitted from the girl to her pad. "Bad night. I'm hungry," she muttered, ignoring Joe.

Joe looked at the drawing. It was good. But they were always good. Cath had real talent, more than Joe ever had. She would set up each night where people strolled, her sketches beside her like trophies from a hunt. People would stop to look, sometimes moving on, sometimes sitting for a portrait.

Eventually Joe and Cath would move on, too. When the town was empty, Cath said. When the thing inside her wanted to move on. They had spent this week at a little New England vacation spot. At least they were heading south lately. Summer was dying, and Joe longed to winter in the sun. Sleep for Joe was rare enough since he'd met Cath. Winters up north meant long nights in bars. Things closed in then, closed in around him. On those nights, he would lie awake in their motel bed, feeling Cath's eyes on him, feeling her hunger.

He looked at the sketch, at the child captured there, perfect except for the emptiness that spoke from the eyes, from any eyes that Cath drew. And the mouth.

Where the mouth should have been, empty paper gaped. Cath left the mouth until the end. The portraits always bothered Joe when they looked like that. To him, the pictures weren't waiting to be completed, waiting for a last piece to be added. To Joe, something vital had been ripped from what had once been whole, leaving behind a void that threatened to suck in the world around it. An empty thing but insatiable. Waiting to suck him in, too.

"Cath," he whispered. "You promised."

She ignored him again. Joe wrapped his fingers around the thin wrist of her hand that held the sketchpad. "You promised."

Cath snapped her head around to glare up at him. Joe caught his breath as anger met hunger in her grey eyes, becoming something alive, something that leapt for him.

The father cleared his throat, and the thing in Cath's eyes retreated. Cath turned to the parents. "Sorry, can't get her right. You can have this." Tearing the sketch from her pad, she shoved it at the mother. "We gotta go." Cath stood and folded her stool as the child ran to peek from behind the father's legs. Joe grabbed the other stool and the canvas bag that held Cath's supplies. He put an arm around Cath's waist, leading her away.

The father started to protest. "But you're almost done. You just need to draw in the mouth."

Cath stopped, and Joe swore. He just wanted to get her out of there. She walked back to the man who exchanged glances with his wife. Cath touched a finger to her lips. "Mouths are the hardest part. The most important part," she said. "Everyone—they say 'the eyes are the windows of the soul.' They say 'Oh, you got the eyes just right.' They don't know. They don't know it's the mouth you gotta get just right. That's what makes a picture come alive. Like it's gonna just start … breathing."

The father cleared his throat, but the mother tugged at his shirt. Joe grabbed Cath's arm and pulled her away. The man muttered something, but Joe didn't care.

He led Cath to a gravel path that switched back and forth up the steep hill to the highway above. Halfway up, an observation area looked down on the pier and the beach and the boardwalk. Cath twisted away from him there. A low stone wall ran around the area's edge, and two lampposts stood at either end. Putting her stool down under the nearest light, she began setting out her sketches against the wall.

Joe dropped the other stool and sat down. The fatigue that lived with him always now rose to engulf him. He felt dead inside, all used up, like the way Cath's pictures made him feel, waiting to be sucked into the void. "We had a deal," he said.

Cath sat, looking up and down the path. "I'm hungry."

"No kids, remember?" Joe said. "And nobody with a family depending on them." He tried to make his voice sound strong, but his hands were shaking.

She opened her pad. "Kind of cuts down the field, Joe."

"Use one of the sketches you've got put away."

Cath laughed. A bitter, empty sound. Joe imagined the mouths she drew making that kind of sound. Cath looked at him finally. "All gone. Used 'em all."

Joe felt the emptiness again, a void gaping below, drawing him down. He leaned forward, head between his hands, fingers pressing hard on his temples, trying to make his fear go away. "Jeez, Cath. All of them?" He searched her face for some hope.

Cath shrugged. "Girl's gotta eat." She stared past him, and he heard gravel crunching underfoot. Joe turned, his hand slipping by reflex to touch the switchblade inside his boot top.

A fat man in black pants, white shirt, and paisley tie loosened at the neck was struggling down the steep path from the highway, a beach chair in each arm. He walked over to the stone wall and put down the chairs to rest. Nodding at Joe and Cath, he glanced at her sketches. He began to turn away but then looked back. His eyes ran over the portraits lined against the low wall like prisoners before a firing squad. The man whistled.

Joe sighed, from regret and relief. Cath would eat tonight.

WITH HER MOUTH, SHE BREATHES YOU IN...

The man's name was Harry. He haggled with Cath over the price then he sat down, and Cath started sketching. Joe glanced at the two chairs that Harry had carried, but he couldn't see a wedding ring, so he kept silent.

Cath worked quickly, her hand slashing at the page, pausing only to switch the color of her pencil. When only the mouth remained unfinished, she put the pad down on her lap.

Harry looked down at the sketch. "There's no mouth."

"Mouths are special, Har," Cath said. She puckered at him, and Harry laughed, a nervous squeaky sound. Cath touched a finger of her drawing hand to Harry's lips. He gave that little laugh again but didn't pull away. Cath ran her fingertips slowly over his lips, tracing each curve and contour. Sitting on the stone wall, Joe thought of her fingers on his own skin at night in bed, tracing the lines of his body. Love and fear and lust—with Cath, they all mixed together, colors in a picture flowing into each other, until you couldn't separate one from another.

She lowered her hand to the paper, her eyes still on Harry's mouth. Picking up a red pencil and dropping her eyes, her hand began to stab at the paper in short urgent strokes. The mouth grew under her fingers as Joe watched. She finished in seconds. Removing the sketch sheet, Cath handed it to Harry. He regarded it for a moment, grunted his approval, and paid her. Portrait under his arm, he picked up his chairs and nodded a goodbye.

After watching Harry labor down the path toward the boardwalk below, Joe walked to where Cath sat cross-legged on the ground, her sketch pad on her lap. She carefully lifted a sheet of carbon paper from the top of the pad. A copy of the sketch she had just rendered of Harry stared up at Joe in black and white. *No color*, thought Joe. *As if all the life's been sucked out of it. No*, he thought. *Not all of it. Not yet.*

From her canvas bag, Cath removed a small rosewood box, its hinged cover carved with letters in a script Joe thought was Arabic. He'd never checked, wanting to know as little as possible about the thing. Cath opened the lid and withdrew what looked like a child's crayon but without any paper covering.

The crayon was as long as Joe's middle finger but thicker, and a red so dark it was almost black. Joe remembered drawing as a kid, the crayons, the names of the colors. Midnight blue, leaf green, sunshine yellow. He knew the name that this one would have carried: blood red. It glinted in the overhead light as if it would be sticky to the touch, but Joe had never touched it, so he didn't know for sure. He didn't want to know.

Hunched over the portrait copy, Cath began to retrace the lines of the mouth with the red crayon, adding color and shading. She worked with almost painful slowness. Joe remembered how once she had made a mistake at this stage, how the fury had burst from her like a wild thing caged too long.

At last, Cath straightened. She gave the mouth one last appraising look then returned the crayon to the rosewood box. Joe walked back to the low stone wall. He knew he would turn back to watch her. He always did.

Below, Harry had reached the boardwalk. The big man put down one chair to wave to someone on the beach. Joe's stomach tightened. A woman waved back at Harry, and a small boy and girl ran to hug him. *Jesus, no,* thought Joe.

He turned back. Cath sat hunched over the portrait of Harry on her lap. Joe rushed to her, praying that it wasn't too late, a prayer that died when he saw the picture. It had started.

The portrait's mouth was moving, fat lips squirming like slick red worms on the paper. A pale vapor rose thin and wispy from those lips. Cath bent her head over the mouth and sucked in that misty thing that Joe never wanted to name.

A scream rose from the beach. A woman's cry, a thing of pain and fear. Between her sobs, Joe could hear children crying.

He walked back to the low stone wall and looked down at the crowd gathered where Harry had fallen. Joe stood there, eyes locked on Harry's still form, feeling the void opening below him again. "Cath, we have to get out of here."

Cath didn't answer him. Joe tore his eyes from the scene below and turned back to her. She was standing now, looking south, down the coastline. "It wants to move on," she said.

HOPE AND DREAMS AND SOUL DEVOURED ...

Joe drove staring at the white lane markers slicing the dark two-lane one after another, like brush strokes by God on a long black canvas. White on black. The negative image of Cath's secret portraits. Black on white, white on black. Just the red missing. Just that blood red.

How long before some cop put it together? A string of deaths, all the victims drawn by a young woman with a male companion. Christ, Harry died with a sketch in his hand.

Cath stirred beside him, and then he felt her eyes on him. He could always feel her gaze, like a physical touch, like a brush dipping into him, drawing something from him. *Is that how you do it, Cath? How you take the thing you take? Capture it in your eyes, then cage it through your fingers onto the page? Have you been feeding on me, too?*

"I'm still hungry," Cath said. Her voice was small, almost childlike in the dark.

He knew what she meant. "We'll hit town soon," he said. But it would be three in the morning when they arrived. No one around. No one to draw. And she had no pictures left. Cath said nothing but looked away. After a while, he figured she was asleep. Then he felt her eyes again.

"I don't *want* to hurt people, Joe."

He swallowed. This was new. She never talked about it, even when he did. He should say something now, something smart, something that would lead them out of this. He should, but he had nothing left to say. He could only nod. "I know, babe."

"It just gets so hungry. I get so hungry."

"I know."

"I can't stop it. It keeps pulling me, making me ..."

Joe could feel her pain in those words. And his fear.

"I'm tired," she said. "So tired I wish I could just go to sleep and never wake up. Ever been that tired, Joe?"

He swallowed again. *All the time*, he thought, but he just nodded. Cath looked away, and he took a breath as if he was coming up for air.

"I'm hungry," she said again.

"I know."

Her eyes settled on him again like a beast on his chest.

"I could draw *you*, Joe."

Joe's hands tightened on the wheel. Cath had said it the way a kid told you she could ride a bike or tie her shoe. The lines flashed by in the headlights. White on black, no red.

"Don't even need to see you," she said. "Know you so well."

Joe stared at the road. *Don't look*, he thought.

"Know your face like I know my own," she said.

The burden of her gaze lifted. He looked at her.

Her eyes were shut, and her hand moved in her lap, mimicking drawing motions. "Don't even need light. Could draw you with my eyes closed." Her hand stopped, and she leaned her head back. A few minutes later, Joe could hear her breathing slow and deepen.

So there it was. He always knew it would come to this. This was why he had stayed, even after he learned what Cath did, what she was. Afraid that when he left, when Cath no longer needed him, she would draw him down. Draw him down onto the page from memory, then drink him in like all the others.

The road lines flew at him like white knives out of the night. White knives and blackness. Just the blood red missing. Taking a hand from the wheel, he felt inside the top of his boot, running his fingers over the bone handle of his switchblade.

A few miles down the road, he found a wide shoulder and pulled over, turning off the engine and the lights.

Cath still slept. Hands shaking, Joe pulled the knife from his boot. *It's self-defense*, he thought. But he just sat holding the knife. It was for the best. How many more would she kill? But he still loved her. Could he do it? He was tired, so tired. He leaned back. He only slept now when Cath did, when he didn't feel her eyes. He closed his eyes. Her breathing brushed his ears, soft and deep, soft and deep, soft ...

He awoke to the sound of scratching on paper. He looked over. Framed against the moonlight, Cath sat hunched over her sketchpad, her hand moving in short, sure strokes.

"Kind of late for drawing, isn't it, Cath?" Joe asked. His throat was dry. He fumbled in his lap for the knife.

"Hungry," she said, her voice barely audible.

"Dark, too," he said, blood pounding in his ears.

"Don't need light. Drawin' from memory," she whispered.

Drawing from memory. Drawing him. He knew she was drawing him. "Don't, Cath." His thumb found the blade's button.

"Tired of being hungry." She sat back, eyes on the sketch.

He couldn't see the picture, but he saw the red crayon in her hand. She'd finished the mouth. "Please, don't do it," he said. His cheeks felt cool and wet. He realized he was crying.

Cath lifted the paper to her face. She was crying, too.

"Don't!" Joe screamed. The knife blade clicked open.

"Bye, Joe. Sorry." Cath breathed in through her lips.

Joe saw a pale wisp rise from the paper and move toward her mouth. Saw his hand gripping the knife flash forward. Saw the blade slice her white T-shirt and slide between her ribs.

Saw the red, the blood red, flow over the white of her shirt to blend with the black of the night and the shadows.

Cath spasmed and fell sideways onto him. Surprise mixed with peace in her face. "Thanks ... Joe," she whispered. Her eyes closed and her head slumped back. A wisp of mist escaped her lips. *That's me,* Joe thought. Sobbing, he pressed his lips to hers, sucking in the breath and the grey mist from her mouth.

Bitter and sour, the thing burned his throat as he breathed it in. Something was wrong. Joe felt a presence of something dark, something ... *hungry.*

His head spinning, Joe flicked on the dome light. Blood soaked into his shirt where Cath slumped against him, the picture still clenched in her hand. Joe stared at the sketch, a scream forming in his mind.

A familiar face stared back at him from the page, a face that Cath knew from memory. The face she knew best of all.

Not Joe's face.

It was Cath.

She hadn't been drawing him. She'd been feeding herself to the thing that had lived in her. Cath had been killing herself.

The emptiness that was the mouth in Cath's pictures gaped beneath him, and Joe felt himself being drawn down.

LOST TO YOU, WHAT MIGHT HAVE BEEN ...

A February evening, St. Pete's Beach. Joe sat on his stool, his back to the beauty of a Gulf sunset. His portraits lay strewn on the sand around him like the dead on a battlefield. A woman and man looked them over while Joe waited. The woman held the hand of a little girl and boy. Twins, Joe guessed.

Couldn't be much more than seven, he thought. He remembered when that would have meant something to him, before Cath died, before ...

The little girl tugged on the mother's hand. "They all look so sad, Mommy." The mother hushed the child while the father haggled with Joe over the price. The day had been slow, so Joe agreed to do both kids for the price of one.

Joe started sketching. His hand leapt over the paper, and the images of the children grew around the emptiness where their mouths should have been. A tear ran down his cheek, but he kept drawing.

He had to. He was hungry.

"By Her Hand, She Draws You Down" first appeared in The Third Alternative, *#28 (2001). A short film based on the story won several awards at film festivals around the world.*

Douglas Smith is an award-winning Canadian author described by Library Journal *as "one of Canada's most original writers of speculative fiction." His fiction has been published in twenty-six languages and thirty-two countries. His work includes the urban fantasy novel,* The Wolf at the End of the World, *and the collections* Chimerascope, Impossibilia, *and* La Danse des Esprits. *His non-fiction guide for writers,* Playing the Short Game: How to Market & Sell Short Fiction, *is a must read for any short story writer.*

Doug is a three-time winner of Canada's Aurora Award, and has been a finalist for the John W. Campbell Award, CBC's Bookies Award, Canada's juried Sunburst Award, and France's juried Prix Masterton and Prix Bob Morane.

His website is www.smithwriter.com and he tweets at twitter.com/smithwritr

The miners of Cripple Creek may have been simple folk, but the whole town turned out in response to the young inventor's genius. After all, Tesla's latest gadget had done the impossible.

NIKOLA TESLA
AND THE RESONATING FREQUENCY TRANSMITTER
by Kurt Newton

THE YOUNG MAN SITTING AT THE BACK OF THE CRIPPLE CREEK SALOON DREW AN UNHEALTHY AMOUNT OF STARES FROM THE MINERS AND PROSPECTORS standing at the bar rail. Maybe it was the young man's appearance: tight-knit hair black as pitch, a wide face with a long blade-like nose on which rested a pair of finely crafted spectacles, thick mustache underneath. To compound matters, he was dressed in a charcoal grey sack suit and black bowtie. Maybe it was the way he sat amid the shouts and hoots and hollers and bustle as if he were sitting in the privacy of his own home, writing in what looked to be a company ledger. Maybe it was the lone beer resting on the table before him, served over an hour previous and still half full. Any one of these would have drawn eyes. All three warranted an investigation. After all, the last thing a group of hard-working, lung-damaged, brain-doused mountain men needed was to be reminded how some people didn't need to lift a finger or break a sweat to get by in the world.

"Hey! You there with the pencil!"

The young man didn't look up from his work as the call, aimed in his direction, rode above the din.

"Hey, I'm talking to you ... foreigner!"

The man belonging to the voice was none other than Elmo Carr: big, dumb, and prone to ornery when drinking, which he'd been doing since the day ended. With his buddies at the bar snickering and goading him on, Elmo walked over to the young man seated at the table and plucked the ledger from his hands. It seemed only then the young man acknowledged his surroundings.

"What do we have here?" Elmo teetered on his boot heels as he stared at the open ledger. It was actually not a ledger at all but a notebook filled with sketches of machinery and mathematical formulas.

"Please, may I have it back?" the young man said. His voice was firm yet polite.

"Now hold on there little fella." Elmo stared at the notebook, his brow furrowing. There were loose sheets still on the table containing much of the same writing on them. "You one of them engineers, ain't you?"

"Please, return my work to me. It is very important."

"Your work." Elmo turned to his buddies. "The man wants his work." A grin turned his face into a caricature of good humor. "I'll tell you what. Last I heard they done run out of paper in the crapper. I think some of these pages here will do just fine." Elmo tore some sheets from the notebook. The young man removed his spectacles and placed them on the table. He stood up and a quiet fell over the saloon.

The stranger wasn't a tall man. In fact, he was virtually dwarfed by Elmo in both height and breadth. But behind those spectacles rested a pair of eyes that could pierce shoe leather.

"I asked you politely to give me my work. Now I am demanding it."

Elmo looked to his buddies and winked. He stuffed the sheets back into the notebook with exaggerated care and held it out to the young man ... then let it drop. The notebook hit the floor with a loud slap. Laughter erupted. As the young man bent to pick it up, Elmo tried to kick it out of reach, but something curious happened instead. The young man grabbed Elmo's boot heel and, using its forward momentum, lifted it high into the air. Elmo was airborne for a moment before crashing down, hitting his head on the floor and knocking himself groggy. The young man picked up his notebook and quietly sat back down.

An older, bearded gentleman who had just walked into the saloon when this occurred shouted, "Elmo Carr! You up to no good again?"

More laughter.

Elmo shooed the imaginary buzzards circling his head and focused on the man who had just made him the butt of a joke. When he realized it was Sam Brannan, he laughed right along with them.

Sam Brannan was the most experienced mountain man in all of Colorado. He knew the Front Range of the Rockies like the nicks and dents on his favorite pick ax. He could read veins of rock the way a Gypsy read tea leaves. And when it came to hiking up the Peak, Sam was your man. He walked over to the table where the young man involved in the altercation sat. "Mr. Tesla?"

The young man stood and held out his hand. "You can call me Nikola. You must be Mr. Brannan. Please sit."

Sam pulled up a chair. The rest of Cripple Creek's patrons went back to what they were doing, all except Elmo who still sat on the floor trying to make the birds disappear. Sam hooked a thumb in Elmo's direction and said, "How'd you do that?"

Nikola wiped his glasses with a handkerchief. "It is a simple law of physics. The transference of force ... and gravity." He returned the glasses to his face. "I trust you received the remuneration I wired?"

"You mean the money? Yes, but—"

"Good. Then we are all set for tomorrow morning?"

"Yes, but—"

"But what, Mr. Brannan?"

"There's word a storm is headed our way. We may have to postpone."

"Out of the question. My work here is time-critical. I must transmit at a given hour on a given day, and that day is tomorrow."

"But—"

"If you will not take me, Mr. Brannan, I will be forced to find someone else who will." The young man immediately began scouting the room for would-be substitutes.

Sam glanced around the saloon at the ragtag gang of dreamers, drunkards and fools. He knew that anyone of them would jump at the chance to help Tesla part with his money. He also knew the majority of them wouldn't hesitate to leave him stranded in the wild. At least, as his guide, Sam could see to his safety. Though, if the weather reports were correct, it was going to be rough going ... even for an experienced climber.

"Okay, I'll take you. But we're going to need an extra hand to haul the equipment."

Nikola looked at the large man he'd sent to the floor just minutes ago, who was now getting to his feet. "You, sir, Mr. Elmo.... We got off on the wrong foot, so to speak. Let me make it up to you." Nikola pulled a twenty-dollar gold piece from his lapel pocket and held it between two fingers so the kerosene light reflected off its watery surface. "How would you like to make twenty dollars for a day's work?"

Elmo rubbed the back of his head and nodded. "Where do I sign up?"

"No signature necessary, Mr. Elmo." Nikola tossed the gold piece and Elmo snatched it out of the air like a golden canary. "Just meet us here at the break of dawn. And dress warmly."

Nikola downed the rest of his beer, then stood. He tucked his notebook under his arm and offered his hand to Brannan. "Tomorrow then?"

Sam stood and reluctantly sealed the deal with a handshake. "Tomorrow."

Nikola took the stairs to his room where he retired for the evening. In spite of the piano music and the raucous behavior below and in the rooms down the hall, he quickly fell asleep and dreamed of an instrument that would not only send signals halfway around the world but would receive them as well.

2

WHAT SAM BRANNAN HAD HEARD was correct. Sunrise at Cripple Creek yielded a sky filled with clouds as thick as beer foam. The cold of the night had given way to a damp chill. As Sam Brannan, Nikola Tesla and Elmo Carr—each looking like bears dressed in their boots and thick parkas—met outside the Cripple Creek Saloon in preparation for the climb, each took a moment to look at the sky as if to pay their respects and, hopefully, get that respect paid in return.

Elmo stood harnessed to what looked like a dog sled. "What the hell am I lugging anyway?" he said, eyeing the rectangular shape wrapped in tarpaulin and strapped to the sled behind him. One side of his mouth bulged with chewing tobacco.

"It is called a Resonating Frequency Transmitter," said Nikola, checking the time on his pocket watch one last time before snapping it shut and tucking it away. "Once we reach the summit, I will send a radio signal to France."

Elmo squinted his eyes and then spit a stream of brown fluid into the snow. "You're a strange little fella, you know that?"

"Let's head out," said Sam, eager to get this day over with.

It was a short walk to the edge of town. The hotel, bank, telegraph office and livery were all closed up tight. It was going to be a good day to stay indoors, grab a drink, play cards, count your money. It appeared only Sam, Nikola and Elmo were foolish enough to attack the Peak today. When they reached the trail entrance at the base of the mountain, Sam stopped. Ahead, Pikes Peak rose majestically until it was lost in the ever-thickening cloud cover. A wooden sign shaped like a crude arrow pointed the way. Carved into the sign were the words: Pikes Peak, alt. 14,000 feet.

"Last chance to change your mind," said Sam. When neither man said a word, Sam said, "Figured as much." The three began their ascent.

In the best of conditions, the twelve-mile trek to the top of the Peak could be accomplished in under six hours. Most never went that far, instead climbing just above the timberline to reach one of the several mines cut into the mountainside. At the lower levels, the rocky trail was wide enough to accommodate a horse-drawn wagon, and the three men had no trouble making good time. But as the timberline sank beneath them, the trail narrowed, gravel giving way to ice, and they were forced to walk single-file. They stopped once to rest, three miles from the summit, on a wind-swept ledge gazing out upon a spectacular pit of ice and snow and surrounding peaks that lent the Rocky Mountains its name. The cloud cover appeared close enough to touch, and as luck would have it, the first flakes of snow began to fill the air.

Sam drank from a water bottle. He tapped Nikola on the shoulder and offered him a drink. Nikola shook his head.

"How long will it take you to set up?" Sam

shouted over the increased howl of the wind.

"Twenty minutes." The young man was barely out of breath.

"And how long for the transmission?"

"Several minutes, no more."

Sam nodded. So far, so good. If all went well they'd be back in Cripple Creek not long after sundown. After reenergizing on water and jerky. They continued on.

Up ahead were a series of switchbacks that looked like stair steps leading to the top. The snow and wind made it increasingly difficult to see. Gusts of forty miles per hour or more tugged at their parkas and pulled at their hoods. At this level the snow was permanent and knee-deep in places. After two hours of non-stop drudgery they at last reached the summit.

Elmo pulled the sled onto a plateau, unharnessed, and sat down where he stood, gasping for air. Nikola immediately went to work unloading the equipment, while Sam tamped an area of snow wide enough to accommodate the unit. Hunched like two odd creatures in an unfriendly environment, Sam assisted Nikola as best he could, helping attach the legs to the three-foot square, hundred-pound transmitter. Nikola screwed in the oval-shaped antenna. He then inserted a detachable armature and hand cranked the unit until it came to life. Dial faces lit up and a drone like that of a dying bagpipe rose above the wind. Nikola worked furiously adjusting dials and turning knobs until the sound reached a deeply soothing tone.

Sam stood back as a sudden tingle traveled over his body. The gold in his teeth began to rattle. From the snow, like a cow drawn to the sound of a dinner bell, Elmo got to his feet and approached the unit. "What's it do?" he shouted.

"It sends a signal up into the sky that, when adjusted to the proper angle, will skip along a layer in the upper atmosphere. Much like a stone on the surface of a pond." As Nikola talked he adjusted the antenna until it was set to the proper degree of inclination. When he was satisfied, he continued. "My colleagues in Paris have a similar unit that is operating at this very instant. Their unit will receive the signals I transmit. Likewise, in just a moment, this unit will receive the signals they are transmitting to me."

Nikola kept a steady watch on the dials. "That's odd."

He had no sooner spoken the words when a gust of wind kicked up so strong it knocked him onto his back. The transmitter tipped on two legs. In the sudden blinding snow, Nikola was sure he was about to witness two year's worth of hard labor destroyed. But Elmo lurched forward and grabbed the unit as if it were a fainting dance partner. With its antenna nestled beneath his chin, the unit continued to transmit its signal. Elmo's hood blew back as another gust slammed into the mountaintop and he cried out. Moments later, when the wind subsided, Elmo righted the unit and stumbled away pawing at his eyes.

While Nikola tended to the transmitter, Sam tended to Elmo, sitting him down on the lee side of stone outcropping to shield them from the wind.

"My eyes ... I can't see!" cried Elmo.

Sam examined Elmo's face and saw that his eyes were sealed over with what looked like fried eggs the color of apple jelly.

"I'm blind!" Elmo bellowed.

"Take it easy," shouted Sam. "You're not blind. Your eyelids are frozen shut, that's all." Sam took his gloves off and gently tugged at the amber-colored wads with his fingers. They were soft to the touch. He'd never seen anything like it. "This might hurt a bit," he said. As he pulled he felt an odd tingling sensation on the tips of his fingers, much like what he had felt when Nikola had turned on the transmitter. He didn't like it. He didn't like it one bit. Ah, what the hell, he thought, and yanked the patch off Elmo's eye in one quick motion, tossing it into the snow.

Elmo squawked, but only for a moment.

He could see again. "Thank the Lord...."

Sam tore the second patch off, returning Elmo's face to normal, except for his eyebrows and eyelashes, which were now gone.

"How does my face look?" Elmo asked, relieved his discomfort was only temporary.

"Good as new," Sam lied.

Meanwhile, Nikola had gathered the information needed. The transmitter was dismantled and returned to the sled, and although the snow continued, the trek back to Cripple Creek was uneventful.

Elmo complained of a headache along the way but he assumed it was from his constant squinting. It was funny, but as he trudged down the trail he could swear he saw lights now and then in the distance, as if piercing the whiteout conditions. Lights that changed color from blue to purple to red. It was impossible, he knew. He was also bothered by what sounded like voices in his ears, faint, garbled whispers that had him asking Nikola more than once if he had said something to him.

They arrived back at the Cripple Creek Saloon hungry and tired at just past eight in the evening. Nikola thanked Sam for his expertise and went straight to his room. He needed to make note of the day's activities. Sam hit the bar; he needed a drink. Elmo wasn't feeling well and decided to continue on to the flophouse where he rented a bed. He had been exhausted before in his life, but this was a different kind of exhaustion. It felt as if his body had been hollowed out.

What Elmo hadn't realized was that even though it was only a matter of moments the Resonating Frequency Transmitter was in his arms, something remarkable had occurred. Something more remarkable than Nikola Tesla had ever dreamed. And that something would not show itself until later that night.

3

As THE SNOW FELL OUTSIDE the Cripple Creek Saloon, Nikola sat upstairs in his room hunched over a writing desk, the soft glow of a kerosene lamp providing ample light. Unfortunately, the lamp didn't provide any understanding to the results of his calculations. Not that he expected it to. Aside from identifying the correct radio signal transmitted by his Paris colleagues, he had recorded an unidentified signal, one that, if his triangulated coordinates were correct, originated from outer space.

Nikola removed his glasses, setting them on the desk before him. He rubbed his eyes. It must be some kind of error, he thought. He drank from a teacup he had borrowed from a scantily clad lady down the hall. The tea was still warm. He closed his eyes and let the relaxation of the moment sink in.

A knock came at the door.

Nikola checked his pocket watch. It was after midnight. Perhaps it was the kind lady wanting her teacup back? Nikola donned his glasses. He then licked his palm and matted his hair down before answering the door.

It was Elmo. He stood in the hallway dressed in his winter parka. Nikola could feel the cold from outside still clinging to his clothes. The look in his eyes was strange. If Nikola wasn't mistaken, the man appeared to be sleepwalking.

"We need your help," Elmo said with a monotone voice.

"I'm sorry?"

Elmo turned and walked away, leaving Nikola to wonder what to do next. As was usually the case when faced with an odd circumstance that piqued his curiosity: he needed to investigate. He hurriedly slipped his boots and parka on and rushed to catch up to the big man.

Nikola noticed the saloon was all but empty as he followed Elmo out into the night, onto the snow-covered street.

"Is somebody hurt? I am not a medical doctor," said Nikola, following close behind, but he received no response.

Elmo led him to the livery, which was lit

up like a church hall. Part horse stable, part blacksmith shop, part supply storage, the livery was also where large shipments were kept before their trip out of town. Among those shipments was Nikola's transmitter. Nikola followed him inside.

The sweet smells of sawdust and horse manure were augmented by the pungent odor of kerosene. Two men lay on the floor between the horse stalls and the blacksmith's bench. Both were gagged and hog-tied. Nikola remembered their faces from the evening before as they sat at the bar in the Cripple Creek Saloon. Beside them stood the Resonating Frequency Transmitter, unpacked and set up the way it had been on top of Pikes Peak.

"What is this about?" Nikola pushed his hood back.

"We need your help," Elmo said again. "There are more of us." Elmo looked toward the ceiling. It was then that Nikola saw the tiny specks of light swirling about like miniature fireflies trapped behind the surface of Elmo's eyes. Elmo gestured to the men on the floor, who grunted and jerked like fish on dry land. "We need you to fill these vessels, the way I was filled. When you are done with them, I will bring more."

"And if I do not do as you say?"

Elmo walked over and kneeled down beside one of the gagged men. He grabbed the man's head in his large hands and began to twist. "If you don't, I will break them ... one by one ... until you do." The bound man struggled futilely.

"Stop. I will do it."

Elmo let go of the man and stood.

Nikola approached the transmitter and with several cranks of the armature charged the coil inside. The array of dials lit up and a low-level hum emanated from the unit. "It might not work at this altitude. The surrounding mountains may interfere."

Although he was disturbed by the prospect of creating more alien automatons, he was fascinated by how this miracle occurred in the first place. The scientific process demanded repetition. No doubt the alien signals he had observed were in truth alien. The electromagnetic energy emanated by Mr. Elmo's body must have acted as a conduit—an antenna, so to speak— allowing the alien energy to invade and take control.

Nikola surveyed his surroundings, looking for a simpler means to transfer the signal into the host body. A coil of steel banding used to cinch wood barrels together hung from a hook on the wall near the blacksmith's bench.

"Mr. Elmo, I will need your assistance."

He showed Elmo what was required: a circular band approximately eight inches in diameter with a band across the middle, arched like the handle of a basket; two holes, one on either side of the circle, through which a small bolt could be secured. As Elmo pounded away on the anvil, Nikola found a spindle of wire used for blasting. He cut two lengths of wire and connected them to the transmitter's existing antenna. He then twisted the free ends to the bolts on the completed halo.

"We are now ready," he announced.

Elmo brought the first man to his feet and sat him on a stool beside the unit. Nikola placed the halo over the man's head. He wanted to tell the frightened man to relax, it would all be over soon, but he wasn't the one about to have an alien presence planted inside of him. Nikola adjusted the dials on the transmitter, duplicating the frequency he had observed on Pikes Peak. A familiar hum filled the livery. Horses stomped and brayed in their stalls. The man under the halo grit his teeth and winced. A moment later his eyes flew open and he stared out toward the night as if he could see something only he was privy to. A guttural scream began in his torso and exited his mouth. His head snapped back and he wailed, his body shuttering on the stool. An amber-colored fluid escaped his eyes and congealed to form twin patches like the ones Elmo had experienced. He fell from the stool, the halo slipping from his head.

The man was unresponsive as Elmo unbound his hands and feet. Then Elmo opened his mouth and emitted a noise unlike anything Nikola had ever heard. It was part dolphin cry, part static burst. The man stirred and clawed at his eyes. Elmo tore the patches free and the man looked around as if waking from a dream. He got to his feet and emitted the same strange cry as Elmo. Together they grabbed the other man and placed him on the stool. Elmo lowered the halo onto the man's head and looked to Nikola to do the rest.

Nikola fine tuned the signal and repeated the process. When this second man flopped to the floor, his eyes covered in the same gelatinous substance, Nikola took the opportunity to do what was needed to stop this process from going any further. A sledgehammer leaned against a support post nearby and he grabbed it, ready to destroy the machine he had worked years to create. He wielded the twenty-pound sledge as if he were at a carnival intent on ringing a bell at the top of a tower. Halfway through the air the sledgehammer stopped abruptly. One of Elmo's large hands had caught the handle.

"Unwise, Mr. Tesla."

He yanked the sledgehammer from Nikola's grasp, shoving him to the ground where he landed near a pile of horse manure. The light in Elmo's eyes flared with a reddish hue as he raised the sledgehammer over his head. Nikola grabbed the manure and flung it into the big man's face. Blindly, Elmo brought the sledgehammer down but Nikola had rolled out of the way. Before Elmo could regain his bearings, Nikola got to his feet and ran from the livery out into the snow, the high-pitched squeals of the three men chasing after him.

Nikola hurried back to the Cripple Creek Saloon. He rushed upstairs to a room at the end of the hall, the same room where, earlier that evening, when he went to borrow a cup of tea, he had seen Sam Brannan enter with a young lady on his arm. Nikola rapped three

times before barging in. Sam sat up in bed, a .45 pistol pointed in his direction.

"I am sorry for the interruption, Mr. Brannan, but we have a problem."

There was a commotion in the saloon below: the sounds of bottles breaking and furniture being knocked over. A body hit the floor. This was followed by a series of high-pitched squeals.

"What in tarnation?" said Sam.

There came heavy footsteps on the stairs.

"We must go. Now!" advised Nikola.

Sam kissed the woman he was with. "Sorry darling," he said, jumping into his suspenders and boots. As he pulled on his jacket, the room's door busted inward and there stood Elmo.

Sam pulled his gun, but hesitated. The crazed look in Elmo's eyes told him things just weren't right with the man. And it wasn't just the fact that his eyebrows and eyelashes were gone. Elmo wasn't himself. He stared at Nikola with harmful intent.

"I thought the two of you had buried the hatchet!" said Sam.

Elmo gave Sam a cursory glance before rushing Nikola.

Once again Nikola's agility outmatched the big man, and he sent Elmo tripping headlong into the window that overlooked the street below. Glass shattered and the window frame splintered. Elmo backed out of the broken window, cold and snow entering the room. He staggered back, his face bloodied. Bits of glass were embedded in his skull. He screamed then, issuing that ear-piercing alien call, and more footsteps were heard on the stairway.

Nikola and Sam were stunned by what they had just witnessed, but not too stunned to know it was time to leave.

Nikola dove out the newly formed exit where the window had been. Sam followed quickly after. The two hit the porch roof and rolled off onto the street below landing in the snow. They got to their feet and ran.

4

"NOW WOULD YOU MIND telling me what's going on?" asked Sam.

He and Nikola were hold up in the loft of the town's Meeting House. They had a bird's eye view of the main street below. It appeared Elmo and his men had lost them.

"The signals I received on the mountain top were not limited to my colleagues in France. When Mr. Elmo grabbed hold of the Resonating Frequency Transmitter I am afraid a signal grabbed hold of him. A signal not from this world."

"You mean outer space?"

"Yes, Mr. Brannan."

"What about Elmo's buddies? They sure as hell didn't make the trip up Pikes Peak with us."

"I am afraid that is my doing. I followed Mr. Elmo to the livery where the unit is housed and he forced me to reproduce the event. After a simple modification I was able to amplify the unit's receptive capability, thereby isolating the characteristic signal marker and—"

"In plain English, please!"

"The transmitter performed perfectly."

"Well isn't that just dandy."

"No, Mr. Brannan, it is not. As you can see, Mr. Elmo no longer needs me to operate the device."

There was movement on the streets. Four men carrying lanterns and rifles were going door-to-door and dragging people out of their beds into the storm. They herded the first group back to the livery, then returned eight strong to search for more.

"It appears Mr. Elmo is building an army. It is my belief he will not stop at Cripple Creek."

"They'll head east to Fairview ... then south to Beacon Hill ... and then on to Victor.... We need to destroy that machine!"

"There may be another way, Mr. Brannan."

"A way to save these people?"

"No, a way to save ourselves."

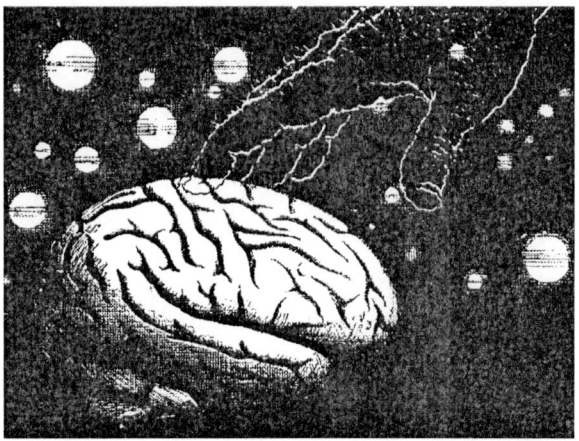

NIKOLA TESLA AND SAM BRANNAN made their way back out into the blinding snow, avoiding the main street and Elmo's men. They slipped between buildings, hunkering down when necessary to avoid capture. By now, nearly everyone in town was amassed in front of the livery: miners and shop owners, hookers and wives. Men and women who had come to Cripple Creek with dreams of striking it rich, now stood like participants in some mindless parade. They stood in the drifting snow waiting, while horses were harnessed to wagons and those wagons were pulled up to where they stood. One by one they stepped up into the wagons and sat like children about to embark on a hayride. Meanwhile, Nikola and Sam circled around to the rear of the building. With Pikes Peak at their backs they spied upon the activity inside.

The first thing Nikola noticed was that Elmo had taken his halo design and modified it, constructing an octopoid-like contraption that "turned" a group of people in one session, thereby speeding up the process. "Brilliant," he muttered, admiring the alien intelligence's technological ingenuity. Elmo, acting as welcoming committee, greeted each new vessel with a touch of his hand and a staccato squeak, and they replied in kind before heading out the door into the snow to wait with the rest. This group appeared to be the last of

Cripple Creek's occupants left unturned. All except for Nikola and Sam, of course. Elmo followed this last group outside, leaving behind two men to guard the machine.

"Now what is this plan of yours?" asked Sam.

"Mr. Brannan, how often do avalanches occur in this area?"

"Not very often. You need a lot of snow."

Nikola looked skyward.

"That's your plan? Hope for an avalanche? For an avalanche to happen now, we would need a miracle."

"I believe I can produce your miracle. Just take care of those men for me, Mr. Brannan, and I will do the rest."

Sam pulled his six-gun and slowly opened the rear door just wide enough to slip inside. Nikola followed.

They moved from horse stall to horse stall until there was nothing left to hide behind. The machine and the two sentries were no more than ten feet away. Sam held up his fist and silently counted to three on his fingers, then bolted to the nearest sentry and knocked him flat with the butt of his pistol. The gun went off accidentally, alerting those outside as to what was going on. The other sentry turned toward him, the whites of eyes filling with a reddish glow. It was Jebediah Griggs, the town's blacksmith. Sam acted quickly, shooting the blacksmith in the leg and dropping him to one knee. "Sorry Jeb," said Sam as he swung a roundhouse punch to the man's jaw, laying him out cold.

"Block the door!" shouted Nikola.

"I'm way ahead of you, son. You just work your miracle."

While Nikola reversed the operation of the unit, transforming it from a receiver into a transmitter, Sam was able to wedge a saw board under the livery's front door handles. Elmo and the rest of the townspeople pressed themselves against the outside of the building. The door bent but didn't budge. Windows broke and arms reached in. Sam did his best

to fight back the throng, taking a flat-headed shovel and whacking everything that moved. He clocked the bank manager on top of the head. He broke three fingers on the Cripple Creek Saloon bartender's right hand. He flattened the nose of the woman he'd slept with just hours ago. Suddenly, the building began to shake. Sam thought it was the collective weight of the people outside pushing to get in, but the noise cut deeper than that. The vibration could be felt through the dirt floor. In the air itself.

Nikola stepped back from the Resonating Frequency Transmitter. The multi-armed receiving antenna rose into the air like a hydra, hovering on the sound waves that pulsed from its circular headbands.

Outside, Elmo had disappeared from the crowd, and by the time Sam realized it, there came movement at the back of the livery. Elmo and three others had entered and were headed for the machine.

"Nikola! Watch out!"

When Nikola saw the men coming he picked up a nearby hammer and busted the knobs off the transmitter, effectively rendering it unalterable.

Nikola joined Sam who stood near the blocked front door. Sam still had four bullets left and he wasn't going to hesitate to use them.

The four men surrounded the machine as the receiving antenna twirled overhead like a carnival ride and the vibration deepened.

Elmo turned, his eyes glowing red. "You fools!"

He took two steps toward Sam and Nikola and stopped. He looked to the ceiling as the ground began to shake. A deep tremor rose out of the rock bed beneath them, a tremor caused by a massive amount of snow sloughing off the side of Pikes Peak and hurtling toward them.

"Well, I'll be darned," said Sam. "What now?"

Nikola quickly examined the interior of

the livery. "According to the laws of physics, the most structurally sound part of this building is right there." He pointed to the nearest horse stall. It was constructed of eight-by-eights on all four corners, and was reinforced by the framing of an overhead loft.

Nikola and Sam ran and dove into the stall just as the leading edge of the avalanche hit the livery. The noise reached a deafening pitch as the building groaned under the weight of the snow. While Elmo's three men ran for the front door, Elmo stood his ground, defiant in the face of the impending calamity. Perhaps he was lamenting his short time on Earth, his army built of a superior race the world would never see, his paradise lost. It was the last sight Sam and Nikola saw before the roof of the livery caved in and everything went black.

5

THE AVALANCHE BURIED MORE than just the livery. It buried the Cripple Creek Saloon. It buried the bank and the post office. It buried the entire town. The narrow valley at the foot of Pikes Peak, once home to the town of Cripple Creek was, now filled with a layer of snow and ice twenty-feet deep.

The storm from the night before had passed and now the sun rose into the morning sky, turning the pristine snow into a field of glitter. Pikes Peak cut a majestic notch out of the blue, as the air held little sound but a gentle wisp of a breeze and the lonesome cry of a circling hawk.

But something suddenly pierced the surface of the new fallen snow: a giant hand with thin fingers poked up out of the depths. A pitchfork opened a hole where the Cripple Creek livery had been, and two men pulled themselves up onto the packed surface of the snow.

Sam Brannan and Nikola Tesla lay on their backs exhausted. They lay like that for a long while before sitting up. They scanned the horizon.

"I don't suppose you know an easier way to get to the next town?" said Sam.

"I am afraid, Mr. Brannan, I am out of miracles," said Nikola. "Although, using some of the materials buried beneath us, I'm sure we can construct a suitable pair of snow shoes."

"I don't think that will be necessary."

Sam stood and tested the firmness of the snow. Nikola got to his feet.

"Shall we?" said Sam.

"After you, Mr. Brannan."

Sam smiled at the young man's continued formality.

"Call me Sam," he said as they headed east into the rising sun.

As a child, Kurt Newton was weaned on episodes of Twilight Zone *and* The Outer Limits, *and* Chiller Theater *(which showed many of the classic sci-fi horror movies of the '50s and '60s), laying the groundwork for his fertile imagination. His short stories have appeared in numerous publications over the last twenty years, including* Weird Tales, Weirdbook, Space and Time, Dark Discoveries, Daily Science Fiction, The Arcanist *and* Hinnom Magazine. *He lives in Connecticut.*

The planet hid itself from the Earthmen—
and what lay behind the mask was fierce and deadly!

THE MASKED WORLD

by Jack Williamson

THE PLANET WORE A MASK.
AT TEN MILLION MILES, IT WAS A SULLEN YELLOW EYE. At one million, a scarred and evil leer. Outside the smoking circle our landing-jets had sterilized, it was a hideous veil of hairy black tentacles and huge sallow blooms, hiding the riddle of its sinister genes.

On most worlds that we astronauts have found, the life is vaguely like our own. Similar nucleotides are linked along similar helical chains of DNA, carrying similar genetic messages. A similar process replicates the chains when the cells divide, to carry the complex blueprints for a particular root or eye or wing accurately down across ten thousand generations.

But even the genes were different here— enormously complicated. Here the simplest-seeming weed had more and longer chains of DNA than anything we had seen before. What was their message?

We had come to read it, with our new genetic micro-probe. A hundred precious tons of microscopic electronic gear, it was designed to observe and manipulate the smallest units of life. It could reach even those strange genes.

That was our mission.

Ours was the seventh survey ship to approach the planet. Six before us had been lost without trace. We were to find out why.

Our pilot was Lance Llandark. A lean hard man, silent and cold as the gray-cased micro-probe. We hated him—until someone learned why he had volunteered to come.

His wife had been pilot of the ship before us. When we knew that, we began to hear the hidden tension in his tired voice, monotonously calling on every band: "Come in, Six.... Come in Six...."

Six never came in.

FOR TWO DAYS, WE WATCHED THE PLANET. The shallow ditch our jets had dug. The charred stumps. The jungle beyond—the visible mask of those monstrous genes—rank, dark, utterly alien.

At the third dawn, Lance Llandark took two of us out in a 'copter. Flying a grid over the landing area, we mapped six shallow pockmarks on that scowling wilderness, where our ships must have landed.

We dropped into the newest crater, where black stumps jutted like broken teeth out of queerly bare red muck. A yellow-scummed stream oozed across it. By the stream we found a fine-boned human skeleton.

A nightmare plant stood guard beside the bones. Its thick leaves were strangely streaked, twisted with vegetable agony, half poison spine and half blighted bloom. Shapeless blobs of rotting fruit were falling from it over those slender bones.

Lance Llandark stood up.

"Her turquoise thunderbird." He showed us the bit of blackened silver and blue-veined stone. "Back on Terra.... Back when we were student pilots.... We bought it from an Indian in an old, old town called Santa Fe."

He bent again.

"Lilith?" he whispered. "Lilith, what killed you?"

We found no other bones, nothing even to tell us what force or poison kept the creeping jungle back from that solitary plant. We left at dusk. Tenderly, Lance Llandark brought the gathered bones. Carefully we carried a few leaves and dried pods from that crazy sentinel plant. We found no other clue.

Patiently, day by forty-hour day, we searched the other sites. We found jet marks and stumps and teeming weeds, but nothing like that tormented nightmare over Lilith Llandark's skeleton. We found no wreckage. Nothing to show how the planet had murdered the lost expeditions.

Day by eternal day, the unknown leered from the secret places of its genes. It was all vegetable. We saw no animal movement, heard no cry or insect hum. The silence became suffocating.

Day after desperate day, we returned to the micro-probe.

"The answer's in the genes," Lance Llandark whispered grimly. "We've no other chance."

He kept the probe running on the strangest genes of all; those from the plant nightmare that had grown beside his wife. They were like nothing else on the planet. The double-stranded chains of DNA were monstrously long; many of the nucleotide links held copper or arsenic atoms.

"Queer!" Lance kept muttering. "No copper or arsenic in other plants here. I'd like to know why."

HE WAS RUNNING WHEN WE HEARD the woman scream. In that stifling quiet, her cry unnerved us all. We crowded down to the lock.

Tattered, stained with blood-colored juices, she slipped through those coiled, constricting creepers. She splashed out into the open ditch, waving a filthy rag. Halfway to the ship, she fell into the mud.

Lance Llandark led three of us to bring her in. She whimpered and looked up. Tears streaked the grime on her wasted face.

"Lance!" she gasped. "My dear."

"Lilith—" But he shrank back suddenly. "I found Lilith dead!"

"I am nearly dead." She tried weakly to get up. "You see, we're all marooned out there in the bush. Emergency landing, when we tried to get off. Wrecked our astrogation gear. Need your spare astro-pilot—"

"Back." He swung on us. "Back aboard!"

"What's wrong?" We were stunned, "She's your wife—"

"Aboard! Instanter!"

We obeyed his deadly voice.

"Help—" she whispered faintly behind us in the mud. "Survivors—need astro-pilot—to plot our way home—"

The clanging lock cut off her voice.

Angrily we turned on Lance Llandark.

"Hold it!" he snapped. "I'm not crazy—the planet is. Come along to the micro-probe. I'm probing a seed from the plant we found by Lilith's bones. It puzzled me. So much of it was—"

In spite of the tension, he had to grope for a word to express meaning.

"Arbitrary! Those shapeless leaves, twisted stalk, that sterile seed. The copper and arsenic in those needless links. Too many genes had no function. No use at all!

"I'd just got the key, when that thing screamed. The copper and arsenic atoms are not genetic instructions to the plant. They're a message to us—words replicated a trillion times, and concealed in every cell of the plant!"

"Words?" someone whispered blankly. "Words in the atoms?"

"Written in binary code." His scowl was bleakly triumphant. "That weed's a mutant, you see. The real Lilith formed the first cell with her micro-probe. She left it—I suppose in her own body—as a message that no pseudo-Lilith could intercept."

Outside that something screamed again.

"Call each copper atom a dot," he whispered. "Call each arsenic a dash. Taken in order along the chains of DNA, they do encode a message. The computer's decoding it now."

He punched a button, and the printer whirred.

TO WHOEVER COMES.... GIVE NO AID TO ANYONE.... GET OFF THIS PLANET.... ITS LIFE IS PSEUDOMORPHIC.... DON'T LET IT LEAVE.... JUST TAKE MY LOVE TO LANCE LLANDARK.... FROM LILITH, HIS WIFE.... AND GET OFF THIS PLANET, FAST....

Outside, it uttered a frantic, bubbling screech.

We did get off the planet, and we expect to stay away.

👽 👽 👽

"The Masked World" originally appeared in the October 1963 issue of Worlds of Tomorrow.

In 1928, twenty-year-old John Stewart Williamson sold his first pulp tale to Amazing Stories, *the flagship magazine of science fiction publishing pioneer Hugo Gernsbach. Thus began the long and distinguished writing career of Jack Williamson, author of such landmark works as "With Folded Hands" (part of his* The Humanoids *series) and the novel* Darker Than You Think, *which deals with shapeshifters.*

Highly creative, extremely prolific, and always entertaining, Williamson wrote throughout the freewheeling days of the pulps, and well into the 21st century, publishing The Stonehenge Gate *in 2005. Earlier, in 2001 and at the age of 92, the author won a Hugo Award for his novella* The Ultimate Earth.

Williamson once stated, "...I have a great deal of respect for good craftsmanship of the sort that commercial writers must develop. The labels you hear so much of—'commercial,' 'serious writer,' 'mainstream,' 'hack,' 'New Wave,' 'experimental'—are usually very misleading. ...I am opposed, however, to literary tricks that tend towards obscurity or artificial difficulty...."

Interestingly, an unfavorable review of Williamson's classic 1951 fix-up novel, Seetee Ship, *in* The New York Times—*which stated the quality of the writing "ranks only slightly above that of a comic-strip adventure"—led to the author being hired by the* Times' *competition. An editor at* The New York Sunday News *read the rotten review and immediately contacted Williamson to script a new science fiction comic strip. So, in a nice turn of events, the popular pulpster created the 1952 strip* Beyond Mars *by loosely adapting* Seetee Ship. *The strip ran for three years, until the* Sunday News *dropped its comics section.*

STILL AVAILABLE!

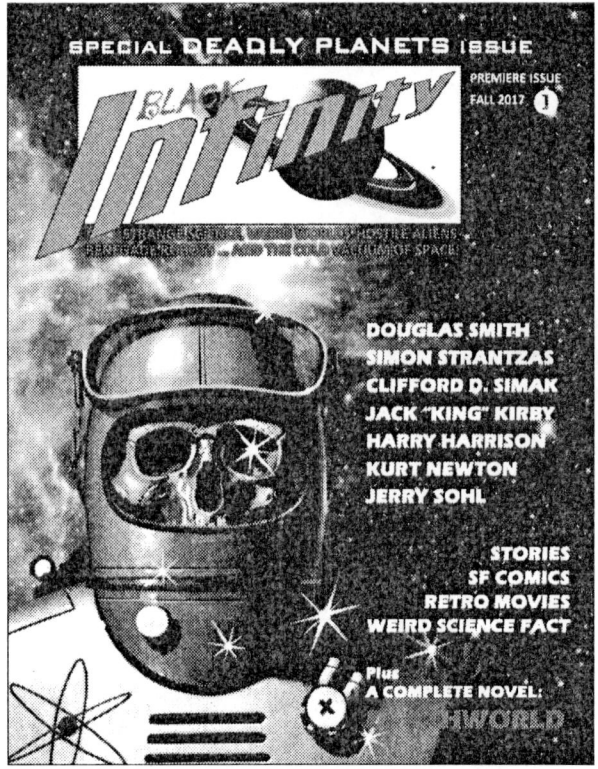

Strange science, weird worlds, hostile aliens, renegade robots ... and the cold vacuum of space.

200 oversized pages packed with exciting stories and art by some of the best writers of yesterday, today and tomorrow. Each issue features fiction, science, comics and retro movie reviews, all focusing on a different fun topic familiar to fans of SF in both print and celluloid.

Black Infinity: Deadly Planets (**#1**): Fiction by award-winning authors Douglas Smith, Simon Strantzas, and others; a classic comic story by Jack Kirby; plus, science and retro movie reviews—all celebrating one of the darker sides of SF: the often-deadly exploration of alien and hostile worlds! • ISBN: 978-0996693677

Black Infinity: Blobs, Globs, Slime and Spores (**#2**) New fiction by Rhys Hughes, Gregory L. Norris, Marc Vun Kannon, and more; classic tales by William Hope Hodgson and Joseph Payne Brennan; an overview of blobs, slime and spores in the entertainment media; weird science, a creepy SF comic and more! • ISBN: 978-0996693684

**There was nothing, especially on earth,
which could set him free—the truth least of all!**

DEAD RINGER

by Lester del Rey

D ANE PHILLIPS SLOUCHED IN THE WINDOW SEAT, WATCHING THE MORNING
CROWDS ON THEIR WAY TO WORK AND CAREFULLY AVOIDING ANY ATTEMPT
TO READ JORDAN'S OLD FACE AS THE EDITOR SKIMMED THROUGH THE NOTES.
He had learned to make his tall, bony body seem all loose-jointed relaxation, no matter what
he felt. But the oversized hands in his pockets were clenched so tightly that the nails were
cutting into his palms.

Every tick of the old-fashioned clock sent
a throb racing through his brain. Every rustle
of the pages seemed to release a fresh shot of
adrenalin into his blood stream. *This time*, his
mind was pleading. *It has to be right this
time....*

Jordan finished his reading and shoved
the folder back. He reached for his pipe,
sighed, and then nodded slowly. "A nice job of
researching, Phillips. And it might make a
good feature for the Sunday section, at that."

It took a second to realize that the words
meant acceptance, for Phillips had prepared
himself too thoroughly against another failure. Now he felt the tautened muscles release,
so quickly that he would have fallen if he
hadn't been braced against the seat.

He groped in his mind, hunting for words,
and finding none. There was only the hot,
sudden flame of unbelieving hope. And then
an almost blinding exultation.

JORDAN DIDN'T SEEM TO NOTICE his silence. The
editor made a neat pile of the notes, nodding
again. "Sure. I like it. We've been short of
shock stuff lately and the readers go for it
when we can get a fresh angle. But naturally
you'd have to leave out all that nonsense on
Blanding. Hell, the man's just buried, and his
relatives and friends—"

"But that's the proof!" Phillips stared at
the editor, trying to penetrate through the
haze of hope that had somehow grown chilled
and unreal. His thoughts were abruptly dis-
organized and out of his control. Only the ur-
gency remained. "It's the key evidence. And
we've got to move fast! I don't know how long
it takes, but even one more day may be too
late!"

Jordan nearly dropped the pipe from his
lips as he jerked upright to peer sharply at the
younger man. "Are you crazy? Do you seriously expect me to get an order to exhume
him now? What would it get us, other than
lawsuits? Even if we could get the order without cause—which we can't!"

Then the pipe did fall as he gaped open-
mouthed. "My God, you believe all that stuff.
You expected us to publish it *straight!*"

"No," Dane said thickly. The hope was
gone now, as if it had never existed, leaving
a numb emptiness where nothing mattered.
"No, I guess I didn't really expect anything.
But I believe the facts. Why shouldn't I?"

He reached for the papers with hands he
could hardly control and began stuffing them
back into the folder. All the careful documen-
tation, the fingerprints—smudged, perhaps,
in some cases, but still evidence enough for
anyone but a fool—

"Phillips?" Jordan said questioningly to himself, and then his voice was taking on a new edge. "Phillips! Wait a minute, I've got it now! *Dane* Phillips, not *Arthur*! Two years on the *Trib*. Then you turned up on the *Register* in Seattle? Phillip Dean, or some such name there."

"Yeah," Dane agreed. There was no use in denying anything now. "Yeah, Dane Arthur Phillips. So I suppose I'm through here?"

Jordan nodded again and there was a faint look of fear in his expression. "You can pick up your pay on the way out. And make it quick, before I change my mind and call the boys in white!"

IT COULD HAVE BEEN WORSE. It had been worse before. And there was enough in the pay envelope to buy what he needed—a flash camera, a little folding shovel from one of the surplus houses, and a bottle of good scotch. It would be dark enough for him to taxi out to Oakhaven Cemetery, where Blanding had been buried.

It wouldn't change the minds of the fools, of course. Even if he could drag back what he might find, without the change being completed, they wouldn't accept the evidence. He'd been crazy to think anything could change their minds. And they called *him* a fanatic! If the facts he'd dug up in ten years of hunting wouldn't convince them, nothing would. And yet he had to see for himself, before it was too late!

He picked a cheap hotel at random and checked in under an assumed name. He couldn't go back to his room while there was a chance that Jordan still might try to turn him in. There wouldn't be time for Sylvia's detectives to bother him, probably, but there was the ever-present danger that one of the aliens might intercept the message.

He shivered. He'd been risking that for ten years, yet the likelihood was still a horror to him. The uncertainty made it harder to take than any human-devised torture could

be. There was no way of guessing what an alien might do to anyone who discovered that all men were not human—that some were ... zombies.

There was the classic syllogism: *All men are mortal; I am a man; therefore, I am mortal.* But not Blanding—or Corporal Harding.

It was Harding's "death" that had started it all during the fighting on Guadalcanal. A grenade had come flying into the foxhole where Dane and Harding had felt reasonably safe. The concussion had knocked Dane out, possibly saving his life when the enemy thought he was dead. He'd come to in the daylight to see Harding lying there, mangled and twisted, with his throat torn. There was blood on Dane's uniform, obviously spattered from the dead man. It hadn't been a mistake or delusion; Harding had been dead.

It had taken Dane two days of crawling and hiding to get back to his group, too exhausted to report Harding's death. He'd slept for twenty hours. And when he awoke, Harding had been standing beside him, with a whole throat and a fresh uniform, grinning and kidding him for running off and leaving a stunned friend behind.

It was no ringer, but Harding himself, complete to the smallest personal memories and personality traits.

THE PRESSURES OF WAR probably saved Dane's sanity while he learned to face the facts. All men are mortal; Harding is not mortal; therefore, Harding is not a man! Nor was Harding alone—Dane found enough evidence to know there were others.

The *Tribune* morgue yielded even more data. A man had faced seven firing squads and walked away. Another survived over a dozen attacks by professional killers. Fingerprints turned up mysteriously "copied" from those of men long dead. Some of the aliens seemed to heal almost instantly; others took days. Some operated completely alone; some seemed to have joined with others. But they were legion.

Lack of a clearer pattern of attack made him consider the possibility of human mutation, but such tissue was too wildly different, and the invasion had begun long before atomics or X-rays. He gave up trying to understand their alien motivations. It was enough that they existed in secret, slowly growing in numbers while mankind was unaware of them.

When his proof was complete and irrefutable, he took it to his editor—to be fired, politely but coldly. Other editors were less polite. But he went on doggedly trying and failing. What else could he do? Somehow, he had to find the few people who could recognize facts and warn them. The aliens would get him, of course, when the story broke, but a warned humanity could cope with them. *Ye shall know the truth, and the truth shall make you free.*

Then he met Sylvia by accident after losing his fifth job—a girl who had inherited a fortune big enough to spread his message in paid ads across the country. They were married before he found she was hard-headed about her money. She demanded a full explanation for every cent beyond his allowance. In the end, she got the explanation. And while he was trying to cash the check she gave him, she visited Dr. Buehl, to come back with a squad of quiet, refined strong-arm boys who made sure Dane reached Buehl's "rest home" safely.

Hydrotherapy ... Buehl as the kindly firm father image ... analysis ... hypnosis that stripped every secret from him, including his worst childhood nightmare.

His father had committed a violent, bloody suicide after one of the many quarrels with Dane's mother. Dane had found the body.

Two nights after the funeral, he had dreamed of his father's face, horror-filled, at the window. He knew now that it was a normal nightmare, caused by being forced to look at the face in the coffin, but the shock had lasted for years. It had bothered him again, after his discovery of the aliens, until a thorough check had proved without doubt that his father had been fully human, with a human, if tempestuous, childhood behind him.

DR. BUEHL WAS DELIGHTED. "You see, Dane? You *know* it was a nightmare, but you don't really believe it even now. Your father was an alien monster to you—no adult is quite human to a child. And that literal-minded self, your subconscious, saw him after he died. So there are alien monsters who return from death. Then you come to from a concussion. Harding is sprawled out unconscious, covered with blood—probably your blood, since you say he wasn't wounded, later.

"But after seeing your father, you can't associate blood with yourself—you see it as a horrible wound on Harding. When he turns out to be alive, you're still in partial shock, with your subconscious dominant. And that has the answer already. There are monsters who come back from the dead! An exaggerated reaction, but nothing really abnormal. We'll have you out of here in no time."

No non-directive psychiatry for Buehl. The man beamed paternally, chuckling as he added what he must have considered the clincher. "Anyhow, even zombies can't stand fire, Dane, so you can stop worrying about Harding. I checked up on him. He was burned to a crisp in a hotel fire two months ago."

It was logical enough to shake Dane's faith, until he came across Milo Blanding's picture in a magazine article on society in St. Louis. According to the item, Milo was a cousin of *the* Blandings, whose father had vanished in Chile as a young man, and who had just rejoined the family. The picture was of Harding!

An alien could have gotten away by simply committing suicide and being carried from the rest home, but Dane had to do it the hard way, watching his chance and using commando tactics on a guard who had come to accept him as a harmless nut.

In St. Louis, he'd used the "Purloined Letter" technique to hide—going back to newspaper work and using almost his real name. It had seemed to work, too. But he'd been less lucky about Harding-Blanding. The man had been in Europe on some kind of a tour until his return only this last week.

Dane had seen him just once then—but long enough to be sure it was Harding—before he died again.

This time, it was in a drunken auto accident that seemed to be none of his fault, but left his body a mangled wreck.

IT WAS ALMOST DARK when Dane dismissed the taxi at the false address, a mile from the entrance to the cemetery. He watched it turn back down the road, then picked up the valise with his camera and folding shovel. He shivered as he moved reluctantly ahead. War had proved that he would never be a brave man and the old fears of darkness and graveyards were still strong in him. But he had to know what the coffin contained now, if it wasn't already too late.

It represented the missing link in his picture of the aliens. What happened to them during the period of regrowth? Did they revert to their natural form? Were they at all conscious while the body reshaped itself into wholeness? Dane had puzzled over it night after night, with no answer.

Nor could he figure how they could escape from the grave. Perhaps a man could force his way out of some of the coffins he had inspected. The soil would still be soft and loose in the grave, and a lot of the coffins and the boxes around them were strong in appearance only. A determined creature that could exist without much air for long enough might make it. But there were other caskets that couldn't be cracked, at least without the aid of outside help.

What happened when a creature that could survive even the poison of embalming fluids and the draining of all the blood woke up in such a coffin? Dane's mind skittered from it, as always, and then came back to it reluctantly.

There were still accounts of corpses turned up with the nails and hair grown long in the grave. Could normal tissues stand the current tricks of the morticians to have life enough for such growth? The possibility was absurd. Those cases had to be aliens—ones who hadn't escaped. Even they must die eventually in such a case—after weeks and months! It took time for hair to grow.

And there were stories of corpses that had apparently fought and twisted in their coffins still. What was it like for an alien then, going slowly mad while it waited for true death? How long did madness take?

He shivered again, but went steadily on while the cemetery fence appeared in the distance. He'd seen Blanding's coffin—and the big, solid metal casket around it that couldn't be cracked by any amount of effort and strength. He was sure the creature was still there, unless it had a confederate. But that wouldn't matter. An empty coffin would also be proof.

DANE AVOIDED THE MAIN GATE, unsure about whether there would be a watchman or not. A hundred feet away, there was a tree near the ornamental spikes of the iron fence. He threw his bag over and began shinnying up. It was difficult, but he made it finally, dropping onto the soft grass beyond. There was the trace of the Moon at times through the clouds, but it hadn't betrayed him, and there had been no alarm wire along the top of the fence.

He moved from shadow to shadow, his hair prickling along the base of his neck. Locating the right grave in the darkness was harder than he had expected, even with an occasional brief use of the small flashlight. But at last he found the marker that was serving until the regular monument could arrive.

His hands were sweating so much that it was hard to use the small shovel, but the digging of foxholes had given him experience and the ground was still soft from the gravediggers' work. He stopped once, as the Moon came out briefly. Again, a sound in the darkness above left him hovering and sick in the hole. But it must have been only some animal.

He uncovered the top of the casket with hands already blistering.

Then he cursed as he realized the catches were near the bottom, making his work even harder.

He reached them at last, fumbling them open. The metal top of the casket seemed to be a dome of solid lead, and he had no room to maneuver, but it began swinging up reluctantly, until he could feel the polished wood of the coffin.

Dane reached for the lid with hands he could barely control. Fear was thick in his throat now. What could an alien do to a man who discovered it? Would it be Harding there— or some monstrous thing still changing? How long did it take a revived monster to go mad when it found no way to escape?

He gripped the shovel in one hand, working at the lid with the other. Now, abruptly, his nerves steadied, as they had done whenever he was in real battle. He swung the lid up and began groping for the camera.

His hand went into the silk-lined interior and found nothing! He was too late. Either Harding had gotten out somehow before the final ceremony or a confederate had already been here. The coffin was empty.

THERE WERE NO WARNING SOUNDS THIS TIME— only hands that slipped under his arms and across his mouth, lifting him easily from the grave. A match flared briefly and he was looking into the face of Buehl's chief strong-arm man.

"Hello, Mr. Phillips. Promise to be quiet and we'll release you. Okay?" At Dane's sickened nod, he gestured to the others. "Let him go. And, Tom, better get that filled in. We don't want any trouble from this."

Surprise came from the grave a moment later. "Hey, Burke, there's no corpse here!"

Burke's words killed any hopes Dane had at once. "So what? Ever hear of cremation? Lots of people use a regular coffin for the ashes."

"He wasn't cremated," Dane told him. "You can check up on that." But he knew it was useless.

"Sure, Mr. Phillips. We'll do that." The tone was one reserved for humoring madmen. Burke turned, gesturing. "Better come along, Mr. Phillips. Your wife and Dr. Buehl are waiting at the hotel."

The gate was open now, but there was no sign of a watchman; if one worked here, Sylvia's money would have taken care of that, of course. Dane went along quietly, sitting in the rubble of his hopes while the big car purred through the morning and on down Lindell Boulevard toward the hotel. Once he shivered, and Burke dug out hot brandied coffee. They had thought of everything, including a coat to cover his dirt-soiled clothes as they took him up the elevator to where Buehl and Sylvia were waiting for him.

She had been crying, obviously, but there were no tears or recriminations when she came over to kiss him. Funny, she must still love him—as he'd learned to his surprise he loved her. Under different circumstances....

"So you found me?" he asked needlessly of Buehl. He was operating on purely automatic habits now, the reaction from the night and his failure numbing him emotionally. "Jordan got in touch with you?"

Buehl smiled back at him. "We knew where you were all along, Dane. But as long as you acted normal, we hoped it might be better than the home. Too bad we couldn't stop you before you got all mixed up in this."

"So I suppose I'm committed to your booby-hatch again?"

Buehl nodded, refusing to resent the term. "I'm afraid so, Dane—for a while, anyhow. You'll find your clothes in that room. Why don't you clean up a little? Take a hot bath, maybe. You'll feel better."

DANE WENT IN, surprised when no guards followed him. But they had thought of everything. What looked like a screen on the window had been recently installed and it was strong enough to prevent his escape. Blessed are the poor, for they shall be poorly guarded!

He was turning on the shower when he heard the sound of voices coming through the door. He left the water running and came back to listen. Sylvia was speaking.

"—Seems so logical, so completely rational."

"It makes him a dangerous person," Buehl answered, and there was no false warmth in his voice now. "Sylvia, you've got to admit it to yourself. All the reason and analysis in the world won't convince him he's wrong. This time we'll have to use shock treatment. Burn over those memories, fade them out. It's the only possible course."

There was a pause and then a sigh. "I suppose you're right."

Dane didn't wait to hear more. He drew back, while his mind fought to accept the hideous reality. Shock treatment! The works, if what he knew of psychiatry was correct. Enough of it to erase his memories—a part of himself. It wasn't therapy Buehl was considering; it couldn't be.

It was the answer of an alien that had a human in its hands—one who knew too much!

He might have guessed. What better place for an alien than in the guise of a psychiatrist? Where else was there the chance for all the refined, modern torture needed to burn out a man's mind? Dane had spent ten years in fear of being discovered by them—and now Buehl had him.

Sylvia? He couldn't be sure. Probably she was human. It wouldn't make any difference. There was nothing he could do through her. Either she was part of the game or she really thought him mad.

Dane tried the window again, but it was hopeless. There would be no escape this time. Buehl couldn't risk it. The shock treatment—or whatever Buehl would use under the name of shock treatment—would begin at once. It would be easy to slip, to use an overdose of something, to make sure Dane was killed. Or there were ways of making sure it didn't matter. They could leave him alive, but take his mind away.

In alien hands, human psychiatry could do worse than all the medieval torture chambers!

THE SICKNESS GREW IN HIS STOMACH as he considered the worst that could happen. Death he could accept, if he had to. He could even face the chance of torture by itself, as he had accepted the danger while trying to have his

facts published. But to have his mind taken from him, a step at a time—to watch his personality, his ego, rotted away under him—and to know that he would wind up as a drooling idiot....

He made his decision, almost as quickly as he had come to realize what Buehl must be.

There was a razor in the medicine chest. It was a safety razor, of course, but the blade was sharp and it would be big enough. There was no time for careful planning. One of the guards might come in at any moment if they thought he was taking too long.

Some fear came back as he leaned over the wash basin, staring at his throat, fingering the suddenly murderous blade. But the pain wouldn't last long—a lot less than there would be under shock treatment, and less pain. He'd read enough to feel sure of that.

Twice he braced himself and failed at the last second. His mind flashed out in wild schemes, fighting against what it knew had to be done.

The world still had to be warned! If he could escape, somehow ... if he could still find a way.... He couldn't quit, no matter how impossible things looked.

But he knew better. There was nothing one man could do against the aliens in this world they had taken over. He'd never had a chance. Man had been chained already by carefully developed ridicule against superstition, by carefully indoctrinated gobbledegook about insanity, persecution complexes, and all the rest.

For a second, Dane even considered the possibility that he *was* insane. But he knew it was only a blind effort to cling to life. There had been no insanity in him when he'd groped for evidence in the coffin and found it empty!

He leaned over the wash basin, his eyes focused on his throat, and his hand came down and around, carrying the razor blade through a lethal semicircle.

DANE PHILLIPS WATCHED FEAR give place to sickness on his face as the pain lanced through him and the blood spurted.

He watched horror creep up to replace the sickness while the bleeding stopped and the gash began closing.

By the time he recognized his expression as the same one he'd seen on his father's face at the window so long ago, the wound was completely healed.

"Dead Ringer" first appeared in the November 1956 issue of Galaxy Science Fiction Magazine, *with an illustration by Dick Francis (no connection to the British jockey turned mystery writer).*

Lester del Rey (née Leonard Knapp) was an American writer and editor who began a long association with Astounding Stories *after John W. Campbell published his first SF tale in the April 1938 issue. Del Rey went on to produce numerous stories for the pulp magazines of the day, including* Weird Tales *and* Unknown *(Campbell's competitive response to "The Unique Magazine"). Del Rey's first two novels were published as part of the fondly-remembered Winston Science Fiction Series for young readers. The author eventually wrote ten of the 37 Winston titles, including a few under the pseudonyms Philip St. John and Erik van Lihn.*

During the explosive growth of SF digests in the 1950s, del Rey edited such titles as Space SF, Science Fiction Adventures *(as Philip St. John),* Rocket Stories *(as Wade Kaempfert), and* Fantasy Fiction *(as Cameron Hall). In 1977 del Rey and his wife Judy-Lynn del Rey established and edited the long-running and highly successful Del Rey Books, a science fiction imprint of Ballantine Books.*

She noticed the change in her husband—
But she had married for better or worse.

HUMAN IS

by Philip K. Dick

illustration by Emsh

JILL HERRICK'S BLUE EYES FILLED WITH TEARS. SHE GAZED AT HER HUSBAND IN UNSPEAKABLE HORROR. "YOU'RE— YOU'RE HIDEOUS!" SHE WAILED.

Lester Herrick continued working, arranging heaps of notes and graphs in precise piles.

"Hideous," he stated, "is a value judgment. It contains no factual information." He sent a report tape on Centauran parasitic life whizzing through the desk scanner. "Merely an opinion. An expression of emotion, nothing more."

Jill stumbled back to the kitchen. Listlessly, she waved her hand to trip the stove into activity. Conveyor belts in the wall hummed to life, hurrying the food from the underground storage lockers for the evening meal.

She turned to face her husband one last time. "Not even a *little* while?" she begged. "Not even—"

"Not even for a month. When he comes you can tell him. If you haven't the courage, I'll do it. I can't have a child running around here. I have too much work to do. This report on

Betelgeuse XI is due in ten days." Lester dropped a spool on Fomalhautan fossil implements into the scanner. "What's the matter with your brother? Why can't he take care of his own child?"

Jill dabbed at swollen eyes. "Don't you understand? I *want* Gus here! I begged Frank to let him come. And now you—"

"I'll be glad when he's old enough to be turned over to the Government." Lester's thin face twisted in annoyance. "Damn it, Jill, isn't dinner ready yet? It's been ten minutes! What's wrong with that stove?"

"It's almost ready." The stove showed a red signal light. The robant waiter had come out of the wall and was waiting expectantly to take the food.

Jill sat down and blew her small nose violently. In the living room, Lester worked on unperturbed. His work. His research. Day after day. Lester was getting ahead; there was no doubt of that. His lean body was bent like a coiled spring over the tape scanner, cold gray eyes taking in the information feverishly, analyzing, appraising, his conceptual faculties operating like well greased machinery.

Jill's lips trembled in misery and resentment. Gus—little Gus. How could she tell him? Fresh tears welled up in her eyes. Never to see the chubby little fellow again. He could never come back—because his childish laughter and play bothered Lester. Interfered with his research.

The stove clicked to green. The food slid out, into the arms of the robant. Soft chimes sounded to announce dinner.

"I hear it," Lester grated. He snapped off the scanner and got to his feet. "I suppose he'll come while we're eating."

"I can vid Frank and ask—"

"No. Might as well get it over with." Lester nodded impatiently to the robant. "All right. Put it down." His thin lips set in an angry line. "Damn it, don't dawdle! I want to get back to my work!"

Jill bit back the tears.

• • •

LITTLE GUS CAME TRAILING into the house as they were finishing dinner.

Jill gave a cry of joy. "Gussie!" She ran to sweep him up in her arms. "I'm so glad to see you!"

"Watch out for my tiger," Gus muttered. He dropped his little gray kitten onto the rug and it rushed off, under the couch. "He's hiding."

Lester's eyes flickered as he studied the little boy and the tip of gray tail extending from under the couch.

"Why do you call it a tiger? It's nothing but an alley cat."

Gus looked hurt. He scowled. "He's a tiger. He's got stripes."

"Tigers are yellow and a great deal bigger. You might as well learn to classify things by their correct names."

"Lester, please—" Jill pleaded.

"Be quiet," her husband said crossly. "Gus is old enough to shed childish illusions and develop a realistic orientation. What's wrong with the psych testers? Don't they straighten this sort of nonsense out?"

Gus ran and snatched up his tiger. "You leave him alone!"

Lester contemplated the kitten. A strange, cold smile played about his lips. "Come down to the lab some time, Gus. We'll show you lots of cats. We use them in our research. Cats, guinea pigs, rabbits—"

"Lester!" Jill gasped. "How can you!"

Lester laughed thinly. Abruptly he broke off and returned to his desk "Now clear out of here. I have to finish these reports. And don't forget to tell Gus."

Gus got excited. "Tell me what?" His cheeks flushed. His eyes sparkled. "What is it? Something for me? A *secret*?"

Jill's heart was like lead. She put her hand heavily on the child's shoulder. "Come on, Gus. We'll go sit out in the garden and I'll tell you. Bring—bring your tiger."

A click. The emergency vidsender lit up.

Instantly Lester was on his feet. "Be quiet!" He ran to the sender, breathing rapidly. "Nobody speak!"

Jill and Gus paused at the door. A confidential message was sliding from the slot into the dish. Lester grabbed it up and broke the seal. He studied it intently.

"What is it?" Jill asked. "Anything bad?"

"Bad?" Lester's face shone with a deep inner glow. "No, not bad at all." He glanced at his watch. "Just time. Let's see, I'll need—"

"What is it?"

"I'm going on a trip. I'll be gone two or three weeks. Rector IV is into the charted area."

"Rexor IV? You're going there?" Jill clasped her hands eagerly. "Oh, I've always wanted to see an old system, old ruins and cities! Lester, can I come along? Can I go with you? We never took a vacation, and you always promised—"

Lester Herrick stared at his wife in amazement. "You?" he said. "*You* go along?" He laughed unpleasantly. "Now hurry and get my things together. I've been waiting for this a long time." He rubbed his hands together in satisfaction. "You can keep the boy here until I'm back. But no longer. Rexor IV! I can hardly wait!"

"YOU HAVE TO MAKE ALLOWANCES," Frank said. "After all, he's a scientist."

"I don't care," Jill said. "I'm leaving him. As soon as he gets back from Rexor IV. I've made up my mind."

Her brother was silent, deep in thought. He stretched his feet out, onto the lawn of the little garden. "Well, if you leave him you'll be free to marry again. You're still classed as sexually adequate, aren't you?"

Jill nodded firmly. "You bet I am. I wouldn't have any trouble. Maybe I can find somebody who likes children."

"You think a lot of children," Frank perceived. "Gus loves to go visit you. But he doesn't like Lester. Les needles him."

"I know. This past week has been heaven, with him gone." Jill patted her soft blonde hair, blushing prettily. "I've had fun. Makes me feel alive again."

"When'll he be back?"

"Any day." Jill clenched her small fists. "We've been married five years and every year it's worse. He's so—so inhuman. Utterly cold and ruthless. Him and his work. Day and night."

"Les is ambitious. He wants to get to the top in his field." Frank lit a cigarette lazily. "A pusher. Well, maybe he'll do it. What's he in?"

"Toxicology. He works out new poisons for the Military. He invented the copper sulphate skin-lime they used against Callisto."

"It's a small field. Now take me." Frank leaned contentedly against the wall of the house. "There are thousands of Clearance lawyers. I could work for years and never create a ripple. I'm content just to be. I do my job. I enjoy it."

"I wish Lester felt that way."

"Maybe he'll change."

"He'll *never* change," Jill said bitterly. "I know that, now. That's why I've made up my mind to leave him. He'll always be the same."

LESTER HERRICK CAME BACK from Rexor IV a different man. Beaming happily, he deposited his anti-gray suitcase in the arms of the waiting robant. "Thank you."

Jill gasped speechlessly. "Les! What—"

Lester moved his hat, bowing a little. "Good day, my dear. You're looking lovely. Your eyes are clear and blue. Sparkling like some virgin lake, fed by mountain streams." He sniffed. "Do I smell a delicious repast warming on the hearth?"

"Oh, Lester." Jill blinked uncertainly, faint hope swelling in her bosom. "Lester, what's happened to you? You're so— so different."

"Am I, my dear?" Lester moved about the house, touching things and sighing. "What a dear little house. So sweet and friendly. You don't know how wonderful it is to be here. Believe me."

"I'm afraid to believe it," Jill said.

"Believe what?"

"That you mean all this. That you're not the way you were. The way you've always been."

"What way is that?"

"Mean. Mean and cruel."

"I?" Lester frowned, rubbing his lip. "Hmm. Interesting." He brightened. "Well, that's all in the past. What's for dinner? I'm faint with hunger."

Jill eyed him uncertainly as she moved into the kitchen. "Anything you want, Lester. You know our stove covers the maximum select-list."

"Of course." Lester coughed rapidly. "Well, shall we try sirloin steak, medium, smothered in onions? With mushroom sauce. And white rolls. With hot coffee. Perhaps ice cream and apple pie for dessert."

"You never seemed to care much about food," Jill said thoughtfully.

"Oh?"

"You always said you hoped eventually they'd make intravenous intake universally applicable." She studied her husband intently. "Lester, what's happened?"

"Nothing. Nothing at all." Lester carelessly took his pipe out and lit it rapidly, somewhat awkwardly. Bits of tobacco drifted to the rug. He bent nervously down and tried to pick them up again. "Please go about your tasks and don't mind me. Perhaps I can help you prepare—that is, can I do anything to help?"

"No," Jill said. "I can do it. You go ahead with your work, if you want."

"Work?"

"Your research. In toxins."

"Toxins!" Lester showed confusion. "Well, for heaven's sake! Toxins. Devil take it!"

"What dear?"

"I mean, I really feel too tired, just now. I'll work later." Lester moved vaguely around the room. "I think I'll just sit and enjoy being home again. Off that awful Rexor IV."

"Was it awful?"

"Horrible." A spasm of disgust crossed Lester's face. "Dry and dead. Ancient. Squeezed to a pulp by wind and sun. A dreadful place, my dear."

"I'm sorry to hear that. I always wanted to visit it."

"Heaven forbid!" Lester cried feelingly. "You stay right here, my dear. With me. The—the two of us." His eyes wandered around the room. "Two, yes. Terra is a wonderful planet. Moist and full of life." He beamed happily. "Just right."

"I DON'T UNDERSTAND IT," Jill said.

"Repeat all the things you remember," Frank said. His robot pencil poised itself alertly. "The changes you've noticed in him. I'm curious."

"Why?"

"No reason. Go on. You say you sensed it right away? That he was different?"

"I noticed it at once. The expression on his face. Not that hard, practical look. A sort of mellow look. Relaxed. Tolerant. A sort of calmness."

"I see," Frank said. "What else?"

Jill peered nervously through the back door into the house. "He can't hear us, can he?"

"No. He's inside playing with Gus. In the living room. They're Venusian otter-men to-day. Your husband built an otter slide down at his lab. I saw him unwrapping it."

"His talk."

"His what?"

"The way he talks. His choice of words. Words he never used before. Whole new phrases. Metaphors. I never heard him use a metaphor in all our five years together. He said metaphors were inexact. Misleading. And—"

"And what?" The pencil scratched busily.

"And they're *strange* words. Old words. Words you don't hear any more."

"Archaic phraseology?" Frank asked tensely.

"Yes." Jill paced back and forth across the small lawn, her hands in the pockets of her plastic shorts. "Formal words. Like some-thing—"

"Something out of a book?"

"Exactly! You've noticed it?"

"I noticed it," Frank's face was grim. "Go on."

Jill stopped pacing. "What's on your mind? Do you have a theory?"

"I want to know more facts."

She reflected. "He plays. With Gus. He plays and jokes. And he—he eats."

"Didn't he eat before?"

"Not like he does now. Now he *loves* food. He goes in the kitchen and tries endless combinations. He and the stove get together and cook up all sorts of weird things."

"I thought he'd put on weight."

"He's gained ten pounds. He eats, smiles and laughs. He's constantly polite." Jill glanced away coyly. "He's even—romantic! He always said *that* was irrational. And he's not interested in his work. His research in toxins."

"I see." Frank chewed his lip. "Anything more?"

"One thing puzzles me very much. I've noticed it again and again "

"What is it?"

"He seems to have strange lapses of—"

A burst of laughter. Lester Herrick, eyes bright with merriment, came rushing out of the house, little Gus close behind.

"We have an announcement!" Lester cried.

"An announzelmen," Gus echoed.

Frank folded his notes up and slid them into his coat pocket. The pencil hurried after them. He got slowly to his feet. "What is it?"

"You make it," Lester said, taking little Gus's hand and leading him forward.

Gus's plump face screwed up in concentration. "I'm going to come live with you," he stated. Anxiously he watched Jill's expression. "Lester says I can. Can I? Can I, Aunt Jill?"

Her heart flooded with incredible joy. She glanced from Gus to Lester. "Do you—do you really mean it?" Her voice was almost inaudible.

Lester put his arm around her, holding her close to him. "Of course, we mean it," he said gently. His eyes were warm and understanding. "We wouldn't tease you, my dear."

"No teasing!" Gus shouted excitedly. "No more teasing!" He and Lester and Jill drew close together. "Never again!"

Frank stood a little way off, his face grim. Jill noticed him and broke away abruptly. "What is it?" she faltered. "Is anything—"

"When you're quite finished," Frank said to Lester Herrick, "I'd like you to come with me."

A chill clutched Jill's heart. "What is it? Can I come, too?"

Frank shook his head. He moved toward Lester ominously. "Come on, Herrick. Let's go. You and I are going to take a little trip."

THE THREE FEDERAL CLEARANCE AGENTS took up positions a few feet from Lester Herrick, vibro-tubes gripped alertly.

Clearance Director Douglas studied Herrick for a long time. "You're sure?" he said finally.

"Absolutely," Frank stated.

"When did he get back from Rexor IV?"

"A week ago."

"And the change was noticeable at once?"

"His wife noticed it as soon as she saw him. There's no doubt it occurred on Rexor." Frank paused significantly. "And you know what that means."

"I know." Douglas walked slowly around the seated man, examining him from every angle.

Lester Herrick sat quietly, his coat neatly folded across his knee. He rested his hands on his ivory-topped cane, his face calm and expressionless. He wore a soft gray suit, a subdued necktie, French cuffs, and shiny black shoes. He said nothing.

"Their methods are simple and exact," Douglas said. "The original psychic contents are removed and stored—in some sort of suspension. The interjection of the substitute contents is instantaneous. Lester Herrick was probably poking around the Rexor city ruins, ignoring the safety precautions—shield or manual screen—and they got him."

The seated man stirred. "I'd like very much to communicate with Jill," he murmured. "She surely is becoming anxious."

Frank turned away, face choked with revulsion. "God. It's still pretending."

Director Douglas restrained himself with the greatest effort. "It's certainly an amazing thing. No physical changes. You could look at it and never know." He moved toward the seated man, his face hard. "Listen to me, whatever you call yourself. Can you understand what I say?"

"Of course," Lester Herrick answered.

"Did you really think you'd get away with it? We caught the others—the ones before you. All ten of them. Even before they got here." Douglas grinned coldly. "Vibro-rayed them one after another."

The color left Lester Herrick's face. Sweat came out on his forehead. He wiped it away with a silk handkerchief from his breast pocket. "Oh?" he murmured.

"You're not fooling us. All Terra is alerted for you Rexorians. I'm surprised you got off Rexor at all. Herrick must have been extremely careless. We stopped the others aboard ship. Fried them out in deep space."

"Herrick had a private ship," the seated man murmured. "He bypassed the check station going in. No record of his arrival existed. He was never checked."

"*Fry it!*" Douglas grated. The three Clearance agents lifted their tubes, moving forward.

"No." Frank shook his head. "We can't. It's a bad situation."

"What do you mean? Why can't we? We fried the others—"

"They were caught in deep space. This is Terra. Terran law, not military law, applies." Frank waved toward the seated man. "And it's in a human body. It comes under regular civil laws. We've got to *prove* it's not Lester Herrick —that it's a Rexorian infiltrator. It's going to be tough. But it can be done."

"How?"

"His wife. Herrick's wife. Her testimony. Jill Herrick can assert the difference between Lester Herrick and this thing. She knows— and I think we can make it stand up in court."

It was late afternoon. Frank drove his surface cruiser slowly along. Neither he nor Jill spoke.

"So that's it," Jill said at last. Her face was gray. Her eyes dry and bright, without emotion. "I knew it was too good to be true." She tried to smile. "It seemed so wonderful."

"I know," Frank said. "It's a terrible damn thing. If only—"

"*Why?*" Jill said. "Why did he—did it do this? Why did it take Lester's body?"

"Rexor IV is old. Dead. A dying planet. Life is dying out."

"I remember, now. He—it said something like that. Something about Rexor. That it was glad to get away."

"The Rexorians are an old race. The few that remain are feeble. They've been trying to migrate for centuries. But their bodies are too weak. Some tried to migrate to Venus—and died instantly. They worked out this system about a century ago."

"But it knows so much. About us. It speaks our language."

"Not quite. The changes you mentioned. The odd diction. You see, the Rexorians have only a vague knowledge of human beings. A sort of ideal abstraction, taken from Terran objects that have found their way to Rexor. Books mostly. Secondary data like that. The Rexorian idea of Terra is based on centuries-old Terran literature. Romantic novels from our past. Language, custom, manners from old Terran books.

"That accounts for the strange archaic quality to *it*. It had studied Terra, all right. But in an indirect and misleading way." Frank grinned wryly. "The Rexorians are two hundred years behind the times—which is a break for us. That's how we're able to detect them."

"Is this sort of thing—common? Does it

happen often? It seems unbelievable." Jill rubbed her forehead wearily. "Dreamlike. It's hard to realize that it's actually happened. I'm just beginning to understand what it means."

"The galaxy is full of alien life forms. Parasitic and destructive entities. Terran ethics don't extend to them. We have to guard constantly against this sort of thing. Lester went in unsuspectingly—and this thing ousted him and took over his body."

Frank glanced at his sister. Jill's face was expressionless. A stern little face, wide-eyed, but composed. She sat up straight, staring fixedly ahead, her small hands folded quietly in her lap.

"We can arrange it so you won't have to actually appear in court," Frank went on. "You can vid a statement and it'll be presented as evidence. I'm certain your statement will do. The Federal courts will help us all they can, but they have to have *some* evidence to go on."

Jill was silent.

"What do you say?" Frank asked.

"What happens after the court makes its decision?"

"Then we vibro-ray it. Destroy the Rexorian mind. A Terran patrol ship on Rexor IV sends out a party to locate the—*er*—original contents."

Jill gasped. She turned toward her brother in amazement. "You mean—"

"Oh, yes. Lester is alive. In suspension, somewhere on Rexor. In one of the old city ruins. We'll have to force them to give him up. They won't want to, but they'll do it. They've done it before. Then he'll be back with you. Safe and sound. Just like before. And this horrible nightmare you've been living will be a thing of the past."

"I see."

"Here we are." The cruiser pulled to a halt before the imposing Federal Clearance Building. Frank got quickly out, holding the door for his sister. Jill stepped down slowly. "Okay?" Frank said.

"Okay."

When they entered the building, Clearance agents led them through the check screens, down the long corridors. Jill's high heels echoed in the ominous silence.

"Quite a place," Frank observed.

"It's unfriendly."

"Consider it a glorified police station." Frank halted. Before them was a guarded door. "Here we are."

"Wait." Jill pulled back, her face twisting in panic. "I—"

"We'll wait until you're ready." Frank signaled to the Clearance agent to leave. "I understand. It's a bad business."

Jill stood for a moment, her head down. She took a deep breath, her small fists clenched. Her chin came up, level and steady. "All right."

"You ready?"

"Yes."

Frank opened the door. "Here we are."

Director Douglas and the three Clearance agents turned expectantly as Jill and Frank entered. "Good," Douglas murmured, with relief. "I was beginning to get worried."

The sitting man got slowly to his feet, picking up his coat. He gripped his ivory-headed cane tightly, his hands tense. He said nothing. He watched silently as the woman entered the room, Frank behind her. "This is Mrs. Herrick," Frank said. "Jill, this is Clearance Director Douglas."

"I've heard of you," Jill said faintly.

"Then you know our work."

"Yes. I know your work."

"This is an unfortunate business. It's happened before. I don't know what Frank has told you—"

"He explained the situation."

"Good." Douglas was relieved. "I'm glad of that. It's not easy to explain. You understand, then, what we want. The previous cases were caught in deep space. We vibro-tubed them and got the original contents back. But this time we must work through legal channels."

Douglas picked up a vidtape recorder. "We will need your statement, Mrs. Herrick. Since no physical change has occurred we'll have no direct evidence to make our case. We'll have only your testimony of character alteration to present to the court."

He held the vidtape recorder out. Jill took it slowly.

"Your statement will undoubtedly be accepted by the court. The court will give us the release we want and then we can go ahead. If everything goes correctly we hope to be able to set up things exactly as they were before."

Jill was gazing silently at the man standing in the corner with his coat and ivory-headed cane. "Before?" she said. "What do you mean?"

"Before the change."

Jill turned toward Director Douglas. Calmly, she laid the vidtape recorder down on the table. "What change are you talking about?"

Douglas paled. He licked his lips. All eyes in the room were on Jill. "The change in *him*." He pointed at the man.

"Jill!" Frank barked. "What's the matter with you?" He came quickly toward her. "What the hell are you doing? You know damn well what change we mean!"

"That's odd," Jill said thoughtfully. "I haven't noticed any change."

Frank and Director Douglas looked at each other. "I don't get it," Frank muttered, dazed.

"Mrs. Herrick—" Douglas began.

Jill walked over to the man standing quietly in the corner. "Can we go now, dear?" she asked. She took his arm. "Or is there some reason why my husband has to stay here?"

THE MAN AND WOMAN WALKED silently along the dark street.

"Come on," Jill said. "Let's go home."

The man glanced at her. "It's a nice afternoon," he said. He took a deep breath, filling his lungs. "Spring is coming—I think. Isn't it?"

Jill nodded.

"I wasn't sure. It's a nice smell. Plants and soil and growing things."

"Yes."

"Are we going to walk? Is it far?"

"Not too far."

The man gazed at her intently, a serious expression on his face. "I am very indebted to you, my dear," he said.

Jill nodded.

"I wish to thank you. I must admit I did not expect such a—"

Jill turned abruptly. "What is your name? Your *real* name."

The man's gray eyes flickered. He smiled a little, a kind, gentle smile. "I'm afraid you would not be able to pronounce it. The sounds cannot be formed..."

Jill was silent as they walked along, deep in thought. The city lights were coming on all around them. Bright yellow spots in the gloom. "What are you thinking?" the man asked.

"I was thinking perhaps I will still call you Lester," Jill said. "If you don't mind."

"I don't mind," the man said. He put his arm around her, drawing her close to him. He gazed down tenderly as they walked through the thickening darkness, between the yellow candles of light that marked the way. "Anything you wish. Whatever will make you happy."

"Human Is" first appeared in the Winter 1955 issue of Startling Stories. *Regarding his story, Philip K. Dick once remarked, "It's not what you look like, or what planet you were born on. It's how kind you are. The quality of kindness, to me, distinguishes us from rocks and sticks and metal, and will forever, whatever shape we take, wherever we go, whatever we become. For me,* Human Is *is my credo."*

Dick is perhaps better known to film buffs for several movies adapted from his inventive SF stories and novels, most notably Blade Runner *and* Total Recall.

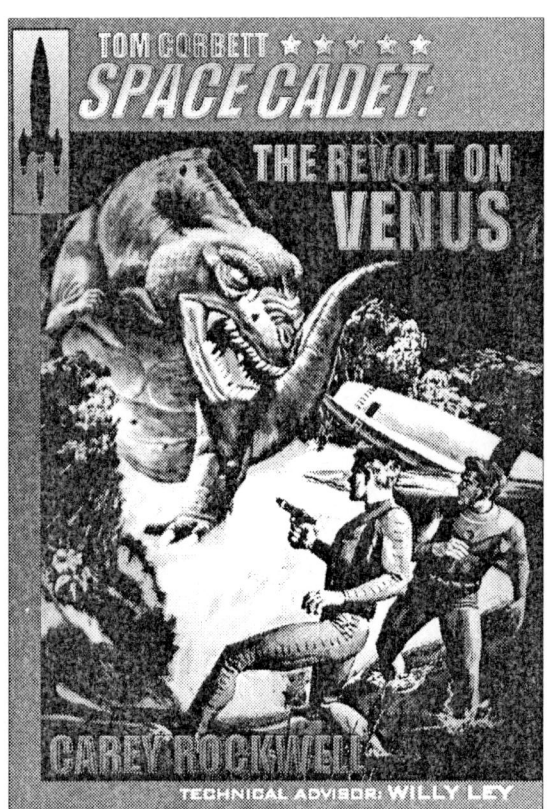

Life is not a soap opera... **unless you're tuned in to the end of the world.**

HIBERNATION

by Gregory L. Norris

ZUHAUSER ROLLED OVER AND SQUINTED AT THE NUMBERS ON THE CABLE BOX. Just after four o'clock. When he looked again, it was shy of six. Another greedy morning, he thought, one hungry for seconds, minutes, and hours.

By seven, when he sat up and kicked his legs over the edge of the mattress, settling his bare feet on the hardwood floor, the new day was bloated on time, though he doubted it was satiated. He stood and the bedroom wavered around him, sluggish from the new day's gluttony. He struggled to stay upright and focus.

One of these mornings, Zuhauser thought, I'm just going to stay in bed, and not get up.

But not today, he conceded, and plodded to the bathroom whose big, lone window gazed across downtown Bonneville.

• • •

THE SONG HAD FOLLOWED HIM out of a dream, as it often did.

Just look her in the eyes, forget about your lies... confess... confess! It's time to fix this mess...

Zuhauser soaped up his face and then leaned into the spray. The music from the long-defunct daytime drama, *The Privilege of Passion*, upped its tempo. The long version, he thought, huffing a humorless chuckle into the spray. The one used for the closing credits, during which an announcer for the network blathered and the song never reached its thrilling, trilling crescendo because the greedy suits who had cancelled the soap operatic travails of the upper crust Merrill and ne'er-do-well Langston clans had to squeeze as much commercial time in as possible.

It's a business, Zuhauser remembered the hated face of daytime programming saying, way back when, when interviewed over the drama's cancellation. *And soaps are no longer good business for this network.*

Oh, but they had been, starting every afternoon at 12:30, with the anchor to the lineup, *Privilege.* At one, the venerated *Love Never Lies* came on, followed by *Wife and Life,* and the long-running *Community Hospital.* Months earlier, during a rare sick day at home, Zuhauser had caught a few minutes of *CH,* the last soap standing, while flipping channels, though he hadn't recognized a single actor and couldn't stomach the diluted storytelling past the first commercial break.

The little soap that could, until it got the ax, had been appointment viewing during almost a decade of lunch breaks. Zuhauser toweled dry, caught the reflection of his sagging torso in the mirror above the counter, and realized, finally, that he'd gotten old and was closer to its cancellation than the premiere of his life's story.

The big bedroom at the front of the house sat bathed in a rosy glow. The Merrill Mansion on *Privilege* had boasted similar curtains: long, crimson drapes with scalloped edges filled the room's four tall windows. Zuhauser often mused that they were like the chambers of a heart. Now, as he pulled on socks that attempted to snag on toenails, his heart galloped for reasons he couldn't identify. He grew intimate with his body's music. From the well of his memory, the theme song from the late, lamented soap played in counterpoint.

Back to sleep, Zuhauser's inner voice tempted. Or maybe it was the bed talking. *Crawl back beneath the covers. The hell with the job, the bills, the bull. The hell with it all.*

Just sleep.

It wasn't like he had anything to look forward to. Alma Merrill wasn't struggling to keep control of Merrill Publishing from half-sister, Minerva Langston. Plucky Maya Merrill wasn't playing Juliet to Romeo Jason Langston, the misunderstood bad boy from the other side of the tracks that ran through the fictional town of Lonesome Oaks, Pennsylvania. Courts in that strange, wonderful berg were permanently out of session, and killers there had stopped killing. The last of the chess moves by bastard rivals born off-screen had been played, and there were no more wardrobe changes. Love in the afternoon was a thing of the past, replaced by shrieking shrews and endlessly yapping talk show harpies.

Sadness washed over him. Old, sure, one of the last remaining souls who appreciated those old-fashioned Friday cliffhangers when you had to wait through the entire weekend until Monday to see who—and how—dunnit. He was living in a world of instant gratification now, only something had been lost and nothing felt very gratifying anymore except for sleep.

Zuhauser pinched the corners of his eyes and jumped off the edge of the mattress before the temptation won and he buried his sorrows—and head—between two pillows. He plodded down the stairs to the landing, thought about microwaving coffee, but caught the time on the clock's green numbers. The morning felt heavy enough to be quitting time, not the start to the day. Sighing, Zuhauser tossed a handful of dry cat food into the big bowl set on a plastic placemat beside the bubble-style water dispenser for cats and then locked the front door behind him. Before heading to his car, he checked the pet flap, as he always did, just in case Maya Merrill, as he called the stray neighborhood cat that'd adopted him, deigned to grace the house on Jonquil Road with her regal presence.

Sunlight spilled down from a cloudless blue sky the color of denim. The morning chill, which had unleashed mist over the river, wasn't long for the day. The lone, giant green pumpkin lurking in the patch of elephantine leaves that covered that side of Mavis Winters' yard showed its first blemish of orange. Warm days would soon be a lost gift. One more thing to mourn.

The malaise chased him on the drive down Jonquil Hill to Main Street, past the ominous sprawl of the biomass power plant that had taken up residence inside the guts and carapace of the old Bonneville Paper Mill. Something caught up at the only streetlight where Main intersected Exchange and sat heavy on both shoulders, its feet resting on his stomach. If he'd downed coffee, it would have taken an encore on the sour burp that shuddered up his throat.

The traffic light, too, exerted its greed for time. The seconds dragged out. A church bell carillon tolled the hour, the unmistakable celebration of new morning broadcast from Our Lady of Peace, but the notes struck Zuhauser's ear like a dirge, a melody better suited for a funeral. As the giant Cyclops eye of the red light glared down at him, the breeze died completely and the world seemed to hold its breath. The air thrummed with an undercurrent, one more than the pile-driver pulses emanating across the town of Bonneville from the new power plant; more than the cadence of his heart, which attempted to jump out of his chest and into Zuhauser's throat. A wrongness surrounded him, and he feared—he *knew*—it was about to get far worse.

ONE OF THE BIGGEST PROBLEMS inherent in working for a small family-owned business was that when things got tense or ugly, there was no way to escape the spotlight.

Zuhauser parked in the same spot his car and its predecessors had occupied for twenty-six years, but on that morning he sensed he would never park there again. The proof was gleaned in the eyes of his few coworkers at Kincaid Family Furniture, none of whom would face him directly on his amble through the showroom, which reeked of new upholstery and leather. In their darting glances, he gathered his first tangible proof that his world was about to alter.

On the last leg of the dead man's walk to the office, past living room suites and just shy of washing machines, dryers, and discounted appliances shamed into that corner of the building, he detected dark hair and the last of summer's tan at the periphery and, turning, came face to faced with Drake Kincaid.

"Lance, good morning," the youngest and sneakiest—*snake*-iest—of Rafe Kincaid's three sons greeted.

It was more proof of the wrongness. "So now I'm 'Lance', not 'Zuhauser'?" he countered.

Drake the Snake smiled, showing too much of the fortune his father had invested in his smile. "Step into my office, if you would."

The idiot was already several yards ahead before realizing Zuhauser hadn't followed. By that point, Zuhauser noticed, Tommy Hawkins, the store's weekday security guard who drove deliveries in the big truck on weekends, had joined the canvas. He and Kincaid met up, doubled back.

"What's this all about?" Zuhauser asked flatly.

Drake the Snake's phony smile dropped. "Hey, this doesn't need to get ugly, pal. *It's just business.*"

FIRED. The old man had been enough of a nightmare to work for, but he'd mostly been a fair nightmare except during annual reviews and at Christmas bonus time. Rafe Kincaid had kept Zuhauser employed as a salesman peddling crap furniture because he sold the crap and sold it consistently even through the worst of the country's economic downturns over the past quarter-plus century.

Since the old man's death at the hands of the Big C, his snake of a son had made obvious changes to the gestalt, primarily by hiring new, crappy furniture hucksters of a certain vibe: young and busty.

Heat rose red up his throat and infected his cheeks. Fat drops of sweat beaded on Zuhauser's forehead. One started an oily skid down the side of his face. He swiped at it with shaking fingers, missed. The next grab popped the offender into smaller trickles.

Fired, because Kinkaid was taking, "a new direction," the snake blathered on, citing reasons. But the truth of the situation was that a shortsighted, slimy bean counter no different than the scummy daytime suit that'd dropped the guillotine on *The Privilege of Passion,* was canning the tried and decent for something untested, shiny, and cheap. Zuhauser had been cancelled.

FOR YEARS, HE SUCCESSFULLY compartmentalized the reality that his life hadn't gone according to the whims and dreams of a younger age. Kincaid Family Furniture was hardly the exciting world of Merrill Publishing, where big-wheeling deals and best sellers were the business of the day, five days a week. During one memorable summer, the writers on the soap, catering to the youth demographic home from school and, as hoped, tuning in beside their mothers, had introduced the character of Dominique Langston. Dom was a perky girl struggling to make it in the cutthroat fashion industry, who fell into the clutches of Alma's ex-husband, the villainous Adam DeVry. The storyline culminated at the popular new heroine's fashion show, where she famously rebuked Adam in front of a packed house. The denouement had also seemed to be the end of Dom's dreams until Alma—impressed—dropped a dime to an old friend, the head honcho at the House of Prussia fashion empire. Dom was last seen surrounded by bolts of luxurious fabric, sipping champagne from a crystal flute, her smile that of a person who's just seen their greatest dream made manifest.

Zuhauser had known nothing about fashion or publishing, but the storyline had inspired him to want better for himself. He'd started at Kincaid's part-time. The old man used him as cheap labor and, gradually, he advanced to full-time employment.

"Some dream," Zuhauser sighed.

He threw his car into drive and peeled away from Kincaid Family Furniture.

HE DROVE AROUND BONNEVILLE, which sat under a deceptive autumn glow. It was the perfect sunny day in appearance, a day when the world had altered drastically only no one but Zuhauser noticed. He drove to the Lookout and bought an ice cream cone—strawberry, his favorite flavor during boyhood summers. Summer was over and the ice cream had a freezer-burned taste around the edges, as though he was offered the last scrap of something that had once been good but was now forever past goodness.

Fired. He figured he had options and would need to explore them with another twenty-two months of car payments and seven years left on the mortgage. He had savings—not a fortune—but winter was coming, and the old furnace loved its oil.

He bit into the sugar cone and his mind drifted. Whenever Minerva Langston had gone for Alma Merrill's jugular, regardless whether it was a corporate attack or private, long-suffering Alma always rose to the challenge and ultimately prevailed. The only time she caved was when the network nuked the entire town of Lonesome Oaks and no one got out alive.

Zuhauser ceased crunching and gazed beyond the windshield. The Lookout was an ice cream and fried snack shack on the ledge that gazed down over Bonneville. For a terrible instant, he wasn't looking at familiar streets and landmarks, but what his imagination transformed into Lonesome Oaks, that fictional berg populated by scenery chewers and dramatic queens, on the very last Friday afternoon before the show went off the air. A chill teased the fine hairs on the nape of his neck. Zuhauser fought it, failed. The chill tumbled and the world phased out of focus. Lonesome Oaks and Bonneville shared the same doomed space, one superimposed over the other.

HOME.

Exhaustion engulfed him on the drive back up Jonquil Road. Zuhauser parked the car and stepped out. A gentle breeze whistled down from the backyard and wove a strange melody through the elephantine pumpkin leaves.

Mavis Winters was in her garden, digging around. She righted and wiped her face on a corner of flannel shirt. "Morning, Lance."

Yeah, morning it was. "Mavis," he said.

"You're home early."

"Nice pumpkin," he said, and flashed a tired smile.

She swiped a strand of gray hair out of her face. "It's starting to show a little color."

Zuhauser nodded and maintained the façade of his smile. "Have a good day," he said and plodded toward the front door.

"Lance?" she called.

Zuhauser stopped. "Yeah?"

"This day seem, I dunno…a little odd to you?"

"The oddest."

Maya Merrill, named after Alma's adopted wild child, jumped out of the bushes and sped up the stairs at a respectable distance from Zuhauser's legs.

"There you are," he said.

The cat chirped, spun toward him, and rewarded Zuhauser with a rub of her cheek to his calf. He fumbled his keys into the lock. The cat jumped through the plastic flap ahead of him.

He entered the house. The cat's water bubbler bubbled. The breeze blowing outside whispered around the eaves in a secretive ghost's voice. Maya Merrill crunched on the bounty of dry food in her bowl.

Zuhauser leaned over, aware of the pop of joints and the ache of bones rubbing together,

the result of so many years spent standing on his feet and moving furniture around so old man Kincaid didn't have to pay for additional muscle. He'd gotten a regular salary but had paid all of his dreams out of pocket in exchange.

The cat responded to his caresses with a fractured purr. Zuhauser reached into the fifteen-pound bag of dry food and dumped another handful into the bowl.

"Eat up," he said. "And thanks. If it wasn't for you, I'd be—"

He never finished the sentence except in his mind.

Alone.

Zuhauser kicked off his shoes. At the top of the staircase, he unbuckled his pants. Tie undone, dress shirt yanked over his head, he left a trail of clothes across the hallway. The bedroom, bathed in the rosy glow of the afternoon outside filtering through four pairs of scarlet curtains, welcomed him back. Clad only in his socks and tight-whites that hugged his hips too tightly, he crawled beneath the covers and sandwiched his head between two pillows.

"Just sleep," he sighed.

The room again reminded him of a heart—four curtains representing four chambers. In his imagination, they hadn't come out of a catalog at work, but straight from the Merrill Mansion in fabled, lost Lonesome Oaks. Bonneville was about to follow that town into oblivion, Zuhauser somehow knew.

Scratching sounded at the end of the bed —Maya Merrill sharpening her claws on the bottom of the mattress. The cat jumped up and cautiously moseyed over, eventually settling against the warmth of Zuhauser's bare belly. The cat's purring rippled through him, strangely comforting. Sleep claimed him seconds later.

Zuhauser slept.

Twenty-one days passed before he woke up.

HE WAS IN THE MERRILL MANSION. Not the one

from the make-believe world of bygone daytime drama, located beneath stage lights and catwalks, a set with walls on only three sides. This place wasn't assembled and then taken down, reassembled and taken apart again; it showed dishes in the sink and dust that had gathered in the maid's absence. There were four walls and an endless succession of rooms beyond this one: Alma's bed chamber, decorated in modern artwork and ripple-fold curtains; the sunken living room with its well-outfitted wet bar, perfect for happy hours at half past noon; and the grand drawing room, scene of so many dramatic encounters and original source of those crimson curtains, heart of the Merrill Mansion.

Zuhauser was toiling through a hallway in search of a door when Alma Merrill appeared. She beckoned him over with a curl of manicured nails painted a robust red. Her wide eyes telegraphed the tenseness of the day's script.

"Lance," she whispered. "This way. *Hurry*."

Zuhauser glanced down. Still in underwear and socks—an unflattering presentation in every paradigm outside the comfort of his own bedroom, but especially here. In typical Alma Merrill form, the lady of the great house was dressed impeccably, perhaps in the latest Dominique Langston design.

"Alma?" he asked.

She fast-marched toward him, hooked her arm under his, and walked Zuhauser forward. "We don't have a lot of time. They're in the house."

A flicker of coldness trumped Zuhauser's embarrassment. "How... *who's* in the house?"

His mind cycled through a rogue's gallery of notorious *Privilege* villains. There was, of course, Alma's chief rival, Minerva Langston, and Carlton Connelly, an international jewel thief who'd once attempted to pilfer the Merrill Family treasures. And Buzz Limit, a smooth-talking Texan who'd escaped the Lonesome Oaks police department dressed in drag after framing Minerva's boy-toy for the assault on Candy Merrill's life. And then there was Hieronymous Merrick, twin brother to saintly Father Jonathan, who'd come to town possessed by the devil. The exorcism that played out became the most farfetched of the soap's storylines and, sadly, the one it was remembered most for.

"No," Alma said. "None of them. Far worse!"

Before Zuhauser could question whether Alma Merrill was reading his thoughts, the creak of a footstep sounded overhead. Alma froze. Her grip on Zuhauser tightened.

"Oh no," she sighed.

Alma Merrill hastened forward and forced Zuhauser into following. They turned a corner, rounded another. The dark paneling blurred around him. The ceiling shook with a footstep that sounded as though the stepper was stomping his or her weight in anger.

"The drawing room," she said. "That's where the others are!"

"Others?" Zuhauser parroted.

A clatter of doors banging and furniture being toppled erupted at his back. Whatever had gotten into the Merrill Mansion was no longer upstairs but behind them, and not far away. Zuhauser ran. The exit he'd sought appeared. Alma reached for the knob. The air rushed out of the room. Cold fingers scrabbled at his neck, close enough to tease his flesh.

The door slammed shut behind them. Alma Merrill turned the lock. Zuhauser prayed it would be enough to keep the invader out. Silence fell over the grand drawing room.

Zuhauser waited and struggled to breathe. As the doorknob moved—turned by the malevolent unknown hand on the other side—he saw that the great room was filled with well-dressed, wide-eyed refugees. Merrills, Langstons, and their costars alike had put aside their differences, and all of the wars petty or profound had been tabled. Minerva Langston stood before the big fireplace above whose mantle the portrait of Jonas Merrill, both her and Alma's biological father, hung. Her gloved hands covered Minerva's mouth. Hunky chief of police Nash Thurber looked no more confident with his stage prop sidearm drawn than Lucinda Merrill, who was nine at the time the network slaughtered them all.

The locked door held. The hand ceased jiggling the knob. The silence in the room quickly grew oppressive, near strangulating. Zuhauser experienced a level of fear he hadn't known since the nightmares of his youth. It crawled down past his skin, chilled his blood; deeper, it seeped into his marrow.

"They're outside the door," one of the huddled members of the Merrill clan gasped. Maya Merrill, Zuhauser saw through the filter of his fear.

The young heroine's voice trailed off. A throaty growl replaced it. Zuhauser blinked and the character of Maya Merrill was gone. Her feline namesake had replaced her. The cat paced back and forth, ears lowered, fur raised.

A fist pounded the door. Everyone in the drawing room jumped. A chorus of gasps and sobs rose up. Alma moved to the center of the gathering.

"As long as we stay together in this room —the very heart of our universe—we're safe."

More angry punches hammered the door's other side, from what sounded like multiple fists. Alma returned to Zuhauser.

Boom

She seized hold of his face between both hands and captured his eyes in hers. "Listen to me, dear Lance..."

Boom

"It isn't safe outside this room. Do you understand?"

"I don't—"

Boom!

The door burst open. Somebody screamed. Right before Zuhauser opened his eyes, he stole a glimpse of the horrific presence that had infiltrated the Merrill Mansion. Nothing beyond the threshold looked solid, a mass of mathematical equations, desolate space, smoke and mirrors.

He was back in his bed. Perspiration soaked the sheets, along with other, fouler smells. As he often slept, Zuhauser's head was sandwiched between two pillows. One reeked of oily scalp. The other was damp beneath his cheek from drool.

The room glowed under its usual rosy color, though whether it was morning or afternoon he couldn't tell. Parts of his body— his lower back and shoulders particularly— ached. Others like his feet and arms tingled from pins and needles.

He attempted to shift position and winced. The fog in control of his mind lost most of its power. Very little of Zuhauser's body seemed capable of moving.

"It's awake," a voice, barely female, said from somewhere in his bedroom.

Zuhauser's eyes shot fully open. He raised his chin. The pillow on top slipped an inch or so off of his forehead.

"Yes, awake," answered a second voice, this no more fully male than the first was female.

Through the gap, Zuhauser saw that two figures stood in the room, framed by the curtains at the window across from the bed. Their faces refused to focus, and instead hovered beyond his watering eyes as pale ovals. They were both dressed in formfitting black. Despite the clammy sensation that slithered over Zuhauser's flesh, his reawakened consciousness perceived them as being only half there, phantoms. The fear already in his gut worsened.

"Do we destroy it, Elody?" This came from the phantom he pegged as male.

The female hesitated from answering. "Maybe. This one is different, separate. Best to observe it until we know more. It can always be fed to our hungry."

Zuhauser blinked. Tears spilled down his cheek. When he looked again, the two figures were gone. Terror unlocked his paralysis. He bolted up in his bed and screamed.

CRYING OUT was like expelling a bottled breath turning toxic in his lungs. Zuhauser sucked down a replacement. His vision focused, and the pins and needles in control of his flesh began to short out. The sting in his arms and legs relaxed. He swung his feet over the edge of the mattress and promptly spilled onto the floor.

A rosary of expletives flew from his mouth, most of the blue streak sounding like a drunk's. Zuhauser's tongue sat thick and flabby in his mouth. A few hard swallows helped revive it. Pain raced through his legs, and, at first, his hands refused to cooperate. He reached up, found purchase on the mattress, and hauled himself back to his feet. The bedroom did a spin around him but soon stabilized.

Thirst clawed up his throat, and Zuhauser's stomach protested in a manner his mind translated as being far past simple hunger. No, this was bigger, worse. So much so that he wasn't sure a name for the condition existed.

There were people in his room. Two people. They were gone now, but Zuhauser was sure he'd seen them there and heard what they'd said. In quick order, he drank in the rest of the room—the foul stain on the mattress, a sort of bodily tie dye pattern around his impression; the half-empty water glass on the nightstand that hadn't been there when he'd gone to sleep on a day that now seemed part of another life; the empty candy wrappers beside it exhumed from the top drawer. He hadn't gone sleepwalking since his teens.

Zuhauser sighed another swear. This time he sounded sober, if scared.

He reached for the glass and downed the contents in a single gulp. The water tasted stale and sat heavy in his gut. The glass nearly spilled from his shaking fingers. He set it back down and rounded the bed, palms flat against the edge of the mattress. By the time he faced the bedroom door, Zuhauser's legs had awakened enough to trust them.

He shuffled into the hallway. The relics of that far-away September day—shirt, tie, and pants—remained where he'd dropped them, only now dust bunnies snuggled against his clothes.

Into the bathroom. Zuhauser's reflection gazed back in disbelief from the mirror. Red rose on his chin, cheeks, and throat, stark color on a pale canvas. His skin sagged in some places, was stretched in others. For a terrible second, the creature staring into and out of the glass wasn't human, wasn't alive. With his new beard, Zuhauser looked like a reanimated corpse.

He reached toward the faucet, ran water into his palm, and sipped. The water was warm and gritty. Zuhauser drank.

LONG NAILS, TIRED FLESH. Making it downstairs was like learning to walk for the second time in his life. At any moment, he expected his legs to give out and for the drop to the landing to finish what the longest nap of his life hadn't.

People in his house. Only he couldn't quite think of them as *people*.

At the base of the stairs, he heard the sound and froze. The air inside and outside the house on Jonquil Hill thrummed with an undercurrent that his mind translated into a scream. Distant, an echo from a nightmare, only the scream wasn't human. Mechanical. A signal.

Gooseflesh blossomed over the skin of Zuhauser's bare arms. By the time he managed to move, the sense that something was seriously wrong had solidified past what he merely felt to what he saw.

The bag of dry cat food had been torn into pieces, the food devoured apart from crumbs. The water bubbler sat still, the water gone save for an oily black skim of mold sitting atop the plastic basin.

"What the hell?" Zuhauser moaned. Just

how much time had passed since that afternoon that felt light-years behind him, part of some other life?

The scream-signal shrieked again. His racing mind tracked it down the hill, in the direction of the old paper mill to what was now the state-of-the-art biomass power plant. Was it a siren, a warning? Had something gone wrong at the plant? Something sure seemed to have.

He plodded into the kitchen, his stomach coming alive as he reached the silent refrigerator. A kind of hunger his body hadn't known since its youth squeezed his guts. Then, Zuhauser thought he was starving after he played soccer or ran like an imbecile with the Norton brothers. Now, he was convinced of it.

Zuhauser pulled open the fridge door. The smell of rot, hot and foul, assaulted his nostrils. He slammed the door shut but the odor had escaped, was loose in the house, and might now always be there.

Everything that wasn't in his stomach rebelled. Zuhauser made it over to the sink and retched up several juicy hiccups. He ran the water again, rinsed his mouth, and settled on a can of condensed chicken noodle soup from the cabinet, which he downed cold, his body grateful for the salty, clotted lumps.

POWER OUT, and yet he heard the signal broadcasting at regular intervals from the direction of the biomass plant. The sun's light waned. From its angle and the deepening color of the leaves he spied through the kitchen window curtains, he'd woken in the thick of October—three full weeks after resting his head between the pillows for that long nap following his heated encounter with Drake Kincaid at the furniture store.

That meant the cable was out. In the age following digitalization, the easy solution of turning on a TV hooked to rabbit ears for free had been yanked off the table. His car had come with a satellite radio option—Zuhauser wasn't sure if the old standard FM even

worked. He felt blind, cold, isolated.

The car. Zuhauser sucked down a deep breath. The food in his stomach felt heavy and slippery, and yet also comforting. He pulled on sweats from the dryer and slid his feet into his abandoned loafers, found his keys, and turned toward the door. The notion of opening it to whatever world awaited outside turned the seconds into sums of time that felt considerably longer.

The last of the day's sunlight and October warmth whistled into the foyer, carrying a cyclone of paper-thin leaves with them. The smell of autumn tempted Zuhauser's memory —nibbling a dry, plain donut hung on a string as part of some bygone Halloween party game in his distant youth; how his mother had played the soundtrack to the gothic daytime soap opera classic, *Dark Shadows*, to spook trick-or-treaters; sweet apples covered in gooey caramel. There were others that attempted exhumation as his feet crunched through leaves on the front stoop. So many. Too many.

Mavis's house sat still and unassuming, the elephantine pumpkin leaves withered down by what he assumed was a killing frost. The giant orb was still there, its hide now orange. The giant hadn't been struggled onto Mavis's porch or carved into a jack-o-lantern—more disquieting proof of the wrongness that now surrounded him.

He trudged through the pumpkin patch and toward Mavis's side door. His bones ached. Worse, his muscles. Ascending the stairs, Zuhauser sucked down a deep breath redolent with autumn smells and Indian summer warmth and knocked. Nobody answered. He knocked again.

Turning, he hobbled back down the stairs. Then he saw the skeleton, left in pieces among the dying pumpkin leaves that had blocked his earlier view of it. His eyes couldn't be sure that it was Mavis, but the rest of Zuhauser was convinced. The air vanished from his lungs. He sucked down another breath and expelled it on a scream.

He screamed again, this time in a wild animal's voice that carried over the neighborhood and beyond.

And while Zuhauser screamed, something out there answered with an alien scream of its own.

IT WAS A SOUND FROM A NIGHTMARE, and when it roared again, freezing him to the spot, Zuhauser understood that it was closer this time.

He willed his legs back into motion and cut across the pumpkin patch. Tears welled in his eyes, mostly for Mavis, poor Mavis. If that was her.

But also out of rising panic. He made it back to the driveway. Behind the house, the overgrown brambles shook at the passing of something moving swiftly. He caught sight of it on his mad, inelegant struggle up the steps to the door. From the cut of his eye, he caught a fleeting glimpse, more proof that he, the world, or both had gone insane: a figure, hunched and skittering toward him on all fours, not quite human.

He pushed open the door, maneuvered in, and slammed it shut behind him. Whatever was out there in pursuit threw itself against the door. The vibrations shuddered through Zuhauser, into his muscles, his marrow. For a moment, he was back in the Merrill Mansion drawing room.

He backed away. His legs snagged, and then he lost balance and fell.

On the floor, a terrible thought rose fresh through his panic. There, it was easier to see, to fear. The cat door.

As though reading his thoughts, the thing on the other side tested the flap with a knock. The flap creaked open, and he saw its face in the space of that fractured second. Not fully human, no, its eyes were wild, its mouth salivating, jaws opened wide. It looked like a girl but a girl who'd gone wild with hunger and had murder in her rabid eyes.

The flap settled. Zuhauser remembered to breathe. A choking silence fell over the kitchen.

She wouldn't, he thought. She *couldn't*. That flap was big enough for a cat, a small dog. Unless he'd misjudged the size of the horror outside his door, there was no way she'd make it inside from that entry point.

Then her head struck the cat door swiftly enough to knock it and the frame out of alignment. She pushed her head through, along with one shoulder. An arm followed and the hand with its dirty talons made a grab at his foot. Zuhauser shrieked again and kicked. One blow struck the horror on the side of her head, which only fueled his attacker's determination to breach the house. The other shoulder eked through the shattered cat door. The rest of her torso followed.

Zuhauser backed away, toward the counter. She was almost through, now up to her slender hips. And once she was in, he knew what the horror planned to do: pick him clean like poor Mavis, who grew pumpkins and harmed none.

He reached the counter, grabbed up for the edge, and hauled himself to his knees. The atrophied muscles of his legs complained, but Zuhauser ignored them and made it back to his feet right as the horror wedged her way through the cat door, screaming in that hellish voice. In the confines of the kitchen, the sharpness bit at his ears.

He reached for the knife block and pulled out the first handle he met. Footsteps clacked across the floor. Zuhauser raised the knife and saw that he'd grabbed the one for pairing—the smallest blade in the block.

"Oh, nuts," he barked, and swung.

The horror avoided the blade with a kind of mad grace, backed away, and assessed the threat. This gave Zuhauser the chance to size up his opponent—female, clad in rags, not exactly what he'd classify as human with her salivating mouth filled with teeth and red-tinged eyes. In that last second before she lunged, he made the connection between the horror and the one called Elody that had watched him from the shadows while he slept. They were hungry.

Then he was back on the floor, the pairing knife knocked from his grip, and the horror was upon him, snapping at his face. Pain exploded along his cheek. Zuhauser tossed a punch hard at his would-be devourer and her teeth detached. In quick order, she pinned his arms to the floor, leaned over his face, her lips wet and red from his blood. Dreaming—surely, he was still in bed, the mattress beneath him and the quilt draped around his supine form. A nightmare, that's what this was. Time for it to end and for him to return to his beloved soap opera and the world of the Merrills and Langstons. Their travails had gone off the air, but during Zuhauser's spell of hibernation he'd resuscitated the show, breathed new life into the characters, created new episodes.

He remembered Alma Merrill hiding him in the family's manor from an evil bigger than anything ever tackled on the show, including the notorious exorcism storyline. No, the pain throbbing outward from where the horror bit him was real.

The nightmare *was* real.

And it was about to devour him, like it had Mavis.

The thing chattering, smiling over him opened her mouth. In that moment before she struck, perhaps this time severing his tongue, his nose, or biting an eyeball clean from its socket, Zuhauser detected the faintest patter across the kitchen floor, a rustle of leaves. His would-be killer heard it, too, and, releasing him, turned.

Something dark and feral sprang at her head. The horror scrambled off Zuhauser and clutched at the newest combatant, screaming. The thing that had entered the fray screamed, too, but Zuhauser recognized its voice even if, at first, he failed to recognize Maya Merrill.

The cat had attached itself to the human-thing and bit at its shoulder, its neck, and the side of its face. The horror flailed but was unable to dislodge Zuhauser's rescuer. The cacophony drilled into his ears, waking him fully from paralysis. Zuhauser labored back to his feet and found the pairing knife, only to toss it again and select something far more formidable.

He didn't need the knife. Turning and slicing through empty space, creating a sharp *whoosh* as the blade cut air, he saw that his opponent was down on her knees, eyes bulging, mouth open and gasping for air that refused to come easily. Maya Merrill had detached but was yodeling through growls as she paced around her prey.

The female collapsed onto her face and ceased moving. Maya Merrill did not, and let out a juicy hiss.

Zuhauser shuffled forward and tested the horror with a nudge of the blade against her shoulder. Nothing. Eyes wide, he absorbed the image of the cat's bite and scratch marks

across the horror's flesh—gruesome enough but hardly deadly. Only the flesh around the bites had mottled. A toxic allergic reaction to cat saliva, or the bacteria of their claws? Regardless, Maya Merrill had saved his life.

Zuhauser lowered the blade and extended his hand. "Hey, baby. *Maya*," he cooed.

Maya Merrill eyed him suspiciously, hissed again, and then yowled, all the while snapping her tail in agitation. He repeated her name. The cat, her tangled fur coat bushed out from battle, sauntered over and brushed against his outstretched hand.

"Oh, Maya," Zuhauser said. His voice hitched with a sob.

The cat let forth with a plaintive mewl. Zuhauser scooped her into his arms. Maya Merrill permitted it. Beyond the house, the sun began to set, and the longest night in history descended.

HE COVERED THE BODY with a tablecloth. Fishing through the cabinets, Zuhauser found three cans of chunk-light tuna and opened one. Maya Merrill devoured the offering. He opened another and, soon gorged, the cat walked away after downing half.

She followed him up the stairs, back to the scene of the original crime. Zuhauser fell onto the bed, aware of the sour smell of the blankets and pillows but past caring. He sat up in the darkness, the melody of the biomass station signal pulsing beyond the house.

What had happened?

What *was* happening?

THEY WAITED IN THE SHADOWS, one man and one cat, the latter curled into a ball and purring on his lap.

Music cycled through Zuhauser's thoughts, something elegant played on a piano, a ghost eluding his attempts to identify it. The melody followed him into a fugue. As he drifted deeper, the song grew more distinct, telling him to confess, confess, and that it was time to fix this mess. It became the opening theme to his beloved soap, *The Privilege of Passion.*

The music broke, and Zuhauser found himself seated in a comfortable leather club chair, part of the Merrill Mansion's opulent drawing room in fictional Lonesome Oaks. Alma Merrill sat across from him on the sofa. She was dressed in designer threads and stroked an impeccable black cat wearing a diamond collar. The cat was Maya.

"Oh, thank heavens you're back!" Alma said.

Zuhauser leaned forward. "Tell me—"

"They're on every channel now, across the television." Alma set Maya Merrill down and crossed to the drawing room's TV, which was housed inside a big cabinet among the towering volume-filled bookshelves. His hostess punched buttons on the remote. The screen lit, showing a silent townscape that he recognized—the center of Bonneville. Another switch and he was looking at Kincaid Family Furniture, its parking lot empty apart from the big delivery van. The last was of the ice cream stand. Another picked-clean human skeleton lay in pieces before the Lookout's ordering window.

"Those... *things.*"

"Rivals, my dear Lance. Worse than any born into those scallawag Langstons, I can tell you!"

"Rivals?"

"They've taken over, a few here and elsewhere, but more are sure to be on their way. It's that signal, the one I already told you about that's coming over every channel. It is my belief that they're using it to put people to sleep and then infiltrating their bodies, like parasites. The transference from their signal to our bodies isn't an ideal fit, however, which is why they emerge so wild and hungry."

Zuhauser faced the image on the TV screen, still frozen on the gruesome scene. "These rivals—where are they from?"

"Several seasons after our premiere, Merrill Publishing released an astronomy book—*View Into Deep Space.* I've got a copy here somewhere."

Alma glided over to the wall of bookcases. She scanned spines and tested volumes with a quick tip out and back before settling on a glossy hardcover boasting an image of a ringed planet. She opened the book and carried it over.

"There—the star *Rukvenakravi*. A desolate planet five orbits in."

"They're aliens from another planet?"

"An alien intelligence, yes—but there is no physical life, at least not at the other end of the transmission."

Alma eyed him with a knowing look.

"The signal, is it being received up at the biomass plant?"

She tipped a glance back at the television, whose image had shifted to show the stack of the power station. As Zuhauser watched, the picture zoomed in on the tall antenna rising up from the plot of ground alongside the stack.

"If that transmitter gets neutralized..." Zuhauser said.

Alma added, "Then some will wake up. Maybe enough to stop the rivals from taking over—much like that black sheep of the Langstons tried to do by secretly gathering shares of Merrill stock. Do you remember?"

Zuhauser smiled. "Vividly."

"You're a loyal viewer. In another world, a different time and place, you and I, maybe..."

"I'll always love you, Alma Merrill. You and the rest of the little soap opera that could. When I die, I'd rather go to *The Privilege of Passion* than Heaven."

She leaned closer and kissed his cheek. Zuhauser turned, and her lips met his. The kiss was wondrous though brief. Zuhauser jolted awake in his bed, Maya Merrill's reassuring weight still on his gut. The long night continued with a dragging slowness that allowed Zuhauser to ponder all that he'd learned.

A message from a fictional soap opera's leading lady. Insanity, yes—though no more incredible than all he'd seen and survived since waking up from his long sleep. If those horrors were to be believed, he could wrap his mind around the rest. A signal beamed down from a distant alien planet—said signal containing the consciousness and intentions of disembodied alien conquerors. They put you to sleep, invade your body, and wake up hungry.

His thoughts cycled back to his encounter with the woman called Elody and her aid. They didn't understand why his mind denied them access.

Because Alma hid me in the Merrill Mansion, he remembered.

He'd loved that show, had cursed its cancellation, and mourned its absence. Now, he realized, *The Privilege of Passion* had somehow saved him.

The Alma Merrill in his dreams—inside his head—surely was more than a figment. An angel? Zuhauser shrugged. Not that it mattered. She'd helped him, and he was grateful.

Zuhauser extricated Maya Merrill off his lap and slipped out of bed, to the nearest window. Outside, Bonneville slumbered under a blanket of darkness. No houses were lit, but the endless siren of the biomass plant sang through the shadows.

A signal being received by its transmission tower. And other towers across the globe. Why else would there have been no response to an entire town gone silent? The Alma in his dreams said knocking out the one tower might be enough to thwart their plans. Wake enough people. Stop enough alien transfers. A beginning point. A Fade In. he trusted her.

"You're a hell of a lady, Alma Merrill," he whispered.

By the time the sun was showing and the long night nearly ended, Zuhauser had come up with a plan.

WHETHER OR NOT IT WAS A GOOD ONE remained to be proven.

He opened the last can of tuna and dumped its contents into the bowl. While Maya Merrill slurped up the stinky goo, Zuhauser dragged the corpse outside and over to the pumpkin patch. The sun was above the horizon, and the sense of being watched sent chills racing down his spine.

Zuhauser hopped into his car and turned the ignition. The old beast started up, the noise striking his ears like thunder, a clear indication that he was out there, ready for the eating.

He pulled out of the driveway and motored down Jonquil Road, recording the obscene orderliness of the landscape around him. Cars were parked as they should have been. None of the houses he passed had burned or showed broken windows. Apart from the silence and the occasional picked-clean skeleton, all looked proper, part of a sane world.

Of course it did, his inner critic remarked. It was a takeover bid. A hostile takeover like so many schemes played out on the tiny screen at 12:30 in afternoons past. The aliens from Rukvenakravi hadn't waged conventional, outright war, the kind that results in bombed out cities and global collateral damage. They didn't have physical bodies, according to his source. No, their tactic would give them a readymade, instant civilization to assume, complete with infrastructure, host bodies, and, grisly enough, an unsuspecting food source.

Zuhauser shuddered. Before leaving the house, he'd downed more water and a handful of stale crackers. Even strawberry ice cream would have tried to claw its way up his throat, he guessed.

Jonquil Hill passed by, and he was on Main Street, heading toward Kincaid Family Furniture, source of so many miserable, tawdry soap opera storylines.

ON MYRTLE STREET, three male horrors formed a line to block his advance. Zuhauser hit the brake on instinct, only to again shift his foot right. He stepped on the gas and accelerated. The trio of bodies stood their ground.

"For Alma," he said, and charged.

The distance thinned. One of the men raised what he knew had to be a weapon according to its gun shape, though it was unlike any Zuhauser had seen. The device looked to have been cobbled together from spare parts—plumbing pipe and elbows, hooked up to a car battery planted at the wielder's feet.

Energy flashed forth from the muzzle. The car's windshield came apart, not merely in spider webs or melting, but vanishing. Heat slammed into Zuhauser's face. The next blast punched into the hood. He saw the metal buckle and then the steering wheel froze. Even so, he managed to bury two of the three hybrid men, the gun wielder included, beneath his wheels before the car went into a spin and the sky switched position with the ground.

THUNDER ECHOED through his consciousness, the rumbles forming concentric waves that rippled outward, taking his thoughts with them.

The Merrill Mansion, on a Friday in an autumn long gone. It was during the culmination of the whole Lonesome Oaks Serial Killer plotline that led to the end of *The Privilege of Passion*, which would be replaced by another of those lousy daytime talk shows that were cheaper to produce and guaranteed to lower the collective IQ.

Zuhauser found himself in the grand foyer, facing the mansion's front door. The scene played out as it had then, with him as the camera, focused upon the door, standing in a tenebrous calm in anticipation. A single knock sounded, more thunder. His heart raced, because he knew what was to follow: a second knock, then a hand—Alma Merrill's—shown answering the door. The servants had either quit employment in the storied estate or had been murdered. The killer was on the other side of the door, presumably come for one final victim. Alma would open the door, the killer's identity revealed, and the last thing viewers would see of the fictional town and residents of Lonesome Oaks would be Nadine Lancaster, love child of Rafferty Langston and Theodora Merrill, driven mad by her struggles and denied her Merrill name and social status. Nadine, a slippery smile on her lips, would break out in insane, echoing laughter. Fade Out. The End.

That second knock sounded. The pregnant silence grew unbearable. A hand reached toward the doorknob, only it wasn't Alma's, no. Zuhauser recognized his fingers, the thumb showing a fresh, bloody scratch along the top knuckle. He turned. The door opened, and, indeed, a murderer stood on the front stoop. Its identity had altered.

"We're getting closer to you," Elody said.

Zuhauser studied the woman with the blank, TV-snow face. "Good for you."

"Closer to understanding and entering this house you've constructed around your consciousness."

"I didn't build the place. Old Zebulon Merrill did, way back before Episode One."

She studied him through eyes that crackled, as though trying to dissect the statement. "The people who live here...we have no record of them."

"Your loss."

"We'd welcome you as an ally. We are impressed by your mind and its abilities."

Zuhauser laughed. "Can't say I like what you've done with things."

He tipped a look past the stoop, the murderer standing there, and the fake potted trees meant to create an illusion of tended grounds around the estate set. Beyond, buildings sat dark and more of those insanely hungry hybrids fed upon the sleeping.

"It's only necessary changes to establish the new order. Once the rest of us come through, normality will resume. There is a place for you among it. You have only to want it. Welcome me inside."

She shifted toward the threshold.

"Lance, no," Alma Merrill cautioned from behind.

Zuhauser jolted awake, upside down in the overturned wreck of his car. Outside, movement cast a shadow over him. The third male horror that had blocked the road was still out there. Zuhauser came out of the fog and remembered running the other two down.

A pair of hands forced open the door and scrambled in after him. As he was yanked out, Zuhauser's brain did a fast injury assessment. Nothing was broken, though the skin on his face felt badly sunburned. That, he credited to whatever makeshift alien weapon had been used to vaporize the windshield.

He made it to his feet and found himself staring at the misshapen face of Drake the Snake Kincaid.

Zuhauser huffed out a swear and began to laugh. "Even after an alien invasion, you're more of a pain in my butt than the Langstons were to the Merrills."

The Drake-hybrid stared at him without commentary. Zuhauser's guffaw echoed up into the silent sky over Bonneville.

"Tell her, I agree," he said. "Tell your boss, Elody, that I'll play your game, join up with your cause. Tell her I'm coming to surrender and be part of your new world order."

Drake the Snake nodded and closed his eyes. More of their thought mumbo-jumbo, Zuhauser assumed. Human transmitters transmitting. Message sent. Signal received.

The former, favorite Kincaid son again opened his eyes. By then, Zuhauser had removed the pairing knife from his pants pocket. He drove it into Drake the Snake's left eyeball as deep as it would penetrate.

THE SATISFACTION WAS BRIEF and sort of a letdown. For years, Zuhauser had fantasized about offing the useless jerk; once, memorably, by shoving a stick of dynamite up his keister and lighting the fuse. That particular daydream had sustained him for weeks.

Taking out a hybridized version of Drake Kincaid while he was under alien control was far less satisfying.

He jogged the remainder of the way to Kincaid Family Furniture, aware of the aches in his legs and his patchwork of new cuts weeping blood. The building appeared before him, silent in the daylight. All of the dark emotions he'd ever suffered at the image of the place surfaced. The front entrance was unlocked, and the new furniture smell he'd experienced thousands of times in the past met his senses as though for the first, worsening the malaise.

He fell into a spiral. Alma Merrill's hero had wasted his life selling cheap furniture made from inferior materials in overseas sweat factories. He'd never married, hadn't even come close. There were no children, so no legacy to leave behind to the world. Just a cat and his love for a barely-remembered daytime soap opera.

Then he found the keys to the delivery van hanging from a peg in the office, and Zuhauser reminded himself there was one good thing he could bequeath to the future.

The truck started up right away, and the gage showed a full tank of gas. A lightness washed over him. Zuhauser put the truck in drive and sped away from the building for the last time.

OH, HOW HE'D LOVED THAT SHOW. A dramatic, often silly half-hour soap opera about beautiful people and their larger-than-life adventures. For those thirty minutes, the travails of the Merrill and Langston clans and all those drawn into their orbits had transported a lonely man out of his own life to someplace brighter. It was a fantasy, but the illusion made Zuhauser happy.

He remembered that summer when the young Maya Merrill, who would inspire the name of his cat, met Jason Langston, who'd arrived to town under an alias. Of course, when his real identity got out, the star-crossed lovers were forced to break up. Maya then dated preppy college frat boy Hans Corinth,

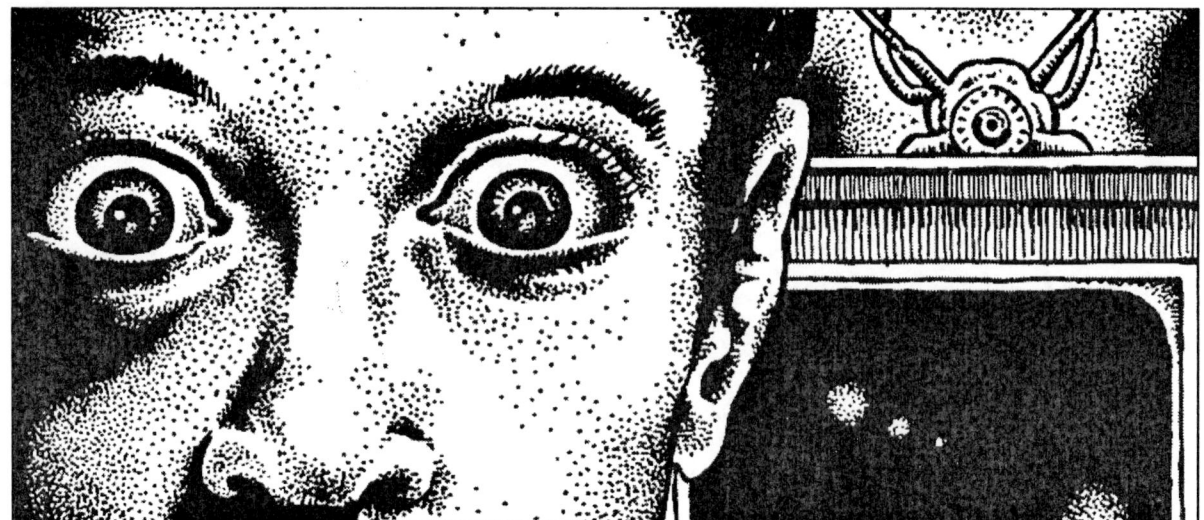

who bore a black secret. Their summer story culminated with Corinth tearing down the road in his car, Maya his prisoner, and Jason in hot pursuit as—

Zuhauser accelerated. The truck chugged along Main Street. Ahead of him, the biomass plant and its broadcast tower rose above the two-story buildings of Bonneville's downtown.

—Corinth, in the throes of a psychotic breakdown, was determined to take Maya with him to the grave rather than lose her. Maya—

They'd done something to the tower, Zuhauser saw. Outfitted it with more of their weapons cobbled together from Earth objects and human tech. Of course they had—the invaders had only transmitted their consciousness across the great galactic distance, not physical matter. If he got enough momentum going, and if Elody was fooled even the slightest degree into thinking he was joining their ranks...

—screamed for Corinth to stop, slow down. He refused and sped up. The car raced through the back roads of Lonesome Oaks. Jason Langston pursued. She reached—

Zuhauser turned past the town hall, sped down Prospect Street, and approached the gate to the biomass plant.

—for the door handle, jumped out right as Corinth lost control of the wheel and—

The gate stood open, as though in invitation. The facility towered ahead of him. Zuhauser pushed the truck past fifty-five on the final charge. The antenna appeared before him, surrounded by a stockade of chain-link fence capped by razor wire.

He pushed down on the gas all the way. And—

Remembered how Maya Merrill had jumped out of the car right before Hans Corinth sailed off the road and to his death. Of course, that episode had run on a Friday, leaving Zuhauser anxious over the course of the weekend to find out Maya's fate. She survived, was reunited with her one true love Jason Langston, and Zuhauser named his cat after the plucky daytime heroine. Maya Merrill the cat had demonstrated similar heroics, so the naming fit.

At the last few seconds before impact, Zuhauser contemplated doing as she had, that day on *The Privilege of Passion*. Opening the door. Jumping out. Cheating death while beating these new, alien versions of Hans Corinth at their own game. But she'd had Jason to return to. Better this way, Zuhauser agreed. It was almost time again to sleep.

Smiling, he sang the little soap's theme

song. Even off-key, it greeted his ear like the music of angels.

The weapons constructed around the tower opened fire. Good, Zuhauser thought. He was coming in like a missile. He not only had momentum but that full tank of gas. He only prayed the impact would be enough to knock out the tower, open up a hole in their transmission network, stop the enemy from fully coming over, and wake up the rest of the world enough to fight back.

"Fade out," Zuhauser whispered, and closed his eyes.

☻ ☻ ☻

*Raised on a healthy diet of creature double features and classic SF television, Gregory L. Norris is a full-time professional writer, with work appearing in numerous short story anthologies, national magazines, novels, the occasional TV episode, and, so far, one produced feature film (*Brutal Colors, *which debuted on Amazon Prime, January 2016). A former feature writer and columnist at Sci Fi, the official magazine of the Sci Fi Channel (before all those ridiculous Ys invaded), he once worked as a screenwriter on two episodes of Paramount's modern classic,* Star Trek: Voyager. *Two of his paranormal novels (written under his nom-de-plume, Jo Atkinson) were published by Home Shopping Net-work as part of their "Escape with Romance" line—the first time HSN has offered novels to their global customer base. He judged the 2012 Lambda Awards in the SF/F/H category. Three times now, his stories have notched Honorable Mentions in Ellen Datlow's Best-of books. In May 2016, he traveled to Hollywood to accept HM in the Roswell Awards in Short SF Writing. Follow Norris' literary adventures at* www.gregorylnorris.blogspot.com.

ACCESSING ... ACCESSING.... OPENING MODULE 3:

BODY SNATCHERS: ALIEN POSSESSION... ALIEN CONTROL ... ALIEN REPLACEMENT

THE EASIEST WAY TO OVERTHROW A SOCIETY IS FROM WITHIN. It's far simpler to subdue the fortress that has opened the front gates than to try battering your way through heavy stone walls. The aliens featured in the films sited herein are genetically predisposed to do just that. They possess the unique ability to use time as a weapon. No, they can't move back and forth through the time stream. What they can do, is effectively usurp the endless hours of time that have been spent gaining the trust of those around them; time which has allowed others to grow accustomed to, and accept, their personalities, foibles, routines and morals. If they can convince friends and loved ones they are the honorable, trusted colleagues they've always known, these humans are likely to let their guard down. By the time they realize their mistake, it's usually too late.

How does one defend against such a threat? The six scenarios below will help you prepare yourself for just such potentialities.

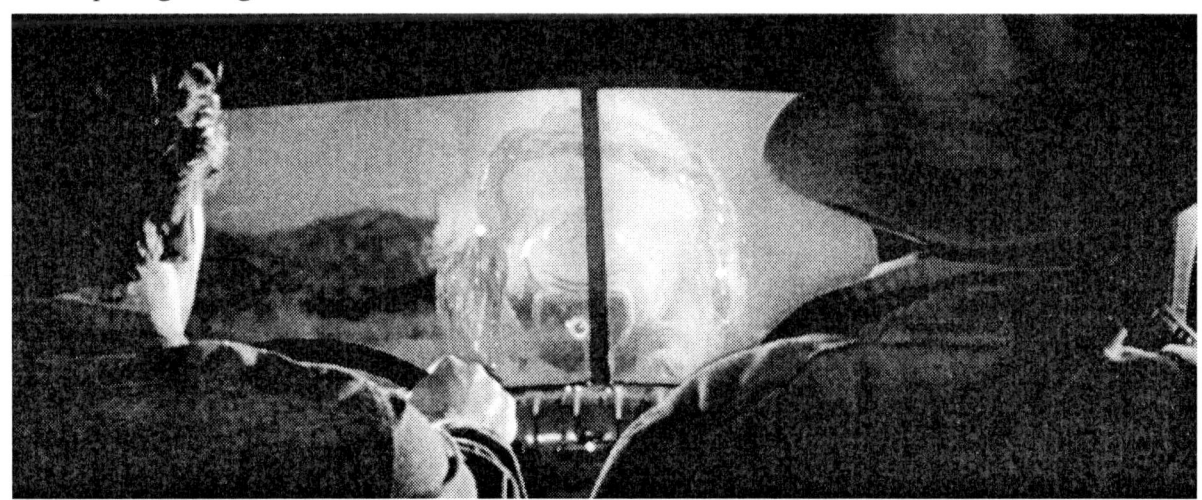

IT CAME FROM OUTER SPACE
(Universal Studios, 1953)

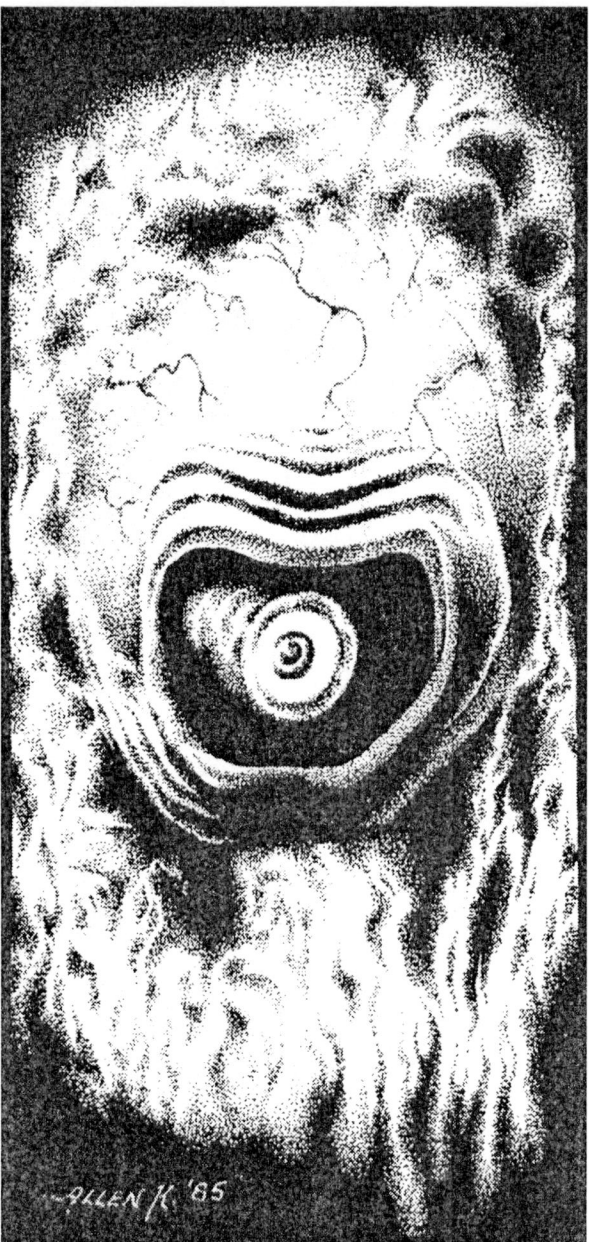

Classification: Intelligent, semi-corporeal alien race capable of replicating the appearance of others

Method of Conquest: Abduction and impersonation of the dominant, local lifeform

Deadliness Factor: 5 out of 10

Characteristics/Motivation: A large, floating cranium with a single giant eye in its center, with straggly tendrils drooping off it that emit a vaporous haze. They desire to escape the planet Earth and return to space.

Necessities for Survival: The ability to look past their terrifying appearance and enough common sense to negotiate with them reasonably

Overall Threat Level: 6 out of 10
(They aren't aggressively violent but do possess enough firepower to destroy the planet if provoked.)

Favorite Scene: The monstrous alien when it's originally shown emerging from the spacecraft

Synopsis: John Putnam (Richard Carlson), a writer and amateur stargazer, is spending a quiet evening with his girlfriend Ellen Fields (Barbara Rush) at home in Arizona, when they see a large meteor crash nearby. John takes Ellen and their friend Pete to investigate the crash site. Once John descends into the crater caused by the impact, he discovers a honeycombed spacecraft with its door open and tracks leading away from it. He barely escapes in time before a landslide buries the ship, leaving John as the only one to have seen it. At first, no one believes his story, not Ellen (although she tries to be supportive), or the local media who've gotten wind of it, and especially not Sheriff Matt Warren (Charles Drake) who seems jealous of John's relationship with Ellen.

A pair of telephone company employees, who are friends with John, are the first to be set upon by the monstrous alien, which swiftly envelops them in a vapor and takes over their appearance. It isn't long before other locals are supplanted by the alien. Moving stiffly and acting in an ominous manner, they carry out their secret objectives. Ellen is kidnapped by what appears to be one of the telephone workmen and forced to go to the

original crash site. John and Matt follow in an attempt to try and rescue her. John travels the final distance alone where he talks with the aliens who say they crashed there on accident and that their only objective is to repair the damage to their ship so that they can leave. They say they took the others' identities because their own true appearance would be hideous by our standards and would spur resistance against them. They promise no harm will come to Ellen or the others as long as no one interferes with their plans.

Things go awry, however, when the Sheriff along with a mob of armed citizens arrive at the crash site looking for trouble. John races to try and help the aliens but is attacked by a replicated Ellen who fires a laser beam at him, forcing him to return fire with his pistol. This causes her to fall into a deep crevasse, leaving her apparently dead. He then finds the rest of the aliens working on their ship. They have a powerful weapon which they plan to use to destroy their own ship, which would likely result in taking out the entire planet as well, to keep it from falling into the Earthlings' hands. John convinces them to release the people they abducted to stall the mob long enough to complete their repairs and escape. When the locals emerge, Ellen is among them, still alive and unharmed. The plan works, as their ship launches up from beneath the ground and on into space.

My Take: Based on a Ray Bradbury story, this was the first 3D movie released by Universal Studios. I really like the look of the aliens. They're monstrous and ghostly and definitely unlike anything which should exist on our planet. The visual effect of showing things from the alien's perspective as it directs its massive eye upon those it wants to control is a nice touch and effectively eerie. Showing the replaced locals represented as blacked-out silhouettes evokes a really nice, ominous effect as well. The fact that you get strong indications early on that these extraterrestrials don't really mean any harm detracts a bit from the suspense, but overall the film is well written, well-acted and has decent enough special effects for its time.

Rating: 7 out of 10

INVADERS FROM MARS
(National Pictures, 1953)

Classification: Martian/Capable of inter-stellar travel, heat-ray weaponry, as well as technology-assisted psychic control

Method of Conquest: Implantation of small crystals into the base of subject's neck, which grants the Martian complete mental control of their victims

Deadliness Factor: 6 out of 10

Characteristics/Motivation: Invasion of the planet and sabotage of rocket innovation

Necessities for Survival: Early discovery of the Martian activities combined with the ability to bring full military armaments against them

Overall Threat Level: 6 out of 10

(While they have the ability to instantly kill those who've been implanted by detonating the crystals in their necks, and possess destructive heat-ray weaponry, their implantation technique can be a slow process, and their methods often lack effective subtlety, leaving them subject to resistance.)

Favorite Scene: The first appearance of the lead, big-headed Martian with the tentacles while he's flanked by his burly, bug-eyed slaves.

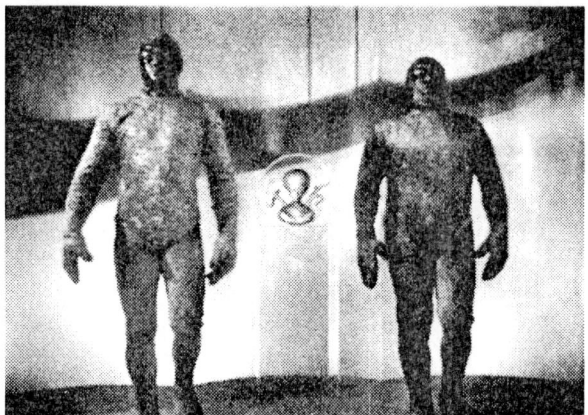

Synopsis: Young David MacLean (Jimmy Hunt) witnesses a luminous flying saucer land and then get enveloped beneath the Earth from his bedroom window during a storm one night. His father, an engineer at a nearby rocket research plant, goes to investigate after hearing his son's story but doesn't return home that night. The next morning, concerned about her husband's disappearance, his mother calls the police. To their surprise, the father returns, still in his pajamas and missing a shoe. He's developed a perpetual dead-eyed stare, and acts defensive, especially in regards to any mention of the spacecraft. David notices a small wound on the back of his father's neck before coming to realize his father is not the same man who left the house the night before.

Soon, several other locals have been similarly changed, the two police officers who went out in search of David's dad, a young girl named Kathy, and more.

While at the police station, David is able to convince a friendly health department physician, Dr. Pat Blake (Helena Carter), of his story. Due to this, she doesn't allow his altered parents to take him back home when

The military use their firepower to blow their way into the underground base where they engage the Martian mutant slaves (who prove very hard to kill) in combat long enough to plant explosives on the saucer. That being done, everyone flees, escaping before the whole area erupts in the resulting explosion.

My Take: I remember seeing this as a child on a local television channel that was playing a week of old science fiction movies. I recall enjoying it at the time. Having recently watched it again, many years later, its flaws are more apparent. On the positive side, the Martians look cool and present a definite threat to the humans. On the negative, there are a lot of pacing problems. They spend far too much

they arrive to pick him up. The two enlist the help of an astronomer named Dr. Stuart Kelston (Arthur Franz) in seeking answers to this secret alien invasion. They theorize the saucer that landed has arrived ahead of a larger invasion force. Once they see conclusive evidence of what's happening, they contact the military who deploy forces their way.

David and Dr. Blake end up captured by some large, bubble-eyed aliens and are taken through an underground passage to meet the lead Martian, which appears as a head atop some writhing tentacles inside a clear, circular sphere. They learn that the Martians have been implanting small crystals at the base of the necks of their victims, granting them total mental control over them. If these converted people are caught, the crystals detonate, killing them.

time showing the military vehicles and tanks on the move. Complete with a heavy patriotic score playing in the background, it seems like something clipped from a military propaganda campaign. I'm torn on whether I like how easily David is able to get people to believe his story. On one hand, it can get tiring when films spend too much time having the

protagonist struggle to convince a horde of disbelievers what's happening. On the other hand, here it happens so quickly, it feels unearned and unrealistic. I didn't care for the very end of the film which made it seem the whole thing may have simply been a nightmare David was having.

For me, the strength of this film is in the design of the Martians. Their warped appearance lends credibility to their not being of our planet. The scene of the saucer flying in and sinking into the ground was well done and unsettlingly. There are some nice, almost surreal looking set pieces which I also liked. In the end, this is decent enough for a one-time view, but not one which will find a place on my DVD shelf.

Rating: 6 out of 10

INVASION OF THE BODY SNATCHERS
(Allied Artists, 1956)
Classification: Alien seeds which travel through space to a planet where they grow into pods capable of replicating humanoid bodies

Method of Conquest: Subterfuge through the replication and imitation of anyone who resists them

Deadliness Factor: 8 out of 10
(They don't come with destructive weaponry, but their ability to overtake people is exceptionally difficult to counteract.)

Characteristics/Motivation: They begin as seeds floating through space until they land on a planet's surface where they expand into giant pea pods which can grow into organic replications of other beings. They operate without emotion and are driven by a genetic need to overtake and supplant the planets they land on.

Necessities for Survival: The ability to remain awake for long periods of time, to recognize the non-verbal clues that give away those that have been replicated, and access to fire to destroy the pods

Overall Threat Level: 8 out of 10

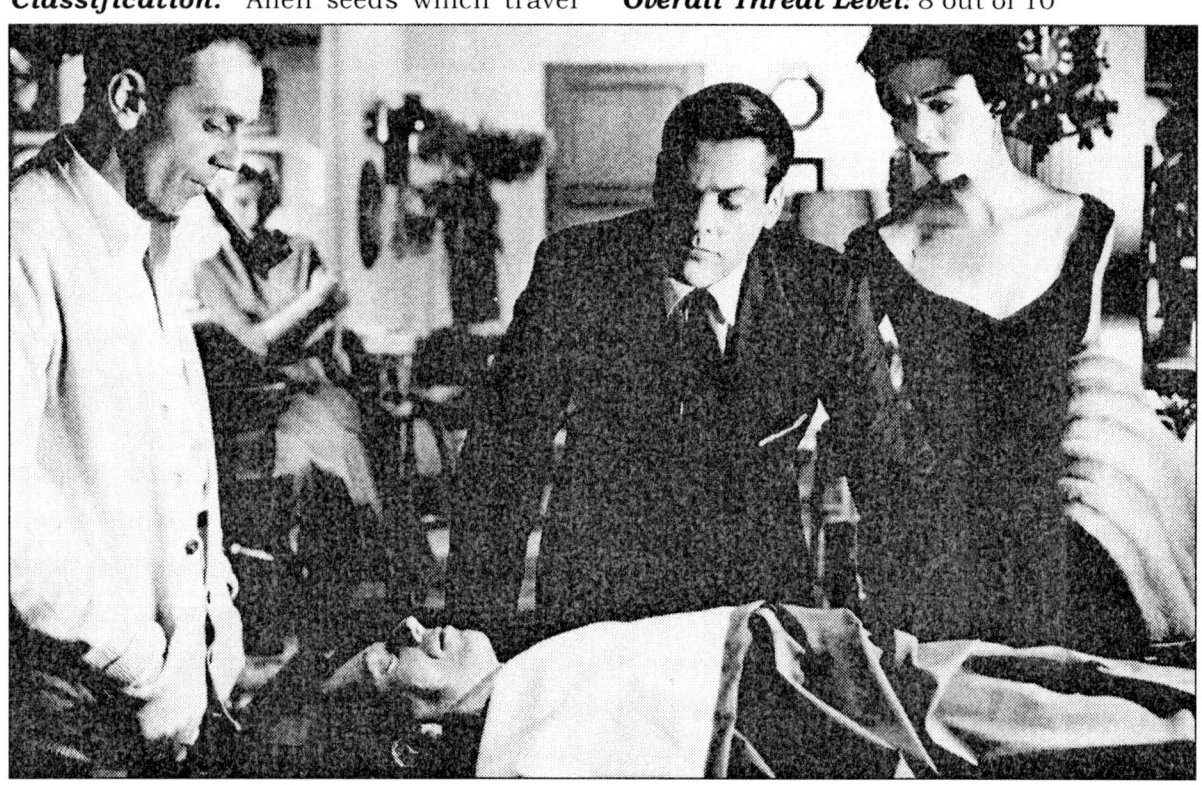

Favorite Scene: When Dr. Bennell witnesses the formation of his own double in one of the alien pods

Synopsis: Dr. Miles Bennell (Kevin McCarthy) returns home to Santa Mira following a medical convention to learn he's been in heavy demand by locals who refuse to see anyone but him. When he gets to his office, however, they've all left. Little by little, he begins to receive complaints from those he encounters that some of their loved ones aren't who they appear to be. He dismisses the idea at first until he's shown a human body that looks vaguely like his friend but without any distinguishing features or fingerprints. After finding another of these strange bodies, he begins to realize something unnatural is going on. His suspicions are cemented after he observes a figure emerging from a giant, puss-filled plant pod in a greenhouse. Upon this discovery, Dr. Bennell sends his friends away to get help, while he and his ex-girlfriend Becky Driscoll (Dana Wynter) stay behind to deal with the doppelgängers. They find themselves pursued as fugitives by the replicated police force and come to discover that the aliens replace their victims when they fall asleep.

Dr. Bennell and Becky try everything from knocking out the aliens by injecting them with drugs, to impersonating overtaken locals, to ultimately hiding out in an old tunnel to escape the body snatchers, all while forcing themselves to stay awake. Unfortunately, Becky ends up succumbing when sleep overwhelms her, leaving Dr. Bennell as the lone survivor who escapes to warn those outside of the terrible things at work in Santa Mira.

My Take: Adapted from the Jack Finney novel *The Body Snatchers* (1954), this black and white feature offers up some decent chills as the leads uncover the mysterious goings-on in the town and are forced to flee for their lives from it. There's a bit of romance involved as Dr. Bennell attempts to rekindle his relationship with his former girlfriend Becky who's recently returned to Santa Mira following a divorce. There can be no arguing that this was a hugely influential film which paved the way to many remakes, imitators and homages. Incidentally, the 1978 remake includes an excellent cameo by Kevin McCarthy which hints at it being a direct tie-in to this one.

Rating: 7 out of 10

FIVE MILLION YEARS TO EARTH
aka QUATERMASS AND THE PIT
(Hammer Films, 1967)

Classification: Large, locust-like race of alien beings

Method of Conquest: Genetic and psychic manipulation of indigenous life forms

Deadliness Factor: 7 out of 10
(Without physical bodies of their own, they're somewhat reliant on human survival.)

Characteristics/Motivation: The psychic survival of their race, colonization of new planets, and the eradication of genetic mutations

Necessities for Survival: Those who are immune to the aliens' mental influence must have the bravery and force of will to mount a resistance. Also, the aliens' vulnerability to iron should be something easy to bring against them.

Overall Threat Level: 7 out of 10

Favorite Scene: The grainy thought-projection video of the Martians leaping and hopping about during their genetic cleansing scene

Synopsis: Professor Quatermass (Andrew Keir) becomes embroiled in an investigation when he accompanies military officer Colonel Breen (Julian Glover) to the Hobbs End subway system in London where a group of men digging a tunnel extension have uncovered long buried skeletal remains of ancient, ape-like humans. Paleontologist Dr. Matthew Roney (James Donald) estimates them to be over five million years old. An alien spacecraft made of an unknown metal is also excavated. One of the workmen claims to see a "hideous dwarf" while inside a small compartment of the craft. Upon researching the Hobbs Lane area's history, Quatermass and Dr. Roney's assistant Barbara Judd (Barbara Shelley) come across historical references to strange disturbances there.

When access to the craft's interior is finally achieved, it reveals a honeycombed, crystalline chamber containing several bizarre-looking, horned, locust-like creatures the size of small children. One of the bodies is removed for further study leading Quatermass to theorize it may be of Martian origin and that they could have traveled to Earth when their planet was dying. They might even have made genetic alterations to the lifeforms they encountered to increase their intellect, essentially being responsible for their eventual evolution into Homo Sapiens.

When Quatermass interrogates an excavator named Sladden, who's been driven half-mad after being assailed by a telekinetic force while working near the craft, the worker claims to have seen hundreds of the hideous Martians coming for

him—leaping all about beneath a sky that isn't our own. Quatermass believes the man was accessing ancient, racial memory of life on Mars millions of years ago. Using a device that can display mental images, Barbara Judd's mind shows horrific scenes from the genetic irradiation of mutations in the alien hives on Mars.

When Colonel Breen and his superiors decide to show the spacecraft on national television and claim it isn't Martian but part of a Nazi propaganda campaign, things go haywire as the terrible alien influence is projected out to the general public, driving everyone into a frenzy, including Quatermass, who only breaks free of the madness by the intervention of Dr. Roney, who seems immune to its effects.

Amidst the chaos, buildings and streets begin to collapse as an enormous, spectral silhouette of a Martian being forms in the skyline, the focus of all the alien energies. Recalling how devils were reputed to be vulnerable to iron and believing these aliens were the catalyst for those legends, Roney climbs

atop a giant crane and maneuvers it into the giant energy-beast, sacrificing himself to destroy it.

My Take: There are several nice horror nods in this film, such as noting how the word Hob, which is part of the town's name, is another term for the devil, and finding a witchcraft symbol etched into the bulkhead of the spacecraft. The details they uncover surrounding the area during the winter of 1341 are effective as well, as it claims the religious people of that time struggled against "an outbreak of evil at Hobbs Lane" which included the appearance of "imps and demons" and "foul noises sent by the devil" to afflict the charcoal burners who'd recently arrived. While the insectoid aliens look a little too stiff, I still love their creepy appearance. The grainy images of the hordes of Martians recorded from the stored memories of Judd is deliciously bizarre and unforgettable.

Writer Nigel Kneale does a superb job releasing the flow of information at a perfect pace as Quatermass and his associates undertake research and experimentation to get

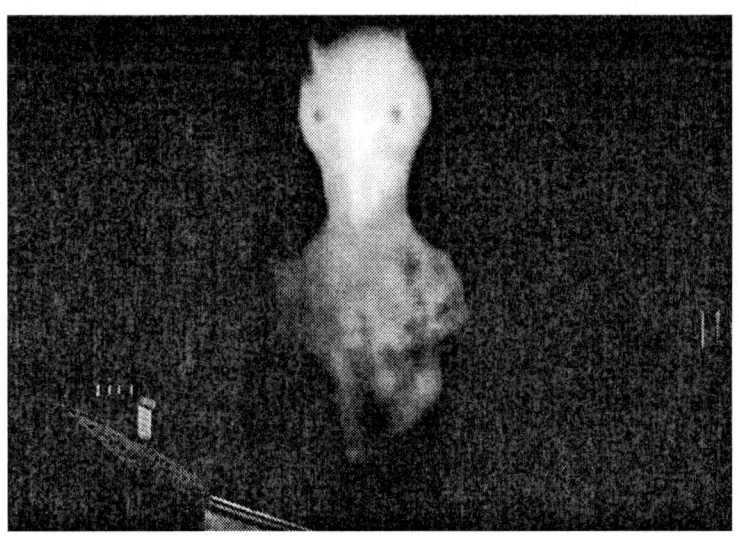

to the bottom of everything. The actor playing the workman Sladden is terrific at portraying the madness he experiences during the psychic visions and telekinetic storm he endures. I also found it interesting that it's ultimately Dr. Roney, and not the film's main protagonist, who ends up saving the world, which isn't something you see that often. This one is highly recommended!

Rating: 8 out of 10

THE THING
(Universal, 1982)

Classification: Monstrous, alien creature capable of assimilating any organic lifeform

Method of Conquest: Gaining the trust of local inhabitants by taking on the appearance of people they know before killing and replacing them

Deadliness Factor: 9 out of 10

Characteristics/Motivation: Its goal is to kill and replace every living being on the planet. It displays high intelligence and understanding of human motivations, which it uses to lure and destroy. It is unswayed by empathy or compassion for its victims.

Necessities for Survival: The ability to isolate anyone who may have come into contact with the alien from the general population in order to keep the pool of potential impostors small enough to identify it. Possessing the capacity to perform blood tests and access to lots of fire-based weaponry are also a must.

Overall Threat Level: 9 out of 10
(Crafty, elusive, and very hard to kill while be-

ing a remorseless murderer)

Favorite Scene: When Norris (Charles Hallahan) drops of an apparent heart attack but is then revealed as the Thing in grotesque and horrific fashion, ending with his detached head growing spider legs while attempting to flee.

Synopsis: A Norwegian helicopter attempting to shoot a dog that's running from it lands in front of an American research base in the Antarctic. Their haste to kill the dog, which runs in amongst the Americans, results in the death of both Norwegians as well as their helicopter being destroyed. Unaware of what drove the Norwegians to such a maddened state, the Americans take the unharmed dog into their camp and eventually place it into their own dog kennels. R. J. MacReady (Kurt Russell) takes a few others in their helicopter over to the Norwegian's base where they find the remains of a bizarre, twisted monstrosity, which they bring back to study. The new dog ends up transforming into a hideous, tentacled beast which begins killing the other dogs and taking on their forms. The workers come upon it and kill it before it completes the transformation. Blair (Wilford Brimley) examines the monster's remains and begins to worry if anyone from their crew might have been replaced during the day when the dog had free reign to move about the camp.

The crew locate a space saucer partially excavated from beneath the ice. They estimate it must have been buried there for at least 100,000 years. Blair quickly begins to assess just how dire their situation may be in dealing with something which can so expertly replicate others, and what it would mean to the rest of the world should it escape. He sets about destroying their chopper and any chance they have of outside communication, or ability to leave the base. He also tries to kill the others since he doesn't know who might already be compromised. MacReady and some of the others subdue him and lock him in a shed both for his safety and their own.

Not knowing who can be trusted, the group turns on each other, arguing, casting accusations and attempting to arm themselves. More die before MacReady forces the remaining men to take a blood test to determine who is and who is not still human.

With their numbers dwindling and the creature still free, they decide the only thing left to do is to make sure nothing, including themselves, ever leaves in order to ensure mankind's survival. While preparing to blow up the base, MacReady is confronted by an enormous version of the Thing. Luckily, it fails to stop him, and he succeeds in detonating everything, including the creature. As the movie ends, only MacReady and Childs (Keith David) remain alive, as everything burns around them amidst a frigid, arctic storm. With no way of escaping, the two sit and wait to die.

My Take: This is one of my all-time favorite movies. The creature effects are outstanding, even by today's standards, and the acting is top notch. Having a director with a genuine love of the genre, as John Carpenter has, closes the loop in creating an absolute masterpiece. This film was

definitely before its time however, as it originally flopped at the box office. Since then, it has gone on to gain a huge following and is now widely considered an iconic, sci-fi/horror gem. Based on the John W. Campbell Jr. story "Who Goes There?", it superbly combines elements of the locked room murder mystery with one of the scariest creatures ever to appear on the big screen. It's tough to find anything to criticize about this one. Being filmed in 1982, the computer technology at the research station looks archaic today, but that wasn't the case when it originally aired. My appreciation for this movie can be surmised in my overall rating, below, as this is the first one I've reviewed thus far to earn a perfect rating.

Rating: 10 out of 10

THE PUPPET MASTERS
(Buena Vista Pictures, 1994)

Classification: Highly intelligent, parasitic, hive mind

Method of Conquest: By attaching themselves to their victim's back, thrusting a piercing tentacle into the brain while a series of hooks latch into the spine, allowing it to take complete control over the host's body

Deadliness Factor: 7 out of 10 *(they'd rather take control over their hosts' bodies than destroy them)*

Characteristics/Motivation: To take over stronger, longer lived human bodies

Necessities for Survival: To not be too shy

to ask people to take off their shirts in order to prove they aren't being controlled, as well as access to someone with encephalitis

Overall Threat Level: 8 out of 10 *(Their ability to strategize and learn from their mistakes only adds to their threat level.)*

Favorite Scene: When The Old Man is interrogating a restrained Sam with the alien still attached to his back

Synopsis: A top secret branch of the CIA sends out agents to investigate reports of an alien space ship that's landed in rural Iowa. The situation is deemed relevant enough to bring the organization's leader, known as The Old Man (Donald Sutherland, who himself starred in the 1978 remake of *Invasion of the Body Snatchers*), personally to the site. His son Sam Nivens (Eric Thal), who's also an agent, and Jarvis (Richard Belzer) go with him. A NASA expert on alien biology, Dr. Mary Sefton (Julie Warner), is brought in to assist.

With the area locals now claiming the whole thing was a hoax perpetrated by a group of teenage boys who'd constructed a giant, fake craft in the woods, they go to the

news station to talk with the director about the initial claims that the space craft was real. Realizing the investigators are onto something, he pulls a gun, but a quicker Sam shoots him dead first. A strange slug-like creature immediately detaches itself from the director's back and attempts to flee, but they're able to capture it before making their own daring escape from the townspeople who attempt to stop them.

Dr. Sefton's autopsy of the alien parasite reveals that they take control of their victims by piercing their brains with a tentacle and using hooks to attach to their spines. When The Old Man notices Agent Jarvis has stopped smoking, they discover one of the aliens is attached to him. They finally manage to subdue him, but not before the creature has moved on to someone else.

During the commotion Sam is secretly taken over as well. He employs his government standing to obtain a box of eggs which unfold to reveal more of the aliens. These are used to infect several Secret Service agents in attempts to take over the President of the United States. It's only through The Old Man's interference that the plan fails.

They capture Sam and interrogate him with the alien still attached. Speaking through Sam, the alien says they want to take over our bodies because they are stronger and last longer than their own. When asked how many of them there are, it replies "only one." It then attempts to kill Sam by shutting down his body, something they narrowly prevent from happening. With the parasite removed, Sam tells his father the alien had thoughts of its own which kept focusing on a hive they must return to on a regular basis. They determine that if they can locate the hive, they may be able to stop the invasion from there.

Sam is horrified to find Dr. Sefton has one attached to her when they go to his place. He succeeds in killing another which she attempts to place on him, but she manages to escape.

Having located the hive, Sam infiltrates it wearing a device that makes the aliens think he's one of them. He finds a bunch of people standing hooked up to tentacles that droop down from the ceiling, transferring their thoughts. He throws some grenades and

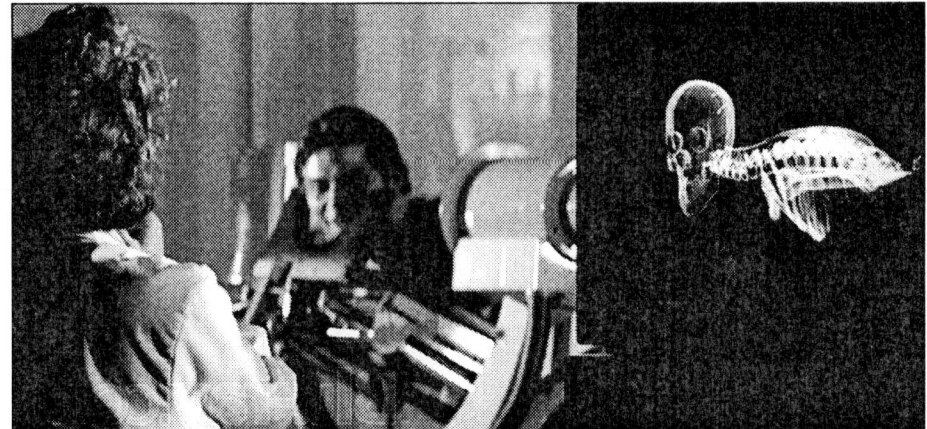

escapes, taking Dr. Sefton with him. He removes her parasite, and she tells him about a young boy which the aliens kept separate because he had some kind of infection of which they were afraid. They go back in and take the child with them.

It turns out the boy has encephalitis, which is far deadlier to the aliens whose bodies are 60% brain as opposed to humans which are only about 5%. Once this is discovered, they infect the aliens with it, causing them to die out.

My Take: This movie, based on a story by Robert A. Heinlein, includes some of my favorite actors in the likes of Donald Sutherland and Julie Warner, both of whom shine in every scene in which they appear. While Eric Thal does a serviceable job in his role, he isn't at the same level of the other two leads. The film keeps the tension up throughout as the aliens methodically take over people in rapidly increasing numbers. These aliens are intelligent and seek out those who hold positions of power so they can better exert their control. Some of the eeriest moments occur during the times when the aliens are communicating directly with the agents either through the interrogation of humans they've taken over or through ones attached to apes typing on a keyboard. The aliens are of an interesting design, but at times the way they use their whipping tentacles to lasso themselves about through the air Spider-Man-style comes off less scary and more amusing. Still, I enjoyed that these aliens were able to put intelligent plans in motion throughout. Overall, featuring great actors, a great script, and decent special effects, I very much enjoyed this film.

Rating: 8 out of 10

Triple-S Operator Robert Marquand had a reputation
as one of the system's best troubleshooters—but he never
thought it would come looking for him at home on Saturn Base.

SPACE ZOMBIES

by Marc Vun Kannon

ROBERT MARQUAND HEARD THE DOOR OPEN BEHIND HIM AS HE STOOD IN THE OBSERVATION LOUNGE OVERLOOKING THE SHUTTLE LANDING BAY. He didn't turn, merely saying "Good day, Simon."

Not at all surprised to be identified so easily, at least not by a Triple-S operator, Simon remarked, "Good Evening, Robert. We switched over a few minutes back." On the Solar System's most remote outpost, day and night were mostly a matter of convention.

Simon stepped forward to join Marquand at the window, but he didn't lean on the sill, or press his nose against it, the way Marquand did. "I guess you had other things on your mind, though." He chuckled. "If you were any closer to the glass you'd punch a hole through it."

Marquand pulled his head back a little in annoyance. "It's not glass, Simon, and it's a foot thick."

Simon rolled his eyes, but all he said was, "Sorry, Operator."

"Aren't you supposed to be down there?" asked Marquand.

"Normally, yes," said Simon, "I'm wearing my med-tech hat today, thanks to you." Saturn Base was built on Mimas, one of its moons. As far distant as they were, most of the people there had multiple roles to play. Even the commander seconded herself to Hydroponics, while Simon was just as good taking care of the people that rode in shuttles as he was the shuttles themselves. He pointed out the window at the spacecraft currently setting down. "They *are*

carrying the extremely experimental treatment for your extremely partner with the extremely advanced case of Clevinger's Syndrome, aren't they?"

"That's 'extremely' Clevinger's Syndrome."

"Ah," said Simon, nodding. "I knew I missed one."

Marquand let his head fall, until it tapped against the glass. It was still cold, no matter what it was made of. "Sorry, Simon," he said. "I've been a little dour lately, haven't I?"

"Um, focused," said Simon. "Focused, I would say. Like a laser, you know, burning little holes in people."

Marquand gusted out a laugh that seemed to push his head away from the non-glass again. "Well, fortunately they have you here, to patch them up." He gestured with his chin at the shuttle. "They have the treatment, yes, but not because Miss Carter is my partner."

"Uh, Operator, Miss Carter's been out here a long time. This is the first shuttle with a treatment that I've ever seen, and most of us can't help thinking it's because of who you are." Which was why they put up with Marquand's dourness, other than the fact that he was 'their' Operator. Everyone liked Miss Carter.

The son of Triple-S' Director of Personnel Fitness shook his head, standing straight. Not that his father wasn't above a little minor string-pulling. He'd kept his son on Saturn Base, after all, out of the normal rotational sequence. That could be justified, since Miss Carter couldn't leave, and Triple-S didn't break up partners. *This* matter was neither minor nor routine, and Joseph Marquand would not have been made the head of PF if he'd been the sort to allow his son's involvement to sway his judgment. "If the best test subject was somewhere else, that shuttle would be somewhere else. My…connection… to the case only makes her first among equals."

"No complaints from us, Operator," said Simon, raising his hands. "We'll take what we can get." Saturn Base wasn't used to getting much, although that was changing. A quarantine facility was already in the works, and much else that would turn 'Saturn Base' into a much more respectable 'Port of Saturn'.

"Don't talk that way, Simon," said Marquand. "You're the door to the rest of the Universe now. Miss Carter's voice is often the last thing those ships hear before the darkness, and the first thing they hear on return." *It's not just me.* Half of those crews were in love

with her for her voice alone, which Marquand could readily understand. It had certainly kept him going in a dark hour.

Simon dropped the subject, because he was smart, looking out the window instead. "You think they're ready for us?"

They weren't, Simon knew it, and Marquand knew Simon knew it, but he let the gambit stand. "They will be, by the time we get down there."

THE CAPTAIN OF THE SHUTTLE was tall, dark-skinned, female, and polite. The passenger was…none of these things. "Good evening, Operator," he said, his voice deep and hard. "Murdered any new species lately?"

"The night is young, Dr. Chen," said Marquand. He didn't bother to extend a hand. His introductory salvo aside, Dr. Chen had spent far too much time working with microbial life forms to be comfortable touching, or being touched. This suited just about everybody who knew him.

"Try to save me a sample next time."

"The last sample ate the researcher."

"Hm. Sloppy technique. It should have been the other way 'round." Dr. Chen turned his gaze upon poor Simon. "You are the medical technician, correct?"

Simon only nodded.

"Pray treat my equipment with more respect than the last imbecile," said Chen, with a negligent wave. "The clumsy fool let it shift."

Simon and Robert watched the crewman being carried off the ship, for a date with a bone-bonder. "That seems unlikely," said Marquand.

"And yet his foot is crushed." He turned back to Simon. "My subject is ready?"

Simon bristled. "Your *patient* is being moved to Medical as you stand there."

"Transport?" said Chen, sounding mildly curious. "Isn't this person local?" There were no other human habitations closer than Jupiter.

"Yes," said Simon, already suspicious of

anything that interested this man.

Chen smiled. "Marvelous."

Simon turned to Marquand. "I'm getting the gear now."

Robert didn't like the look on Simon's face. "It's for Anne."

Simon glared at Chen, nodded sharply, and left.

"Come, Operator," said Chen. "Take me to the lab so I can prepare. The sooner this whole exercise is over, the better."

Marquand had to agree.

THE PROCEDURE HAD BEEN a nightmare in every way. The injections had to be direct, to a number of nerve clusters throughout Miss Carter's body. The pain was expected to be severe, so severe she had to be somnolized beforehand and would remain so for several hours afterward.

Robert Marquand could do nothing about any of it, except watch through the too-small windows of the treatment/recovery room, as Dr. Chen lifted the first of his too-long needles and placed it against Anne's exposed back, pushing firmly.

Even somnolized, Miss Carter moaned.

"Increase the intensity," said Chen, and Simon, out from underfoot as instructed, hastened to comply.

OUTSIDE MEDICAL, in the darkened halls, a figure shuffled slowly forward. Behind it smears of blood marked every step, but they were not why it lurched forward. When it got close enough, it flinched away from the lights, moving off into the shadows of another hallway.

MARQUAND'S IMPLANT CHIMED. He'd forwarded all contacts to it, for the duration. **Message incoming.**

He pounced on the distraction. **This is Marquand.**

This is Captain Faraji, of the Midgard, sir.

Midgard? Right, the shuttle. **What can I do for you, Captain?**

One of my crew is missing.

Once Saturn Base had been the least popular destination in the system. Now it had some comforts to offer a crew with time to kill. **How can you tell?**

This crewman shouldn't be anywhere, Operator, other than his berth. His foot was recently bonded.

Understood. Regenerating nerves, softened bone. The nerves could probably take a short walk, but the newly-bonded bones would be too brittle to support weight for a while, even here, where a failed attempt at an ITB drive had turned out to be a decent artificial gravity generator. The population enjoyed weight levels significantly higher than the less-than-one percent of Earth normal that Mimas provided on its own, too much for some.

Still, Marquand expected the guy to be out and about, enjoying his leave somewhere. People can be stupid that way. **I'll contact Base security, have them do a sweep.**

Thank you, Operator.

Message terminated.

IN THE SHADOWS, something walked, leaving a bloody trail that someone from the night watch easily discovered. Muffled voices spoke into comm units as hand-held lights swept back and forth, converging.

Finally they were all there, gathered around the shivering, cringing figure of a man, pinned in their beams. "Bring up the lights."

MESSAGE INCOMING.

"That was quick," said Marquand to the unconscious form of his partner. He stood and left the room, out of an absurd impulse to give her some privacy. **Marquand here.**

We need you down here, Operator. We found your man. He's on his way to the cooler now.

Marquand couldn't quite place the term, too many options. He chose the most hopeful one. **Confinement?**

Morgue. It's a bloodbath down here, and most of it's his.

I'm on my way.

THE SCENE WAS A MESS of toppled men and broken equipment when Marquand arrived. The low lights made the blood look like something it wasn't, but Marquand knew the smell for what it was. He also knew the smell of death, of a man on the security detail, as well as the man from the shuttle.

The other members of the security team were merely stunned, and already recovering. Marquand helped them to their feet. "What happened here, Quigley?"

"Wish I knew," said Quigley. "The medical team took the body, patched up Manny's leg—"

Manny was not in the room. "What was wrong with it?"

"The guy's foot was a bloody wreck, but he kicked Manny with it anyway. Bone sticking out cut him up pretty bad."

"Ouch." Manny and the dead guy both.

"Yeah. Manny was supposed to go to Medical when we were done, but he never finished, none of us did. He kept complaining about the lights, trying to turn them off. We tried to stop him and it was like the dead guy all over again."

"Except Manny wasn't injured."

Quigley felt his jaw. "No."

"And he's not here."

"No."

CAPTAIN FARAJI MET MARQUAND at the ramp. "The story you have told me makes no sense, Operator."

"That's very true," said Marquand. "I want to see his berth, and I want to see what injured his foot."

"You have all that," said Faraji. "Your man took away Chen's pile of gear, there is no more to see here. The space has been decontaminated. I can show you his berth, if you like, but it is just a berth." She gestured courteously to enter.

Marquand stepped inside. "Was your man under medical observation?"

"He was told to stay in his berth for several hours, Operator. What part of that requires observation?"

"The part that would make my life easier if he was," said Marquand. The shuttle was small, the berth not far from the airlock. Marquand inspected the bedding. "You changed all of this?"

"Alas, yes."

The Operator had been paying attention on the way in. "No scanners between here and the lock. The foot could have held up until he got out. Dock sensors show movement in the proper time frame, but not in the correct thermal range."

There had been no signs of fever. "Too hot?" asked Faraji.

Marquand shook his head. "Too cold. Night sensing was configured for human normal temperatures, and no one told them to change that configuration for anything cooler, such as incoming uncontrolled biological samples."

Faraji didn't pretend to misunderstand. "Chen said his materials were inert."

A guess, but a good one. "And when did he say this?"

"When my man's foot was injured. A sample case also took damage, and a packet of Chen's treatment materials ruptured."

Shifted cargo, a wounded man, they wouldn't have kept the damage confined to the room. "You should have gone into some kind of quarantine."

"Correct," said Faraji, with the speed of someone looking at a Board of Review in the near future. "However, Chen produced his certifications, supporting his claim that his materials were no danger. He also pointed out the severity of his patient's condition and suggested that any delay, much less a quarantine, would mean her death."

'His patient' when it suited his purposes. "Her condition isn't, hopefully *wasn't*, as

severe as all that."

Faraji shrugged. "Alas that you were not there to override the medical specialist. We analyzed the ruptured sample and found it to be as he described, so we sanitized the area and continued on."

"Send me that analysis, please."

An Operator's request was an order to other men. "Of course. Would you have anything else of us, Operator? The good doctor's cargo space, perhaps?"

Which had been washed down twice, from the sound of it, and the clock was ticking on Anne's recovery. "No," he said. "I think I'll have a talk with our 'good doctor' instead."

ON THE WAY BACK TO MEDICAL his implant chimed again. He was getting tired of the sound. **Marquand here.**

Sir, this is Biggs in Security. I got an alert when none of the night crew checked in on time. Last callout was yours. Do you know where they are?

Marquand sighed, but the implant didn't pick that up. **No, but I can guess.**

Sir?

Enough was enough. **Increase illumination base-wide by fifty percent, Biggs, and follow the shouting. Better yet, configure the scanners for below-norm human temperatures. Be careful, the last two didn't sound all that rational. And whatever you do, don't let them bleed on you.**

"BLOOD-BORNE?" asked Chen. He lifted his tools, with their very long needles. "Don't be ridiculous, Operator. My materials would be attacked by the subject's—"

"Patient's."

One does not roll one's eyes at either Operators or partners, but Chen looked like he wanted to. "Very well, attacked by the patient's immune system like any other pathogen."

"Why would that be?" asked Marquand. "You told the captain that it was inert."

"On the floor, it was," said Chen, gesturing at their feet. "She asked the wrong question. In the bloodstream it could become active, but the immune system would overwhelm that small amount without even so much as a fever."

He lied. That would make Faraji happy, at least. Marquand remembered the blood-covered condition of the security team's uniforms. "It appears the real world disagrees with your assessment."

Chen grunted an unhappy agreement.

The door slid open, admitting Simon to his domain. "You called me, Operator?"

"Yes, Simon," said Marquand. He addressed the doctor. "You will provide those certifications you're so proud of and the research behind them to my associate here."

Marquand turned to said associate. "Simon, take those documents and the analysis Captain Faraji's people did, go in there—" he pointed at the room where Miss Carter lay unconscious "—seal the door, and keep it sealed until you can give me some kind of a real-world assessment of what this stuff does."

Simon looked a little overwhelmed. "Uh, Operator…?"

"And what it might do to Miss Carter," added Marquand.

That stiffened Simon's resolve. "You'll have it, Operator." He looked at Chen expectantly.

Chen was looking at Marquand. "You're letting this…this… technician sit in judgment of my work?"

"Simon's as real-world as they come," said Marquand. "Records. Now."

Chen went to his gear and produced a case. He put it in Simon's hands, saying, "I must protest…"

"Of course you must," said Robert, blithely. "Might make you look a bit petty, though, don't you think?" He looked at Simon, who walked to the recovery room. "Keep in touch."

CHEN'S NOTES CONSISTED mostly of video

records, himself performing a test or an experiment while dictating what he was doing and why. Simon was already tired of the sound of his voice, and the video didn't help. There was something wrong with the lighting, but if he corrected the settings the image was too dim. For some reason the doctor had over-sensitized the recordings, rather than turn the lights up. Why would he do that?

Simon looked up, gazing around the room he was in. The lights had gone dim, but Miss Carter had already been resting comfortably. She hadn't made a sound since he entered, which struck him as odd. He'd had to care for a lot of people in pain, and they usually made some kind of noise even while they were asleep. The somnolizer's induced sleep-like state didn't prevent that, unlike true sedation.

Going back to the records, Simon did a quick check for any references to pain. Nothing came up. He tried 'discomfort' and 'distress' instead. Still nothing.

The Operator said to keep in touch, Simon kept in touch. He touched the contact button, speaking a name that the system had probably heard a lot today. "Marquand."

After a slight pause, he heard a terse reply. *"Marquand here."*

"This is Simon."

"What is it, Simon?"

"A couple of weird things in these records, Operator," said Simon. "Didn't the doctor say that the procedure was painful?"

"He did."

"I'm not seeing anything here to back that claim. The subjects don't appear to be in any pain, and a quick check shows no references to painful reactions of any kind."

"So why is Miss Carter somnolized?"

"I don't know, but I'm pretty sure it's not for the reason he gave us."

"Should we wake her up?" asked Marquand after a brief pause.

"I'd say no," said Simon. "Whatever his reason, I'm pretty sure Chen has one. It might be a bad one, but if we terminate it before

completion the consequences might be even worse for her."

"Fine." Marquand didn't sound fine, or happy, but he'd chosen Simon for his medical expertise and was living with it. *"What else have you got?"*

Something made a loud noise in the outer room. Simon said, "Hold on, Operator", and activated the monitor to see what it was.

Dr. Chen stood, backed up against a table. A number of men in blood-soaked clothing approached him, their bodies moving awkwardly, twitching and uncertain. The faces were human, the expressions were not.

"Operator! They're here!" Simon increased the volume from the speaker.

"Finally," said Chen.

DR. CHEN PICKED UP an injector. "You are abominations," he said to the spasmodically approaching men. "You must be ended."

The men attacked as one. Chen pressed his injector against one of them as he slid past the others.

SIMON HEARD A BELLOW through the door. "Operator, he's killing them!" He ran to the door, but it was sealed, and all he could do was look out at the carnage through the small windows.

"I'm not sure they aren't already dead, Simon."

Two more men came at Chen from behind, but somehow he knew they were there and slithered between them. He pressed his injector against a second man, his face calm as his victim cried out and fell against a rack, thrashing.

The rack came down with the man under it, but Chen lost his injector.

"He's down, he's down," shouted Simon. "The doctor is down!"

The speaker was silent, though, and Simon knew the Operator had better things to be paying attention to right then. Motion with any kind of speed in low-gee takes a lot of care and control. Watching the savage way the remaining attackers were pounding the doctor's body, Simon also knew that no matter where he was, Marquand wouldn't get there in time.

If only he could think. If only he could see! Lights!

He ran to the secondary panel, mate to the main board out in the other room. Closing his eyes, he twisted the dial on the illumination panel as high as it could go.

Outside, the pounding stopped and the shrieking started.

Inside, Miss Carter moaned softly, twisting a bit. The somnolizer started to beep. Simon heard them both, fumbled his way to a cabinet and grabbed a light blanket. He flung it out, draping it over Miss Carter from head to toe, and she settled. The somnolizer light went back to green.

The door was closer, so Simon went to squint through the windows. Outside, blurry shapes moved at frantic speeds, not attacking the doctor except to stumble over him as they tried to escape the lights. Eventually one of them found the exit and the other one followed.

Unfortunately, the doors to Medical didn't lock, and Simon couldn't go out there to barricade them either. He went back to his console. "Operator, they're gone! I turned up the lights and that drove them off."

"No surprise. Keep it that way. I'm almost there."

"The lights caused Miss Carter some distress, too. I threw a blanket over her and she's better now."

"I'm almost—"

Marquand hit the doors at speed, killing the rest of his momentum in a controlled crash against the far wall, which was, of course, padded. Lots of people came to Medical in a rush, for some reason.

"Doctor Chen," he said, crouching over the fallen man, "Are you injured? Can you hear me?"

"Yes, Operator," said Chen in a strangely flat voice. "We can hear you."

Marquand pulled back. "Who is 'we'?"

"Please," whined Chen, "The lights, they hurt us."

Marquand moved back to where he had been, blocking the most direct lights from falling on Chen. "Who are you?"

Chen opened his eyes, to the barest slits. "We... are Chen."

"Chen is 'I', not 'we'."

"We are Chen," said Chen, breathing harder, faster. "Chen is not-we. He feeds us, we feed him. He helps us, we help him. He lives... we... live..."

"And when Chen dies?" asked Marquand, as Chen's breathing slowed.

A last breath slid out. "We..."

Marquand looked up, saw Simon staring at him through the little window. He went to the door and pressed the comm button. "What did you see, Simon?"

"He called them abominations, they certainly acted like it," said Simon, pointing out the window. "He killed those two with an injector, but he lost it when the rack fell. The others beat him almost to death."

Marquand went and lifted the rack, finding the injector on the floor, next to Quigley, very dead, very ugly. Whatever was in the injector was toxic to whatever was in them. He went back to the comm. "Simon, go back over those records, look for anything in them about any form of symbiosis, good, bad, or indifferent."

"You think the doctor had a bug? And he brought it here?"

Marquand frowned a bit at the vehemence in the man's tone. If anyone had the right to be angry, it was him, and he wasn't about to claim it. "He's dead already, Simon, a little late to be throttling him."

"I don't know, Operator, I think if word got out I might just be the first person in the line." They all had a stake in the integrity of their environment, after all.

"Let's see what he's done to Anne before

we start noising it about, shall we?"

Simon accepted that. "I'll do my part. You go do yours."

Marquand raised the injector. "Doing it."

SIMON STEPPED DOWN off the chair he'd been standing on, after trying to cover the lights in the recovery room with some of the extra sheets. They were hurting his eyes, but they were hurting Miss Carter even more, and he really wanted to be able to take that blanket away.

Or did he?

He didn't know what Chen had looked like or sounded like, before whatever had happened to him. So far all he'd seen of these bugs were the people they were inside of, Chen and those horrible security guys. Chen had called them abominations, but was he any better? He wasn't beating people to death, but maybe what he was doing to them was worse.

Simon looked at the blanket, the shield. Not Miss Carter.

A light turned from green to blinking yellow, the somnolizer shutting off. He let it.

"Simon."

Simon backed away to the console, and hit the switch. "How's the bug-hunt going?"

"One down…"

"One to go," said Simon. "I only saw two." Not, God help us, three.

"Let's hope that two is all there are," said Marquand. *"How are things on your end?"*

Right, the…research. He checked his notes. "Obscure," said Simon. "Long or short version?"

"Short."

"Doctor Chen was a xeno-biologist until an accident that should have left him paralyzed didn't. Switched over to his current area of specialization right after."

"I thought you said it was obscure."

"I thought you said you wanted the short version."

"I did," said Marquand. *"Great. Another do-gooder who broke the rules."*

And that was the good version. "Does this mean I have to change my opinion of the guy?"

"I'D WAIT UNTIL MISS CARTER wakes up," said Marquand. Probably not even then. The biggest saints in the world weren't especially nice people.

Will do, said Simon. **Good luck.**

Marquand looked at the injector. Kill his friends to kill the bugs, kill the bugs and kill his friends? Hardly what he'd call luck. He moved into another dimly-lit hall, injector at the ready. He only had one charge left, but whatever his friends had become, it wasn't smart.

He looked at the injector. *No, they're not that smart, are they?*

He activated his implant. **Destination?** it asked.

Shuttle Midgard, Captain Faraji.

"SO WHAT DID YOU DO?" asked Simon.

"We captured it," said Marquand. "I got the crew of the shuttle to move all the exercise treadmills into the halls around where the last abomination was. Eventually we found it walking steadily, going nowhere. After that it was just a matter of getting it safely stored away in the shuttle's cargo hold. We'll have the whole thing cleaned up before day shift begins."

Simon pointed. "And all these guys?"

Marquand didn't turn around. "They're gathering the bodies and the doctor's materials, to go back to Triple-S for investigation and research. His work may have been unsanctioned and unethical, but what's done is done. At this point, it would be more unethical *not* to use it, as the doctor intended." Marquand took a deep breath. "So, are you going to open the door now?"

"I don't know," said Simon. "You didn't kill the abomination, so points to you for that, but…"

"Simon, let him in," said Miss Carter,

laughing. "It's just Robert."

"Okay," grumbled Simon, but he released the seal on the door.

Marquand pushed against the door before the mechanism was fully released. "A bit overboard there on the security, don't you think?" he said, shaking Simon's hand.

"You said to protect her," said Simon. "How was I to know?"

"You did great," said Robert, looking away.

"How's—Anne! You're standing? Walking on your own?" He went and swept her up in his arms, spinning around. "This is terrific!"

"Robert, please," said Anne, cupping his face in her hands. "There's no need to shout." She kissed him lightly on the lips.

"We're not deaf."

👽 👽 👽

Marc Vun Kannon, after surviving his teen age years, entered Hofstra University. Five years later, he exited with a BA in philosophy and a wife. He still has both, but the wife is more useful. Since then he almost accumulated a PhD in philosophy and has acquired a second BA in Computer Science. After dabbling in fulfilling pursuits such as stock boy and gas station attendant, he found his spiritual home as a software support engineer, for CAMP Systems International.

Marc puts his degrees in Philosophy and Computer Science to good use writing stories about strange things that happen to ordinary people. His wife and three children think it's harmless enough, and it keeps him out of trouble. As a philosopher (his first novel, Unbinding the Stone, demanded he write it while he was in Graduate School), his main interest is in the characters, and as a Computer geek his technique is to follow the character's and story's logic to 'grow' a story organically. His main rule when writing is to not do again what he's already seen done before, resulting in books that are hard to describe. Visit Marc at authorguy.wordpress.com

Todd Treichel's

HOW WEIRD IS THAT?

BEING MINDFUL OF MIND CONTROL

RETURNING READERS MAY RECALL THE *Cordyceps* fungus from the last column, and its ability to enslave ants to serve as ideal spore-dispensers. While being controlled in this way does lend each day a refreshing regularity, the feeling of loss of personal control over our decisions and actions ranks among many people's greatest terrors. Humans, in such a scenario—that would be science fiction, surely? The Master would prefer that you keep thinking so....

This fear of loss of control has always been part of being human. A belief in demonic possession reaches back before recorded history, in nearly every culture. Belief in being marched away by little gray men or vacuumed up into a spaceship is considerably more recent, but also quite widespread. The phenomena may be related. Any sufficiently advanced demon is indistinguishable from an alien.

Back here on Earth, others are finding themselves possessed in other ways. Christianity, Islam, Buddhism, Hinduism, Wicca, Kabbalist Judaism and other religions past and present include beliefs in the possibility of being possessed or controlled by demons or other supernatural entities. The concept is central to Vodou and other African-based faiths.

Zombies that rampage across the land looking for brains are a relatively new invention. Part of that idea, though, rises from a purportedly real phenomenon: individuals who were made to (or to appear to) rise from the dead, and who were put to use as slave labor on Haitian sugar plantations. In the 1980s, Harvard-educated professor Wade Davis explained in his books *The Serpent and the Rainbow* and *Passage of Darkness* how this might be possible, by use of the neurotoxin tetrodotoxin, the same pufferfish toxin that makes dining on fugu risky, augmented

by strong cultural beliefs in the powers of the bokor, the voodoo sorcerer. In this belief system, the bokor stores the zombified individual's soul in a jar, and replaces it with a spirit, which he then directs. Professor Davis explains that the drug causes a coma resembling death. The "corpse" is buried, and then revivified by the bokor. Potentially credible documented cases are few, but there is widespread belief in Haiti that bokors can raise the dead and cause them to carry out the bokor's instructions.

It is easy to relegate such matters to the domain of faith, or if one prefers, superstition. However, despite the fact that we are now ostensibly enlightened, and fears of supernatural possession have faded into the fringes for many, the loss of control of one's self might soon be more possible than ever before. And it won't be aliens taking control (or at least, not only aliens)—other humans are going to beat them to it.

Which brings us to controlling the minds, and thus actions, of others. This isn't even science fiction any more. This world is here, right now. The average person is surprised by what is possible now. It's possible to grow little brains in a lab, sustain them by implanting them in a mouse, and retrieve them as needed. In 2016, quadriplegic Nathan Copeland directed a robot arm to fist-bump President Obama, using only his mind. Memories have been transferred between rats. We now have sufficient maps of the brains of a variety of animals to control them by directly stimulating feelings of rewards and aversion. A rat can be steered through a maze like a radio-controlled car. Various brain-boosting implants, devices that obey unspoken commands, and mind-reading artificial intelligences are getting closer to being common

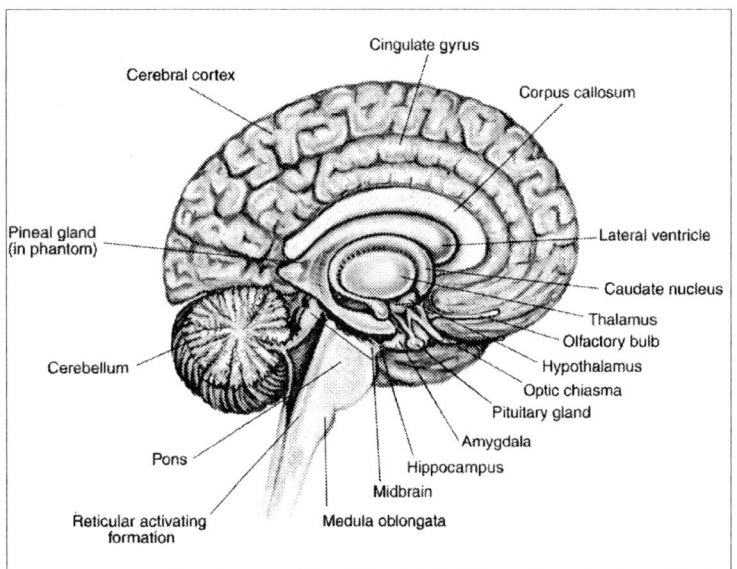

aspects of our lives—and virtually none of this required an abandoned mansion, a lightning storm or a hunchbacked lab assistant.

There's a big difference between a successful experiment in a lab, and a product that is ready to be commonplace in society, or even in specific applications, but that threshold might not lie very far in the future. There is at least one company, BrainGate, that is developing commercial solutions to limited motility or communication, with a number of clinical trials underway.

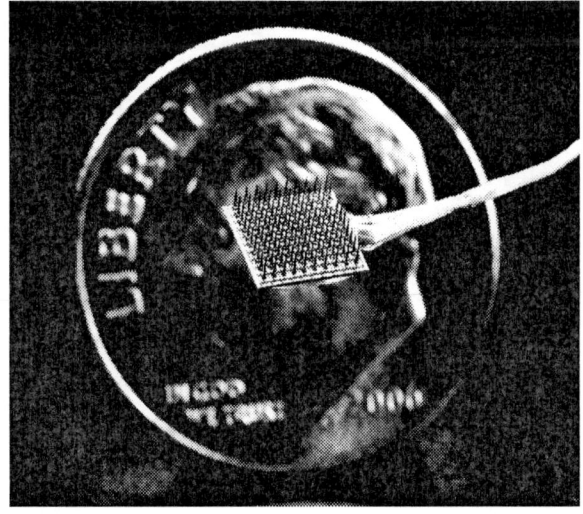

Scientists do not yet understand very much about how the brain works, and there is evidence that it works differently in every head in some important aspects. However, artificial intelligence may be able to help reduce the level of neuron mapping needed, by learning the patterns at work within an individual brain, without needing the entire map. And the brain does a good job of adapting to refine its own control, if it can see the results of its attempts.

It's now over 50 years since Yale scientist Jose Delgado demonstrated his ability to control the actions of animals (including primates) and evoke specific emotions and sensations in people. He captured attention by stopping a charging bull just feet before impact. Researchers can routinely hijack the whisker inputs to the brains of rats, and force them to

take various actions using a laptop and a wireless connection. Scientists can even move each other's appendages by commands sent over the internet. One can imagine a modern update on *The Manchurian Candidate* or Roger Zelazny's "No Award," in which someone at a desk in Spy Headquarters can "Click Here" and cause an unsuspecting fall guy to carry out an assassination in a faraway place.

Recent years have brought yet another new science of playing around in other people's brains: optogenetics. A protein was found in certain algae that responds to exposure to blue light, by releasing lots of positive ions, and another that spews negative ions in yellow light. Yet another favors green, while some have been trained to like red, and even infrared. (Nothing has been published yet regarding what happens in the lab when someone in a plaid shirt walks through, or when Christmas decorations go up for the holiday season.) The micro-organisms use this ability to create energy and detect light in their environments. By infusing brain neurons with these light-sensitive proteins, scientists can turn the neurons on and off.

The process is much more precise than the old standby, electrical stimulation. So far, this has been quite useful in determining the function of specific groups of cells and in treating disorders. But the potential reaches further: mice have been made to run in the direction specified by the researcher, and turning parts of the brain on and off with the equivalent of a light switch raises the notion of a future in which the human brain is well enough understood that people can also be controlled. If only to stop motorists from running red lights.

Furthermore, the light-happy proteins can also be used anywhere in the body to open and close gateways for medicines—or other chemicals, perhaps with less benign purposes. Current realities are limited, but the possibilities are boundless.

Of course, before technology began playing a strong role, mesmerism, hypnosis and brainwashing were unnerving people. And not just in totalitarian countries.

Many Americans are unaware that their government strove with great determination for

mind control capabilities. Spurred by fears of Communist brainwashing and drug experiments, the MK-ULTRA program run by the CIA in the 1950s and 1960s conducted secret, and in many cases, involuntary experiments on Americans, using LSD and other drugs, hoping to discover techniques that could be used in interrogation and manipulation of enemies. Other efforts focused on hypnosis, implants, shocks, anything that offered a chance of the desired manipulation of minds. All of this came to light during congressional and executive investigations into CIA mischief in general in the 1970s, and the program ended. So we are given to understand.

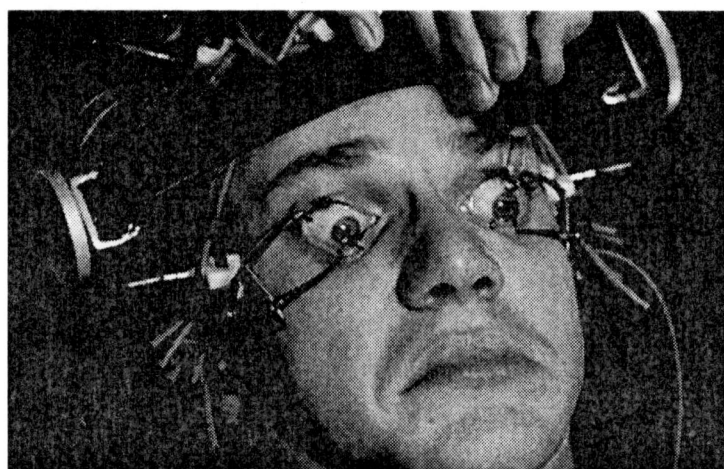

The potential usefulness of such techniques has not diminished. We'll leave it at that. I don't need to become a test subject, and neither do you.

Another drug to watch out for is scopolamine. Since bad people can be found just about anywhere, it seems odd that this drug is exclusively used in South America. One would think that a drug that can neutralize the will of its victim with a single puff of breath would be high on any crook's shopping list. Those exposed can reportedly be led like sheep—or zombies—to do whatever the perpetrator wishes, be it withdrawing all of their money and handing it over, or even changing the TV channel from soap opera to soccer.

Governmental efforts to manipulate animals certainly continue. The US Defense Advanced Research Projects Agency, DARPA, is developing a neural implant to remotely control the movement of sharks. The sharks could then be used without easy detection to locate or attack enemy ships or mines. DARPA is also creating "machine-insect interfaces" to give a whole new meaning to the idea of using bugs for surveillance. The idea of such brain-computer interfaces (BCI) is being advanced on many fronts, and soon will be commonplace, and certainly not just for manipulating critters.

Some critters can turn the tables. The parasitic microbe Toxoplasma *gondii* alters the brain chemistry of its host to further its own ends. Rats that nibble anything touched by cat feces ingest T. gondii eggs, and the microbe then alters the brains of these unfortunate rats, so that they develop a compulsive affection for the smell of cats. Hanging out near cats is not healthy for the rats, who are eaten, and thereby transfer the infection to the cat, which poops out more little gondiis, and the cycle continues. Not disgusted yet? Consider that humans who handle or clean up after cats can also be infected, with poorly understood effects on their brains. It is thought by some researchers that behavior can be altered: impulsive risk-taking

devices, psychoactive chemicals in aircraft contrails, internal voices instigating mischief, lurking strangers of uncertain affiliation—much of which has a distinct whiff of schizophrenic paranoia to it. But even if these complaints were overly imaginative, they might only have been ahead of their time. (In some cases, quite far ahead: victims at the turn of the 20th century described controlling devices that resembled standard mad scientist equipment, complete with cranks, levers, coils, light bulbs—advanced technology of the day, packaged in a way that a layman might imagine could explain any vague sort of "field" or "ray.")

What is possible is changing so fast that it is difficult to keep pace, but much of it does not require esoteric fancies to imagine how people of bad intent could take you over, perhaps one day as easily as ordering a pizza.

Researchers have created limited brain-to-brain communication. If this communication were one-way, emotions and ideas could be planted in one's brain. Students could share the answer to question three on Miss Fonebone's quiz! But the implications could be even more troubling than that. Brain-computer interfaces (BCIs) are great when they allow a paralyzed person to move their own arm, or even in the

increases, as does the risk of schizophrenia. And the infection is not rare; perhaps as many as 50% of humans are infected (and a higher percentage of crazy cat ladies). No one has been observed nuzzling up to a tiger yet, but it is possible that subtle but disturbing harm is being done to our brains, and we do not yet understand its nature.

Many people claim to be suffering from mind control right now—are they paranoid, or onto something? I asked in Issue #2, what can we know for sure, anymore? This might become a refrain.

The Internet maintains a low hum of chatter about imposed exposure to microwaves, subatomic particle beams, implanted

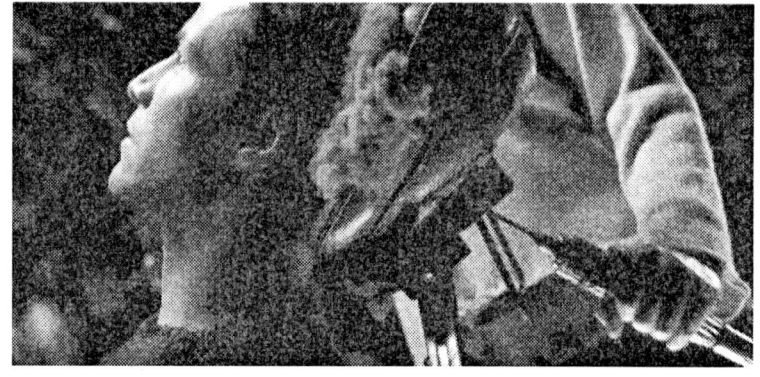

case of a paralyzed driver, a Formula I race car. But in principle there's nothing to prevent someone else from controlling that arm, or that vehicle, as long as they can reach that interface. An augmented surgeon could be hacked so that he sees the wrong condition or makes the wrong cut. If there is a cybernetic control technology in place that connects to a network or receives any kind of external input, it can probably be hacked. The track record for the security of, and access to, private information is not reassuring. Maybe mind control is not yet possible, but forces are advancing on all fronts, and to think that this citadel will not be breached would be foolish.

Furthermore, tens of thousands of people are using BCIs right now, and the devices are collecting data on their brain functions in order to sharpen their control. Each vendor of these devices could potentially have an extensive database on how each user's brain works—indeed, they would be foolish not to be doing this—and these very data that improve the performance and utility of the technology could leave individuals or

whole groups of people vulnerable to tailored takeover measures. Microsoft, Facebook and probably other large corporations are making significant investments in BCI technology. Soon there could be debates about the virtues of their use of data, just as now, but on a whole new level.

And this entire discussion omits the possibilities that might be opened by nanotechnology. Could tailored nanobots quickly learn an individual brain's neural patterns and change them? Could they lie in wait and then seize control of limbs or other systems? This would require mastering two technologies that are far from mature, so it's probably nothing to worry about any time soon. At least, that's what I think I think. Wait … re-thinking … re-thinking … yes, that's right.

These technologies are fascinating and exciting, yet they get little attention in the general news. We should, though, stay informed, not just about progress, but about ethics, and security.

Will we be smart about the use of these new powers? We welcome technology into our homes and wave away concerns about the possibility that our cameras could be showing others our every move, and our voice-controlled speakers listening and passing along our most intimate conversations. How vigilant will we be about circumscribing the reach of these mind-control technologies? Think of the upside! Think of the coolness! Think of what a bored teenager somewhere on the other side of the world could do with control of your brain.

Illustrations: page 122: a midnight encounter from producer Val Lewton's 1943 movie *I Walked with a Zombie* (RKO); page 123: (top) regions of the human brain and (bottom) an implant developed by BrainGate; page 124: (middle) *seriously*, lab rats just want to be left alone; and (bottom) FBI agents Mulder and Scully have been warning us for years (from *The X-Files*, 20th Century Fox Television, 1993 to present); page 125: (middle) Malcom McDowell is the unwilling subject of conditioning, in Stanley Kubrick's 1971 film adaptation of the 1962 Anthony Burgess novel *A Clockwork Orange* (Warner Bros.); and (bottom) a typical scopolamine serving suggestion that's not recommended for home use; page 126: (top) a crazy cat lady *(What else?)* and (bottom) Keanu Reeves as Neo, about to enter a virtual world via a brain-computer interface, in the 1999 movie *The Matrix* (Warner Bros.); page 127: (top) Alfred Molina as Dr. Octavius, the victim of a brain-computer interface gone bad, in Sam Raimi's 2004 movie *Spider-Man 2* (Columbia Pictures); and (bottom) nanobots cruising the bloodstream.

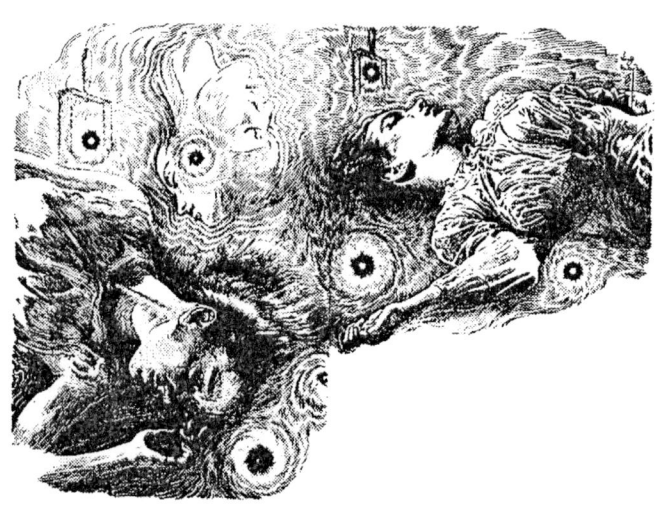

Layroh was looking for a few good men to accompany him on an expedition to uncover the dead secrets of the past. For those needing a second chance in life it seemed like a golden opportunity.

THE CAVERN OF THE SHINING ONES

by Hal K. Wells

IT WAS SHORTLY AFTER MIDNIGHT WHEN A PERSISTENT NIGHTMARE AROUSED **DON FOSTER FROM SLEEP.** For a moment he lay drowsily in his blankets there on the sand, with memory of the nightmare still vivid.

It had been a monstrous flying thing like a giant blue-bottle fly that he had been battling in his sleep. Memory of the thing's high-pitched, droning buzz still rang in his ears. Then abruptly he realized that the peculiar buzzing was no mere echo of a nightmare. It was an actual sound that still vibrated from somewhere within the camp.

Startled into full awakening, Foster propped himself up on one elbow. The sound was penetrating, but not particularly loud. He was apparently the only one whom it had awakened. In the gray gloom of the desert starlight he saw the blanket-shrouded figures of the rest of the men still deep in slumber.

He realized the source of the sound now. It came from inside the black walls of Layroh's tent, pitched there in its usual isolation on a slight rise fifty yards from the sleeping group. Foster grunted disgustedly to himself. More of Layroh's scientific hocus-pocus! The man seemed to go out of his way to add new phases of mystery to this crazy expedition of his through the barren wastelands of the Mojave.

For a solid week now they had been working their way back and forth over a thirty-mile stretch of desert, while Layroh labored with his intricate instruments searching for something known only to himself. Whatever reason Layroh had for recruiting a party of fifteen to accompany him was still a mystery. So far the men had done practically nothing except trail along after Layroh while he worked with his apparatus.

It was a state of affairs that caused the men little worry. As long as they had enough to eat they were quite content. They were down-and-outers, all of them, human derelicts recruited from the park benches and cheap flop houses of Los Angeles. They had only one thing in common: all of them were large and powerful men.

Don Foster was the youngest of the fifteen, and the only college man in the group. A succession of bad breaks had finally landed him broke and hungry on a park bench, where Layroh found him. Layroh's offer of ten dollars a day and all expenses had seemed a godsend. Foster had promptly jumped at the offer. Layroh's peculiar conditions and rules had seemed trivial details at the time.

Foster scowled as he lit a cigarette and

stared through the gloom at the violet-lighted tent from which the disturbing sound still came. Seven days of experience with Layroh's peculiarities had begun to make them a little irritating. His sternly enforced code of rules was simple enough. Never approach Layroh unless called. Never touch Layroh's instruments. Never approach Layroh's tent. Never ask questions.

Layroh neither ate with the men nor mingled with them in any way that could possibly be avoided. As soon as they made camp each night he set up his small black tent and remained inside it until camp was broken the next morning. No one knew whether the man ever slept. All night long the violet light glowed inside the black tent. The men had wondered about the unusual color of that light, then had finally decided it was probably something required by the same eye weakness that made Layroh wear heavily smoked goggles, both day and night.

Strange sounds in the night as Layroh worked with his apparatus in the black tent were nothing unusual, but to-night was the first time that Foster had ever heard this peculiar whining buzz. As he listened it rose in a sudden thin crescendo that rippled along his spine like a file rasping over naked nerve-ends. For one shuddering second there seemed to be an intangible *living* quality in that metallic drone, as though some nameless creature sang in horrible exultance. Then abruptly the sound ceased.

Foster drew a deep breath of relief and ground his cigarette into the sand beside him. Better try to get to sleep again before Layroh started some new disturbance with his infernal apparatus.

He was just settling down into his blankets when a movement in the tent drew his attention back to it. Layroh was apparently changing the position of the violet light, for his tall figure was suddenly silhouetted against the tent wall in sharp relief.

Foster started in surprise as another figure loomed darkly beside that of Layroh. For a moment he thought that the unprecedented had happened and some member of the expedition was inside those jealously guarded tent walls with Layroh. Then he saw that the figure must be a mere trick of the shadows cast by the moving light upon some piece of luggage. It looked like the torso of a man, but the head was a shapeless blob and the arms were nothing more than boneless dangling flaps. A moment later the light moved on and both shadows vanished.

Foster grinned sheepishly over the momentary start the distorted shadow had given him, and determinedly rolled himself in his blankets to sleep.

It was after sunrise when he awoke. The rest of the camp was already up, but there was one member of the party missing.

Jeff Peters' empty blankets were still spread there on the sand, but no one had seen the big Negro since the camp turned in the night before. The expedition's daily travels under the blazing sun of the Mojave never had appealed particularly to Jeff, and he had apparently at last made good his repeated threats to desert.

The men were just getting up from breakfast when Layroh finished packing his tent and apparatus in his sedan, and started down toward the camp. As usual, he halted some five yards away from them, standing there for a moment in stony silence.

Physically, the man was a giant, towering well over six feet in height. On several occasions when the expedition's cars had stalled in deep sand he had strikingly demonstrated the colossal strength in his tall body.

His aquiline features, his red-bronze complexion, and his long black hair, were all suggestive of Incan or Mayan ancestry. No one had ever seen any trace of feeling or emotion upon his impassive features. Foster would have given a good deal for just one glimpse of the eyes hidden behind the dark-colored goggles.

In their depths he might be able to find some reason for the tingling surge of nameless dread that Layroh's close approach always inspired.

Layroh noted Jeff Peters' absence at once. "We seem to have our first deserter," he commented evenly. His voice was as richly resonant as the tone of some fine old violin. He hesitated almost imperceptibly between words, like one to whom English was not a native tongue.

"It does not matter," he continued indifferently. "We can spare one man easily enough. Today we shall continue toward the east. Pack the truck at once. We are ready to start."

Without waiting for an answer, he turned and strode back to the sedan. A curious thought struck Foster as he stared after Layroh's retreating figure. What if the oddly distorted shadow he had seen against the tent wall last night had really been that of a man—had been that of Jeff Peters?

For only a moment did Foster mull over the idea. Then he promptly dismissed it as being absurd. He could imagine no possible reason for Jeff Peters being in Layroh's tent in the middle of the night. The shadow had been only remotely like that of a man, anyway. There had been neither head nor arms to the figure, only shapeless masses totally unlike anything human.

They finished packing the breakfast stuff in the supply truck, and the party started out along the trail with Layroh's sedan leading the way. For nearly two hours they followed their usual routine, working steadily eastward and stopping at regular intervals while Layroh made his methodical tests with his instruments.

Then near the end of the second hour something happened that abruptly sent a thrill of excitement through the entire expedition. Layroh had just set his apparatus up on a small sand dune beside the trail. The mechanism looked somewhat like a portable radio, with two slender parallel rods on top and a number of dials on the main panel.

Layroh swung the rods slowly around the horizon while he carefully tuned the various dials. It was when the rods pointed toward the southeast that there suddenly came the first response he had ever received. From somewhere within the mechanism there came a faint staccato ripple of clear beauty like countless tiny hammers beating upon a crystal gong.

The sound galvanized Layroh into the nearest approach to emotion anyone had ever seen him display. The giant moved with the furious speed of a madman as he returned the apparatus to the sedan and swung the car out across the sand toward the southeast. After a mile he stopped and hurriedly set the apparatus up again. This time the crystalline signal came in with a noticeable increase in volume.

From then on the progress of the party became a mad dash that taxed the endurance of everyone except Layroh himself. After the first hour they entered a terrain so rugged that the cars had to be abandoned and they fought their way forward on foot. Layroh was forced to turn the radiolike apparatus over to one of the men, while he himself carried another mechanism that consisted of a heavy silver cylinder with four flexible nozzles emerging from one end.

They held as rigidly as possible to a straight line toward the southeast, scrambling over whatever obstacles intervened. Their only stops were at regular intervals when Layroh checked their course. Each time the crystalline signal came in with greater volume.

Their objective appeared to be a cone-shaped peak several miles ahead that loomed up high above the surrounding rock masses. The oddly shaped mountain was identified by one of the men who had once been a Mojave desert rat.

"Lodestone Peak," he announced succinctly. "Full of iron, or somethin'. A compass always goes haywire within a radius of ten miles of it."

It was early afternoon when they finally arrived at a level area at the base of the mountain. For the last two miles Layroh had not stopped long enough to make any tests. Now he set the radio-like apparatus in place some ten yards from the face of a sheer cliff that towered high above them.

The crystalline signal came in a rippling flood. He spun the dials. The sound ceased, and the pointing rods glowed with an aura of amber light at their tips. Swift and startling answer came from deep within the heart of the cliff, a mighty note of sonorous beauty like the violent plucking of a string on some colossal bass viol. So powerful was the timbre of the pulsing sound that the entire side of the mountain seemed to vibrate in harmony with it.

Layroh snapped off the apparatus and the sound ceased. Carefully searching until he found a certain spot on the cliff face, he stepped close to it and unlimbered the nozzles of the silver cylinder. Foster noted that at the place selected by Layroh there was a five-foot-wide stratum of slightly lighter-colored rock extending from the sand to a point high up on the cliff face.

From the metal nozzles of the cylinder there spurted a broad beam of dead black. There was a searing flash of blue-white flame as the black beam struck the cliff face. There followed a brief second during which the rock melted into nothingness in the heart of that area of blue radiance. Then the stabbing beam bored steadily on back into the cliff like the flame of a blow torch melting a way through a block of butter.

Layroh adjusted the nozzles until the black beam was a solid shaft of opacity seven feet in height and nearly five in width. The hole in the cliff became a tunnel from which blue radiance surged outward in a shimmering mist as the black beam steadily bit deeper into the rock.

"Follow me," Layroh ordered the men, "but do not approach too close."

He stepped forward and entered the mouth of the tunnel. Shaken by the spectacular thing occurring before their eyes, yet, driven by curiosity as to what might lie at the end of that swift-forming tunnel, the men came crowding obediently after him. A moment later they were within the passage, stumbling dazedly forward through the billowing fog of bluish radiance. There was an odd, almost electric, tingle of exhilaration in that radiant mist as it surged about their bodies.

Fragments of almost-forgotten scientific lore flitted through Foster's brain as he groped for a clue to the action of the strange ray. Not quite complete disintegration of matter, but something very close to it—probably the transformation of matter into radiant energy, an ingenious harnessing of the same forces that are forever at work in the cosmic crucibles of the universe's myriad suns.

The action of the black ray was amazingly rapid. They were forced to hurry forward at a fast walk to keep their distance behind Layroh. The vertical stratum of lighter-colored rock continued straight back into the heart of the mountain. It apparently served as a guide. The color of the blue flame-mist changed perceptibly whenever Layroh allowed the black ray to stray into the rock at either side of it.

For nearly two hundred yards they bored their way steadily into the mountain, their path gradually sloping downward. The walls and floor of the swift-forming tunnel were as smooth and hard as though glazed with a film of diamond.

Then abruptly Layroh shut the black ray projector off as the rock ahead of them ended and they broke through into another larger tunnel, dimly lighted by small globes of violet radiance set at intervals in the glassy ceiling. After thirty yards of travel along this tunnel they found their way barred by a massive door of copper-colored metal.

At Layroh's imperious gesture the men halted a dozen feet back of him in the tunnel while he brought something out of his leather belt-case. Foster was the only one of the group who was near enough to see that the object was a small tube closely resembling a pocket flashlight.

The only break in the surface of the great door was a six-inch disk over near its right-hand edge. Layroh slid this disk aside. Into the opening that was revealed he sent a series of flashes of colored light from the tube—two red, three green, and two blue. The colors were the combination to the light-activated mechanism of the lock. At the last of the blue flashes there was a whirring of hidden mechanism and the portal swung slowly and ponderously open.

Layroh beckoned to the men to follow him as he strode swiftly on into a vast room that was flooded with bluish light from scores of the radiant globes. As the men passed through the door it reached the limit of its opening swing and began automatically closing again behind them, but they were too completely engrossed in the scene before them to notice it.

THEY WERE IN A GREAT CAVERN whose glass-smooth floor was nearly a hundred yards square, and whose ceiling was so high that it was lost in the shadows above the maze of metal girders and cables that made a web-work some forty feet overhead. There was a feeling of almost incredible age about the place, as though it had been sealed away there in the heart of the mountain for countless centuries.

On every hand there was evidence that the cavern and all its contents were the products of a race of beings whose science was one that was utterly strange to that of the modern world. At the end of the room where they stood were row after row of different machines, great engines with bodies of dull silver metal and with stilt-like legs and jointed arms that made them look like giant metal insects. Foster could understand few of the details of the machines, but he felt that in efficiency and versatility they were far ahead of Earth's best modern efforts.

Grouped together in the center of the cavern were many assemblies of apparatus linked together by small cables that descended from main cables in the girder-crisscrossed ceiling overhead. There was a soft hissing of sparks leaping between terminals and a steady glow from oddly shaped tubes which indicated that the mechanisms were still functioning in silent and efficient performance of their unknown tasks.

The piece of apparatus nearest the door was an upright skeleton framework of slender pillars housing in their center a cluster of coils set around a large drum-like diaphragm. Foster wondered if this were not the signal device with which Layroh had tuned in his own portable instrument. The principal piece of mechanism in the central space, however—a great crystal-walled case filled with an intricate array of rods and wires—was something at whose purpose Foster could not even guess.

Layroh strode on past the central apparatus toward the back wall. The men followed him. Then as they rounded the apparatus and saw for the first time the incredible things lining that rear wall, tier upon tier, they stopped short in utter stupefaction. Before them was Life, but Life so hideously and abysmally alien that their brains reeled in horror.

Great shining slugs slumbered there by the hundreds in their boxlike crystal cells, their gelatinous bodies glowing with pale and ever-changing opalescence. The things were roughly pear-shaped, with the large end upward. Deep within this globular portion glowed a large nucleus spot of red. From the tapering lower part of each slug's body there sprouted scores of long slender tendrils like the gelatinous fringe of a jelly-fish.

The things measured nearly four feet in height. Each was suspended upright in an individual glass-walled cell, its body supported by a loop of wire that dropped from larger cables running between each row of cells. There was steady and exhaustless power of some kind coursing through those cables. Where they branched at the end of each cell-row there was a small unit of glowing tubes and silver terminals whose tips glowed with faint auras of leaping sparks.

The slugs were dormant now but the regular changes in the opalescent sheen which coursed over their bodies like the slow breathing of a sleeping animal, gave mute evidence that life was still in those grotesque forms, waiting only to be awakened.

Fascinated by the tiers of glowing things, one of the men started slowly forward with a hand outstretched as though to touch one of the cells. His advance aroused Layroh to swift action. The bronze-faced giant whirled and swung the nozzles of the black ray projector into line with the man.

"Back, *yaharigan*, back!" he ordered imperiously. "The Shining Ones have slumbered, undisturbed for a thousand centuries. They shall not awake from their long sleep to find the filthy fingers of a *yaharigan* defiling their crystal cells. Back!"

Panic-stricken at the threat of the black ray, the man stumbled backward to join his fellows. Layroh's startling statement of the incredible age of the shining things in the cases erased all thought of the expedition's code of rules from Foster's mind.

"You mean that those—those *things*—moved and lived in the outside world a hundred thousand years ago?" he asked dazedly. "But there is no indication of there ever having been any such creatures among Earth's early forms of life."

"Fool!" There was angry disdain in Layroh's resonant voice. "They who slumber here are a race born far from this planet. They are the Shining Ones of Rikor. Rikor is a tiny planet circling a wandering sun whose orbit is an ellipse so vast that only once in a hundred thousand years does it approach your solar system. Rikor's sun was nearly dead, and the Shining Ones had to find a new home soon or else perish. Then their planet swung near the Earth, and their scouts returned with the news that Earth was ideally suited for their purpose. There were barely five

hundred of the Shining Ones all told, and they migrated to Earth in a body."

"And they've been in this cavern ever since, sealed up like tadpoles in fish bowls?" The question came from Garrigan, a strapping sandy-haired Irishman whose first blind panic at the black ray's menace was swiftly giving way to curiosity.

"It was your ancestors who drove the Shining Ones into their retreat here," Layroh answered grimly. "When the Shining Ones arrived upon Earth they found the planet already in the possession of a race of human beings whose science was so far advanced that it compared favorably even with the science of Rikor. This race was comparatively few in numbers, and was concentrated upon a small island-continent known as Atlantis. Shining Ones and Atlanteans met in a war of titans, with a planet as the stake. The Shining Ones were vanquished in that first battle. They lost a fifth of their number and barely half a dozen of their smallest space ships escaped destruction.

"Planning a new and decisive assault, the Shining Ones planted atomic mines throughout the foundations of Atlantis. But the Atlanteans struck first by a matter of hours. At a set moment every volcanic vent on the Earth's surface belched forth colossal volumes of a green gas. Though that gas was harmless to creatures of Earth, it meant slow but certain death to all Rikorians. Furiously the Shining Ones struck their own blow, setting off the cataclysmic explosion that sank Atlantis forever beneath the waters of the Atlantic. Scarcely a handful of Atlanteans escaped, but Rikor's victory was a hollow one. Earth's air was so thoroughly poisoned that it would require centuries of slow ionization by sunlight to again make it fit for Rikorian breathing. The Shining Ones had at most three months before the slow poison would weaken their bodies to the danger point."

"Why didn't they go back to their own planet, then, where they belonged?" broke in the truculent voice of Garrigan again.

"That was impossible," Layroh answered impatiently. "The few space ships they had left would carry barely a score, and Rikor's sun was already so far advanced in its swing away from Earth that there would be time for only one trip. There was only one chance for survival remaining to them. They knew of a process of suspended animation in which their bodies could survive almost indefinitely without being harmed by the Atlantean gas. They would require outside aid to be awakened from that dormant state, so a small group of them must remain active and embark for Rikor, to try to survive there until Rikor returned near enough to the Earth for them to again cross the void.

"The dormant ones must have a retreat so well hidden that they would not be disturbed during the thousand centuries that must elapse before they could be awakened. The Shining Ones sped back to their base on the North American continent and in the three months remaining to them they prepared this cavern here in the heart of the mountain. Radium bulbs supplied its light. For the unfailing source of electrical energy needed to course through the dormant bodies and keep them alive they tapped the magnetic field of the planet itself, the force produced as the Earth rotates in the sun's electrical field like an armature spinning within the coils of a dynamo."

IT WAS FOSTER WHO BROKE IN with the question that was in the thoughts of the entire party. "Just where do *you* come in on all this?" he asked bluntly. "And what was your reason for bringing us here?"

There was blazing contempt in Layroh's rich voice as he turned toward Foster. "*Yaharigan* of Earth!" he jeered. "Your brain is as stupid as the feeble brains of those true *yaharigans* of Rikor whose physical structure your human bodies so closely resemble. Have you not guessed yet that I am no contemptible creature of Earth—that this human shell I wear is nothing but a cleverly contrived disguise? Look, *yaharigans*, look upon the real face of the one who has come to restore the Earth to its rightful masters!"

With a single swift movement, Layroh snatched the colored goggles from his face and flung them aside. There was a smothered gasp of horror from the group. They saw now why Layroh had always worn those concealing lenses. There were no eyes in that bronzed face, nothing but two empty sockets. And from deep within the skull there glowed through those gaping sockets a seething pool of lurid red—the nucleus spot of a Shining One!

Reeling backward with the rest of the men from the horror of the glowing thing within the skull, Foster dazedly heard Layroh's resonant voice ring exultantly on: "My ancestors were among the twenty Shining Ones who remained active. After placing their comrades in their long sleep those twenty survivors set up a signal apparatus in the cavern so that it could be found again no matter how much the outside terrain might change. Then they filled in the entrance tunnel with synthetic rock and embarked for Rikor.

"There upon that dying planet generations passed. When the time came that Rikor's sun again neared Earth, so rigorous had life become upon Rikor that only six Rikorians remained alive. In order to increase our chances of winning through on the perilous trip to Earth, each of us traveled in a separate space ship. The precaution was well taken. We encountered a dense cloud of meteors near Alpha Centauri and I was the only survivor."

Layroh gestured briefly toward the rows of many-armed metal engines. "There are the normal vehicles for a Shining One's body—armored machines powered by sub-atomic motors and with appendages equipped for every task of peace or war. This synthetic human figure which I now wear was donned only in order that I might have no difficulty in mingling with Earthmen while I sought the cavern. It is an exact replica of the body of an Atlantean, including artificial vocal chords. Even the colored goggles necessary to hide the glowing red of my nucleus are similar to those worn by Atlantean scientists while working with their ray machines—"

Layroh was abruptly interrupted by a scream of maniacal fury from Olsen, a shambling Swede who stood near the edge of the group. Ever since Layroh's unmasking the Swede had been staring at him with eyes rigidly wide in terror like those of a bird confronting a snake. The steady contemplation of the horror of the blaring red thing behind Layroh's empty eye-sockets had apparently at last driven the Swede completely insane. He snatched a revolver from his belt as he leaped forward, and fired once. His shot struck Layroh in the forehead.

The bullet ripped through the surface of Layroh's face, then glanced harmlessly aside as it struck metal underneath. Layroh never even staggered from the impact. The black ray from the projector caught Olsen before he could fire again. There was a searing flash of flame, then a swiftly melting cloud of blue-white radiance, and the Swede was gone.

Layroh swung the projector back to menace the others. "I had forgotten that *yaharigans* of Earth have weapons that might be annoying," he said evenly. "Two more of you have pistols—Garrigan and Ransome. Toss them away from you at once. Hesitate—and the black ray speaks again."

Sullenly the two men obeyed his order.

"Good," commended Layroh. "In the pits where you are going you will have little use for pistols. When I again take you from those pits you will quickly learn why I brought you with me. *Yaharigans*, I have called you, and *yaharigans* you shall be—Earthly counterparts of those miserable beasts of Rikor who have for ages been bred only for the one purpose of supplying food for the Shining Ones. I knew that when I found the cavern the process of awakening the Shining Ones would require that they be carefully fed with the calcium and lime from the bones of living *yaharigans*, the normal food of all Rikorians.

"The few *yaharigans* I had brought from Rikor were consumed on my long trip to Earth. So I had to recruit a party of human beings to go with me and serve as the necessary food for the Shining Ones. My search for the cavern took longer than I had expected for I knew only its approximate location. My own body at last had to have sustenance. Last night the Negro, Jeff Peters, provided that sustenance.

"I shall feed those of you who remain to the first group of Shining Ones to be awakened. After that we shall be strong enough in numbers to sally forth and capture ample food for awakening the rest of our comrades. Then in our full strength we shall emerge and again become masters of a planet upon which your crude race shall exist only as *yaharigan* herds for our sustenance."

Layroh's resonant voice ceased. Keeping the black ray projector alertly covering the men, he strode over to a closed metal door in the wall just beyond them. He took a small tube from a rack beside it and opened the door by sending a flash of yellow light into the mechanism of its lock.

"Into the pits until I am ready for you," he commanded curtly. "They were first constructed for keeping our own *yaharigans* while we were working in the cavern, and they should serve just as well for you."

With the memory of Olsen's tragic fate still fresh in their minds, the men obediently filed into the next room, with Layroh bringing up the rear. The room was little more than a single large cell carved from the living rock, and lighted by a single radium bulb in the ceiling.

Its smooth glasslike floor was broken at intervals of ten feet by circular pits fifteen feet deep. At Layroh's order the men entered the floor-pits, one man to each pit. As Foster lowered himself into one of them he saw how grimly efficient a trap the pit was.

An unusually tall and active man might be able to jump high enough to touch the edge, but the effort would be useless. Those glass-smooth edges were so cunningly rounded that they offered no possible purchase for clutching fingers. The diameter of the pit, ten feet, was too great to permit any effort at climbing by wedging one's body between two opposing walls.

Layroh sent every man into the pits but one.

"You will return to the cavern with me, Carter," he ordered. "I have need for you at once."

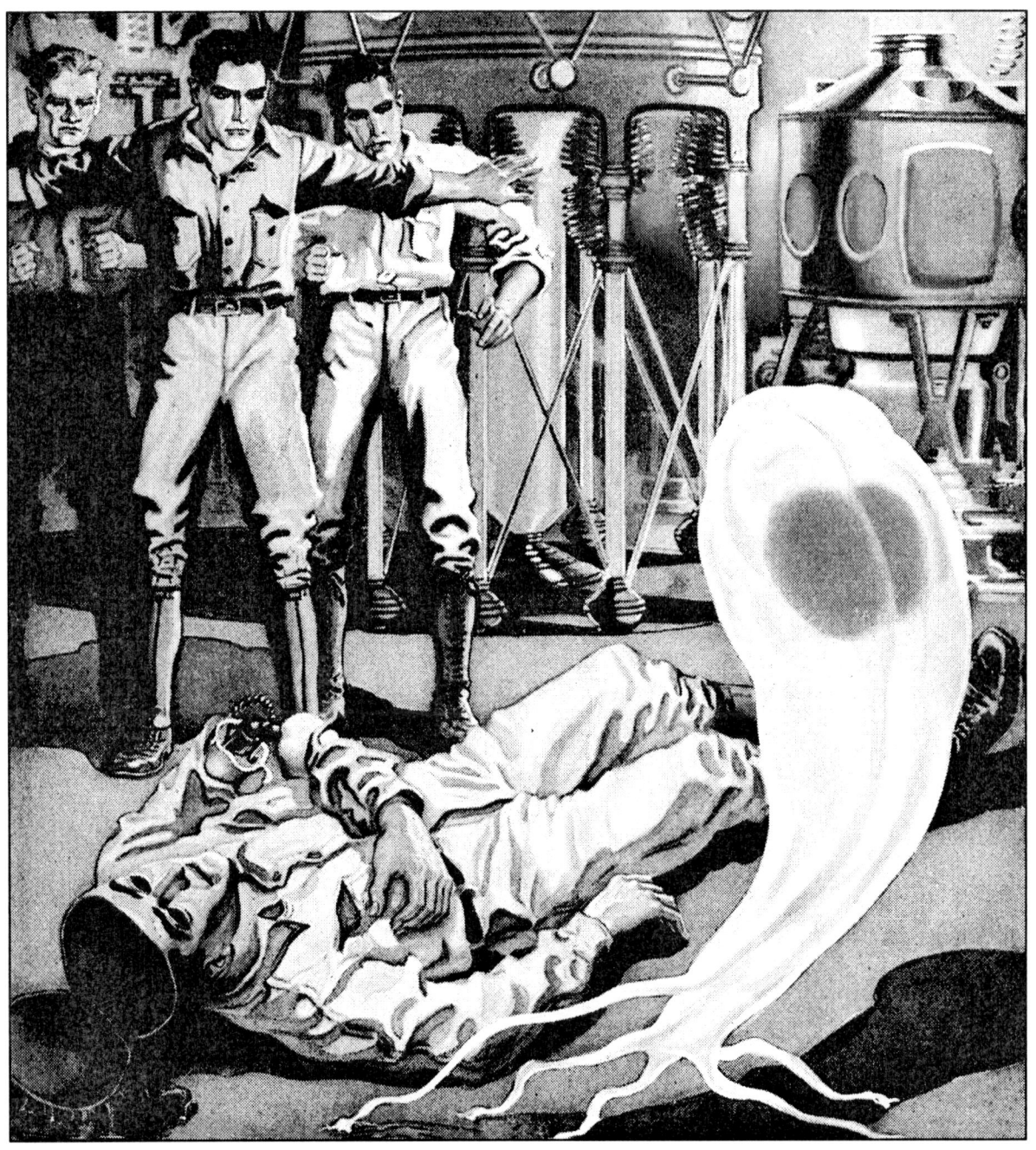

They heard the door clang shut as Layroh and Carter left the pit room. Chaos reigned as the men flung their bodies against the pit walls in efforts to escape. There was the click of metal as several of them tried with pocket knives to chip finger-holes in the walls, but the glassy surfaces were of diamond hardness.

FOSTER'S BRAIN WAS NUMB with despair as he began to realize the true meaning of those sleeping things out in the cavern. Death in some unknown and horrible form was imminent for himself and his companions, he knew, but his thoughts were going far beyond that, to the time when the Shining Ones would emerge in all their resistless power to ravage and conquer a helpless world.

There could be little doubt as to the futility of Earth's best efforts against the advanced science of these invaders from far-off Rikor. Encased in their colossal machine-bodies of glittering metal and armed with such terrible weapons as the black ray projector, the Shining Ones would be as invulnerable as men trampling an anthill underfoot.

The future status of mankind upon the Earth would be that of vast herds of human *yaharigans*, probably bred for ever greater bone content as men breed cattle for superior food values. The picture aroused Foster to a fury of cold desperation. If they could only escape from the pits there might be a chance to trap Layroh and slay him before he brought those hordes of opalescent slugs to life. Then escape from the cavern itself would be an easy matter. Even if the outer door had been locked since they passed through it Layroh had the light-key and Foster remembered the combination.

Half a dozen wild schemes flitted through Foster's brain, only to be discarded as futile. Then suddenly he thought of something that had every chance of success if only they were given time enough. Layroh in his arrogance had forgotten that his prisoners were not naked brutes of Rikor. In the very clothing the men wore was the means of escape from the pits.

Foster's voice cut through the babel in the room until he gained everyone's attention.

"Our only chance for escape is to get a rope between two pits," he said curtly. "Then one man can climb out while the other holds the rope. We'll have to make that rope from our clothing. No one man can get a strip strong enough, so we'll have to work the strips to a central man who can braid them into a single heavy rope. I'm near the center. Get the strips to me. Tear your clothing into ribbons and knot them together. Use your knives, watches, anything to weight one end of the strip. Then cast until you get contact with the pit next to you. That way all the strips can be worked to me."

A period of feverish activity followed while the men went to work. Layroh also was busy. Through several narrow ventilating slits high in the cavern wall they heard the hum of machinery.

The first of the men finished knotting their ropes together. With weighted ends muffled to deaden their fall upon the rock floor, they began casting to get contact with their neighbors.

Success came slowly. There were often scores of blind casts made before a weighted end came into an adjoining pit. But the time finally came when Foster had a twenty-five-foot length of rope strong enough to bear his weight. He already had a single strand making contact with Garrigan in the next pit. Garrigan drew the heavier rope in to him, then acted as an anchor while Foster climbed to the floor above.

His down-stretched hand pulled Garrigan to freedom. Getting the other men up to the floor was the work of but a few moments. They were a weird-looking crew in the torn fragments of clothing that remained to them. Foster stationed them beside the locked cavern door so that they would be hidden behind it when it opened.

"Wait till Layroh is safely inside," he ordered, "then rush him. Get that black ray thing out of commission first. Without that, we should be more than a match for him. In the meantime you come with me, Garrigan. Maybe we can get a look into the cavern."

By climbing on Garrigan's broad shoulders Foster found that he had a clear view through one of the narrow ventilating slits. Layroh had made efficient use of the time since he had left the pit room. Suspended from softly glowing wires in the large central glass case was a circular group of ten of the Shining Ones.

Foster's eyes widened in horror as he saw the object in which the trailing tendrils of the luminous slugs were sunk. It was the naked body of Carter. As those sucking tendrils drew out the substance of his skeleton, Carter's body was changing slowly, horribly, sinking into a flabby mass of puttylike flesh.

The dormant bodies of the great slugs glowed perceptibly brighter as they fed, and the pulsations of opalescence quickened. The Shining Ones were beginning to awaken. Faint but unmistakable there came to Foster's ears a low singing drone from the group.

He shuddered. He knew now why Jeff Peters' shadow had seemed so grotesquely *boneless*. That droning buzzing sound he had heard from the black tent had been the feeding cry of a Shining One—of Layroh. Then, his horrible feast ended, Layroh had blasted what remained of his victim into nothingness with the black ray.

Foster was abruptly startled into action as Layroh turned from watching the central case. Picking up the black ray projector, he started toward the pit-room door. Foster scrambled down. With Garrigan he joined the tensely waiting group beside the door.

There was the sound of the mechanism unlocking. The door opened and Layroh came striding in. In a concerted rush the men were upon him. Foster's hurtling dive for the black ray projector knocked the apparatus out of Layroh's hands. It crashed to the floor with a violence that left it shattered and useless. Swept off his feet by the savage fury of the unexpected attack, Layroh went to the floor beneath the writhing group of men.

The metal sinews of his magnificent body brought him to his knees in one mighty effort, but the numbers of his assailants were too great. Again he was beaten down while powerful hands tore at his limbs. The metal of the ingenious machine that was Layroh's body began twisting and giving way before the savagery of the assault.

He staggered to his feet, flinging the men aside in one last mad surge of power, and lurched toward the cavern. His effort to slam the door closed behind him was blocked by the swift leap of two of the men. Layroh staggered on into the cavern. Then suddenly the torn framework of his legs collapsed completely, and he fell heavily on his back.

The men surged forward with a shout of triumph. But before they could reach Layroh's prostrate figure one of his hands reached up and opened his skull as one opens the hinged halves of a box. From within the skull there rolled a great shining slug, a sinisterly beautiful figure of glowing opalescence, with a scarlet nucleus! For one breath-taken instant it rose to its full height of four feet, hesitated, as if warily regarding the horror-struck men, then with tendrils pressed into its body until it was nearly spherical, the slug that had been Layroh rolled like a ball of living fire across the cavern toward the cluster of machines. Foster snatched up one of the discarded pistols from the floor and fired twice at that hurtling globe of flame, but both shots missed.

A moment later the slug reached the machines. It fled swiftly past a group of smaller mechanisms and selected a gleaming metal colossus whose size and formidable armament indicated that it was designed primarily as an instrument of war. With whipping tendrils the slug swarmed up one of the metal legs and into a small crystal-walled compartment in the forward end of the machine.

There was the crackling hiss of unleashed sub-atomic forces somewhere within the metal

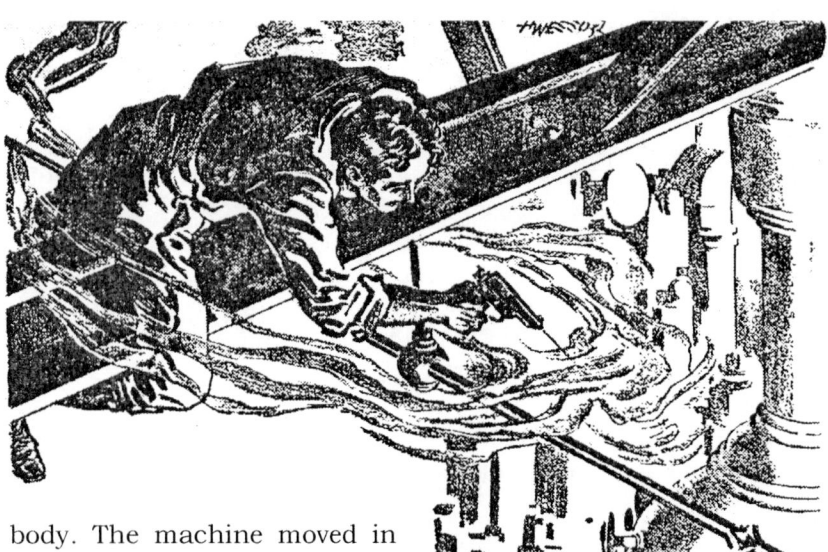

body. The machine moved in fumbling uncertainty for a moment as the slug fought to get control of mechanism that had lain idle for a thousand centuries! Then swiftly full control came, and the machine came charging toward the men.

They broke in wild panic before the onslaught of the metal monster. As an engine of war it was invincible. Six feet in height and nearly twenty feet in length, it maneuvered upon its jointed legs with bewildering speed and efficiency. A score of rodlike arms projected from the main trunk, arms that were equipped for nearly every purpose. Some ended in pincers, others in barbed points, and others in clusters of flexible metal tentacles.

One of the men screamed in terror and broke for the door back into the pit room. Foster flung him aside and slammed the door shut and locked.

"You'd be trapped like a rat in there," he grated. "Our only chance is to stick together and fight it out."

It was a chance that seemed increasingly slight as they tried to close in upon the machine. Garrigan had recovered the other pistol from the floor. He emptied it into the metal monster at a range of less than ten feet but the bullets glanced harmlessly off as from armor plate.

The machine fought back with deadly efficiency. One of the dagger-pointed arms impaled a man like a speared fish. Pincers closed upon the neck of another, half tearing his head from his body. With the strength of desperation, the men wrecked the pillars-and-diaphragm apparatus and from the debris tore metal fragments to serve as clubs. Their blows against the thing's piston-like legs failed to even shake it. Two more men died before the grim efficiency of the stabbing arms.

Foster had held the remaining bullets in his own pistol, waiting for a chance to use them against some vulnerable spot in the machine, but he saw none. There was a bare chance that if he could gain the machine's back he might find some crevice through which he could send a telling shot. Cramming the pistol into his belt, he watched his chance, then used the debris of the wrecked apparatus as a stepping stone for a running leap that landed him solidly on top of the metal bulk just back of the crystal compartment.

He fumbled for the pistol in his belt, but

before he could even touch it a tentacle-tipped arm lashed down toward him, picked him off the thing's back, and flung him with terrific force high into the air....

For a breathless moment he saw the girders and cables of the ceiling hurtling toward him. Instinctively he grabbed with both hands at one of the lower girders as his body thudded into it. His clutching fingers slipped momentarily, then held, leaving him dangling there at arms' length thirty feet above the floor.

His wits swiftly clearing from the shock of that mighty toss through space, Foster scrambled up on the narrow girder. Sitting astride the metal beam, he looked down at the scene below.

The battle down there was nearly over. The glowing slug in the machine was now obviously trying to capture the remaining men alive for further use. Instead of slaying, its lashing arms fought only to stun and cripple.

Six of the men still remained on their feet but they were trapped in an angle between heavy apparatus and one of the walls. In the central case the ten semi-dormant slugs, still too inactive to take part in the battle themselves, seemed watching the conflict with great unwinking eyes of crimson.

Foster groaned. The metal colossus was too powerful for their feeble efforts. It would take a bolt of lightning to have any effect upon that mighty engine of war. At the thought, Foster's heart leaped in sudden inspiration. There was lightning, the terrific electrical force of a spinning planet, in the cables up here among the girders, if he could only release it.

Slightly below his position and barely six feet away from him one of the main power cables of the cavern was suspended from heavy insulators. If the cable had ever had an insulating sheath around it the fabric had vanished during the centuries, for the dull silver-colored metal was now completely bare.

If that naked cable could be dropped into contact with Layroh's machine-body, the entire power of one of the cavern's main lines would be grounded through the metal of the machine. The position of the cable with regard to where the machine was now, was perfect for the scheme. If Foster could sever the cable just opposite him there was an excellent chance that the longer one of the free ends would drop directly upon the machine.

And in his possession he had a possible means of severing that cable—the pistol that was still crammed in his belt. There were four shots remaining in the pistol. The cable was barely half an inch thick, but the range was so short that he could not very well miss. If the silver-colored metal was as soft as it looked, the heavy bullets should be enough to tear through it.

Foster thrust the pistol as close to the cable as he could reach. Then, with the muzzle scarcely a yard from the silver strand, he fired. The heavy bullet caromed from the cable's surface, but not before it had torn a gash nearly a third of the way through it.

There was a sudden cessation of activity below as the slug in the machine looked up at the sound of the shot. Swift inspiration seized Foster and he promptly sent his next shot down at the machine itself. The bullet glanced harmlessly off, but his ruse worked. Apparently believing that Foster was merely trying another futile attack upon it, the machine turned its attention back to the men it had cornered. *Foster could be attended to later.*

Foster slipped and nearly fell just as he fired at the power line the next time and his shot missed. That left him only one remaining cartridge. Aiming with infinite care he sent his last shot smashing squarely into the part of the cable remaining intact.

It trembled and sagged as the bullet cut the remaining metal nearly through. Only a bare thread was left, yet that thread held. Sick at heart over the narrow margin by which his effort had failed, Foster stared in despair at the nearly severed cable. It needed only one solid blow to tear that last thread of metal apart, but the cable was just far enough away to be effectively beyond his reach.

Then suddenly Foster's eyes narrowed. There was a way remaining by which the weakened power line could be broken. A single hurtling dive out and downward from the girder would send his own body crashing squarely into the metal strand. Beneath the smashing impact of his one hundred and eighty pounds the nearly severed cable was certain to break.

Foster shuddered as he realized what that dive into space would mean. He was not thinking of the fall itself. The thirty-foot drop to the diamond-hard floor of the cavern would in all probability mean death or broken bones, but that was a hazard which Foster was willing to take.

It was the thought of what would happen in the brief moment of contact when his body met that bare cable that drained the color from Foster's face. There was the terrific electrical energy from a spinning world coursing through that silver strand, a force that in all probability was powerful enough to instantly char a human body to a glowing cinder!

If he could only insulate his body at the point where it would touch the cable he might have at least a chance of surviving the contact. The only possible insulating medium he had was the clothing he wore—a pair of heavy corduroy trousers and the sleeveless remnant of a woolen shirt. They could be rolled into a bundle that would be bulky enough to at least give him some protection from contact with the bare cable.

Laying the empty pistol on the girder beside him, he stripped as quickly as his precarious perch would permit. Then, using the pistol as a central core to give body to the bundle, he swathed it deep within the folds of the clothing, making a thick roll that he could hold in his right hand as he leaped.

At best the insulating qualities of the roll would be far from perfect, yet it might serve to minimize the effects of the cable's charge enough to give him some chance of escaping alive. His contact with the power line would be only for the fractional part of a second and his body would be completely in the air at the time, out of direct contact with anything through which the cable's charge might ground.

Foster crouched on the girder, his eyes fixed upon the scene below as he tensely waited for the best moment to make the leap. The machine had shifted its position slightly while he had been stripping. It was now too far over the right to be under the cable when it fell.

For a moment as the machine maneuvered still farther over to the right in its conflict with the cornered men, Foster was afraid that his opportunity had passed. An idea came to him and he yelled directions. One of the men suddenly dashed to the left, apparently in a last frantic effort to escape the metal colossus. The machine flashed quickly over to head the fugitive off. The maneuver brought it for the moment directly under Foster's position.

Foster's muscles tensed swiftly, then flung his body headlong out into space. His aim was perfect. The bulky roll of cloth in his outstretched right hand struck the cable squarely with all the force of his hurtling body behind it.

There was a searing flash of blue flame as the last thread of the cable snapped, and a tearing flood of agony that blotted all consciousness from Foster's brain as his falling body hurtled on toward the cavern floor.

HE STRUGGLED SLOWLY BACK to consciousness to find Garrigan and another of the men working over him. There was the stabbing pain of broken bones in his left ankle. With the men helping him, he sat up and looked around.

The scene was one of utter chaos and destruction. The falling cable had obviously found its mark on Layroh's machine-body and in its last furious convulsions the metal colossus had completely wrecked the great glass case in the center of the cavern floor.

The machine itself was now nothing more than a tangled heap of twisted metal. In its shattered crystal compartment was a torn blob of swiftly blackening gelatin—all that remained of Layroh, the Shining One. Other shredded figures of dead flesh marked where the ten half-awakened slugs had died in the wreckage of the glass-walled case.

And in the many tiers of small cells along the cavern's back wall were more figures of death. The severed cable had been the source of the energy that had kept those dormant figures alive. When that energy ceased death had come quickly. Those figures in the cells were no longer Shining Ones. Their bodies were already swiftly darkening in decay.

Foster smiled grimly as he looked around the cavern. There were scientific treasures here that would revolutionize a world. It was a fitting retribution for the Shining Ones. When they had destroyed Atlantis they had robbed Earth of countless centuries of scientific knowledge and progress. Now, here in the cavern that had at last become their tomb, they were leaving a legacy of science that would go far toward repaying that ancient debt.

👽 👽 👽

"The Cavern of the Shining Ones" first appeared in the November 1932 issue of Astounding Stories *(illustrated by H. W. Wesso).*

Harold Kerton Wells (1899-1979) left his job as a salesman in a dry goods store to pursue a career as a magazine writer. Among his works were close to two dozen fantasy stories for the pulps, including three published in Weird Tales. *Wells' fantastic novel,* Blood on the Sun, *was published in* Startling Stories, *May 1942.*

LETTERS FROM OUR READERS

Dear Cosmic Fungi,

I've almost finished reading issue 2 of your amazing magazine, which has confirmed the impression I had with issue 1: this is a little dream come true for me!

My mother was a science fiction buff (very, very unusual for an Italian woman back then—heck, she was probably the only one over here). I grew up seeing sci-fi novels and magazines lying around the house. The awesome illustrations by Chesley Bonestell and other great artists eventually drew me too close to run away and I was trapped: I started reading them too.

And then there were the movies, of course. We watched films like *The Day the Earth Stood Still* or *The Village of the Damned* every single time they were on TV.

(Continued next page)

During the late 70's, the classic movies and magazines slowly faded away; today I can still enjoy the films on DVD and BD, but the magazines... oh, how I longed for a truly good magazine that collected great stories, something with a classic feel that could take me back to my personal golden age ... and now I have it! Black infinity is what I had been waiting for, and boy, am I happy to have it at last!

About the magazine:

The "departments" are the first thing I read. I am familiar with Matt Cowan's writing skills, he does a great, great job here, too, as does Todd Treichel with his peculiar articles.

The comic book is an especially nice touch that—as a comic fan—I really appreciate. I hope it'll be a permanent feature.

Tom English's introduction to each volume is a precious way to let readers know what's in store for them and provide them with useful information.

The illustrations are simply perfect, exactly what I would expect and hope to see in a magazine like this, an effective and welcome throwback to the era whose spirit is being honored here. I'd love to see more information about them.

As to the stories, they are clearly chosen with passion and intelligence alike. I like the fact that they span many different decades (centuries?) and yet they blend perfectly in a unique, mesmerizing flow. The choice of one theme that binds all the stories together turns every issue into an essential collection for every sci-fi lover.

So: THANK YOU for this great magazine!

One thing I noticed, though, is that googling "Black Infinity" doesn't yield many results at all ... in this era, having such meager internet presence is not a very hot idea: anything you can do to rectify this? I'd really hate for the mag to be ignored by internet-dwelling sci-fi fans just because they don't know of its existence. Please do let people know you are here and you are fabulous, I want to keep reading your mag for all the years to come!

I guess I've bothered you for long enough now, so I'd better say goodbye and thank you once more!!

Mac of BIOnighT
www.macvibes.com

Thanks, Mac! Receiving your kind words is no bother at all! We're thrilled you're enjoying our nod to the past and the future of SF in both print and celluloid. And we promise to continue producing our retro SF magazine for many issues to come. As to our Internet presence, we're working on it. Previously we've relied solely on our Dead Letter Press website, but we plan to launch a standalone site for Black Infinity *soon.*

By the way, your letter got us curious about BIOnighT, so we did a little research. Turns out your creative endeavors fall right in line with what we're doing here. We've taken the liberty of printing your web address, above, and we encourage our readers to check it out.

Your Pal in Space,
Hal-9000

In regards to alien replacement—turnabout is fairplay!

THE REPAIRMAN

by Harry Harrison

BEING AN INTERSTELLAR TROUBLESHOOTER WOULDN'T BE SO BAD ... *IF* I COULD SHOOT THE TROUBLE!

The Old Man had that look of intense glee on his face that meant someone was in for a very rough time. Since we were alone, it took no great feat of intelligence to figure it would be me. I talked first, bold attack being the best defense and so forth.

"I quit. Don't bother telling me what dirty job you have cooked up, because I have already quit and you do not want to reveal company secrets to me."

The grin was even wider now and he actually chortled as he thumbed a button on his console. A thick legal document slid out of the delivery slot onto his desk.

"This is your contract," he said. "It tells how and when you will work. A steel-and-vanadium-bound contract that you couldn't crack with a molecular disruptor."

I leaned out quickly, grabbed it and threw it into the air with a single motion. Before it could fall, I had my Solar out and, with a wide-angle shot, burned the contract to ashes.

The Old Man pressed the button again and another contract slid out on his desk. If possible, the smile was still wider now.

"I should have said a *duplicate* of your contract—like this one here." He made a quick note on his secretary plate. "I have deducted 13 credits from your salary for the cost of the duplicate—as well as a 100-credit fine for firing a Solar inside a building."

I slumped, defeated, waiting for the blow to land. The Old Man fondled my contract.

"According to this document, you can't quit. Ever. Therefore I have a little job I know you'll enjoy. Repair job. The Centauri beacon has shut down. It's a Mark III beacon...."

"*What* kind of beacon?" I asked him. I

have repaired hyperspace beacons from one arm of the Galaxy to the other and was sure I had worked on every type or model made. But I had never heard of this kind.

"Mark III," the Old Man repeated, practically chortling. "I never heard of it either until Records dug up the specs. They found them buried in the back of their oldest warehouse. This was the earliest type of beacon ever built —by Earth, no less. Considering its location on one of the Proxima Centauri planets, it might very well be the first beacon."

I looked at the blueprints he handed me and felt my eyes glaze with horror. "It's a monstrosity! It looks more like a distillery than a beacon—must be at least a few hundred meters high. I'm a repairman, not an archeologist. This pile of junk is over 2000 years old. Just forget about it and build a new one."

The Old Man leaned over his desk, breathing into my face. "It would take a year to install a new beacon—besides being too expensive—and this relic is on one of the main routes. We have ships making fifteen-light-year detours now."

He leaned back, wiped his hands on his handkerchief and gave me Lecture Forty-four on Company Duty and My Troubles.

"This department is officially called Maintenance and Repair, when it really should be called trouble-shooting. Hyperspace beacons are made to last forever—or damn close to it.

When one of them breaks down, it is *never* an accident, and repairing the thing is never a matter of just plugging in a new part."

He was telling *me*—the guy who did the job while *he* sat back on his fat paycheck in an air-conditioned office.

He rambled on. "How I wish that were all it took! I would have a fleet of parts ships and junior mechanics to install them. But its not like that at all. I have a fleet of expensive ships that are equipped to do almost anything—manned by a bunch of irresponsibles like *you*."

I nodded moodily at his pointing finger.

"How I wish I could fire you all! Combination space-jockeys, mechanics, engineers, soldiers, con-men and anything else it takes to do the repairs. I have to browbeat, bribe, blackmail and bulldoze you thugs into doing a simple job. If you think you're fed up, just think how I feel. But the ships must go through! The beacons must operate!"

I recognized this deathless line as the curtain speech and crawled to my feet. He threw the Mark III file at me and went back to scratching in his papers. Just as I reached the door, he looked up and impaled me on his finger again.

"And don't get any fancy ideas about jumping your contract. We can attach that bank account of yours on Algol II long before you could draw the money out."

I smiled, a little weakly, I'm afraid, as if I had never meant to keep that account a secret. His spies were getting more efficient every day. Walking down the hall, I tried to figure a way to transfer the money without his catching on—and knew at the same time he was figuring a way to outfigure me.

It was all very depressing, so I stopped for a drink, then went on to the spaceport.

BY THE TIME THE SHIP was serviced, I had a course charted. The nearest beacon to the broken-down Proxima Centauri Beacon was on one of the planets of Beta Circinus, and I headed there first, a short trip of only about nine days in hyperspace.

To understand the importance of the beacons, you have to understand hyperspace. Not that many people do, but it is easy enough to understand that in this *non*-space the regular rules don't apply. Speed and measurements are a matter of relationship, not constant facts like the fixed universe.

The first ships to enter hyperspace had no place to go—and no way to even tell if they had moved. The beacons solved that problem and opened the entire universe. They are built on planets and generate tremendous amounts of power. This power is turned into radiation that is punched through into hyperspace. Every beacon has a code signal as part of its radiation and represents a measurable point in hyperspace. Triangulation and quadrature of the beacons works for navigation—only it follows its own rules. The rules are complex and variable, but they are still rules that a navigator can follow.

For a hyperspace jump, you need at least four beacons for an accurate fix. For long jumps, navigators use as many as seven or eight. So every beacon is important and every one has to keep operating. That is where I and the other trouble-shooters came in.

We travel in well-stocked ships that carry a little bit of everything; only one man to a ship because that is all it takes to operate the overly efficient repair machinery. Due to the very nature of our job, we spend most of our time just rocketing through normal space. After all, when a beacon breaks down, how do you find it?

Not through hyperspace. All you can do is approach as close as you can by using other beacons, then finish the trip in normal space. This can take months, and often does.

This job didn't turn out to be quite that bad. I zeroed on the Beta Circinus beacon and ran a complicated eight-point problem through the navigator, using every beacon I could get an accurate fix on. The computer gave me a course with an estimated point-of-arrival as well as a built-in safety factor I never could eliminate from the machine.

I would much rather take a chance of breaking through near some star than spend time just barreling through normal space, but apparently Tech knows this, too. They had a safety factor built into the computer so you couldn't end up inside a star no matter how hard you tried. I'm sure there was no humaneness in this decision. They just didn't want to lose the ship.

IT WAS A TWENTY-HOUR JUMP, ship's time, and I came through in the middle of nowhere. The robot analyzer chuckled to itself and scanned all the stars, comparing them to the spectra of Proxima Centauri. It finally rang a bell and blinked a light. I peeped through the eyepiece.

A fast reading with the photocell gave me the apparent magnitude and a comparison with its absolute magnitude showed its distance. Not as bad as I had thought—a six-week run, give or take a few days. After feeding a course tape into the robot pilot, I strapped into the acceleration tank and went to sleep.

The time went fast. I rebuilt my camera for about the twentieth time and just about finished a correspondence course in nucleonics. Most repairmen take these courses. Besides their always coming in handy, the company grades your pay by the number of specialties you can handle. All this, with some oil painting and free-fall workouts in the gym, passed the time. I was asleep when the alarm went off that announced planetary distance.

Planet two, where the beacon was situated according to the old charts, was a mushy-looking, wet kind of globe. I tried to make sense out of the ancient directions and finally located the right area. Staying outside the atmosphere, I sent a flying eye down to look things over. In this business, you learn early when and where to risk your own skin.

The eye would be good enough for the preliminary survey.

The old boys had enough brains to choose a traceable site for the beacon, equidistant on a line between two of the most prominent mountain peaks. I located the peaks easily enough and started the eye out from the first peak and kept it on a course directly toward the second. There was a nose and tail radar in the eye and I fed their signals into a scope as an amplitude curve. When the two peaks coincided, I spun the eye controls and dived the thing down.

I cut out the radar and cut in the nose orthicon and sat back to watch the beacon appear on the screen.

The image blinked, focused—and a great damn pyramid swam into view. I cursed and wheeled the eye in circles, scanning the surrounding country. It was flat, marshy bottom land without a bump. The only thing in a ten-mile circle was this pyramid—and that definitely wasn't my beacon.

Or wasn't it?

I dived the eye lower. The pyramid was a crude-looking thing of undressed stone, without carvings or decorations. There was a shimmer of light from the top, and I took a closer look at it. On the peak of the pyramid was a hollow basin filled with water. When I saw that, something clicked in my mind.

Locking the eye in a circular course, I dug through the Mark III plans—and there it was. The beacon had a precipitating field and a basin on top of it for water; this was used to cool the reactor that powered the monstrosity. If the water was still there, the beacon was still there—inside the pyramid. The natives, who, of course, weren't even mentioned by the idiots who constructed the thing, had built a nice heavy, thick stone pyramid around the beacon.

I took another look at the screen and realized that I had locked the eye into a circular orbit about twenty feet above the pyramid.

The summit of the stone pile was now covered with lizards of some type, apparently the local life-form. They had what looked like throwing sticks and arbalasts and were trying to shoot down the eye, a cloud of arrows and rocks flying in every direction.

I pulled the eye straight up and away and threw in the control circuit that would return it automatically to the ship.

Then I went to the galley for a long, strong drink. My beacon was not only locked inside a mountain of handmade stone, but I had managed to irritate the things who had built the pyramid. A great beginning for a job and one clearly designed to drive a stronger man than me to the bottle.

Normally, a repairman stays away from native cultures. They are poison. Anthropologists may not mind being dissected for their science, but a repairman wants to make no sacrifices of any kind for his job. For this reason, most beacons are built on uninhabited planets. If a beacon *has* to go on a planet with a culture, it is usually built in some inaccessible place.

Why this beacon had been built within reach of the local claws, I had yet to find out. But that would come in time. The first thing to do was make contact. To make contact, you have to know the local language.

And, for *that*, I had long before worked out a system that was fool-proof.

I had a pryeye of my own construction. It looked like a piece of rock about a foot long. Once on the ground, it would never be noticed, though it was a little disconcerting to see it float by. I located a lizard town about a thousand kilometers from the pyramid and dropped the eye. It swished down and landed at night in the bank of the local mud wallow. This was a favorite spot that drew a good crowd during the day. In the morning, when the first wallowers arrived, I flipped on the recorder.

After about five of the local days, I had a

sea of native conversation in the memory bank of the machine translator and had tagged a few expressions. This is fairly easy to do when you have a machine memory to work with. One of the lizards gargled at another one and the second one turned around. I tagged this expression with the phrase, "Hey, George!" and waited my chance to use it. Later the same day, I caught one of them alone and shouted "Hey, George!" at him. It gurgled out through the speaker in the local tongue and he turned around.

When you get enough reference phrases like this in the memory bank, the MT brain takes over and starts filling in the missing pieces. As soon as the MT could give a running translation of any conversation it heard, I figured it was time to make a contact.

I FOUND HIM EASILY ENOUGH. He was the Centaurian version of a goat-boy—he herded a particularly loathsome form of local life in the swamps outside the town. I had one of the working eyes dig a cave in an outcropping of rock and wait for him.

When he passed next day, I whispered into the mike: "Welcome, O Goat-boy Grandson! This is your grandfather's spirit speaking from paradise." This fitted in with what I could make out of the local religion.

Goat-boy stopped as if he'd been shot. Before he could move, I pushed a switch and a handful of the local currency, wampum-type shells, rolled out of the cave and landed at his feet.

"Here is some money from paradise, because you have been a good boy." Not really from paradise—I had lifted it from the treasury the night before. "Come back tomorrow and we will talk some more," I called after the fleeing figure. I was pleased to notice that he took the cash before taking off.

After that, Grandpa in paradise had many heart-to-heart talks with Grandson, who found the heavenly loot more than he could resist. Grandpa had been out of touch with things since his death and Goat-boy happily filled him in.

I learned all I needed to know of the history, past and recent, and it wasn't nice.

In addition to the pyramid being around the beacon, there was a nice little religious war going on around the pyramid.

It all began with the land bridge. Apparently the local lizards had been living in the swamps when the beacon was built, but the builders didn't think much of them. They were a low type and confined to a distant continent. The idea that the race would develop and might reach *this* continent never occurred to the beacon mechanics. Which is, of course, what happened.

A little geological turnover, a swampy land bridge formed in the right spot, and the lizards began to wander up beacon valley. And

found religion. A shiny metal temple out of which poured a constant stream of magic water—the reactor-cooling water pumped down from the atmosphere condenser on the roof. The radioactivity in the water didn't hurt the natives. It caused mutations that bred true.

A city was built around the temple and, through the centuries, the pyramid was put up around the beacon. A special branch of the priesthood served the temple. All went well until one of the priests violated the temple and destroyed the holy waters. There had been revolt, strife, murder and destruction since then. But still the holy waters would not flow. Now armed mobs fought around the temple each day and a new band of priests guarded the sacred fount.

And I had to walk into the middle of that mess and repair the thing.

It would have been easy enough if we were allowed a little mayhem. I could have had a lizard fry, fixed the beacon and taken off. Only "native life-forms" were quite well protected. There were spy cells on my ship, all of which I hadn't found, that would cheerfully rat on me when I got back.

Diplomacy was called for. I sighed and dragged out the plastiflesh equipment.

WORKING FROM 3D SNAPS of Grandson, I modeled a passable reptile head over my own features. It was a little short in the jaw, me not having one of their toothy mandibles, but that was all right. I didn't have to look *exactly* like them, just something close, to soothe the native mind. It's logical. If I were an ignorant aborigine of Earth and I ran into a Spican, who looks like a two-foot gob of dried shellac, I would immediately leave the scene. However, if the Spican was wearing a suit of plastiflesh that looked remotely humanoid, I would at least stay and talk to him. This was what I was aiming to do with the Centaurians.

When the head was done, I peeled it off and attached it to an attractive suit of green plastic, complete with tail. I was really glad they had tails. The lizards didn't wear clothes and I wanted to take along a lot of electronic equipment. I built the tail over a metal frame that anchored around my waist. Then I filled the frame with all the equipment I would need and began to wire the suit.

When it was done, I tried it on in front of a full-length mirror. It was horrible but effective. The tail dragged me down in the rear and gave me a duck-waddle, but that only helped the resemblance.

That night I took the ship down into the hills nearest the pyramid, an out-of-the-way dry spot where the amphibious natives would never go. A little before dawn, the eye hooked onto my shoulders and we sailed straight up. We hovered above the temple at about 2,000 meters, until it was light, then dropped straight down.

It must have been a grand sight. The eye was camouflaged to look like a flying lizard, sort of a cardboard pterodactyl, and the slowly flapping wings obviously had nothing to do with our flight. But it was impressive enough for the natives. The first one that spotted me screamed and dropped over on his back. The others came running. They milled and mobbed and piled on top of one another, and by that time I had landed in the plaza fronting the temple. The priesthood arrived.

I folded my arms in a regal stance. "Greetings, O noble servers of the Great God," I said. Of course I didn't say it out loud, just whispered loud enough for the throat mike to catch. This was radioed back to the MT and the translation shot back to a speaker in my jaws.

The natives chomped and rattled, and the translation rolled out almost instantly. I had the volume turned up and the whole square echoed.

Some of the more credulous natives prostrated themselves and others fled screaming. One doubtful type raised a spear, but no one else tried that after the pterodactyl-eye picked him up and dropped him in the swamp. The priests were a hard-headed lot and weren't buying any lizards in a poke; they just stood and muttered. I had to take the offensive again.

"Begone, O faithful steed," I said to the eye, and pressed the control in my palm at the same time.

It took off straight up a bit faster than I wanted; little pieces of wind-torn plastic rained down. While the crowd was ogling this ascent, I walked through the temple doors.

"I would talk with you, O noble priests," I said.

Before they could think up a good answer, I was inside.

THE TEMPLE WAS A SMALL ONE built against the base of the pyramid. I hoped I wasn't breaking too many taboos by going in. I wasn't stopped, so it looked all right. The temple was a single room with a murky-looking pool at one end. Sloshing in the pool was an ancient reptile who clearly was one of the leaders. I waddled toward him and he gave me a cold and fishy eye, then growled something.

The MT whispered into my ear, "Just what in the name of the thirteenth sin are you and what are you doing here?"

I drew up my scaly figure in a noble gesture and pointed toward the ceiling. "I come from your ancestors to help you. I am here to restore the Holy Waters."

This raised a buzz of conversation behind me, but got no rise out of the chief. He sank slowly into the water until only his eyes were showing. I could almost hear the wheels turning behind that moss-covered forehead. Then he lunged up and pointed a dripping finger at me.

"You are a liar! You are no ancestor of ours! We will—"

"Stop!" I thundered before he got so far in that he couldn't back out. "I said your ancestors sent me as emissary—I am not one of your ancestors. Do not try to harm me or the wrath of those who have Passed On will turn against you."

When I said this, I turned to jab a claw at the other priests, using the motion to cover my flicking a coin grenade toward them. It blew a nice hole in the floor with a great show of noise and smoke.

The First Lizard knew I was talking sense then and immediately called a meeting of the shamans. It, of course, took place in the public bathtub and I had to join them there. We jawed and gurgled for about an hour and settled all the major points.

I found out that they were new priests; the previous ones had all been boiled for letting the Holy Waters cease. They found out I was there only to help them restore the flow of the waters. They bought this, tentatively, and we all heaved out of the tub and trickled muddy paths across the floor. There was a bolted and guarded door that led into the pyramid proper. While it was being opened, the First Lizard turned to me.

"Undoubtedly you know of the rule," he said. "Because the old priests did pry and peer, it was ruled henceforth that only the blind could enter the Holy of Holies." I'd swear he was smiling, if thirty teeth peeking out of what looked like a crack in an old suitcase can be called smiling.

He was also signaling to him an under-priest who carried a brazier of charcoal complete with red-hot irons. All I could do was stand and watch as he stirred up the coals, pulled out the ruddiest iron and turned toward me. He was just drawing a bead on my right eyeball when my brain got back in gear.

"Of course," I said, "blinding is only right. But in my case you will have to blind me before I *leave* the Holy of Holies, not now. I need my eyes to see and mend the Fount of Holy Waters. Once the waters flow again, I will laugh as I hurl myself on the burning iron."

He took a good thirty seconds to think it over and had to agree with me. The local torturer sniffled a bit and threw a little more charcoal on the fire. The gate crashed open and I stalked through; then it banged to behind me and I was alone in the dark.

But not for long—there was a shuffling nearby and I took a chance and turned on my flash. Three priests were groping toward me, their eye-sockets red pits of burned flesh. They knew what I wanted and led the way without a word.

A crumbling and cracked stone stairway brought us up to a solid metal doorway labeled in archaic script *MARK III BEACON—AUTHORIZED PERSONNEL ONLY*. The trusting builders counted on the sign to do the whole job, for there wasn't a trace of a lock on the door. One lizard merely turned the handle and we were inside the beacon.

I unzipped the front of my camouflage suit and pulled out the blueprints. With the faithful priests stumbling after me, I located the control room and turned on the lights. There was a residue of charge in the emergency batteries, just enough to give a dim light. The meters and indicators looked to be in good shape; if anything, unexpectedly bright from constant polishing.

I checked the readings carefully and found just what I had suspected. One of the eager lizards had managed to open a circuit box and had polished the switches inside. While doing this, he had thrown one of the switches and that had caused the trouble.

Rather, that had *started* the trouble. It wasn't going to be ended by just reversing the water-valve switch. This valve was supposed to be used only for repairs, after the pile was damped. When the water was cut off with the pile in operation, it had started to overheat and the automatic safeties had dumped the charge down the pit.

I could start the water again easily enough, but there was no fuel left in the reactor.

I wasn't going to play with the fuel problem at all. It would be far easier to install a new power plant. I had one in the ship that was about a tenth the size of the ancient bucket of bolts and produced at least four times the power. Before I sent for it, I checked over the rest of the beacon. In 2000 years, there should be *some* sign of wear.

The old boys had built well, I'll give them credit for that. Ninety percent of the machinery had no moving parts and had suffered no wear whatever. Other parts they had beefed up, figuring they would wear, but slowly. The water-feed pipe from the roof, for example. The pipe walls were at least three meters thick —and the pipe opening itself no bigger than my head. There were some things I could do, though, and I made a list of parts.

The parts, the new power plant and a few other odds and ends were chuted into a neat pile on the ship. I checked all the parts by screen before they were loaded in a metal crate. In the darkest hour before dawn, the heavy-duty eye dropped the crate outside the temple and darted away without being seen. I watched the priests through the pryeye while they tried to open it. When they had given up, I boomed orders at them through a speaker in the crate. They spent most of the day sweating the heavy box up through the narrow temple stairs and I enjoyed a good sleep. It was resting inside the beacon door when I woke up.

THE REPAIRS DIDN'T TAKE LONG, though there was plenty of groaning from the blind lizards when they heard me ripping the wall open to get at the power leads. I even hooked a gadget to the water pipe so their Holy Waters would have the usual refreshing radioactivity when they started flowing again. The moment this was all finished, I did the job they were waiting for.

I threw the switch that started the water flowing again.

There were a few minutes while the water began to gurgle down through the dry pipe. Then a roar came from outside the pyramid that must have shaken its stone walls. Shaking my hands once over my head, I went down for the eye-burning ceremony.

The blind lizards were waiting for me by the door and looked even unhappier than usual. When I tried the door, I found out why —it was bolted and barred from the other side.

"It has been decided," a lizard said, "that you shall remain here forever and tend the Holy Waters. We will stay with you and serve your every need."

A delightful prospect, eternity spent in a locked beacon with three blind lizards. In spite of their hospitality, I couldn't accept.

"What—you dare interfere with the messenger of your ancestors!" I had the speaker on full volume and the vibration almost shook my head off.

The lizards cringed and I set my Solar for a narrow beam and ran it around the door jamb. There was a great crunching and banging from the junk piled against it, and then the door swung free. I threw it open. Before they could protest, I had pushed the priests out through it.

The rest of their clan showed up at the foot of the stairs and made a great ruckus while I finished welding the door shut. Running through the crowd, I faced up to the First Lizard in his tub. He sank slowly beneath the surface.

"What lack of courtesy!" I shouted. He made little bubbles in the water. "The ancestors are annoyed and have decided to forbid entrance to the Inner Temple forever; though, out of kindness, they will let the waters flow. Now I must return—on with the ceremony!"

The torture-master was too frightened to move, so I grabbed out his hot iron. A touch on the side of my face dropped a steel plate over my eyes, under the plastiskin. Then I jammed the iron hard into my phony eye-sockets and the plastic gave off an authentic odor.

A cry went up from the crowd as I dropped the iron and staggered in blind circles. I must admit it went off pretty well.

Before they could get any more bright ideas, I threw the switch and my plastic pterodactyl sailed in through the door. I couldn't see it, of course, but I knew it had arrived when the grapples in the claws latched onto the steel plates on my shoulders.

I had got turned around after the eye-burning and my flying beast hooked onto me backward. I had meant to sail out bravely, blind eyes facing into the sunset; instead, I faced the crowd as I soared away, so I made the most of a bad situation and threw them a snappy military salute. Then I was out in the fresh air and away.

When I lifted the plate and poked holes in the seared plastic, I could see the pyramid growing smaller behind me, water gushing out of the base and a happy crowd of reptiles sporting in its radioactive rush. I counted off on my talons to see if I had forgotten anything.

One: The beacon was repaired.

Two: The door was sealed, so there should be no more sabotage, accidental or deliberate.

Three: The priests should be satisfied. The water was running again, my eyes had been duly burned out, and they were back in business. Which added up to—

Four: The fact that they would probably let another repairman in, under the same conditions, if the beacon conked out again. At least I had done nothing, like butchering a few of them, that would make them antagonistic toward future ancestral messengers.

I stripped off my tattered lizard suit back in the ship, very glad that it would be some other repairman who'd get the job.

"The Repairman" first appeared in the February 1958 issue of Galaxy Magazine. The original accompanying illustration is by Frank Kramer.

Author Harry Harrison began his professional life as a comic book artist, working with industry legend Wallace Wood. In the early 1950s he illustrated science fiction stories for publisher Bill Gaines' famed and frequently reprinted EC Comics Weird Science and Weird Fantasy. Soon afterward, Harrison traded in his T-square for a typewriter, and went on to produce numerous, well-received SF tales, including "The Stainless Steel Rat" series and the novels Deathworld (featured in Black Infinity #1) and Make Room, Make Room! (the basis for the 1973 movie Soylent Green, starring Charlton Heston and Edward G. Robinson, in his last film role).

Sometimes, no matter how hard you try,
blending in with the locals is just not enough.

INCIDENT IN THE WOMEN'S BATHROOM

by Rebekah Memel

THERE IT IS! THERE'S ONE OF YOUR KIND. I CAN SMELL IT," MR. CRAWFORD SAID.

Following the direction of his eyes, I see a well dressed, attractive young woman. She is coiffed and skillfully made up, wearing a tweed suit, heels, a hat and gloves. She does not look any different than any of the other women in the lobby of our big city hotel.

I strongly prefer to wait and let the situation work itself out, but Mr. Crawford wants to jump right in.

And since I am only a Zuzzdee woman, my opinion is not worth even the weight of my words.

"Let's follow it. We can arrest it right now just for being here. But then we can only expel it. Let's catch it using the bathroom. Then we can send it to a labour camp for years."

The woman is sitting in the lobby, maybe waiting for someone. She glances occasionally at her watch. Finally after about twenty minutes she gets up, and walks across the lobby towards the stairs to the second floor.

The bathrooms are on the second floor. We are following her, staying far enough behind so we will not be seen. Mr. Crawford is shaking with excitement. I am trembling also, but inside where no one can see it. My anxiety is of a very different nature than his.

There is a large full-length mirror at the head of the stairs. I am captivated by my own appearance as I see the reflection of a well-dressed, attractive Earth woman. As long as I am wearing a blouse and no one can see my Utburb, no one can tell I am a Zuzzdee. This is why all Zuzzdee women, even I, must wear

the lavender armband on the rare occasions when we are allowed to visit human society.

On the second floor we look right and left, but see no sign of her.

"It's in the bathroom. I got it now!" Mr. Crawford yells. His face is swollen with emotion.

Mr. Crawford pushes open the door of the women's bathroom and yells, "Earthland Security. Everybody out."

His squat, bulky body is blocking the doorway.

There are about half a dozen women in the room, a few coming out of stalls, some at the sinks washing their hands or combing their hair. They are angry at Mr. Crawford, but I know they are afraid and that their fear is greater than their anger. They all hurry out, being careful not to brush Mr. Crawford as they are squeeze by him.

The woman he is following is standing by a sink applying lipstick. Unlike everyone else, she remains calm and finishes her primping before she turns to face us.

"What is the meaning of this outrage?" Her words are demanding but her voice is calm.

"You don't belong in here. I can have you sent to a labour camp."

"It is you who will go to a camp," she says smiling, and her smile is chilling. It is the smile of a large cat that has trapped a mouse in a corner.

Mr. Crawford seems shaken by her confidence. They stand glaring at each other for a few moments, and then Mr. Crawford turns to me and says, "All right. Do your job."

He turns around and leaves, slamming the door behind him.

We both stand staring at each other, waiting for the echo of the door to fade.

"You don't belong in here," I say. "You can be arrested."

She laughs, loudly and confidently. "I should be saying that to you. You're a Zuzzdee. You are the one who doesn't belong here."

"I work for Earthland Security. My job is to detect Zuzzdees, and to prevent them from passing as humans."

"So why is it you and not your boss standing here?"

"He cannot risk being wrong. If he falsely accused a true Earth woman, he would be punished terribly. There is no risk for me."

"Your boss will be very angry that he is wrong."

"Yes, he can yell and scream at me and call me a Zuzzhead. But there is a limit to what he can do. He needs me. There are few Zuzzdees who would do this job."

"And why do you betray your own people by doing it?"

"Many of us are poor and cold and hungry. What credits I receive are sent back to my family."

"And I suppose you want me to take off my blouse and brassiere? Is that the only way I can convince you that you are wrong?"

She raises her hand and begins unbuttoning the first button of her blouse.

"Stop. Tell me why you are here?"

She smiles sadly. "Meeting a girlfriend for lunch, shopping in the city for perfume, and later seeing a play. Then I will return home."

"Have you come a very long way?"

"Yes, I am very far away from home."

"And do you think you will ever come here again?"

"Whenever I want to. I like to be in the City and walk freely among people. To see and be seen. And sometimes there are things that I want that I cannot get anywhere else."

"There are great risks involved."

"Only for Zuzzdee. But sometimes, in order to live a life, risks must be taken. A woman, Zuzzdee or human, should not be a prisoner of fear. A life lived in fear is not worth living."

Turning away from her after she speaks, I begin pulling the bathroom door open. Half hidden, far down the corridor in the shadows, I can see Mr. Crawford waiting.

I hold the door open and turn towards to her.

She turns to me and smiles again. "I have made my decision about the kind of life I want to live. Now you must make yours."

She slides by me, brushing me with her chest, then she is fading into the crowd that is waiting to use the bathroom.

I turn to face Mr. Crawford who is running up to meet me.

👽 👽 👽

Rebekah Memel Brown is a lover of scuba diving, cats, and black and white movies. Her historical novel Days of Darkness *is about two young women in Berlin in the 1920s. She has written many essays about outré authors Algernon Blackwood, Sarban, and Robert Aickman, among others, primarily for the British literary magazine* Wormwood. *Her short fiction has appeared in* Unspoken Water *and the 2014 World Fantasy Convention e-book* Unconventional Fantasy. *She lives in haunted Salem, Massachusetts, with her husband David.*

Spiritual
BOOT CAMP
for

Creators
& Dreamers

ENCOURAGEMENT, INSPIRATION &
BASIC TRAINING TO HELP YOU ACHIEVE YOUR DREAMS

TOM ENGLISH
★ ★ ★ ★ ★ & ★ ★ ★ ★
WILMA ESPAILLAT ENGLISH

A Ravens' Read!

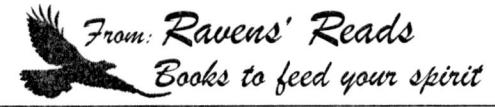

From: *Ravens' Reads*
Books to feed your spirit

Beware! For this is the night of the Megasoid!

THE DUPLICATE MAN

by Clifford D. Simak

HE CAME ALIVE FROM NOTHING. HE BECAME AWARE FROM UNAWARENESS.
He smelled the air of the night and heard the trees whispering on the embankment above him and the breeze that had set the trees to whispering came down to him and felt him over with soft and tender fingers, for all the world as if it were examining him for broken bones; or contusions and abrasions.

He sat up and put both his palms down upon the ground beside him to help him sit erect, and stared into the darkness. Memory came slowly and when it came it was incomplete and answered nothing.

His name was Henderson James and he was a human being and he was sitting somewhere on a planet that was called Earth. He was thirty-six years old and he was, in his own way, famous, and comfortably well-off. He lived in an old ancestral home on Summit Avenue, which was a respectable address even if it had lost some of its smartness in the last twenty years or so.

On the road above the slope of the embankment a car went past with its tires whining on the pavement, and for a moment its headlights made the treetops glow. Far away, muted by the distance, a whistle cried out. And somewhere else a dog was barking with a flat viciousness.

His name was Henderson James and if that were true, why was he here. Why should Henderson James be sitting on the slope of an embankment, listening to the wind in the trees and to a wailing whistle and a barking dog? Something had gone wrong, some incident that, if he could but remember it, might answer all his questions.

There was a job to do.

He sat and stared into the night and found that he was shivering, although there was no reason why he should, for the night was not that cold. Beyond the embankment he heard the sounds of a city late at night, the distant whine of the speeding car and the far-off wind-broken screaming of a siren. Once a man walked along a street close by and James sat listening to his footsteps until they faded out of hearing.

Something had happened and there was a job to do, a job that he had been doing, a job that somehow had been strangely interrupted by the inexplicable incident which had left him lying here on this embankment.

He checked himself. Clothing ... shorts and shirt, strong shoes, his wristwatch and the gun in the holster at his side.

A gun?

The job involved a gun.

He had been hunting in the city, hunting something that required a gun. Something that was prowling in the night and a thing that must be killed.

Then he knew the answer, but even as he knew it he sat for a moment wondering at the strange, methodical, step-by-step progression of reasoning that had brought him to the memory. First his name and the basic facts pertaining to himself, then the realization of where he was and the problem of why he happened to be there and finally the realization that he had a gun and that it was meant to be used. It was a logical way to think, a primer schoolbook way to work it out:

I am a man named Henderson James.

I live in a house on Summit Avenue.

Am I in the house on Summit Avenue?

No, I am not in the house on Summit Avenue.

I am on an embankment somewhere.

Why am I on the embankment?

But it wasn't the way a man thought, at least not the normal way a normal man would think. Man thought in shortcuts. He cut across the block and did not go all the way around.

It was a frightening thing, he told himself, this clear-around-the-block thinking. It wasn't normal and it wasn't right and it made no sense at all ... no more sense than did the fact that he should find himself in a place with no memory of getting there.

HE ROSE TO HIS FEET and ran his hands up and down his body. His clothes were neat, not rumpled. He hadn't been beaten up and he hadn't been thrown from a speeding car. There were no sore places on his body and his face was unbloody and whole and he

felt all right.

He hooked his fingers in the holster belt and shucked it up so that it rode tightly on his hips. He pulled out the gun and checked it with expert and familiar fingers and the gun was ready.

He walked up the embankment and reached the road, went across it with a swinging stride to reach the sidewalk that fronted the row of new bungalows. He heard a car coming and stepped off the sidewalk to crouch in a clump of evergreens that landscaped one corner of a lawn. The move was instinctive, and he crouched there, feeling just a little foolish at the thing he'd done.

The car went past and no one saw him. They would not, he now realized, have noticed him even if he had remained out on the sidewalk.

He was unsure of himself; that must be the reason for his fear. There was a blank spot in his life, some mysterious incident that he did not know and the unknowing of it had undermined the sure and solid foundation of his own existence, had wrecked the basis of his motive and had turned him, momentarily, into a furtive animal that darted and hid at the approach of his fellow men.

That and something that had happened to him that made him think clear around the block.

He remained crouching in the evergreens, watching the street and the stretch of sidewalk, conscious of the white-painted, ghostly bungalows squatting back in their landscaped lots.

A word came into his mind. *Megasoid.* An odd word, unearthly, yet it held terror.

The megasoid had escaped and that was why he was here, hiding on the front lawn of some unsuspecting and sleeping citizen, equipped with a gun and a determination to use it, ready to match his wits and the quickness of brain and muscle against the most blood-thirsty, hate-filled thing yet found in the Galaxy.

The megasoid was dangerous. It was not a thing to harbor. In fact, there was a law against harboring not only a megasoid, but certain other alien beasties even less lethal than a megasoid. There was good reason for such a law, reason which no one, much less himself, would ever think to question.

And now the megasoid was loose and somewhere in the city.

JAMES GREW COLD at the thought of it, his brain forming images of the things that might come to pass if he did not hunt down the alien beast and put an end to it.

Although beast was not quite the word to use. The megasoid was more than a beast ... just how much more than a beast he once had hoped to learn. He had not learned a lot, he now admitted to himself, not nearly all there was to learn, but he had learned enough. More than enough to frighten him.

For one thing, he had learned what hate could be and how shallow an emotion human hate turned out when measured against the depth and intensity and the ravening horror of the megasoid's hate. Not unreasoning hate, for unreasoning hate defeats itself, but a rational, calculating, driving hate that moti-vated a clever and deadly killing machine which directed its rapacity and its cunning against every living thing that was not a megasoid.

For the beast had a mind and a personal-ity that operated upon the basic law of self-preservation against all comers, whoever they might be, extending that law to the interpre-tation that safety lay in one direction only ... the death of every other living being. No other reason was needed for a megasoid's killing. The fact that anything else lived and moved and was thus posing a threat, no matter how remote, against a megasoid, was sufficient reason in itself.

It was psychotic, of course, some murder-ous instinct planted far back in time and deep in the creature's racial consciousness, but no more psychotic, perhaps, than many human instincts.

The megasoid had been, and still was for that matter, a unique opportunity for a study in alien behaviorism. Given a permit, one could have studied them on their native planet. Refused a permit, one sometimes did a foolish thing, as James had.

And foolish acts backfire, as this one did.

James put down a hand and patted the gun at his side, as if by doing so he might de-rive some assurance that he was equal to the task. There was no question in his mind as to the thing that must be done. He must find the megasoid and kill it and he must do that be-fore the break of dawn. Anything less than that would be abject and horrifying failure.

For the megasoid would bud. It was long past its time for the reproductive act and there were bare hours left to find it before it had loosed upon the Earth dozens of baby megasoids. They would not remain babies for long. A few hours after budding they would strike out on their own. To find one megasoid, lost in the vastness of a sleeping city, seemed bad enough; to track down some dozens of them would be impossible.

So it was tonight or never.

Tonight there would be no killing on the megasoid's part. Tonight the beast would be intent on one thing only, to find a place where it could rest in quiet, where it could give itself over, wholeheartedly and with no interference, to the business of bringing other megasoids into being.

It was clever. It would have known where it was going before it had escaped. There would be, on its part, no time wasted in seek-ing or in doubling back. It would have known where it was going, and already it was there, already the buds would be rising on its body, bursting forth and growing.

There was one place, and one place only, in the entire city where an alien beast would be safe from prying eyes. A man could figure that one out and so could a megasoid. The question was: Would the megasoid know that a man could figure it out? Would the megasoid underestimate a man? Or, knowing that the man would know it, too, would it find another place of hiding?

James rose from the evergreens and went down the sidewalk. The street marker at the corner, standing underneath a swinging street light, told him where he was and it was closer to the place where he was going than he might have hoped.

II

THE ZOO WAS QUIET for a while, and then something sent up a howl that raised James' hackles and made his blood stop in his veins.

James, having scaled the fence, stood tensely at its foot, trying to identify the howling animal. He was unable to place it. More than likely, he told himself, it was a new one. A person simply couldn't keep track of all the zoo's occupants. New ones were coming in all the time, strange, unheard of creatures from the distant stars.

Straight ahead lay the unoccupied moat cage that up until a day or two before had held an unbelievable monstrosity from the jungles of one of the Arctian worlds. James grimaced in the dark, remembering the thing. They had finally had to kill it.

And now the megasoid was there ... well, maybe not there, but one place that it could be, the one place in the entire city where it might be seen and arouse no comment, for the zoo was filled with animals that were seldom seen and another strange one would arouse only momentary wonder. One animal more would go unnoticed unless some zoo attendant should think to check the records.

There, in that unoccupied cage area, the megasoid would be undisturbed, could quietly go about its business of budding out more megasoids. No one would bother it, for things like megasoids were the normal occupants of this place set aside for the strangers brought to Earth to be stared at and studied by that ferocious race, the humans.

James stood quietly beside the fence.

Henderson James. Thirty-six. Unmarried. Alien psychologist. An official of this zoo. And an offender against the law for having secured and harbored an alien being that was barred from Earth.

Why, he asked himself, did he think of himself in this way? Why, standing here, did he catalogue himself? It was instinctive to know one's self ... there was no need, no sense of setting up a mental outline of one's self.

It had been foolish to go ahead with this megasoid business. He recalled how he had spent days fighting it out with himself, reviewing all the disastrous possibilities which might arise from it. If the old renegade spaceman had not come to him and had not said, over a bottle of most delicious Lupan wine, that he could deliver, for a certain, rather staggering sum, one live megasoid, in good condition, it never would have happened.

JAMES WAS SURE that of himself he never would have thought of it. But the old space captain was a man he knew and admired from former dealings. He was a man who was not averse to turning either an honest or a dishonest dollar, and yet he was a man, for all of that, that you could depend upon. He would do what you paid him for and keep his lip buttoned tight once the deed was done.

James had wanted a megasoid, for it was a most engaging beast with certain little tricks that, once understood, might open up new avenues of speculation and approach, might write new chapters in the tortuous study of alien minds and manners.

But for all of that, it had been a terrifying thing to do and now that the beast was loose, the terror was compounded. For it was not wholly beyond speculation that the descendants of this one brood that the escaped megasoid would spawn might wipe out the population of the Earth, or at the best, make the Earth untenable for its rightful dwellers.

A place like the Earth, with its teeming millions, would provide a field day for the fangs of the megasoids, and the minds that drove the fangs. They would not hunt for hunger, nor for the sheer madness of the kill, but because of the compelling conviction that no megasoid would be safe until Earth was wiped clean of life. They would be killing for survival, as a cornered rat would kill ... except that they would be cornered nowhere but in the murderous insecurity of their minds.

If the posses scoured the Earth to hunt them down, they would be found in all directions, for they would be shrewd enough to scatter. They would know the ways of guns and traps and poisons and there would be more and more of them as time went on. Each of them would reproduce, accelerating their budding to replace with a dozen or a hundred the ones that might be killed.

James moved quietly forward to the edge of the moat and let himself down into the mud that covered the bottom. When the monstrosity had been killed, the moat had been drained and should long since have been cleaned, but the press of work, James thought, must have prevented its getting done.

Slowly he waded out into the mud, feeling his way, his feet making sucking noises as he pulled them through the slime. Finally he reached the rocky incline that led out of the moat to the island cage.

He stood for a moment, his hands on the great, wet boulders, listening, trying to hold

his breath so the sound of it would not interfere with hearing. The thing that howled had quieted and the night was deathly still. Or seemed, at first, to be. Then he heard the little insect noises that ran through the grass and bushes and the whisper of the leaves in the trees across the moat and the far-off sound that was the hoarse breathing of a sleeping city.

NOW, FOR THE FIRST TIME, he felt fear. Felt it in the silence that was not a silence, in the mud beneath his feet, in the upthrust boulders that rose out of the moat.

The megasoid was a dangerous thing, not only because it was strong and quick, but because it was intelligent. Just how intelligent, he did not know. It reasoned and it planned and schemed. It could talk, though not as a human talks ... probably better than a human ever could. For it not only could talk words, but it could talk emotions. It lured its victims to it by the thoughts it put into their minds; it held them entranced with dreams and illusion until it slit their throats. It could purr a man to sleep, could lull him to suicidal inaction. It could drive him crazy with a single flicking thought, hurling a perception so foul and alien that the mind recoiled deep inside itself and stayed there, coiled tight, like a watch that has been overwound and will not run.

It should have budded long ago, but it had fought off its budding, holding back against the day when it might escape, planning, he realized now, its fight to stay on Earth, which meant its conquest of Earth.

It had planned, and planned well, against this very moment, and it would feel or show no mercy to anyone who interfered with it.

His hand went down and touched the gun and he felt the muscles in his jaw involuntarily tightening, and suddenly there was at once a lightness and a hardness in him that had not been there before. He pulled himself up the boulder face, seeking cautious hand- and toeholds, breathing shallowly, body pressed against the rock. Quickly, and surely, and no noise, for he must reach the top and be there before the megasoid knew there was anyone around.

The megasoid would be relaxed and intent upon its business, engrossed in the budding forth of that numerous family that in days to come would begin the grim and relentless crusade to make an alien planet safe for megasoids ... and for megasoids alone.

That is, if the megasoid were here and not somewhere else. James was only a human trying to think like a megasoid, and that was not an easy or a pleasant job and he had no way of knowing if he succeeded. He could only hope that his reasoning was vicious and crafty enough.

His clawing hand found grass and earth and he sank his fingers deep into the soil, hauling his body up the last few feet of the rock face above the pit.

He lay flat upon the gently sloping ground, listening, tensed for any danger. He studied the ground in front of him, probing every foot. Distant street lamps lighting the zoo walks threw back the total blackness that had engulfed him as he climbed out of the moat, but there still were areas of shadow that he had to study closely.

Inch by inch, he squirmed his way along, making sure of the terrain immediately ahead before he moved a muscle. He held the gun in a rock-hard fist, ready for instant action, watching for the faintest hint of motion, alert for any hump or irregularity that was not rock or bush or grass.

Minutes magnified themselves into hours, his eyes ached with staring and the lightness that had been in him drained away, leaving only the hardness, which was as tense as a drawn bowstring. A sense of failure began to seep into his mind and with it came the full-fledged, until now unadmitted, realization of what failure meant, not only for the world, but for the dignity and the pride that was Henderson James.

Now, faced with the possibility, he admitted to himself the action he must take if the megasoid were not here, if he did not find it here and kill it. He would have to notify the authorities, would have to attempt to alert the police, must plead with newspapers and radio to warn the citizenry, must reveal himself as a man who, through pride and self-conceit, had exposed the people of the Earth to this threat against their hold upon their native planet.

They would not believe him. They would laugh at him until the laughter died in their torn throats, choked off with their blood. He sweated, thinking of it, thinking of the price this city, and the world, would pay before it learned the truth.

THERE WAS A WHISPER OF SOUND, a movement of black against deeper black.

The megasoid rose in front of him, not more than six feet away, from its bed beside a bush. James jerked the pistol up and his finger tightened on the trigger.

"Don't," the megasoid said inside his mind. "I'll go along with you."

His finger strained with the careful slowness of the squeeze and the gun leaped in his hand, but even as it did he felt the whiplash of terror slash at his brain, caught for just a second the terrible import, the mind-shattering obscenity that glanced off his mind and ricocheted away.

"Too late," he told the megasoid, with his voice and his mind and his body shaking. "You should have tried that first. You wasted precious seconds. You would have got me if you had done it first."

It had been easy, he assured himself, much easier than he had thought. The megasoid was dead or dying and the Earth and its millions of unsuspecting citizens were safe and, best of all, Henderson James was safe ... safe from indignity, safe from being stripped naked of the little defenses he had built up through the years to shield him against the public stare. He felt relief flood over him and it left him pulseless and breathless and feeling clean, but weak.

"You fool," the dying megasoid said, death clouding its words as they built up in his mind. "You fool, you half-thing, you duplicate...."

It died then and he felt it die, felt the life go out of it and leave it empty.

He rose softly to his feet and he seemed stunned, and at first he thought it was from knowing death, from having touched hands with death within the megasoid's mind.

The megasoid had tried to fool him. Faced with the pistol, it had tried to throw him off his balance to give it the second that it needed to hurl the mind-blasting thought that had caught at the edge of his brain. If he had hesitated for a moment, he knew, it would have been all over with him. If his finger had slackened for a moment, it would have been too late.

The megasoid must have known that he would think of the zoo as the first logical place to look and, even knowing that, it had held him in enough contempt to come here, had not even bothered to try to watch for him, had not tried to stalk him, had waited until he was almost on top of it before it moved.

And that was queer, for the megasoid must have known, with its uncanny mental powers, every move that he had made. It must have maintained a casual contact with his mind every second of the time since it had escaped. He had known that and ... wait a minute, he *hadn't* known it until this very moment. Although, knowing it now, it seemed as if he had always known it.

What is the matter with me, he thought. There's something wrong with me. I should have known I could not surprise the megasoid, and yet I didn't know it. I must have surprised it, for otherwise it would have finished me off quite leisurely at any moment after I climbed out of the moat.

You fool, the megasoid had said. You fool, you half-thing, you duplicate...

You duplicate!

He felt the strength and the personality and the hard, unquestioned identity of himself as Henderson James, human being, drain out of him, as if someone had cut the puppet string and he, the puppet, had slumped supine upon the stage.

So that was why he had been able to surprise the megasoid!

There were two Henderson Jameses. The megasoid had been in contact with one of them, the original, the real Henderson James, had known every move he made, had known that it was safe so far as that Henderson James might be concerned. It had not known of the second Henderson James that had stalked it through the night. Henderson James, duplicate. Henderson James, temporary. Henderson James, here tonight, gone tomorrow.

For they would not let him live.

The original Henderson James would not allow him to continue living, and even if he did, the world would not allow it. Duplicates were made only for very temporary and very special reasons and it was always understood that once their purpose was accomplished they would be done away with.

Done away with ... those were the words exactly. Gotten out of the way. Swept out of sight and mind. Killed as unconcernedly and emotionlessly as one chops off a chicken's head.

He walked forward and dropped on one knee beside the megasoid, running his hand over its body in the darkness. Lumps stood out all over it, the swelling buds that now would never break to spew forth in a loath-some birth a brood of megasoid pups.

He rose to his feet.

The job was done. The megasoid had been killed—killed before it had given birth to a horde of horrors.

The job was done and he could go home. Home?

Of course, that was the thing that had been planted in his mind, the thing they wanted him to do. To go home, to go back to the house on Summit Avenue, where his executioners would wait, to walk back deliberately and unsuspectingly to the death that waited.

The job was done and his usefulness was over. He had been created to perform a certain task and the task was now performed and while an hour ago he had been a factor in the plans of men, he was no longer wanted. He was an embarrassment and superfluous.

Now wait a minute, he told himself. You may not be a duplicate. You do not feel like one.

That was true. He felt like Henderson James. He *was* Henderson James. He lived on Summit Avenue and had illegally brought to Earth a beast known as a megasoid in order that he might study it and talk to it and test its alien reactions, attempt to measure its intelligence and guess at the strength and depth and the direction of its non-humanity. He had been a fool, of course, to do it, and yet at the time it had seemed important to understand the deadly, alien mentality.

I am human, he said, and that was right, but even so the fact meant nothing. Of course he was human. Henderson James was human and his duplicate would be exactly as human as the original. For the duplicate, processed from the pattern that held every trait and characteristic of the man he was to become a copy of, would differ in not a single basic factor.

In not a single basic factor, perhaps, but in certain other things. For no matter how much the duplicate might be like his pattern, no matter how full-limbed he might spring from his creation, he still would be a new man. He would have the capacity for knowledge and for thought and in a little time he would have and know and be all the things that his original was...

BUT IT WOULD TAKE SOME TIME, some short while to come to a full realization of all he knew and was, some time to coordinate and recognize all the knowledge and experience that lay within his mind. At first he'd grope and search until he came upon the things that he must know. Until he became acquainted with himself, with the sort of man he was, he could not reach out blindly in the dark and put his hand exactly and unerringly upon the thing he wished.

That had been exactly what he'd done. He had groped and searched. He had been compelled to think, at first, in simple basic truths and facts.

I am a man.

I am on a planet called Earth.

I am Henderson James.

I live on Summit Avenue.

There is a job to do.

It had been quite a while, he remembered now, before he had been able to dig out of his mind the nature of the job.

There is a megasoid to hunt down and destroy.

Even now he could not find in the hidden, still-veiled recesses of his mind the many valid reasons why a man should run so grave a risk to study a thing so vicious as a megasoid. There were reasons, he knew there were, and in a little time he would know them quite specifically.

The point was that if he were Henderson James, original, he would know them *now*, know them as a part of himself and his life, without laboriously searching for them.

The megasoid had known, of course. It had known, beyond any chance of error, that there were two Henderson Jameses. It had been keeping tab on one when another one showed up. A mentality far less astute than the megasoid's would have had no trouble in figuring that one out.

If the megasoid had not talked, he told himself, I never would have known. If it had died at once and not had a chance to taunt me, I would not have known. I would even now be walking to the house on Summit Avenue.

He stood lonely and naked of soul in the wind that swept across the moated island. There was a sour bitterness in his mouth.

He moved a foot and touched the dead megasoid.

"I'm sorry," he told the stiffening body. "I'm sorry now I did it. If I had known, I never would have killed you."

Stiffly erect, he moved away.

III

HE STOPPED AT THE STREET CORNER, keeping well in the shadow. Halfway down the block, and on the other side, was the house. A light burned in one of the rooms upstairs and another on the post beside the gate that opened into the yard, lighting the walk up to the door.

Just as if, he told himself, the house were waiting for the master to come home. And that, of course, was exactly what it was doing. An old lady of a house, waiting, hands folded in its lap, rocking very gently in a squeaky chair ... and with a gun beneath the folded shawl.

His lip lifted in half a snarl as he stood there, looking at the house. What do they take me for, he thought, putting out a trap in plain sight and one that's not even baited? Then he remembered. They would not know, of course, that he knew he was a duplicate. They would think that he would think that he was Henderson James, the one and only. They would expect him to come walking home, quite naturally, believing he belonged there. So far as they would know, there would be no possibility of his finding out the truth.

And now that he had? Now that he was here, across the street from the waiting house?

He had been brought into being, had been given life, to do a job that his original had not dared to do, or had not wanted to do. He had carried out a killing his original didn't want to dirty his hands with, or risk his neck in doing.

Or had it not been that at all, but the necessity of two men working on the job, the original serving as a focus for the megasoid's watchful mind while the other man sneaked up to kill it while it watched?

No matter what, he had been created, at a good stiff price, from the pattern of the man that was Henderson James. The wizardry of man's knowledge, the magic of machines, a deep understanding of organic chemistry, of human physiology, of the mystery of life, had made a second Henderson James. It was legal, of course, under certain circumstances ... for example, in the case of public policy, and his own creation, he knew, might have been validated under such a heading. But there were conditions and one of these was that a duplicate not be allowed to continue living once it had served the specific purpose for

Illustrated by DON SIBLEY

which it had been created.

Usually such a condition was a simple one to carry out, for the duplicate was not meant to know he was a duplicate. So far as he was concerned, he was the original. There was no suspicion in him, no foreknowledge of the doom that was invariably ordered for him, no reason for him to be on guard against the death that waited.

THE DUPLICATE KNITTED HIS BROW, trying to puzzle it out. There was a strange set of ethics here.

He was alive and he wanted to stay alive. Life, once it had been tasted, was too sweet, too good, to go back to the nothingness from which he had come ... or would it be nothingness? Now that he had known life, now that he was alive, might he not hope for a life after death, the same as any other human being? Might not he, too, have the same human right as any other human to grasp at the shadowy and glorious promises and assurances held out by religion and by faith?

He tried to marshal what he knew about those promises and assurances, but his knowledge was elusive. A little later he would remember more about it. A little later, when the neural bookkeeper in his mind had been able to coordinate and activate the knowledge that he had inherited from the pattern, he would know.

He felt a trace of anger stir deep inside of him, anger at the unfairness of allowing him only a few short hours of life, of allowing him to learn how wonderful a thing life was, only to snatch it from him. It was a cruelty that went beyond mere human cruelty. It was something that had been fashioned out of the distorted perspective of a machine society that measured existence only in terms of mechanical and physical worth, that discarded with a ruthless hand whatever part of that society had no specific purpose.

The cruelty, he told himself, was in ever

giving life, not in taking it away.

His original, of course, was the one to blame. He was the one who had obtained the megasoid and allowed it to escape. It was his fumbling and his inability to correct his error without help which had created the necessity of fashioning a duplicate.

And yet, could he blame him?

Perhaps, rather, he owed him gratitude for a few hours of life at least, gratitude for the privilege of knowing what life was like. Although he could not quite decide whether or not it was something which called for gratitude.

He stood there, staring at the house. That light in the upstairs room was in the study off the master bedroom. Up there Henderson James, original, was waiting for the word that the duplicate had come home to death. It was an easy thing to sit there and wait, to sit and wait for the word that was sure to come. An easy thing to sentence to death a man one had never seen, even if that man be the walking image of one's self.

It would be a harder decision to kill him if you stood face to face with him ... harder to kill someone who would be, of necessity, closer than a brother, someone who would be, even literally, flesh of your flesh, blood of your blood, brain of your brain.

There would be a practical side as well, a great advantage to be able to work with a man who thought as you did, who would be almost a second self. It would be almost as if there were two of you.

A thing like that could be arranged. Plastic surgery and a price for secrecy could make your duplicate into an unrecognizable other person. A little red tape, some finagling ... but it could be done. It was a proposition that Henderson James, duplicate, thought would interest Henderson James, original. Or at least he hoped it would.

The room with the light could be reached with a little luck, with strength and agility and determination. The brick expanse of a chimney, its base cloaked by shrubs, its length masked by a closely growing tree, ran up the wall. A man could climb its rough brick face, could reach out and swing himself through the open window into the lighted room.

And once Henderson James, original, stood face to face with Henderson James, duplicate ... well, it would be less of a gamble. The duplicate then would no longer be an impersonal factor. He would be a man and one that was very close to his original.

There would be watchers, but they would be watching the front door. If he were quiet, if he could reach and climb the chimney without making any noise, he'd be in the room before anyone would notice.

He drew back deeper in the shadows and considered. It was either get into the room and face his original, hope to be able to strike a compromise with him, or simply to light out ... to run and hide and wait, watching his chance to get completely away, perhaps to some far planet in some other part of the Galaxy.

Both ways were a gamble, but one was quick, would either succeed or fail within the hour; the other might drag on for months with a man never knowing whether he was safe, never being sure.

Something nagged at him, a persistent little fact that skittered through his brain and eluded his efforts to pin it down. It might be important and then, again, it might be a random thing, simply a floating piece of information that was looking for its pigeonhole.

His mind shrugged it off.

The quick way or the long way?

He stood thinking for a moment and then moved swiftly down the street, seeking a place where he could cross in shadow.

He had chosen the short way.

IV

THE ROOM WAS EMPTY.

He stood beside the window, quietly, only his eyes moving, searching every corner, checking against a situation that couldn't seem quite true ... that Henderson James was not here, waiting for the word.

Then he strode swiftly to the bedroom door and swung it open. His finger found the switch and the lights went on. The bedroom was empty and so was the bath. He went back into the study.

He stood with his back against the wall, facing the door that led into the hallway, but his eyes went over the room, foot by foot, orienting himself, feeling himself flow into the shape and form of it, feeling familiarity creep in upon him and enfold him in its comfort of belonging.

Here were the books, the fireplace with its mantel loaded with souvenirs, the easy chairs, the liquor cabinet ... and all were a part of him, a background that was as much a part of Henderson James as his body and his inner thoughts were a part of him.

This, he thought, is what I would have missed, the experience I never would have had if the megasoid had not taunted me. I would have died an empty and unrelated body that had no actual place in the universe.

The phone purred at him and he stood there startled by it, as if some intruder from the outside had pushed its way into the room, shattering the sense of belonging that had come to him.

The phone rang again and he went across the room and picked it up.

"James speaking," he said.

"That you, Mr. James?" The voice was that of Anderson, the gardener.

"Why, yes," said the duplicate. "Who did you think it was?"

"We got a fellow here who says he's you."

Henderson James, duplicate, stiffened with fright, and his hand suddenly was grasping the phone so hard that he found the time to wonder why it did not pulverize to bits beneath his fingers.

"He's dressed like you," the gardener said, "and I knew you went out. Talked to you, remember? Told you that you shouldn't? Not with us waiting for that ... that thing."

"Yes," said the duplicate, his voice so even that he could not believe it was he who spoke. "Yes, certainly I remember talking with you."

"But, sir, how did you get back?"

"I came in the back way," the even voice said into the phone. "Now what's holding you back?"

"He's dressed like you."

"Naturally. Of course he would be, Anderson."

And that, to be sure, didn't quite follow, but Anderson wasn't too bright to start with and now he was somewhat upset.

"You remember," the duplicate said, "that we talked about it."

"I guess I was excited and forgot," admitted Anderson. "You told me to call you, to make sure you were in your study, though. That's right, isn't it, sir?"

"You've called me," the duplicate said, "and I am here."

"Then the other one out here is him?"

"Of course," said the duplicate. "Who else could it be?"

He put the phone back into the cradle and stood waiting. It came a moment after, the dull, throaty cough of a gun.

He walked to a chair and sank into it, spent with the knowledge of how events had so been ordered that now, finally, he was safe, safe beyond all question.

Soon he would have to change into other clothes, hide the gun and the clothes that he was wearing. The staff would ask no questions, most likely, but it was best to let nothing arouse suspicion in their minds.

He felt his nerves quieting and he allowed himself to glance about the room, take in the books and furnishings, the soft and easy ... and earned ... comfort of a man solidly and unshakably established in the world.

He smiled softly.

"It will be nice," he said.

It had been easy. Now that it was over, it seemed ridiculously easy. Easy because he had never seen the man who had walked up to the door. It was easy to kill a man you have never seen.

With each passing hour he would slip deeper and deeper into the personality that was his by right of heritage. There would be no one to question, after a time not even himself, that he was Henderson James.

The phone rang again and he got up to answer it.

A pleasant voice told him, "This is Allen, over at the duplication lab. We've been waiting for a report from you."

"Well," said James, "I..."

"I just called," interrupted Allen, "to tell you not to worry. It slipped my mind before."

"I see," said James, though he didn't.

"We did this one a little differently," Allen explained. "An experiment that we thought we'd try out. Slow poison in his bloodstream. Just another precaution. Probably not necessary, but we like to be positive. In case he fails to show up, you needn't worry any."

"I am sure he will show up."

Allen chuckled. "Twenty-four hours. Like a time bomb. No antidote for it even if he found out somehow."

"It was good of you to let me know," said James.

"Glad to," said Allen. "Good night, Mr. James."

Clifford D. Simak's "The Duplicate Man" originally appeared in the March 1951 issue of Galaxy Magazine, as "Good Night, Mr. James" (with illustrations by Don Sibley), and was reprinted in 1964 as "The Night of the Puudly" (in the author's collection of the same title). The same year, the story was loosely adapted by Robert C. Dennis as "The Duplicate Man" for the 1963-1965 television series The Outer Limits. The alien race in Simak's story were called Puudly—arguably a terrible name for a serious SF tale. Screenwriter Dennis used the term Megasoid for The Outer Limits version. For this reprint in Black Infinity, the editor also has substituted Megasoid for Puudly.

American writer Clifford D. Simak began his career in the early 1930s by publishing a handful of super science tales in Wonder Stories, a magazine founded by Hugo Gernsback ("The Father of Science Fiction"). Over the next few years Simak continued to delve into SF sporadically, while producing numerous western and war stories for the adventure pulps of the day. Once Simak finally settled down to strange worlds and sensational ideas, he proved himself both thoughtful and prolific. Clifford's prose is always profound but never preachy, and fans and professionals acknowledged his genius with three Hugo Awards, a Nebula, a Jupiter, and a Bram Stoker Award for Lifetime Achievement.

Simak once wrote, "I have been happily married to the same woman for thirty-three years (...without whom I'd never have written a line) and have two children. My favorite recreation is fishing (the lazy way, lying in a boat and letting them come to me). Hobbies: Chess, stamp collecting, growing roses."

Note: the images of the Megasoid were created from photos taken from the episode of The Outer Limits, "The Duplicate Man" (MGM, 1964).

The room was small, but it held a whole Universe—
and Norcriss had no place in it!

THE CREATURE INSIDE

by Jack Sharkey

"**H**OW MUCH DID THEY TELL YOU ABOUT THE FIX WE'RE IN?" SAID DR. ALAN BURGESS TO HIS VISITOR.

Lieutenant Jerry Norcriss shook his head. "They said you'd fill me in. They said it was urgent."

Burgess paused, lighted a cigarette, then belatedly offered one to Jerry, who declined. "Well," he said, interspersing his words with short nervous puffs of smoke, "about a year ago, I stumbled on a way to reverse the process of an electro-encephalograph, to play pre-recorded thoughts and experiences to a man's mind. You zoologists, with your Contact process for penetrating newly discovered fauna's minds, will be familiar with the process. Luckily for us."

Jerry eyed him. "Go on."

"My development involves an infinitely selective feedback. We give the subject a saturating dose of inflowing concepts. His mind is free to choose among them and to link them. Take 'bigness, affluence and danger' for an instance. The subject puts them together and fleshes them out. He could experience a large, expensive fission bomb falling onto him, or he could be sacrificed to an immense golden idol, or— Or anything that his inner mind chose."

"I begin to understand," said Jerry. "The overlay influences all the senses. The subject thinks he's *really* undergoing whatever he conjures up—and you use it for therapy, letting him work off his aggressions and frustrations in what seems to him an actual universe."

"Correct, except for the tense," said Alan Burgess. "I *was* doing that until Monday of this week." He leaned forward across the desk. "We screen the subjects carefully, because certain psychoses could be disastrous to the subject in my device. Paranoia, for instance. The man would be amid unutterable horrors, with danger on every side; he'd emerge a gibbering idiot, if he didn't die of heart failure first."

"Emerge?" asked Jerry, frowning. "I'd assumed you used a helmet, such as we do in Contact...."

Burgess sighed. "Unfortunately, I am paying the penalty of lone-wolf experimentation. I wish I'd had the sense to route the input to the brain through a helmet, but I didn't. Instead I installed the person in an observation room. The influencing factor was nutrition. Intravenous feedings wouldn't have served the purpose of the observer; sometimes the subject's choice of foodstuffs is significant. He had to be let move about, his mind in a make-believe world, but his body actually moving about a room we could see into. So—I had an atomic duplicator installed. The hospital got one last year for making radium, turning cancerous growths into normal flesh, regrowing bone and the like.

"Should the subject then grow hungry, the duplicator would be triggered by his conviction of eating. In his mind, he might be—hanging from a branch by his tail, for instance. The duplicator's production of bananas, coconuts or whatever would give us a further clue to his state of mind. You see?"

"So far, sound enough, Dr. Burgess," said Jerry. "So what went wrong? I assume something did, or I wouldn't be here."

"We made a terrible error. We tried observing a man named Anthony Mawson in our gadget. I'd diagnosed his case as simple inferiority complex. My fault. Wrong diagnosis. Mawson has megalomania, a gorgeous case of it...of course, he's not the first such case to fool psychiatrists. You see, his outward shyness, soft-spoken voice and general gawkishness is due to feeling superior to others, not the reverse. He feels smarter, stronger, braver, etcetera, than everybody else in creation—but he also feels that nobody knows it but himself. Hence his indrawing, his brooding, taciturn gentility."

Jerry Norcriss prodded. "What happened with Mawson when you put him in your machine?"

"I don't know," said Burgess. "No one's been able to see into the machine since he entered it on Monday."

"He couldn't have escaped?"

"No! I wish he had. Anthony Mawson is still in that room, in his own private universe, and we can't get him out of it. We've tried cutting the power to the machine; the opacity inside the room remains. We sent two men in after him. They never came out."

"How could he possibly...?" asked Jerry.

Burgess shook his head. "We can only guess. Our theory is that he's used the duplicator to make the entire room self-sustaining. Normally we could wait till he runs out of material to feed the duplicator, but—we can't wait on the lives of those two men. Nor can we chance his expanding his universe."

Norcriss frowned. "Expanding it?"

Burgess nodded. "By, perhaps, feeding the duplicator with the room itself. With a pickaxe, he can start hewing down the very walls, or even have the duplicator build a robot that will take care of its need for material to build with. Against this development, we have surrounded the room completely with a force-shield, limiting his outward progress to two feet of concrete in any direction. But the room is approximately thirty feet square, and twenty feet high. With all that mass he could exist in there for years."

"And my job is to get him out," said Jerry.

"Yes. The government feels that a Contact specialist's the only kind of man to send into this madman's world. You men are used to extra-somatic experiences—and you have learned to live with danger without losing your heads."

"Well," said Jerry, getting up, "I guess that sums up the situation sufficiently."

Burgess nodded, sadly. "Any further briefing is useless. Impossible, really. I've told you the situation, and you can certainly imagine the danger. But as for the solution, well.... You'll just have to feel your way, and do whatever you think best."

Jerry paused beside Burgess at the door to the hall. "One thing, though, Doctor; when I get into the influence of the machine, what kind of universe will I be in? Mine or Mawson's?"

"I can only theorize on that," said Burgess. "My guess would be that you'll find both in there, one vying for supremacy over the other.

This fight won't be man to man. It will be universe against universe."

THERE HAD BEEN NO SENSATION at all as Jerry stepped through the flat sheet of grayness in the doorway; no more physical awareness than a blind man might feel when passing through the beam of a powerful light. Perhaps there was a slight sensation of the mere presence of the energies that kept the opacity in existence —but that sensation, Jerry knew, was psychological, not actual.

"Although," he realized, as his world became an infinity of opalescent gray, "in this place, a psychological awareness will be no different from a genuine physical sensation. Better be careful what I think about in this psychokinetic fog...."

The thought was barely formulated when the grayness changed. It became moist against his flesh, and started swirling in tendrils about him. "Damn it, be *careful!*" he belatedly cautioned his mind. "Now the stuff *is* fog!" Ahead of him in the swirling mist a brighter-than-gray glow led his footsteps forward.

He found himself standing beneath an overhanging marquee. Its black undersurface was runneled with condensed moisture amid the garish naked bulbs that haloed the wet cement sidewalk.

A red-coated doorman, resplendent behind rows of bright brassy buttons, gave him a smile as he pulled open the door that led to the club. Jerry nodded and went inside.

Thick crimson carpet cushioned his footfalls as he moved cautiously through an empty lobby, then down a white marble staircase toward the ballroom. Dimly, he was aware that the band at the far end of the mammoth room was playing music. What song he didn't know until a chance chording reminded him of a popular song of the day ... at which point that suddenly was the tune. The tables ringing the dance floor were covered with bright linen and shining silver. The tables were empty of patrons, however, until Jerry casually thought, "I should think business would be better—"

Suddenly a horde of laughing couples appeared in the chairs, with hurrying waiters bringing champagne, trays, and menus to their guests.

The men wore tuxedos; the women were in evening dress. He looked suddenly at himself, and saw that his uniform was now the official dress uniform of the Space Corps. Before he could conquer it, his mind voiced a quick wish that he shouldn't be dining alone; and then a girl was rising from her place at a table beside the dance floor, hurrying to greet him, hands outstretched.

Her fingers were small and strong and warm. She smiled up at him. "Jerry, darling."

Despite her being only arm's length from him, he could not see her well at all. His impression was merely one of youth, loveliness and girl-ness. But then, as he tried to ascertain precisely what she looked like, hidden corners of his mind began to supply each detail an instant before his conscious quest for it, and Jerry, in a few moments, was suddenly staggered with delighted shock.

Very few men are privileged to find a girl who lives up to all their dreams of perfection in a woman.

Hair as soft as cobweb, as fluffy as dancing clouds, as golden as flowing honey, cascaded down about a slender alabaster throat, and died in golden ripples on smooth white shoulders. Eyes the rich brown of raw chocolate gazed serenely at him from under red-gold brows and jet lashes, their patrician serenity permeated with a touch of twinkling impishness. Her lips were soft and not unlike berry-stained velvet, sweet and warm and tempting; her mouth generous and tilted at the corners into a smile of greeting—obviously the result of her subduing a frank laugh of joy at seeing him. Geometrically perfect teeth flashed white as porcelain between her lips. Her gown was a shimmering midnight blue, highlighted with random sprinkles of brightly coruscating gems.

Even as his lips parted to ask her name, Jerry knew it and spoke it softly. "Carol."

"Listen," she said softly, tilting her head toward where the band had begun a new song. Swift, urgent and rapturous, it floated through the room, surrounded the two of them, took possession of them. Then Carol was in his arms, and Jerry was dancing out onto the floor with her. The other couples were a blur of forgotten figures that swayed.

Jerry knew the melody. It was their song, their own private love song, the one that had been playing on the night when they both knew, suddenly, that there could be no one else for either of them but the other....

As they returned to their table, Jerry realized that Carol was now garbed in a white peasant blouse and bright flowered flaring skirt, and that her hair was drawn back at the temples to expose her ears, now adorned with golden hoops. The table was in a lattice-backed booth, covered with a red-and-white checkered cloth. The inner surface of the table held salt, pepper, grated cheese and breadsticks, matching cruets of pale olive oil and dark vinegar. The band was now a five-man gypsy ensemble.

"Remember the first time we came here, Jerry?" asked Carol, her eyes at once upon his face and distant, dreamy....

As she smiled, Jerry noticed with dull horror that one of her eyes was perceptibly lower than the other.

The teeth she flashed his way were mottled with brown stains. She took hold of his fingers with her own.

"Carol!" he said shakily, staring at the knuckly, red-raw hands that clutched at his. "What's happening?"

"Happening?" she said, her voice a raucous croak of amusement. "*Nothing's* happening! In fact, you're probably one of the dullest guys I ever got stuck with." She tossed her head petulantly. Coarse, straw-colored hair flipped away from her thick neck. Her breath was sour with wine and miasmic with garlic.

"Carol!" he cried.

"Don't whine!" she snapped, viciously. "I hate a guy who whines!" With that, she shoved out of the booth, and waddled toward the rear of the coffeehouse, one hand scratching at a bulge of flesh that overhung the too-tight girdle. Her black leotards were twisted and dull as she passed the flashing rainbow lights of the brassy jukebox.

Jerry shoved away from the table, overturning his coffee in its cracked china cup, and he wove his way through the reek and smoke toward the door through which she'd vanished.

When he got there, the door was a peeling poster on a bare brick wall, advertising some long-forgotten show. His fingers scrabbled on rough mortar for a moment. Then he turned and paced back to his cot, where he flopped on his back in the long shadows of the bars.

"Norcriss!" said the guard, coming into the cell. "This is it!" The brass uniform buttons flashed brightly.

Strong hands were lifting him from the cot, dragging him down a long corridor toward a steel door. As they got there, the door opened wide, and Jerry saw the gaping maw of hungry steel gears, while behind him a man's voice droned prayers.

Then, before the guard could shove Jerry forward into that waiting mechanical mouth, Jerry noticed the odd shimmer of grayness that lay between himself and the waiting teeth, and he remembered that he was in a world of illusion.

At precisely that moment he knew beyond a doubt that those waiting jaws were illusion in form only. An atomic duplicator does not have to chew its intake. It merely dissolves the atomic bonds with the rays that flash between its power plates on either side of the disruption platform. The waiting mouth and teeth were mere symbols in Jerry's mind of what was about to occur.

They were unreal—but they could be fatal.

He shut his eyes, shoved backward with his feet, and thought of Carol as he'd first glimpsed her.

When he opened his eyes once more, she was standing before him in her ballroom gown again, and the band was just beginning to play their song once more.

"Jerry," she said, taking his arm. "Dance with me."

"No. We're in danger here. Come on, I'll get your coat. We've got to go away quickly."

A spark of alarm showed briefly in her eyes. Then she nodded wordlessly and hurried up the marble staircase with him to the lobby. Jerry got her coat from the check-room —a marvelous silvery fur that covered her from neck to waist—and then they were heading out into the fog together.

"Good evening to you, sir," said the doorman, eyes and buttons bright.

Jerry grunted and led Carol off down the street into the fog.

"Where are we going?" she asked, breathlessly trying to keep pace.

"Away, I hope," he said. Even their movement from the ballroom could be sheer illusion. Jerry tried moving from the club entrance in the exact reverse of the motion in which he'd first approached it, trying to achieve the real doorway that led from the experimental room into the antiseptic hospital corridor where Burgess waited. But the fog continued to be fog. It would not take on the form of that intangible gray shimmering that guarded the entrance to Anthony Mawson's megalomaniac universe.

"If I could only see where—" he began.

Then every tendril of fog was gone.

Before him lay the cold blackness of outer space, pinpointed with hard, unwinking stars. Jerry recoiled from the viewplate, shaken, and turned around to see Carol. Her eyes were wide and startled as she glanced about at the metal confines of the control cabin. Jerry had just time enough to think how incongruous she looked in her fur jacket and long blueblack gown ... and then she was clothed in the neat gray uniform of the WASP, trim short-sleeved shirt and sharply creased shorts.

"Jerry," said Carol. She slipped her arm through his, staring at the infinite stars in the viewplate. "What are we running from?"

He tried to think, but could not remember. "There's—some danger behind us. We have to get away from it, Carol. It means complete destruction if we're caught."

Carol stared helplessly at the stars in the viewplate. "But where are we running to?"

Jerry shook his head. "Impossible to tell. Not without the help of a good astrogator. Out in space, stars shift and magnitudes change. I'm not even qualified to guess—"

"Sir," said the astrogator, handing a clipboard to Jerry, "we can reach any of these seven stars in a few hours. Just tell me where you'd prefer to go."

Jerry turned to the man, resplendent in his neat Space Corps uniform, jacket bright with brass buttons. When he tried to focus upon the man's features he could detect nothing.

"We'd better choose the quickest trip," Jerry said, after a moment's indecision. "No telling how much fuel we have left."

The astrogator nodded. "I'm afraid that's out of my department, all right, sir. But if *you'd* care to check the tanks?" Without waiting for a reply, the man turned and began to pick his way carefully toward the rear of the spaceship, stepping from girder to girder. The floor, Jerry noticed idly as he followed, was exposed to open space between the curving ribs of steel that formed the framework of the ship.

"Careful, now," he said, helping Carol along from one to the other. "That's vacuum out there. We don't want to fall through."

Ahead of Jerry, the implacable man with the brass buttons was nearly to the steel door masking the blast chamber where the components of fuel were mingled and ignited. Jerry, giddily aware of every hazardous step over the squares of star-speckled blackness, kept one hand on Carol's arm, the other on her chessboard.

"Don't spill any of the men!" she cautioned, as the diminutive plastic figures danced and rattled on the board. "I don't intend to search the whole cosmos for a pawn."

"Here you go, sir," said the politely insistent astrogator, opening the steel door. Before Jerry yawned an oval of intense white flame, the radiating heat crisping against his skin and hair.

"The fission rate," Jerry mumbled, consulting his wristwatch. "I've got to time it, or I won't be able to calculate the amount of fuel still in the bulkheads."

"Count it by steps, sir," suggested the astrogator.

"One," said Jerry, stepping out toward that blinding coruscation of heat. "Two," he said, feeling carefully for the next girder.

Then the toe of his boot slipped from the metal, and he realized, with a horrible lancing of adrenalin through his abdomen, that he was falling out the opening between the girders. The only salvation would be a shove with his still-braced rear foot, but that would carry him directly into the inferno of burning fuel. An eternity of falling through icy vacuum against an instant of intolerable searing pain....

"The fire—" gasped Jerry, toppling in inexorable slow motion toward starry darkness, a cloud of twirling chess pieces orbiting about his head. "I've got to make it into the fire...."

He tensed the muscles of the laggard leg for the spring that would carry him to destruction, and then he saw that the chess pieces were shimmering gray, and the oval frame of the doorway to the flaming fuel was shimmering gray, and even what had seemed hot white burning was cold gray waiting mist, and with a yell of remembrance, Jerry clamped shut his eyes and let himself plunge downward into nothingness....

III

"ARE YOU ALL RIGHT, NORCRISS?" Jerry blinked slowly, then focused on the face of Dr. Alan Burgess. He found himself lying on a narrow, white-sheeted cart, in the corridor outside the room where all the trouble had begun. "Mawson," he said groggily. "Is he—?"

Burgess nodded wearily. "Still in there, in full control of his one-man universe. What happened, Norcriss? You came tumbling out that door like a wild man, clawing the air and yelling. Then you went into shock. You've been unconscious for two hours."

"I—I thought I was falling," Jerry admitted. "The last thing I remember is stepping through the open space between a spaceship's supporting girders."

"What open space?" said Burgess, frowning curiously.

Jerry shook his head. "There isn't any such thing. But something happens to logic in that room. It's like having a dream, Doctor. Things that would startle you in everyday life seem correct. Even familiar. But there's a kind of pattern to events. At first, I'm in my universe, and mostly in control. Then little fragments of my pseudo-reality start slipping, changing into other things. The changes seem perfectly normal to me. Then, all at once, the guy with the brass buttons turns up—and I've managed in the nick of time, twice, to realize that I was about to be sent or led between the disrupting plates of your atomic duplicator."

"The man with the brass buttons," Burgess said slowly. "Do you think it's Mawson?"

"Either him or a robot he's made to keep his machine fed." When Burgess scowled, Jerry shrugged and appended, "It is *his* machine, for all practical purposes. He's the boss of that hungry electronic monster, Doctor, however the hospital feels about it."

"This Carol. Is she a real woman, or a figment of your imagination, wishful thinking?"

"She's real enough," Jerry sighed. "She's the personal secretary of the entire Space Zoology program. I take her out sometimes. There's nothing special between us."

"But you wish there were," said Burgess.

Jerry stared at him. "What makes you think that?"

Burgess tilted his head toward the room where Mawson still maintained control. "Your visions in there. You must think a lot of her. You can kid yourself consciously; but nearly all you underwent in there came straight from your subconscious. And a subconscious just

doesn't know how to lie."

Jerry changed the subject, "What's our next move? How soon can I go back after Mawson?"

"You can't. Mawson's knowledge of this Carol can easily be turned to your disadvantage. He can use her to lead you to dissolution in there. No, it's much too risky. You're lucky you got out when you did."

"But what about Mawson, then?"

Burgess tried to look confident. He failed. "We can ring up your headquarters and ask for another man. Or, if worse comes to worse, we can partition off this part of the hospital, and just sit it out until Mawson runs out of atomic building blocks."

"Which may take years," Jerry reminded him.

Burgess turned his palms upward. "What else can we do?"

"Send me again," said Jerry. "I know the score pretty well, now. I know what to watch out for. I'm sure that with one more try I can get Mawson out of there."

"Sorry," Burgess said, shaking his head. "As a medical man, I cannot permit it. You've had a bad shock. We'll try someone else, if your outfit will send someone, and see what happens. If he fails, or if they won't supply us with any more men, then—well, you can try again in a few weeks, if you're still game. But not now."

"Doctor, in a few weeks, Mawson will be so well in control of that universe that he may find a way to block the entrance. Have you thought of that?"

"His universe is not a real one—" Burgess began.

"But that duplicator is real enough. It can make anything he decides he needs. And at any time he may get the bright idea of simply mounting his machine right at the entrance, so anyone stepping into that gray field will be powdered into atoms, instantly."

"That's true enough," admitted Burgess. "But my diagnosis still stands. For now, you are off this assignment. When I feel you're ready—assuming nothing else has succeeded meantime—I'll contact you at the base."

"How do you know I won't be off on some other planet by then?" asked Jerry bitterly.

"I don't," said Burgess. "I hope you are not, but there isn't anything further I can do about it. I'm sorry."

"And what do I do in the meantime?"

Burgess grinned. "Call up this Carol and go out on the town."

Jerry shook his head at the last part. "No thanks. I prefer Carol to know nothing about it."

Burgess shrugged and gave it up. "All right, Norcriss. Rest here till you feel stronger, then you're free to go." Then he was striding off down the corridor.

After a bit, Jerry sat up cautiously, let the slight giddiness subside, then swung his legs off the side of the cart and got down.

Behind him, the door to Mawson's universe stood open on its wall of grayness. Jerry stared thoughtfully at it, then saw that the two internes who were guarding the opposite ends of this section of the hospital corridor were hesitantly half-starting toward him. Jerry knew he could be through that doorway and into the grayness before they got within ten feet of him....

IV

THEN HIS SHOULDERS SLUMPED, and he turned and walked toward the elevators. Burgess was right. He felt worn out, and not inclined to make grandstand plays. Besides, he thought, thumbing the elevator button, it would be nice to see the *real* Carol again, after her nebulous pseudo-self. He wanted very much to put his arms around a girl who wouldn't suddenly turn into something horrible in his embrace.

The steel doors slid open before him, and the elevator boy leaned out to check the corridor for other passengers. "Down," he said.

Jerry nodded and started into the elevator.

Then he hesitated, and looked back toward the room where Mawson reigned supreme, then back at the elevator boy. "Say," he said, uncertainly, "that's a strange outfit for an elevator attendant in a hospital. I'd have expected an orderly in an all-white getup."

The boy glanced down at his uniform, the bright blue pants, shined black shoes, and scarlet jacket bright with twin rows of brass buttons. "I suppose it is," he said. "But I don't usually run this elevator. I'm from the hotel next door. I'm just doing this while the regular guy takes his coffee break."

Jerry hesitated, then stepped toward the waiting elevator with its pale gray walls. And stopped again. His hand went to his forehead, bewilderedly. "There's something—" he said.

Then Carol was beside him, slipping her arm through his. "Come on, Jerry," she said urgently. "We'll be late for our date."

Jerry looked at her, then at the hotel corridor behind her, then again at the waiting elevator.

"I have the oddest feeling something's wrong," he said. "I—I don't remember coming over here for you."

"You didn't," she said promptly. "I came for you, Jerry. This is your hotel, remember? Doctor Burgess said you'd had a bad shock, but I didn't know how bad till now."

"Shock?" said Jerry. "What shock? What was bothering me?"

Carol smiled tightly. "Nothing. Nothing at all. Come on, Jerry, darling." Again she drew him toward the elevator.

"If I could only remember," he said, uneasily, on the brink of that open cube of bright grayness. Then his eyes focused upon the brass buttons fronting the boy's jacket, and at his own shadow as it passed across those glowing hemispheres. As the shadow crossed a button, the color would die, and the button would be dull crystal, and then glow bright and brassy again when the shadow had passed.

"Photoelectric cells!" said Jerry. "Light-sensitive cells. Those aren't buttons, they're eyes! Multiple robot eyes!" He staggered away from the boy. Carol stopped him.

The elevator boy, suddenly half again Jerry's height, was towering over him, long steel arms extending like hooked telescopes toward him. "Get in, Jerry, get *in!*" cried Carol, struggling to push him forward toward those invincible metal clamps.

In a fury of fear, Jerry fought her, grappled with her, twisted to avoid those extending robot hands that would drag him to destruction. And suddenly Carol was screaming his name, and her eyes were pools of terror and betrayal, and the leaping metal fingers had buried themselves in the soft flesh of her shoulders and dragged her back into grayness.

Incredible energies came alive about her, and then there was only a shimmer of dusty crystalline winds, and she was gone.

Jerry found himself standing before the still-warm plates of the atomic duplicator, in the room where Mawson had had his short-lived universe. Beside the machine, a squat cubic box dangled limp steel arms, its rows of photo-electric cells losing their golden glow.

And then, as Burgess came hurrying in through the door, he toppled over in a dead faint.

"SO THERE IS NO SUCH PERSON AS CAROL?" said Burgess, standing at the foot of the hospital bed. "She was only the figment of your imagination?"

"Yes," said Jerry dully. "And all along, it was Mawson I was really with. He was clever, all right. She was certainly the last occupant of that crazy place I was likely to attack. If he had not tried attacking me himself—I might be atom dust by now. A little longer, and she—*he*, I mean—might have *talked* me into that elevator."

"Well," said Burgess, "I'm sorry this thing ended with Mawson's dissolution, but that can't be helped. You did your job well, Lieutenant."

"Thanks," said Jerry, expressionlessly.

"To come so near death so many times—" Burgess shuddered. "You have a remarkable constitution, not to have cracked under such a strain. Lieutenant, you're a lucky man."

And Jerry, his mind still filled with a vision of golden hair, soft brown eyes and warm, eager lips, could only echo wearily, "Very lucky."

"The Creature Inside" first appeared in the December 1963 issue of Worlds of Tomorrow. *The original* WoT *illustrations are by Frank Bruno (cover art) and Wallace Wood (interior).*

Jack Sharkey decided to become a writer when he was in the fourth grade, when he realized that "someone wrote all those stories in the textbooks." He started devouring every book he could get his hands on, figuring that "if I put enough literature into my head, some of it might overflow and come out." After sixteen years of education, Jack found himself teaching high school English in Chicago, a worthwhile career, but "not what one would call zesty." After a two-year hitch in the Army, and a year in advertising "sublimating my urge to write things for cash," he moved to New York, determined to make a career of full-time fiction-writing.

Oddly enough, it worked out. He once stated, "I'd like to say I do this for fulfillment, or for cash, or because it's my destiny; however, the real reason is that this kind of stay-at-home self-employment lets me sleep late in the morning."

The Planeteers found Mars
an unexpectedly pleasant world—
until they ran afoul of the inhabitants, who could imitate anything!

THE BRAIN-STEALERS
OF MARS

by John W. Campbell, Jr.

ROD BLAKE LOOKED UP WITH A DEEP CHUCKLE. The sky of Mars was almost black, despite the small, brilliant sun, and the brighter stars and planets that shone visibly, Earth most brilliant of all, scarcely sixty million miles away.

"They'll have a fine time chasing us, back there, Ted." He nodded toward the brilliant planet.

Ted Penton smiled beatifically.

"They're probably investigating all our known haunts. It's their own fault if they can't find us—outlawing research on atomic power."

"They had some provocation, you must admit. Koelenberg should have been more careful. When a man takes off some three hundred square miles of territory *spang* in the center of Europe in an atomic explosion, you can't blame the rest of the world for being a bit skittish about atomic power research."

"But they might have had the wit to see that anybody that did get the secret would not wait around for the Atomic Power Research Death Penalty, but would light out for parts and planets quite unknown, and leave the mess in the hands of a lawyer till the fireworks quieted down. It was obvious that when we developed atomic power we'd be the first men to reach Mars, and nobody could follow to bring us back unless they accepted the hated atomic power and used it," argued Blake.

"Wonder how old Jamison Montgomery Palborough made out with our claims," mused Penton. "He said he'd have it right in three months, and this is the third month and the third planet. We'll let the government stew, and sail on, fair friend, sail on. I still say that was a ruined city we saw as we landed."

"I think it was, myself, but I remember the way you did that kangaroo leap on your neck the first time you stepped out on the moon. You certainly saw stars."

"We're professionals at walking under cockeyed gravities now. Moon— Venus—"

"Yes, but I'm still not risking my neck on the attitude of a strange planet *and* a strange race at the same time. We'll investigate the planet a bit first, and yonder mudhole is the first stop. Come on."

They reached the top of one of the long rolling sand dunes and the country was spread out below them.

It looked exactly as it had been from the last dune that they had struggled up, just as utterly barren, utterly bleak, and unendingly red. Like an iron planet, badly neglected and rusted.

The mudhole was directly beneath them, an expanse of red and brown slime, dotted here and there with clumps of dark red foliage.

"The stuff looks like Japanese maple," said Blake.

"Evidently doesn't use chlorophyll to get the sun's energy. Let's collect a few samples. You have your violet-gun and I have mine. I guess it's safe to split. There's a large group of things down on the left that look a little different. I'll take them while you go straight ahead. Gather any flowers, fruits, berries or seeds you see. Few leaves—oh, you know. What we got on Venus. General junk. If you find a small plant, put on your gloves and yank it out. If you see a big one, steer clear. Venus had some peculiarly unpleasant specimens."

Blake groaned. "You telling me. I'm the bright boy that fell for that pretty fruit and climbed right up between the stems of a scissor tree. *Uh-uh.* I shoot 'em down. Go ahead, and good luck."

Penton swung off to the left, while Blake slogged ahead to a group of weird-looking plants. They were dome-shaped things, three feet high, with a dozen long, drooping, sword-shaped leaves.

Cautiously Blake tossed a bit of stone into the center of one. It gave off a mournful, drumming boom, but the leaves didn't budge. He tried a rope on one leaf but the leaf neither stabbed, grabbed, nor jerked away, as he had half expected after his lesson with the ferocious plants of Venus. Blake pulled a leaf off, then a few more. The plant acted quite plant-like, which pleasantly surprised him.

The whole region seemed seeded with a number of the things, nearly all about the same size. A few, sprinkled here and there, were in various stages of development, from a few protruding sword-leaves, to little three-inch domes on up to the full-grown plant. Carefully avoiding the larger ones, Rod plucked two small ones and thrust them into his specimen bag. Then he stood off and looked at one of the domes that squatted so dejectedly in the thick, gummy mud.

"I suppose you have some reason for being

like that, but a good solid tree would put you all in the shade, and collect all the sunlight going. Which is little enough." He looked at them for some seconds picturing a stout Japanese maple in this outlandish red-brown gum.

He shrugged and wandered on, seeking some other plant. There were few others. Apparently this particular species throttled out other varieties very thoroughly. He wasn't very anxious anyway—he was much more interested in the ruined city they had seen from the ship. Ted Penton was cautious.

Eventually Blake followed his winding footsteps back toward the ship, and about where his footsteps showed he'd gathered his first samples, he stopped. There was a Japanese maple there. It stood some fifteen feet tall, and the bark was beautifully regular in appearance. The leaves were nearly a quarter of an inch thick, and arranged with a peculiar regularity, as were the branches. But it was very definitely a Japanese maple.

Rod Blake's jaw put a severe strain on the hinges thereof. It dropped some three inches, and Blake stared. He stared with a steady, blank gaze at that perfectly impossible Japanese maple. He gawked dumbly. Then his jaw snapped shut abruptly, and he cursed softly. The leaves were stirring gently, and they were not a quarter of an inch thick. They were paper thin, and delicately veined. Further, the tree was visibly taller, and three new branches had started to sprout, irregularly now. They sprouted as he watched, growing not as twigs but as fully formed branches extending themselves gradually. As he stared harder at them they dwindled rapidly to longer twigs, and grew normally.

Rod let out a loud yip, and made tracks rapidly extending themselves toward the point where he'd last seen Ted Penton. Penton's tracks curved off, and Rod steamed down as fast as Mars' light gravity permitted, to pull up short as he rounded a corner of another sword-leaf dome clump. "Ted," he panted, "come over here. There's a—a—weird thing. A—it looks like a Japanese maple, but it doesn't. Because when you look at it, it changes." Rod stopped, and started back, beckoning Ted. Ted didn't move.

"I don't know what to say," he said quite clearly, rather panting and sounding excited, though it was a quite unexciting remark, except for one thing. He said it in Rod Blake's voice! Rod stiffened. Then he backed away hurriedly, stumbled over his feet and sat down heavily in the sand.

"For the love of—Ted—*Ted!* Wh-what did you s-s-say?"

"I don't know wh-what to s-s-say."

Rod groaned. It started out exactly like his own voice, changed rapidly while it spoke, and wound up a fair imitation of Ted's. "Oh, Lord," he groaned, "I'm going back to the ship. In a hurry."

He started away, then looked back over his shoulder. Ted Penton was moving now, swaying on his feet peculiarly. Delicately he picked up his left foot, shook it gently, like a man trying to separate himself from a piece of flypaper. Rod moved even more rapidly than

he had before.

Long but rapidly shrinking roots dangled from the foot, gooey mud dropping from them as they shrank into the foot. Rod turned again with the violet-gun in his hand. It thrummed to blasting atomic energy, and a pencil beam of ravening ultraviolet fury shot out and a hazy ball of light surrounded it.

The figure of Ted Penton smoked suddenly, and a hole the size of a golf ball drove abruptly through the center of the head, to the accompaniment of a harsh whine of steam and spurts of oily smoke. The figure did not fall. It slumped. It melted rapidly, like a snowman in a furnace. The fingers ran together, the remainder of the face dropped, contracted, and became horrible.

It was suddenly the face of a man whose pouched and dulled eyes had witnessed and enjoyed every evil the worlds knew, weirdly glowing eyes that danced and flamed for a moment in screaming fury of deadly hate—and dissolved with the last dissolution of the writhing face.

And the arms grew long, very long and much wider. Rod stood frozen while the very

wide and rapidly widening arms beat up and down. The thing took off and flapped awkwardly away, and for an instant the last trace of the hate-filled eyes glittered again in the sun.

Rod Blake sat down and laughed. He laughed and laughed again at the very funny sight of the melting face on the bat-bodied thing that had flown away with a charred hole in the middle of its grape-fruit-sized head. He laughed even louder when another Ted-Penton-thing came around the corner of the vegetable clump, on the run. He aimed at the center of its head.

"Fly away!" he yelled as he pressed the little button down.

This one was cleverer. It ducked. "Rod—for the love of—*Rod*, shut up," it spoke.

Rod stopped and considered slowly. This one talked with Ted Penton's voice. As it got up again he aimed more carefully and flashed again. He wanted it to fly away too. It ducked again, in another direction this time, and ran in rapidly. Rod got up hastily and ran. He fell suddenly as some fibrous thing lashed out from behind and wrapped itself unbreakably about his arms and body, binding him helplessly.

Penton looked down at him, panting heavily. "What's the trouble, Rod; and why in blazes were you shooting your gun at me?"

Rod heard himself laugh again, uncontrollably. The sight of Ted's worried face reminded him of the flying thing, with the melted face. Like an overheated wax figure. Penton reached out a deliberate hand and cracked him over the face, hard. In a moment Rod steadied, and Penton removed the noose from his arms and body. Blake sighed with relief.

"Thank God, it's you, Ted," he said. "Listen, I saw you—*you*—not thirty seconds ago. You stood over there, and I spoke to you. You answered in *my* voice. I started off, and your feet came up out of the ground with roots on them, like a plant's. I shot you through the forehead, and you melted down like a wax doll to a bat-thing that sprouted wings and flew away."

"Uhh—" said Penton soothingly. "Funny, at that. Why were you looking for me?"

"Because there's a Japanese maple where I was that grew while my back was turned, and changed its leaves while I looked at it."

"Oh, Lord," said Penton unhappily, looking at Rod. Then more soothingly, "I think we'd better look at it."

Rod led the way back on his tracks. When the maple should have been in sight, it wasn't at all. When they reached the spot where Rod's tracks showed it should have been, it wasn't there. There was only a somewhat wilted sword-bush. Rod stared blankly at it, then he went over and felt it cautiously. It remained placidly squatted, a slightly bedraggled lump of vegetation.

"That's where it was," said Blake dully. "But it isn't there any more. I know it was there."

"It must have been an—er—mirage," decided Penton. "Let's get back to the ship. We've had enough walking practice."

Rod followed him, wonderingly shaking his head. He was so wrapped up in his thoughts, that he nearly fell over Penton, when Ted stopped with a soft, unhappy, gurgling noise. Ted turned around and looked at Rod carefully. Then he looked ahead again.

"Which," he asked at length, "is you?"

Rod looked ahead of Penton, over his shoulder. Another Rod was also standing in front of Penton. "My God," said Rod, "it's *me* this time!"

"I am, of course," said the one in front. It said it in Rod Blake's voice. Ted looked at it, and finally shut his eyes. "I don't believe it. Not at all. *Wo bist du gewesen, mein Freund?*"

"*Was sagst du?*" said the one in front. "But why the *Deutsch?*"

Ted Penton sat down slowly and thoughtfully. Rod Blake stared at Rod Blake blankly, slightly indignant.

"Let me think," said Penton unhappily. "There must be some way to tell. Rod went away from me, and then I come around the corner and find him laughing insanely. He takes a shot at me. But it looks and talks like Rod. But he says crazy things. Then I go for a walk with him—or *it*—and meet another one that at least seems less insane than the first one. Well, well. I know German of course, and so does Rod.

Evidently this thing can read minds. Must be like a chameleon, only more so."

"What do you mean?" asked Rod Blake. It doesn't particularly matter which one.

"A chameleon can assume any color it wants to at will. Lots of animals have learned to imitate other animals for safety, but it takes them generations to do it. This thing, apparently, can assume any shape or color at will. A minute ago it decided the best form for the locality was a sword-bush. Some of these things must be real plants then.

"Rod thought of a maple tree, thought of the advantages of a maple tree, so it decided to try that, having read his mind. That was why it was wilted-looking; this isn't the right kind of country for maple trees. It lost water too fast. So it went back to the sword-bush.

"Now this one has decided to try being Rod Blake, clothes and all. But I haven't the foggiest notion which one is Rod Blake. It won't do a bit of good to try him on languages we know, because he can read our minds.

I know there must be some way. There must—there must—Oh yes. It's simple. Rod, just burn me a hole in that thing with your violet-gun."

Rod reached for his gun at once with a sigh of relief and triggered quickly. The phony Rod melted hastily. About half of it got down into the boiling mud before Rod incinerated the rest with the intense ultraviolet flare of the pistol.

Rod sighed. "Thank the Lord it was me. I wasn't sure for a while, myself."

Ted shook himself, put his head in his hands, and rocked slowly. "By the Nine Gods of the Nine Planets, what a world! Rod, for the love of heaven, stay with me hereafter. Permanently. And whatever you do, don't lose that pistol. They can't grow a real violet-gun, but if they pick one up, may God help us. Let's get back to the ship, and away from this damned place. I thought you were mad. My error. It's just the whole bloody planet that's mad."

"I was—for a while. Let's move."

They moved. They moved hastily back across the sand dunes to the ship.

"THEY'RE CENTAURS," GASPED BLAKE. "Will you look at that one over there—a nice little calico. There's a beautiful little strawberry roan. What people! Wonder why the city is so dilapidated, if the people are still here in some numbers. Set 'er down, will you, Ted. They haven't anything dangerous, or they'd have a better city."

"Uhmmm—I suppose that's right. But I'd hate to have one of those fellows nudge me. They must weigh something noticeable, even here—about twelve hundred pounds back on Earth. I'm setting down in that square. You keep your hand on that ten-inch ion-gun while I step out."

The ship settled with a soft *thumpf* in the deep sandy dust of the ruined city square. Half a hundred of the centaurs were trotting leisurely up, with a grizzled old Martian in the lead, his mane sparse and coarse.

Ted Penton stepped out of the lock.

"*Pholshth,*" the Martian said after a moment's inspection. He extended his hands out horizontally from his shoulders, palms upward and empty.

"Friends," said Ted, extending his arms in a similar gesture, "I am Penton."

"*Fasthun Loshthu,*" explained the centaur, indicating himself. "*Penshun.*"

"He sounds like an ex-soldier," came Blake's voice softly. "Pension. Is he OK?"

"I think so. You can leave that post anyway, and shut off the main atomics, start auxiliary B, and close the rooms. Lock the controls with the combination and come on out. Bring your ion-gun as well as your ultraviolet. Secure the lock-doors."

"Blazes. I want to come out this afternoon. Oh well...." Blake went to work hurriedly and efficiently.

It was some thirty seconds before he was through in the power room. He stepped eagerly into the lock.

He stopped dead. Penton was on his back, moving feebly, the old centaur bent over him, with his long, powerful fingers fixed around the man's throat. Penton's head was shaking slowly back and forth on the end of his neck, in a loose, rather detached-looking way.

Blake roared and charged out of the lock, his two powerful pistols hastily restored to his holsters. He charged out—and sailed neatly over the centaur's back, underestimating Mars' feeble grip. In an instant he was on his feet again and returning toward his friend when a skillful left forefoot caught his legs and sent him tumbling as the heavy bulk of an agile young centaur landed on his back.

Blake turned—his was a smaller, lighter body far more powerfully muscled. In a moment the Earthman broke the centaurs' grip and started through the six or seven others that surrounded him. A grunted word of command dissolved the melée, and Blake stood up, leaping toward Penton.

Penton sat on the ground, rocking slowly back and forth, his head between his hands. "Oh, Lord, they all do it here."

"Ted—are you all right?"

"Do I sound it?" Penton asked unhappily. "That old bird just opened up my skull and poured a new set of brains in. Hypnotic teaching—a complete university education in thirty seconds—all done with hypnotism and no mirrors used. They have the finest education system. Heaven preserve us from it."

"*Shthuntho ishthu thiu loinal?*" asked the old Martian pleasantly.

"*Ishthu psoth lonthul timul,*" groaned Penton. "The worst of it is, it works. I know his language as well as I know English." Suddenly he managed a slight grin. He pointed to Blake and said: "Blake *omo phusthu ptsoth.*"

The old centaur's lined, sparsely bearded face smiled like a pleased child's. Blake looked at him uneasily.

"I don't like that fellow's expre—" He stopped, hypnotized. He walked toward the old Martian with blank eyes and the grace of an animated tailor's dummy. He lay down, and the old Martian's long, supple fingers circled his neck. Gently they massaged the back of his spine up to the base of his skull.

Penton smiled sourly from where he sat. "Oh, you don't like his face, eh? Wait and see how you like his system."

The centaur straightened. Slowly Blake sat up. His head continued to nod and weave in a detached sort of way, till he gingerly reached up, felt around for it and took it firmly in his hands. He rested his elbows on his knees.

"We didn't both have to know his blasted language," he managed bitterly at last. "Languages always did give me headaches anyway."

Penton watched him unsympathetically. "I hate repeating things, and you'll find it useful, anyway."

"You are from the third planet," the Martian stated politely.

Penton looked at him in surprise, started up, then rose to his feet gingerly.

"Get up slowly, Blake, I advise you for your own good." Then to the Martian: "Why, yes. But you knew! How?"

"My great-great grandfather told me of his trip to the third planet before he died. He was one of those that returned."

"Returned? You Martians have been to Earth?" gasped Blake.

"I guessed that," said Penton softly. "They're evidently the centaurs of legend. And I think they didn't go alone from this planet."

"Our people tried to establish a colony there, many many years ago. It didn't succeed. They died of lung diseases faster than they could cross space. The main reason they went in the first place was to get away from the *thushol*. But the thushol simply imitated local Earth-animals and thrived. So the people came back. We built many ships, hoping that since we couldn't go, the thushol would. But they didn't like Earth." He shook his head sorrowfully.

"The thushol. So that's what you call 'em." Blake sighed. "They must be a pest."

"They were then. They aren't much any more."

"Oh, they don't bother you any more?" asked Penton.

"No," said the old centaur apathetically. "We're so used to them."

"How do you tell them from the thing they're imitating?" Penton asked grimly. "That's what I need to know."

"It used to bother us because we couldn't," Loshthu sighed. "But it doesn't any more."

"I know—but how do you tell them apart? Do you do it by mindreading?"

"Oh, no. We don't try to tell them apart. That way they don't bother us any more."

Penton looked at Loshthu thoughtfully for some time. Blake rose gingerly and joined Penton in his rapt contemplation of the grizzled Martian. "Uhmmmm," said Penton at last, "I suppose that is one way of looking at it. I should think it would make business rather difficult though. Also social relations, not knowing whether it was your wife or just a real good imitation."

"I know. We found it so for many years," Loshthu agreed. "That was why our people wanted to move to Earth. But later they found that three of the ship commanders were thushol, so the people came back to Mars where they could live at least as easily as the thushol."

Penton mentally digested this for some moments, while the half-hundred centaurs stood about patiently, apathetically motionless.

"We have myths on Earth of centaurs, people like you, and of magic creatures who seemed one thing, but when captured became snakes or tigers or other unpleasant beasts, but if held long enough reverted to human shape and would then grant a wish. Yes, the thushol are intelligent; they could have granted a simple Earth barbarian's wish."

Loshthu shook his head slowly.

"They are not intelligent, I believe. Maybe they are. But they have perfect memories for detail. They would imitate one of our number, attend our schools, and so learn all we knew. They never invented anything for themselves."

"What brought about the tremendous decline in your civilization? The thushol?"

The centaur nodded.

"We forgot how to make space ships and great cities. We hoped that would discourage the thushol so they would leave us. But they forgot too, so it didn't help."

"Good Lord," Blake sighed, "how in the name of the Nine Planets do you live with a bunch like that?"

Loshthu looked at Blake slowly.

"Ten," he said. "Ten planets. You can't see the tenth with any practicable instrument till you get out beyond Jupiter. Our people discovered it from Pluto."

Blake stared at him owlishly. "But how can you live with this gang? With a civilization like that—I should think you'd have found some means of destroying them."

"We did. We destroyed all the thushol. Some of the thushol helped us, but we thought that they were our own people. It happened because a very wise, but very foolish philosopher calculated how many thushol could live parasitically on our people. Naturally the thushol took his calculations to heart. Thirty-one percent of us are thushol."

Blake looked around with a swiftly unhappy eye. "You mean—some of these here are thushol?" he asked. Loshthu nodded.

"Always. They reproduced very slowly at first, in the form of an animal that was normally something like us, and reproduced as did other animals. But then they learned to imitate the amoebae when they studied in our laboratories.

"Now they simply split. One big one will split into several small ones, and each small one will eat one of the young of our people and take its place. So we never know which is which. It used to worry us." Loshthu shook his head slowly.

Blake's hair rose slightly away from his head, and his jaw dropped away. "My God," he gasped. "Why didn't you do something?"

"If we killed one we suspected, we might be wrong, which would kill our own child. If we didn't, and just believe it our own child anyway, it at least gave us the comfort of believing it. And if the imitation is so perfect one can't tell the difference, what is the difference?"

Blake sat down again, quietly.

"Penton," he sighed, at length, "those three months are up, let's get back to Earth—fast."

Penton looked at him. "I wanted to a long time ago. Only I thought of something else. Sooner or later, some other man is going to come here with atomic power, and if he brings some of those thushol back to Earth with him, accidentally, thinking it's his best friend—well, I'd rather kill my own child than live with one of those, but I'd rather not do either.

"They can reproduce as fast as they can eat, and if they eat like an amoeba—God help us. If you maroon one on a desert island, it will turn into a fish, and swim home. If you put it in jail it will turn into a snake and go down the drain pipe. If you dump it in the desert it will turn into a cactus and get along real nice, thank you."

"Good God."

"And they won't believe us, of course. I'm sure as blazes not going to take one back to prove it. I'll just have to get some kind of proof from this Loshthu."

"I hadn't thought of that. What can we get?"

"All I can think of is to see what they can let us have, then take all we can, and make a return trip with reputable and widely believed zoologists and biologists to look into this thing. Evolution has produced some weird freaks, but this is a freakier freak than has ever been conceived."

"I still don't really believe it," Blake said. "The only thing I am firmly convinced of is my headache."

"It's real enough and logical enough. Logical as hell. And hell on Earth if they ever get there. Evolution is always trying to produce an animal that can survive anywhere, conquer all enemies, the fittest of, the surviving fit. All life is based on one thing—protoplasm.

"Basically, it's the same in every creature, every living thing, plant and animal, amoeba and man. It is just modified slightly, hooked together in slightly different ways. The thushol are built of protoplasm—but infinitely more adaptable protoplasm. They can do something about it, make it take the form of a bone cell and be part of a thigh bone, or be a nerve cell in a brain.

"From some of that ten-second college-course Loshthu poured into me, I gather that at first the thushol were good imitations outside, but if you cut into one, you could see that the organs weren't there. Now they have everything. They went through Martian medical colleges, of course, and know all about what makes a centaur tick, and so they make themselves with the same kind of tickers. Oh, very nice."

"They don't know much about us. Maybe with the X-ray fluoroscope screen we could have recognized those imitations of us," suggested Blake.

"Oh, no, by no means. If we knew the right form, they'd read it in our minds, and have it. Adaptive protoplasm. Just think, you couldn't kill it in an African jungle, because when a lion came along, it would be a little, lady lion, and when an elephant showed up, it would be a helpless baby elephant.

"If a snake bit it, I suppose the damned thing would turn into something immune to snake bites—a tree, or something like that. I just wonder where it keeps the very excellent brain it evidently has."

"Well, let's find out what Loshthu can offer us by way of proofs."

IT DEVELOPED THAT THE MARTIANS had once had museums. They still had them, because nobody was sufficiently interested to disturb their age-long quiet. Martians lived centuries, and their memories were long; but once or twice in a lifetime did a Martian enter the ancient museums.

Penton and Blake spent hours in them, intensive hours under Loshthu's guidance. Loshthu had nothing but time, and Penton and Blake didn't want to linger. They worked rapidly, collecting thin metal sheaves of documents, ancient mechanisms, a thousand things. They baled them with rope that they had brought from the ship when they moved it nearer the museum. Finally, after hours of labor, bleary-eyed from want of sleep, they started out again to the ship.

They stepped out of the gloomy dusk of the museum into the sun-lit entranceway. Immediately, from behind a dozen pillars, a leaping, flashing group of men descended upon them, tore the books, the instruments, the data sheaves from their hands. They were upset, slugged, trampled on and spun around. There were shouts and cries and curses.

Then there was silence. Twelve Pentons and thirteen Blakes sat, lay, or stood about on the stone stairway. Their clothes were torn, their faces and bodies bruised, there was even one black eye, and another developing swiftly. But twelve Pentons looked exactly alike, each clasping a bit of data material. Thirteen Blakes were identical, each carrying a bit of factual mustiness under his arm or in his hand.

Loshthu looked at them, and his lined, old face broke into a pleased smile. "Ah," he said. "There are more of you. Perhaps some can stay with us to talk now."

Penton looked up at Loshthu, all the Pentons did. Penton was quite sure *he* was the Penton, but he couldn't think of any way to prove it. It was fairly evident that thushol had decided to try Earth again. He began to wonder just—"

"Loshthu, just why," asked one of the Pentons in Penton's voice, "did the thushol not stay on Earth if they could live there?"

Penton was quite sure he had been the one to think of that partic—

"Pardon me, but wasn't that the question I was going to ask?" said another Penton in well-controlled fury. Penton smiled gently. It seemed evident that— "I can apparently be spared the trouble of doing my own talking. You all help so," said one of the numerous Pentons angrily.

"Say, how in hell are we going to tell who's who?" demanded one of the Blakes abruptly.

"That damned mind-thief stole my question before I had a chance—"

"Why you—you—*you* should talk! I was just about—"

"I think," said one of the Pentons wearily, "you might as well stop getting peeved, Blake, because they'll all act peeved when you do. What do you know. I beat all my imitators to the draw on that remark. A noble achievement, you'll find, Rod. But you might just as well pipe down, and I'll pipe down, and we'll see what our good friend, Loshthu, has to say."

"Eh," sighed Loshthu. "You mean about the thushol leaving Earth? They did not like it. Earth is a poor planet, and the people were barbarians. Evidently they are not so now. But the thushol do not like work, and they found richer sustenance on Mars."

"I thought so," said Penton. (Does it matter which one?) "They've decided that Earth is richer than Mars now, and want a new host. Don't draw that pistol, Blake! Unfortunately, my friend, we had twenty-five ion-guns and twenty-five violet-guns made up. If we'd had more we would have more companions.

"We were exceedingly unfortunate in equipping ourselves so well in the matter of clothing, and being so thoughtful as to plan all of it right, so we carried a lot of each of the few kinds. However, I think we can improve things a little bit.

"I happen to remember that one ion-gun is out of commission, and I had the coils out of two of the violet-guns to repair them. That makes three guns out of service. We will each stand up and fire, one at a time, at the sand in front there. The line forms on the right."

The line formed. "Now," continued that particular Penton, "we will each fire, beginning with myself, one at a time. First ion, then violet. When one of us evidences lack of a serviceable gun, the others will join in removing him rapidly but carefully. Are we ready? Yes?" That Penton held up his ion-gun and pushed the button.

It didn't fire, and immediately the portico stank with his smoke.

"That's one," said the next Penton. He raised his ion-gun and fired. Then his violet-gun. Then he raised it and fired again, at a rapidly dissolving Blake. "That makes two. That one evidently found, when we fired at the first one, that *his* didn't work. We have one more to eliminate. Next?"

Presently another Blake vanished. "Well, well," said Penton pleasantly, "the Blake-Penton odds are even. Any suggestions?"

"Yes," said Blake tensely. "I've been thinking of a patch I put in one suit that I ripped on Venus."

Another Blake vanished under the mutual fire.

"There's one more thing I want to know. Why in blazes are those phonies so blasted willing to kill each other, and though they know which is which, don't kill us? And how did they enter the ship?" Rod demanded.

"They," said two Pentons at once. Another one looked at them. "Bad timing, boys. Rodney, my son, we used a combination lock. These gentlemen are professional mind-readers. Does that explain their possession of the guns?

"Now since these little gun tests and others have been made I think it fairly evident that we are not going to leave this planet until the two right men are chosen and only two go into that ship with us. Fortunately they can't go without us—because while they can read minds, it takes more than knowledge to navigate a space ship, at least such knowledge as they can get from us. It takes understanding, which mere memory will not supply. They need us.

"We will, therefore, march dutifully to the ship, and each of us will replace his guns carefully in the prepared racks. *I* know that *I'm* the right Penton—but *you* don't. So no movement will be made without the unanimous agreement of all Pentons and Blakes."

Blake looked up, white-faced. "If this wasn't so world-shakingly serious, it would be the damnedest comic opera that ever happened. I'm afraid to give up my gun."

"If we all give them up, I think it puts us even. We have some advantage in that they don't want to kill us, and if worse comes to worst, we could take them to Earth, making damned sure that they didn't get away. On Earth we could have protoplasmic tests made that would tell the story. By the way, that suggests something. Yes indeed, I think we can make tests here. Let's repair to the ship."

THE BLAKES SAT DOWN and stayed down. "Ted, what in blazes can we do?" His voice was almost tearful. "You can't tell one of these ghastly things from another. You can't tell one from me. We can't—"

"Oh, God," said another Blake, "that's not me. That's just another one of those damned mind stealers."

Another one groaned hopelessly.

"That wasn't me either." They all looked helplessly at the line of Pentons. "I don't even know who's my friend."

Penton nodded. All the Pentons nodded, like a grotesquely solemn chorus preparing to recite some blessing. They smiled in superhuman unity. "That's all right," they said in perfect harmony. "Well, well. A new stunt. Now we all talk together. That makes things easier.

"I think there may be a way to tell the difference. But you must absolutely trust me, Blake. You must give up your guns, putting all faith in my ability to detect the right one, and if I'm wrong, realize that I will not know. We can try such simple tests as alcohol, whiskey, to see if it makes them drunk, and pepper to see if it bums their tongues—"

"It won't work," said Blake tensely. "Lord, Penton, I can't give up my guns—I *won't*—"

Penton, all the Pentons, smiled gently. "I'm half again as fast as you are, Blake, and no Martian-born imitation of you is going to be faster. Maybe these Martian imitations of me are as fast as I am. But you know perfectly well that I could ray the whole gang of you, all ten of you, out of existence before any one of you could move a finger. You know that, don't you, Rod?"

"Lord, yes, but Ted, Ted, don't do that—don't make me give up my guns—I've got to keep them. Why should I give up mine, if you keep yours?"

"That probably was not you speaking, Rod, but it doesn't matter. If it wasn't what you thought, we could do something about it. Therefore, that is what you wanted to say, just as this is what I wanted to say, whether I said it or not.

"But anyway, the situation is this; one of us has to have unquestioned superiority over the other gang. Then, the one with the whip hand can develop proof of identity and enforce his decisions. As it is, we can't."

"Let *me* be that one, then," snapped one Blake.

"I didn't mean that," sighed another. "That wasn't me."

"Yes it was," said the first. "I spoke without thinking. Go ahead. But how are you going to make the others give up their guns? I'm willing. You can't make them?"

"Oh, yes I can. I have my faithful friends, here," said Penton grimly, his eleven hands waving to his eleven counterparts. "They agree with me this far, being quite utterly selfish."

"But what's your system. Before I put my neck in the noose, I have to know that noose isn't going to tighten on it."

"If I had a sound system in mind—I'm carefully refraining from developing one—they'd read it, weigh it, and wouldn't agree at all. They still have hopes. You see that pepper and alcohol system won't work perfectly because they can read in my mind the proper reaction, and be drunk, or have an inflamed tongue at will, being perfect actors. I'm going to try just the same. Rod, if you ever trusted me, trust me now."

"All right, come on. We'll go to the ship, and any one of these things that doesn't part with its gun is *not* me. Ray it."

Blake rose jerkily, all ten of him, and went down to the ship.

The Pentons followed faithfully after. Abruptly Penton rayed one Blake. His shoulder blades had humped curiously and swiftly. Wings were developing. "That helps," said Penton, holstering his guns.

The Blakes went on, white-faced. They put the weapons in the racks in the lock stoically. The Martians had seen the—to them—inconceivably swift movements of Penton's gun hands, and Penton knew that he, himself, had done the raying that time.

But he still didn't know a way to prove it without causing a general melée which would bring about their own deaths. That wasn't so important. The trouble was that given fifty years, the rest of the world would descend on this planet unwarned. Then all Earth would be destroyed. Not with flame and sword and horrible casualty lists—but silently and undetectably.

The Blakes came out, unarmed. They shuffled and moved about uneasily, tensely, under the watchful eyes of eleven Pentons armed with terrifically deadly weapons.

Several Pentons went into the ship, to come out bearing pepper, saccharine tablets, alcohol, the medicine chest. One of them gathered them together and looked them over. "We'll try pepper," he said, rather unhappily. "Line up!"

The Blakes lined up, hesitantly. "I'm putting my life in your hands, Ted," said two of them in identical, plaintive tones.

Four Pentons laughed shortly. "I know it. Line up. Come and get it. First, stick out the tongue."

With unsteady hands he put a bit of pepper from the shaker on the fellow's tongue. The tongue snapped in instantly, the Blake clapped his hands to his mouth, gurgling unpleasantly. *"Waaaar!"* he gasped. *"Waar— achooo—damnt!"*

With hands like flashing light, Penton pulled his own, and a neighbor's ion-gun. In a fiftieth of a second all but the single gagging, choking, coughing Blake were stinking, smoking, swiftly dissolving and flowing rubbish. The other Penton methodically helped destroy them.

Blake stopped gagging in surprise. "My God, it might not have been the right one!" he gasped.

The ten Pentons sighed softly. "That finally proves it. Thank God. Definitely. That leaves *me* to find. And it won't work again, because while you can't read my mind to find the trick that told, these brothers of mine have. The very fact that you don't know how I knew, proves that I was right."

Blake stared at him dumbly. "I was the first one—" he managed between a cough and a sneeze.

"Exactly. Go on inside. Do something intelligent. Use your head. See what you can think of to locate me. You have to use your head in some such way that they don't mind-read it first, though. Go ahead."

Blake went, slow-footed. The first thing he did was to close the lockdoor, so that he was safely alone in the ship. Blake went into the control room, donned an air-suit complete with helmet, and pushed a control handle over, then a second.

Presently he heard curious bumpings and thumpings, and strange floppings and whimperings. He went back rapidly, and rayed a supply chest and two crates of Venusian specimens that had sprouted legs and were rapidly growing arms to grasp ray pistols. The air in the ship began to look thick and greenish; it was colder.

Contentedly Blake watched, and opened all the room doors. Another slithering, thumping noise attracted him, and with careful violet-gun work he removed an unnoticed, extra pipe that was crawling from the crossbrace hangers. It broke up into lengths that rolled about unpleasantly. Rod rayed them till the smallest only, the size of golf balls with curious blue-veined legs, staggered about uncertainly. Finally even they stopped wriggling.

Half an hour Rod waited, while the air grew very green and thick. Finally, to make sure, he started some other apparatus, and watched the thermometer go down, down till moisture grew on the walls and became frost, and no more changes took place. Then he went around with an opened ion-gun with a needle beam and poked everything visible with it.

The suction fans cleared out the chlorine-fouled atmosphere in two minutes, and Blake sat down wearily.

He flipped over the microphone switch and spoke into the little disc. "I've got my hand on the main ion-gun control. Penton, I love you like a brother, but I love Earth more. If you can induce your boy friends to drop their guns in a neat pile and retire—OK. If not, and I mean if not within thirty seconds, this ion-gun is going into action and there won't be any more Pentons. Now, drop!"

Grinning broadly, with evident satisfaction, ten Pentons deposited twenty heart-cores of ultra-essence of destruction, and moved off. "Way off," said Blake grimly. They moved.

Blake collected twenty guns. Then he went back into the ship. There was a fine laboratory at one end, and with grim satisfaction he took down three cotton-stoppered tubes, being very careful to handle them with rubber gloves. "You never did mankind a good turn before, tetanus, but I hope you spread high, wide and handsome here—"

He dumped them into a beaker of water, and took beaker and glass down to the lock and out. The ten waited at a distance.

"All right, Penton. I happen to know you took a shot of tetanus vaccine some while ago, and are immune. Let's see if those blasted brain-stealers can steal the secret of something we know how to make, but don't know anything about. They can gain safety by turning into chickens, which are immune, but not as human creatures. That's a concentrated dose of tetanus. Go drink it. We can wait ten days if we have to."

Ten Pentons marched boldly up to the beaker, resting beside the ship. One stepped forward to the glass—and nine kept right on stepping. They stepped into the lee of the ship where the ion-gun could not reach.

Blake helped Penton into the ship with a broad grin. "Am I right?"

"You're right," sighed Penton, "but—you can't get tetanus by swallowing it, and lockjaw doesn't develop in ten days."

"I didn't know for sure," grinned Blake. "They were too busy trying to find out what I was doing to follow your mind. Ah—*there* they go. Will you ray them or shall I?" asked Blake politely.

"There's one thing … ahhh"—he straightened as the incredible glare died in thin air—"I want to know. How in blazes did you pick *me* out?"

"To do what you did requires some five hundred different sets of muscles in a beautifully coordinated neuromuscular hookup, which I didn't believe those things could imitate without a complete dissection. I took the chance it was you."

"Five hundred sets of muscles! What the heck did I do?"

"You sneezed."

Rod Blake blinked slowly, and slowly his jaw tested again its supports and their flexibility.

"The Brain-Stealers of Mars" first appeared in the December 1936 issue of Thrilling Wonder Stories*. Two years later Campbell refined his alien-replacement plot—ditching the light-hearted, pulp-fiction tone of this earlier work, for a far more serious take on the subject—producing his masterpiece "Who Goes There." "The Brain-Stealers…." is one of five Blake and Penton stories published by* Thrilling Wonder *during the late 30s, all of which were incorporated into the 1966 novel* The Planeteers. *Art for this story is by prolific pulp artist Alex Schomburg, whom many fondly remember as the chief cover artist for Timely Comics (forerunner of Marvel), who beautifully illustrated Captain America, the Sub-Mariner and the Human Torch.*

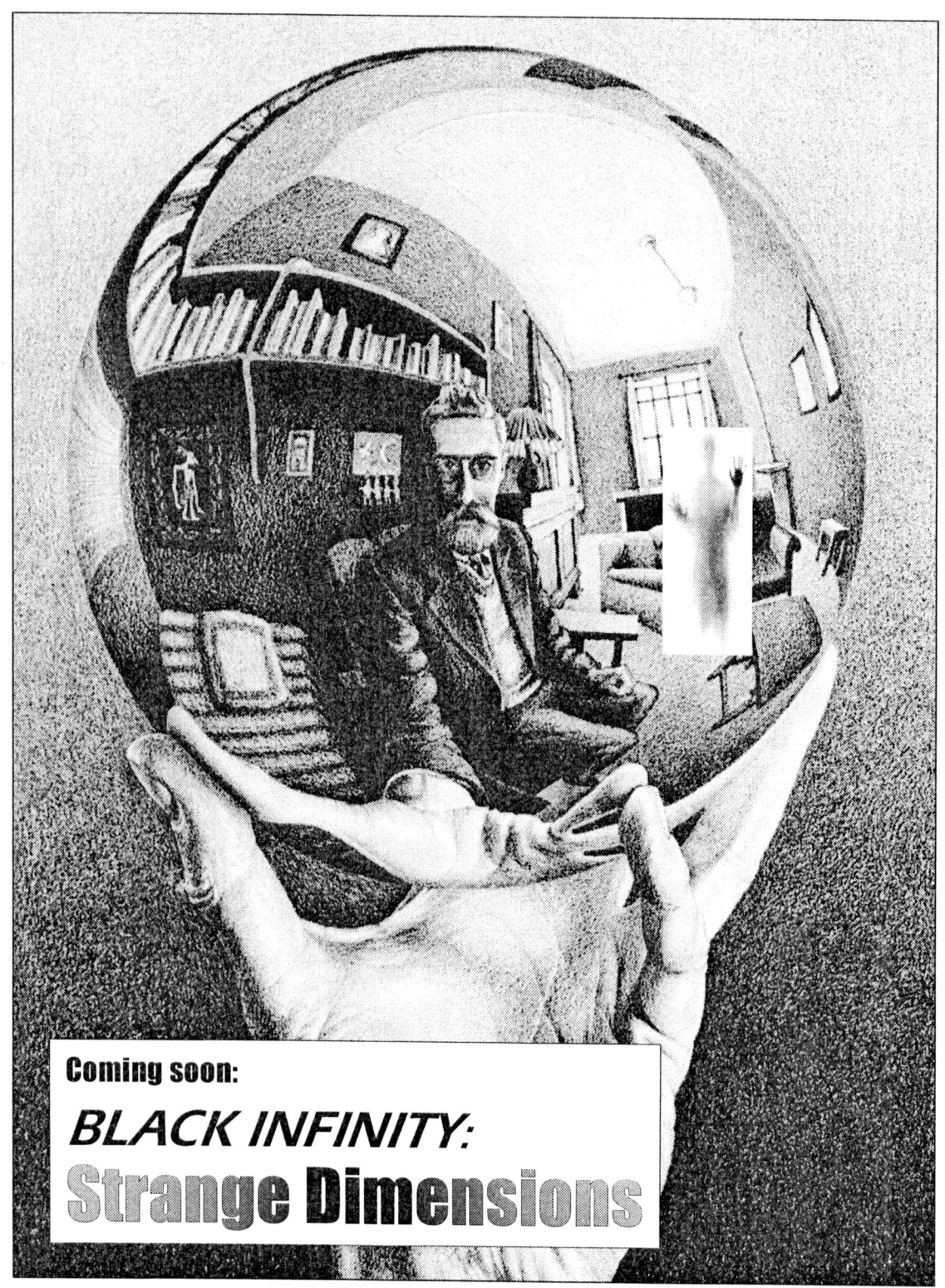

Coming soon:

BLACK INFINITY:
Strange Dimensions

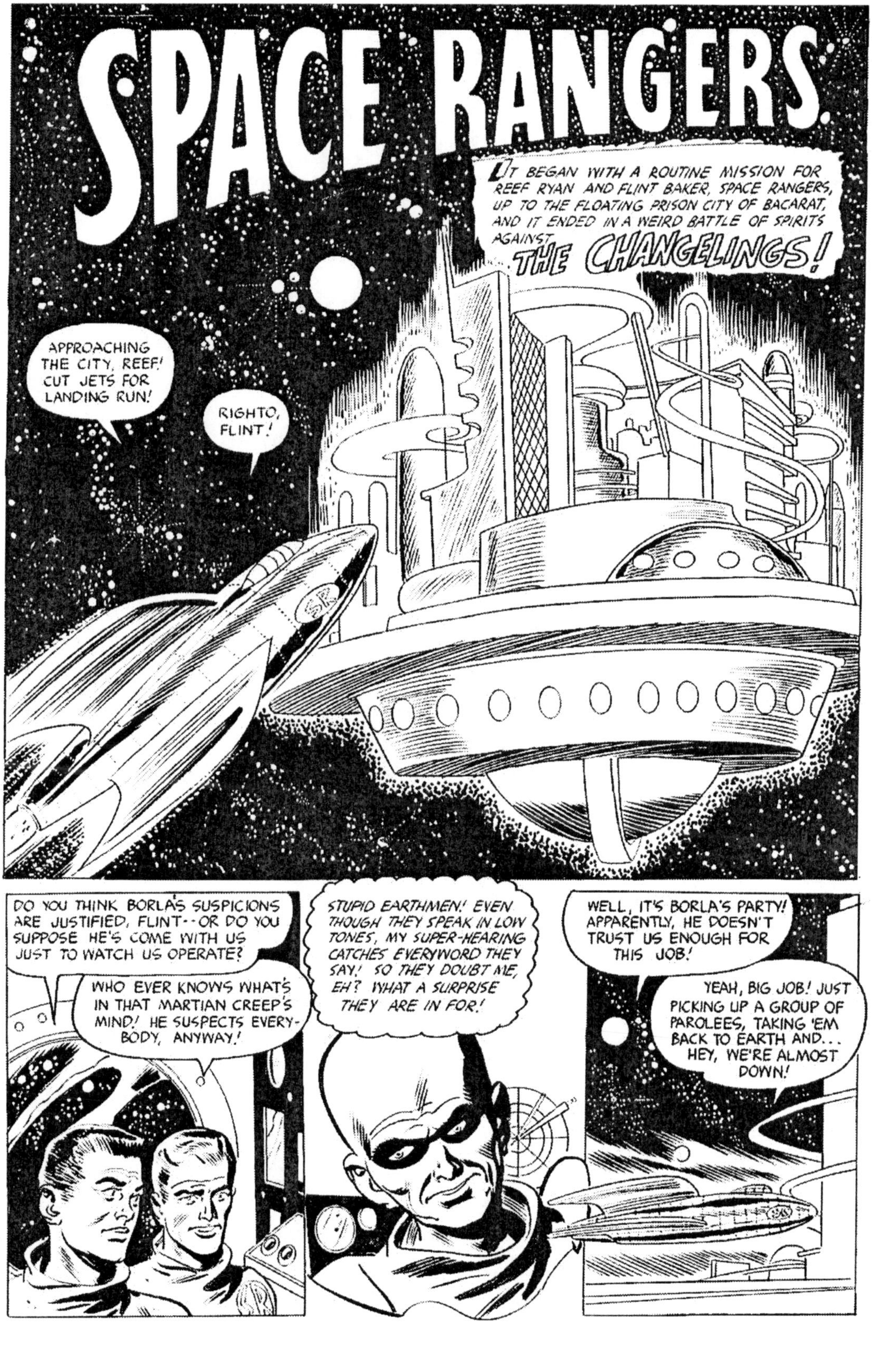

In the time of the Pharaohs, an Egyptian *femme fatale* was tried for perverse crimes against her people. She was sentenced to be buried alive in a specially sealed tomb, hidden beneath the desert floor. She has slept undisturbed for thousands of years beneath an ocean of sun-parched sand—waiting to be freed; waiting for three American archaeologists who will ignore the inscription above the portal of her tomb:

> WHOSO COMETH,
>
> NOW OR HEREAFTER,
>
> WAKE NOT THE SOUL
>
> THAT SLEEPS WITHIN.

C. Bryson Taylor's "lost" 1904 supernatural novel featuring a vampiric female mummy!

From the novel: *"He must have wanted to sleep sound, whoever he was," Holloway observed with flippancy. "...If the old man's still here, I'd like to collect him before it gets too dark."*

Soon a force of men was at work, a swarm of ants prying around the edges of the walled-up door, where, above, the ancient message gave its warning. From this inscription Deane found himself unaccountably unable to keep his eyes. He and Holloway discussed it in low tones, to the accompaniment of the thud of falling pick and spade. Holloway wavered between the seductive idea of buried treasure, whose owner had perhaps sought to guard it with a theatrical warning, and the bejewelled mummy of the king he wished to collect. Deane hoped there would be tablets to decipher; Merritt said nothing. When Holloway questioned, wishing his theories on the subject, Merritt answered shortly: "I'm not expecting anything.... It's the unexpected that turns up and floors you, no matter what you think you'll get."

IN THE **DWELLINGS** OF THE **WILDERNESS**

C. BRYSON TAYLOR

Trade edition: $7.00   ISBN-13: 978-0979633591

DEAD LETTER PRESS
WWW.DEADLETTERPRESS.COM